Bad Traffic

Simon Lewis

D0255921

Bad Traffic

Simon Lewis

Bournemouth Libraries	
WI	
300026201	
Askews	2009
AF	£7.99

THANKS

For help and inspiration, thanks to: Mark and Nat, Mum and Rog, Dad and Janet, Noe, Shen Ye, Du Yingnan, Joyce Sun, Xiao Song, Dan, Ed and Fran, Ya Ou, Gareth, Ling Ling and the Mingtownsfolk, Charles, the Readys, Kat, Yen, Chris T. and the Dali people, Matt, Nick, Daren, Kate, and all at Rough Guides.

BAD TRAFFIC

Copyright © Simon Lewis 2008

First published by Sort Of Books, 2008

No part of this book may be reproduced in any form without permission from the publisher except for the quotation of brief passages in reviews.

Sort Of Books, PO Box 18678, London NW3 2FL

Typeset in Melior and Frutiger to a design by Henry Iles

Printed in the UK by Clays Ltd, St Ives plc

2

Distributed by the Penguin Group in all territories excluding the United States and Canada:
Penguin Books, 80 Strand, London WC2 0RL.

384pp

A catalogue record for this book is available from the British Library

ISBN 978-0-9548995-5-4

This work was supported by a grant from the Arts Council, England

Contents

交通差

INSPECTOR JIAN

(1

THIS MAN HAVE COME FROM CHINA TO FIND HIS DAUGHTER WHO HAVE SOME TROUBLE. HE DOES NOT SPEAK ENGLISH.

Jian walked into Leeds University and handed his message, written for him on the back of an aeroplane boarding pass, to the front desk security guard. This was the first black person he had ever met and he noted the paleness of the man's palms and the brown tea in his mug. It seemed to have milk in it, the way Mongolians liked it.

The guard took his time, turning the boarding pass over and considering the flight number – AR574 from Beijing Capital Airport – and, in irritation, Jian's fingers tightened on the handle of his suitcase. He wiped sweat beads off his forehead.

He was wondering whether to give the guard a cigarette to help move things along when the man looked up, and the whites of his eyes seemed to shine out of his face. He beckoned for Jian to follow.

The corridors were painted rather an informal yellow. He was led past a lounge area, like the one at the airport, and a refectory noisy with the alien clamour of metal cutlery on plates. Students bustled round. Jian was used to towering over people but it wasn't going to happen here, a lot of these guys were over one eighty. Some of the girls too. There were many different races but everyone seemed to be getting along.

He was led to a door labelled '106' and ushered into an office where a middle-aged woman addressed him in a witter as meaningless as birdsong. Her hair was blonde, her eyes a disconcerting green. She wasn't wearing a uniform but she appeared to have her own desk, so was presumably of more consequence than the guard. He replied, in Mandarin Chinese, '*Wo zhao wo de nu'er...* I'm looking for my daughter.' No one would understand, but it satisfied a need to hear his own voice and words he could comprehend, it soothed away the unfamiliarity. The guard and the woman babbled, and he said – surely it was obvious – 'Get a translator.'

Back home Jian had rank and status and was used to people rushing to do his bidding. But he was nothing here, just a nuisance. If he wanted things done he'd have to do them himself.

He stalked out, the guard following at his heels. The bulky suitcase made him list to one side as he retraced his steps to the refectory. He stood on a chair and stepped up from it onto a tabletop. A girl twirling yellow noodles onto a fork looked at him with alarm and slid her tray away.

He cleared his throat and yelled, '*You ren hui shuo zhong guo hua ma?...* Does anybody here speak Mandarin Chinese?'

A hush fell. The noodles slipped off the fork. Someone laughed nervously. Making a scene didn't worry him, he didn't feel any pull of social convention here. These people weren't his people, he could make monkey noises and it wouldn't matter. He bellowed his question again, so even the queue over by the vending machines in the corner shut up and looked at him.

The guard beckoned him down with angry sweeps of his arm. Jian ignored him and scanned the crowd, picking out the Asian faces. All he saw was curiosity or alarm. Perhaps no one could help him, perhaps there was no one he could speak to in this whole peculiar city.

'Anybody?'

Another security guard was coming, this one portly and white. The guards looked at each other and Jian recognised the silent communication that passed between them, he knew it well – citizen acting up, placate and eject. The black guard put a hand on his leg.

Jian told him, 'You don't understand. My daughter is in trouble.' But of course no one was listening.

(2

The call had come thirty-two hours previously, at around 11pm, Chinese time.

Jian was pouring Chivas Regal into a crystal glass. When the mobile trilled he winced theatrically for the benefit of the girl opposite, to show how much he resented the interruption.

He finished pouring, making sure her measure was the more generous, and topped up the glasses with a green tea mixer. The trick was to pick the most sugary brand available, then the girl tended not to notice how drunk she was getting.

The mobile trilled on. If she complained about how much whisky he'd given her, he'd blame it on the distraction.

This was her first visit to the flat in the new housing development and he was anxious she find it pleasing. It was just the sort of chic little penthouse, he hoped, that a classy mistress of a certain age might like to be shacked up in, but you could never second-guess the tastes of these modern girls.

So far it was going well. She'd admired the equestrian statue above the compound's arched entrance and the portico with the name of the development in English, 'UBBER WEST SIDE'. She'd even commented that when the water feature was working, you'd be able to see the moon reflected in it.

All the buildings were named after foreign cities. They were in 'Lisbon', and he'd looked it up on a map in case she asked about it. Ah yes, he knew Portugal, home of the indomitable Figo. They generally performmed well in the group stages, then flopped in the quarter finals.

Inside the flat, the gold-effect taps and Western toilet had met the lady's approval, as had the glass coffee table held up by bronze-effect lions. She talked of completing the place with modern-art-type pictures and European historical-style chairs.

When she'd wondered aloud how much he paid, he had deflected her curiosity with an airy wave. It would not do for her to find out that the lease was free, a reward from the developer for helping to smooth the project through. As well as introducing its financiers to the more flexible local politicians, he had overseen, in his official capacity, the requisition of the land from those peasants who had been under the impression that because they'd farmed it for generations, it belonged to them.

Now, he reckoned, all he had to do was get her a bit tipsy, then manoeuvre her into the bedroom – to admire the black sheets, perhaps. When she saw the erotic print above the bed he would smile, making an effort to look twinkling rather than wolfish. It was important that she didn't look out of the window, so he had already drawn the curtains and fastened them with the tasselled gold rope.

It was true, he reflected, that women made you feel younger. He felt about fourteen – all nerves, uncertainty and plans.

No one rang him after ten.

Teasingly she said, 'Is it a girlfriend?'

He worried that it was. But no.

'It's my daughter.'

He went into the kitchen to answer it.

This was Wei Wei's second call today. When she'd phoned earlier she'd sounded downbeat, and had told him her marks were slipping. It had not been a convenient time, he had been at a noisy banquet with portly dignitaries, he had downed a lot of toasts, and now he guiltily reflected that perhaps his attempts to jolly her along had seemed brusque and formulaic.

He yawned. Certainly he had drunk rather too much at the banquet, and he hoped that he would be up to his later duties. Well, he had his bottle of blue pills. The problem was the pounding headache they gave you in the morning.

With his mouth still stretched wide, he pressed 'start call'.

'Dad, help me, help me,' sobbed Wei Wei, above background clamour. 'Help me. Help.'

He snapped his mouth shut. A clatter, a clunk, a gurgle, and the phone was silent.

'Wei Wei?'

He reeled, looked at the mobile as if it were some horrific object, then pressed it hard to his head.

'Wei Wei? Is that you? Wei Wei?'

But there was only a flat drone, the connection had been severed. He shook the mobile as if that would make it work, then looked for last number redial. It did not feel appropriate somehow, to be, at a time of crisis, navigating chirpy graphics and menus on a tiny screen.

He called her back. After eight rings, she said something curt and upbeat in English.

'Wei Wei? What happened?' But it was just her voicemail. He said, 'What's going on? Call me back now.' Then hung up.

He rang back again, but this time the call was not connected. An incongruously calm recorded voice, not his daughter, said something in English. He tried again and again, and got only that infuriating message.

'*Baba bang wo*... Dad, help me.' Her words reverberated like an echo. He leaned his forehead against the cold metal of the extractor fan and ordered himself to go over what had happened before forming conclusions.

Plea, noises, silence, the impossibility of reconnection. His daughter had called, in a state of distress, and begged for help. Then she'd dropped the phone or perhaps it had been ripped from her grasp.

He shuddered at this, and slapped a palm against the wall, and the windowframe rattled. In a window of 'Hamburg', the block opposite, a woman cleaning her teeth looked across sharply.

Then the battery had run out, or been taken out, or the phone had broken. Perhaps it had been hurled away and shattered. No – then it would have clunked more.

His forehead was cold, but his cheeks were heating up. And what about that background bawling? Babies crying, rubber squeaking, pumps pumping? It could even have been mocking laughter. It was impossible to know, the noises were so ambiguous, and already his memory was compromised by his interpretations.

What now? He pressed his head harder against the unyielding metal. He felt something give, and the whole fan came away from the wall. He caught it and pushed it back.

Did he have any other numbers for her? No. Why, he did not even know the address where she lived. How ridiculous, how remiss, to have no way of contacting your own daughter but one mobile number. He stepped back, the extractor fan clattered to the floor and screws pinged about the kitchen.

The only connection he had to her life in England was the address of her college, which would be on the prospectus, in her room.

He walked into the lounge, hardly noticing the absence of the girl, and barked his shin on the edge of the coffee table.

Perhaps it was a joke, perhaps she was just having a bad day, there was every chance it would prove a false alarm and another line would be added to the already lengthy text on how his daughter caused him stress.

He'd catch the first flight to Beijing in the morning, but he would have to get busy now, pulling in some serious favours to arrange an express British visa. Hopefully he could be met at the airport by an official from the embassy, then he could be on a flight to London tomorrow afternoon. He gathered up keys, wallet and cigarettes and, though he felt better at least to be active, a cold stone of dread had settled in his stomach.

The girl called from the bedroom. 'Darling, all you can see from here are the slagheaps. I didn't realise we were so close. There'll be filthy coal dust blowing in. It's hardly ideal.'

He opened the front door.

'Darling?'

3

'*Xiansheng*'. Jian heard a word he understood and turned sharply. A gangly white youth was standing by the guard. The lad said, '*Wo hui shuo zhong wen yi dian'r...* I can speak little Chinese.' His tones were flat, but comprehensible. Jian looked at him with open-mouthed astonishment. A white person speaking Chinese was like a dog walking on two legs – a good trick but there was something unnatural about it.

'I am learn Chinese here. I can help you.'

Jian stepped off the table and the security guard let go. He kept it simple.

'I have come to find my daughter. Her name is Wei Wei, she's twenty-one, she's studying Tourism and Leisure.'

Speaking the banal facts seemed an oddly poignant act. Perhaps they would evoke her, and she would breeze around the corner – that fake Louis Vuitton bag hanging off one shoulder, hair swinging, chatting on a mobile, some no-good lad following at her heels. The image was achingly precise. He rubbed his face.

'I have reason to believe she's in trouble.'

Back in Room 106 there was more of the clack and cluck of the English language. Jian wondered if he could smoke but couldn't see an ashtray and he didn't want to distract them by trying to ask for one.

The lad said, 'It's not school law to tell out information about student. Can you prove you her father?'

'Here's my passport. Same name.'

'Your visa is dated today.'

'I just got here.'

Jian had used his clout to get himself attached as technical advisor to a delegation from Daqing oil extraction facility number three, on a junket to the United Kingdom to explore new refining techniques.

The oil men had been drinking on the plane and expected him to join them. He'd explained that he had a stomach upset and they'd assumed he was afraid of flying and ribbed him about it. He hadn't slept at all on the twelve-hour flight.

When they had landed in London he'd taken the group translator aside and made her write him the note, and promise not to talk about it. Unable to read a single sign, he'd got lost in the Underground on the way from Heathrow to King's Cross. Getting a train ticket to Leeds hadn't been easy either, and had involved soliciting aid from strangers, as had finding the right platform and even opening the train door. Just about every single thing was different from home and it was infuriating to be made so helpless.

He'd assumed there'd be hot food on the train, but all he could get was pricey sandwiches. The bread had tasted like foam, and had grease smeared on it, and the filling was not tofu, as he'd assumed, but hard yellow cheese which made him feel ill. Now he was tired, hungry and jet-lagged.

He was given a manila folder. A passport photo of his daughter was clipped to it. He touched the edge, careful not to put a coarse finger across her face.

'That's her.'

Big dark eyes looked blankly out. In pictures she cultivated a model's vacuity and this image was giving nothing away. Sleek hair flowed from a centre parting. She'd bleached the ends brown. Last time he'd seen her, it had been dark red. Her mouth was closed, as always in pictures, to cover the gap between her front teeth. She was so self-conscious about that gap, she didn't understand that the small imperfection didn't mar her beauty but completed it.

'That's her.'

And now, the student explained, they were going to the Tourism and Leisure department to talk to her tutor. He made it sound like they were on some guided tour. Clearly he was enjoying this practical use for all his effort.

The student asked where he was from.

'The north east.'

'It must be very beautiful up in there,' said the lad. 'But cold yes?'

'Ugly and cold.' Jian was in no mood for chit-chat. But this lad was useful, and had to be treated with respect.

'What do you do?'

'I'm a policoman.'

'Do you have any friends in this country?'

'No.'

'Do you have a place to stay?'

'No.'

He'd sort out a hotel when this was done with. He'd also get something to eat, shave, and have a shit. But he couldn't think about mundane details now, not until his mind was put at rest.

He was escorted to a Room 317, where he paced while a South Asian lady with a dot on her forehead tapped on a keyboard. A display of portrait photos hung on the wall. He guessed they were the members of staff for the department: they had the same thing back at the station.

The student said, 'She have found your daughter on the computer. Your daughter teacher Mister Delaware.'

'Where is he?'

'Let us go and see.' There were five in his little group – the wary black security guard, the woman with green eyes, the student exalting in his usefulness, and this lady with the dot. They stopped outside a classroom and through a glass panel in the door a man could be seen lecturing students.

'Teacher Delaware will be finish in about twenty minutes.'

Jian shoved the door and strode up to Delaware. Twenty or so surprised faces watched him brandish the folder, jabbing at the passport picture.

'Please, I need to find my daughter, where is this girl?'

The others came in and a discussion began, with people talking over each other and looking flustered and students craning forward to watch the show. These people used a lot of hand gestures. It made them look excitable.

Delaware dressed very casually for a teacher. He made a placating signal – hands raised, then lowered – said something to his class and studied the passport photo. He didn't recognise her, Jian could tell, and he began to dislike the man, knowing in his stomach that he would bear no good news. He dug folders from a briefcase and showed a list of names with rows of ticks next to them, and the student translated.

'Here her name, see? This is how we write it in English. These the records of the classes Wei Wei went to. She here at start of course, in September last year.'

All the names had a row of ticks beside them, extending to the edge of the form. Except Wei Wei's. There were only three ticks by her name.

'She here only three week.'

'No no no. She rings me every week and tells me how her studies are going. There's a mistake.'

'These records...' now a faltering tone showed that the lad thought of his language skills as a curse – he was to deliver ill tidings. 'These records say she no here. She no go to lecture or hand in work since after that time.'

Jian realised his mouth was open, and closed it.

'She said she was learning about the hotel trade and all that kind of thing. She was a member of the East Asian student society and she was going to act in a play. She was here. She was learning here, and he was her teacher.'

Jian pointed at Delaware, who raised his eyebrows at the security guard.

'No here,' said the student. 'She go, long time ago. She no come here for... four months. Four month no come here.'

The room seemed to be tipping upside down, so Jian put his hand on the whiteboard for support. Suddenly the world was a strange place, he was in the territory of dreams, everything seemed normal but the details were all wrong. He was surrounded by words but he couldn't read them, the faces around him were the wrong shape and a man with blue eyes was telling him he didn't know his own daughter.

'You're telling me that my daughter rang me every week to lie to me?' He pressed his palms against his face. The sad thing was, he could believe it. He felt ashamed of her, then of himself. 'Oh fuck.'

'Let us now go out.'

'Go where? That's it. Where am I going to go? Where?'

He kicked a chair, and the security guard put a hand on his arm.

'Now how am I going to find her?'

The student said, 'The college have records. Know where she was living.'

(4

Standing outside the university, Jian looked gloomily at a billboard across the street. The giant image of a pretty Asian girl flanked by a black man and a white man seemed to be taunting him. It was impossible to tell what it was advertising.

The student had called a taxi for him. When it came he showed the driver a print-out teacher Delaware had made, lines of squiggles which apparently showed the address his daughter had given when she enrolled.

In the back seat, Jian took from his briefcase a slim hardback book. Wei Wei had sent a portrait photo to a magazine and been invited to Beijing to take part in a 'prestigious modelling competition'. He'd forbidden it: he knew what those competitions involved. She'd thrown a sulk, and to mollify her he'd paid for this portfolio of fashion images to be made.

Before leaving home he'd scoured the house for recent pictures, and because he couldn't find any better alternatives he'd bought a copy of the dumb book along. He flicked through it. In one image she posed in a tight military uniform, cradling a gun, legs wide apart, lipstick as red as the star on her beret. In another she was in a red qipao slit right up the thigh, and here she was in a little black dress cocking a champagne glass and a cigarette holder. The photos had captions – guff like 'woman is beauty' and 'true love is forever' in Chinese, and other stuff in English, the language of fashion and modernity.

He thought what a good actress she was – just from the pictures you could tell she was inhabiting each role. She'd had to do a lot of acting on the phone for all those months. But he hadn't made it difficult for her. Their Friday night exchanges had been ritualised, absent of true communication. Are you well? How is college? How are your marks? How is the food? Yes, great, okay, rubbish. Only on food had they gone into any detail. She'd tell him about the strange things she was eating and the tastes she missed. He'd emphasise the importance of a good education and they'd say brisk goodbyes. Every remembered word bought a wince – what a tower of deceit.

The cab passed houses with slanting slate roofs, given a look of ruddy health by their red brick walls and wide windows. The front doors looked flimsy and none of the windows had bars, even on the ground floor. It was remarkable how much care had been lavished on the little gardens. No one seemed to be growing vegetables and no dogs were chained up. There was no litter, the trees were bushy, the pavements flat and smooth. Everything spoke of contented prosperity. But, with no streetlife – no food stalls or vendors, and not even many pedestrians – it was all rather dreary.

The cab pulled up and the driver tapped a meter. It said seventeen. Jian gave him two of the orangey-brown notes and received three chunky gold coins in return. He tried to calculate how much that had been in yuan. A not unreasonable thirty. No – an outrageous three hundred. Standing on the pavement, he watched the taxi pull away. Had he just been conned?

He was standing outside a row of three-storey houses. He checked the printout. Among the squiggles were digits – thirty-four, the same number displayed on a wooden panel on the house before him. The path to the door passed a brick mounting that held rubbish bins. Odd place to put them, in the way of visitors.

He rang the bell and planned what to say to his daughter. He'd play it cool and ask her how she was eating. She'd apologise for stressing him out like that. She'd be impressed that he had come all this way out of paternal concern and would apologise for her unfilial behaviour. He'd be magnanimous. He would not get angry, not yet. The door was opened.

5

An unfamiliar Asian girl held the door on a chain.

Jian said, '*Ni hui shuo zhong wen ma?*... Do you speak Chinese?'

'*Hui.*' A mainlander – that was lucky.

He held the vanity book open at an image of Wei Wei looking dreamy with a fake butterfly in her hair.

'*Zheige nu'hai zhu zai zher ma?*... Does this girl live here?'

'No.'

'Did she live here?'

'Yes. A long time ago.'

'I'm trying to trace her. She's missing.'

He flashed his PSB namecard. The logo of Tian'anmen Gate was in red above embossed black characters. He'd had them specially made, in thicker card than the government issued.

'Come in.'

He had said it out loud, just like that, without thinking. Missing. Now the heavy word clattered round inside his head.

The hallway was carpeted. He bent to take his shoes off but she told him not to bother and led him past bicycles into a cramped kitchen. On a plate sat some half-eaten bread and paste dish.

'I interrupted your dinner.'

'It's okay.'

'What is that?'

'Pizza.'

'Is it tasty?'

'It's simple to cook.'

'You eat with a knife and fork. That's clever.'

'It's easy.'

'What's your name?'

'Song.'

The only time Wei Wei had ever talked about her flatmates was to call a certain Song 'a top-class bitch'. The girl wore glasses and had bad skin but there was a good figure beneath the jeans and jumper. Her accent was Beijing, a croaky 'r' inflection at the end of words. She seemed okay to him.

'When did Wei Wei live here?'

'She moved in in September of last year, and she moved out again after three months.'

'Did she say where she was going?'

'No. She moved out in secret, when we were all at college.'

'She didn't leave a note?'

'No. She ran away owing a lot of rent. Three hundred and sixty pounds.'

'Did she leave anything?'

'We put it in a box. I'll get it.'

Song left the dingy kitchen. Jian opened drawers. He found food in the cupboards, bottles under the sink. A cork noticeboard held postcards, bills, restaurant flyers, time-tables, phone numbers and the like. A magazine on the table had glossy images of good-looking people on the cover, and inside were bad photos of these people doing ordinary things, shopping or just walking in the street. Good-quality paper, though. So much of detective work was about spotting things that didn't quite fit – but he couldn't do that here, where everything was strange to him. The girl returned with a cardboard box.

'This is the stuff she left. You're lucky we haven't thrown it away.'

Books, pens, folders – she'd left behind everything associated with her course. Even though she was writing in English, he still recognised her slapdash hand. In notebook margins she had doodled elaborate question marks, turning them into spirals and swirls. Across the cover of a textbook she had scrawled 'dull dull dull', and that symbol he hoped she'd grown out of, a flower with a happy face. He put the relics carefully into his suitcase.

'Is this an official investigation? You're going to struggle without a translator.'

He said, 'You didn't like her.'

'She never talked to us, she was hardly even civil. Except when my boyfriend came round. An English boy. Then she'd put make-up on and walk round in a nightdress. She was flower crazy.' A flirt. 'She liked to show that her English was better than mine, so she used long words to him. I think she looked them up in the dictionary before coming in.'

She slopped the remains of the pizza into a bin and dropped the plate into the sink with an irritable clatter. There was a catch in her voice as she said, 'He kissed her.'

'I see. And?'

'And that was the kind of person she was. She was trouble.'

'I need to see her old room.'

'We got someone in as soon as we realised she wasn't coming back. Mili is in there now.'

'I have to have a look around.'

'Mili doesn't like anyone going in there.'

'If you fail to co-operate with the investigation, that will be noted in my report.'

She rolled her eyes.

'Be quick.'

She led him up two sets of stairs. It didn't feel right to be walking on carpet in shoes. The walls were wallpapered and the lights had tasselled shades. It was civilised and girly and he felt like a trespasser. Song knocked on a door and, when there was no reply, opened it.

Plastic figurines were displayed on shelves and posters of Japanese cartoon characters covered the walls. He'd imagined there would be something of his daughter left, some lingering presence, but of course there was nothing. He'd fooled himself. He'd intended to treat the place as a crime scene but what had really motivated him was a pilgrim's crude need to see.

But now he was here, he had to try. The main light was dim, so he replaced it with the much brighter bulb from the hallway. He got down on all fours and examined the carpet.

'Please be quick. Mili might come home any minute.'

The bed was on a baseboard on castors. He tried to peer under it but the bottom was only a few centimetres off the floor. He shifted a bedside table and a robot-shaped alarm clock fell off. Song watched him from the doorway as he dragged the bed away.

'You're a northeasterner, aren't you, like her? Which city?'

'Qitaihe.'

'What's it like?'

'It's a pearl.'

Qitaihe might be home but Jian had no illusions. It was a town of dour apartments built around state-owned factories and surrounded by freezing wilderness. Time was you could at least make an honest living, but now the hurricane of capitalism was sweeping the country, the inefficient factories were closing, and workers who'd been promised an iron rice bowl – a job for life – were getting thrown onto the street. The biggest industry was the prison, whose inmates made counterfeit watches for the entrepreneurs of the People's Liberation Army. It was a mean town and getting meaner.

The carpet below the bed was dusty and pale. What filthy things they were, just a dirt trap, and what a strange idea to fill your house with them, then not even take your shoes off. The thing must be full of evidence, dust and hair, and who knew what else. Something gleamed by the skirting board. He slipped it in his pocket while the girl talked on.

'Have you heard of Scotland?'

'It's in England.'

'It's the name for the northern area. It's cold and wild, like the northeast. Scottish people are fierce and direct, they make good friends and terrible enemies, and they like drinking and they're not so good at business. Just like northeastern-ers in China.'

'People from cold places are all the same.'

He found a black hair and pulled it straight. It ran from his fingers to his elbow, and it was half bleached. Wei Wei had thick, strong hair. He wrapped it round his finger and pulled it tight so that it caused pain and redness, and it didn't break. It was his daughter's, he was sure of it. When he unwound the hair it left a white striation with a blush either side. He laid it between pages in her vanity book.

'What kind of trouble is she in?'

'I cannot divulge that information.'

'How come you're on your own?'

'My colleagues are following other lines of inquiry.'

He put the bed and table back and changed the bulbs and closed the door on the room and the girl was visibly relieved.

'I really think you're going to need a translator.'

'Where's your toilet?'

The bathroom was cluttered, with pebbles, candles and shells among all the bottles and vials. The showerhead was above the bath, like in a hotel. He sat on the lowered toilet seat and pulled out his find.

A pewter jewellery box, oval, big enough for a few rings. An image of a phoenix was etched on the lid. It was a fake antique, made in a factory on the outskirts of Shenzhen, and aged by being left in strong tea. He knew because the stall-holder had told him all about it when he'd tried to buy it. The stallholder had insisted that the public security man take this thing of little value for free, as he himself could not in all honesty receive money for such a trifle from an esteemed official. Jian had given it to his daughter before she left for England. She'd said it would prove very useful, that she'd keep her best earrings in it.

The phoenix was depicted at the moment of rebirth. The flames were crudely sketched, but the bird was well done, all its feathers delineated, its neck craning away from the fire, wings spreading. So what it was a fake? Someone had taken a lot of care to scratch the picture into the metal. Or maybe they did it with lasers, the way they carved signature chops.

The lid fitted too tight. It would take nimble fingernails to prise off, his own were too thick. He found nail clippers and used the nail-file attachment as a lever.

Inside the box were two pink pills, a half-smoked hand-made cigarette and a package of glossy paper, a couple of centimetres long. He unfolded the package into a flat square. Half a gram or so of white powder gathered in the creases. Drugs. It wasn't even a surprise.

(6

He'd suspected Wei Wei was doing drugs back home. She'd go to that sleazy YES! disco dressed up like a tramp, and get up to who knew what with the disreputable elements that hung round there. He'd tried to get the place shut down on grounds of moral pollution, but no chance of that – the proprietor also owned a sauna where you could get a massage and something else, and city bureaucrats got their something else for free. He'd personally overseen the beating-up of the club's drug dealers – and she'd got mad because they were friends.

He'd hoped a stint at a foreign college would knock some sense into her. And look what she'd done. She'd dropped out of her course, taken drugs, argued with that sensible girl and run away from this comfy house. She'd lied to him for months on end, and now who knew where she had gone and what trouble she'd got herself into. He wanted to punch something in his frustration. Damn her that she caused him such hurt.

The handmade cigarette was four centimetres long with a blackened end. He split it, revealing crispy shreds of tobacco and green fragments of plant matter. It was too old to smell, but presumably it was dope. Rolled-up paper had been inserted to act as a filter. He slid it out with the nail file and uncurled it.

The paper was glossy and white. It had two straight edges and two rough, showing it had been ripped from the corner of something, perhaps a magazine or book cover. It was unmarked except for a curling red line, part of a larger design, possibly a letter.

Jian put the paper in his namecard holder and dropped the rest of the cigarette and the pills and the powder into the toilet and flushed it. The sound awakened a response, and he remembered he needed a shit. He normally took a dump every morning, and his regularity was reassuring to him, but of course now, with the time difference, and staying up for hours, his system was out of whack.

The porcelain was unpleasantly cold. He hadn't used Western toilets much. More and more, he saw them around, but he stuck with what he knew, the squat variety. He realised that other bare arses had sat here recently, including that of the fetching Song. A strange intimacy to share.

So his daughter had moved here in September of last year. She'd attended her course for three weeks and she'd lived in this house for three months. In December she'd run away to save herself from paying rent. It was March now. So what was she doing between dropping out and leaving here? And why did she drop out so quickly? And what had she been doing for the many months that she'd lied to him? And what had happened to her now? That was a lot of questions, but of course only one mattered.

There was no toilet paper bin by the loo, so he wrapped the used sheets in clean sheets and put them in the only bin he could see, under the sink. His turd was not the usual colour and it took two flushes to get it away.

Back in the kitchen, Song was tackling the washing-up. He guessed his presence had made her self-conscious about it. He didn't want to leave. Where would he go? Who else could he to talk to?

Did Wei Wei use a knife and fork?

'I guess.'

He'd never seen that, didn't know she was capable of it.

'What did your boyfriend tell you she said to him?'

'Ex-boyfriend. We split up. What are you studying, oh that is so interesting, tell me more. The importance of – what was her catchphrase? Grace. How she wanted to live like an artist. She got it all out of magazines. She was a silly country girl desperate to look sophisticated. Now I've got all upset again.' The washing-up gloves made decisive slaps as she took them off. She wiped a tear away. 'I wish she'd stayed at home.'

'What else do you remember? What else?'

'She once said how sick she was of oily Cantonese muck and how she wanted proper Chinese food.'

That seemed odd. He did not remember her saying the same to him.

'Where would she get Cantonese food?'

'She usually had takeout.'

'Usually?' She had told him she was cooking for herself. Even about the food, then, she had been lying.

'So who eats takeout and complains about it?'

Jian's eyes were drawn to the restaurant flyers on the corkboard. A couple were for pizza places, with shocking pictures of the lurid things. He answered his own question. 'Waitresses. She worked in a restaurant.'

'That would make sense.'

He could see it. The course had bored her stupid, so she'd stopped attending. Fearing that he'd stop her allowance, she hadn't told him. Needing to do something, she'd got a job in a restaurant. It was a good supposition. He was excited, the detective in him exalted at leads, and while there were leads there was hope.

'There can't be many Chinese restaurants.'

'No, they're everywhere. English people like Chinese food.'

Jian took the flyers down and picked out the ones with Chinese characters on. The flyer for the Wild Crane was flimsy and yellow with a green bamboo design on the cover. He put it aside. The second was glossier, with thicker paper. On the cover a stylised image of a pink lotus flower hung over the name, The Floating Lotus, written in fluid running script. Inside was a long list of dishes, and on the back an address. Jian took out the slip of roach paper from the drugs cigarette and placed it against the bottom right-hand corner of the back page. It was a match, with the red line the bottom curl of the number nine, the last digit of the restaurant telephone number.

'I'm taking this,' he said. 'Thank you for your co-operation.'

7

'I hope you find her,' said Song, seeing Jian out. 'I hope nothing bad has happened.'

It was getting dark and the streetlights were on, glowing orange and not the white he was used to. He approached a pedestrian walking a dog and held up the flyer, but the guy just babbled and walked away.

After ten minutes he still hadn't seen a taxi. They did not seem to be as prevalent here as they were at home, and no wonder, when they cost so much. He supposed they didn't cruise residential areas. Frustrated and at a loss, he got on a bus, hoping it would take him back to the centre of town. At least he knew there was a cab rank outside the station. Even buying a bus ticket required educated guesses and keen observation – no conductor, so does money go to the driver or into a machine? How much money? These chunky gold ones? How many? He was given novel coins in his change – hexagonal ones, copper ones.

He hadn't been on a bus in a decade, it was not done for a man in his position. Tired, he pressed his fingers against closed eyes. It was the early hours of the morning back home – he should be tucked up in bed with some chick to warm his feet. He didn't feel right and wondered if he'd caught an illness. Perhaps he just wasn't used to this climate or this air. He spat on the floor, smeared the goo with his heel, then lit a 555.

He didn't know why his daughter had gone wayward. Probably she blamed him for the car crash that had killed her mother. He'd been driving a station Toyota and he'd been drunk and pushing it hard, but the lorry hadn't even bothered to indicate, and its driver had been even drunker. Whichever way you looked at it – and he'd looked at it from all the ways you could look at it – it wasn't his fault.

He'd made sure the lorry driver had got a harsh sentence. Now, though, he envied that driver. The man had served his time and paid his dues. How was he supposed to pay his? He blinked hard and rubbed his face to jolt his mind out of that particular, well-worn, track.

Two women were looking at him and tutting. He scowled right back and in his head confronted them, saying, 'What? Am I in a zoo? You never seen a Chinese guy before?' The bus was passing fields and trees, which couldn't be right, so he dropped his cigarette and got off at the next stop.

It was dispiriting. If he couldn't even get around, or have a conversation, how could he conduct an investigation? Jet-lag, fatigue, all-pervasive foreignness, the unique and unsettling experience of anonymity and powerlessness – it was affecting the way he thought. He did not feel like a successful, wealthy and high-ranking policeman any more. He put his hand in front of his face. He was this dense flesh and nothing else, a middle-aged man, big but running to fat, with a lot on his mind.

He stepped into the street and a car honked at him and he had to scuttle forward sharply. Traffic here came from the wrong direction. He'd remembered fine earlier, but now he was slipping. He got the same number bus going in the other direction.

He counted out three hundred and sixty pounds and wondered who the figures depicted on the notes were. The woman on the back of them all was presumably the

Queen or Madam Thatcher. It was a beautiful currency, very artistic, but he was getting through it at a frightening rate.

He got off at a stop he recognised and rang the bell at number thirty-four. Song answered.

He said, 'It's not an official investigation. I'm Wei Wei's father.'

Embarrassment, then consternation, passed across her features.

'This is the rent she owed.'

He gave her the money. Some people would just pocket it, but he was sure she was an honest citizen. It would go where it was supposed to and a wrong would be righted. Now she looked at him as if seeing him for the first time.

'There's one condition.'

'Which is?'

He held up the flyer for the Floating Lotus.

'Come and have a drink with me.'

8

'My daughter called and begged me to help her. Now I don't know where she is.'

'Oh dear.' Song bit her fingernail. His distress had made her sad.

Now that Song was leading him, Jian was passive, and instead of trying to figure out his environment he just let it happen. The illuminated signs outside the bus window all said the same thing – 'You do not understand.'

'She's probably just ashamed that she dropped out and wanted to spare your feelings. And now she's got into some little trouble. There's probably a man involved,' she said, with the confidence of youth and inexperience. 'Women do stupid things over men. If she's at this restaurant, I'll take off, okay? Leave you alone for a reunion.'

Indeed, it was quite possible that Wei Wei was working at the restaurant. Maybe she was doing well, had found something she could throw herself into. He pictured her waiting tables, dreaming of stardom as an actress or model, living with some guy. A local difficulty had occurred – jail, pregnancy, a perception of failure – and she'd called him in a moment of weakness, then lost her phone or her nerve. Perhaps she'd called during a bad trip, and afterwards forgotten she'd called at all. She'd be so surprised to see him, she'd drop a plate.

The more he thought about her, the more elusive she seemed. He could conjure her features, but not arrange them into an expression. He could remember her character –

moodiness, kindness, thoughtlessness, romanticism – only in the abstract, without the accompaniment of illustrating incidents. He saw her doing little things that meant nothing – washing, humming, tapping her feet with her headphones on. The dumbest of details came to mind – a smiling sunflower, a fake bag, that green gonk that dangled off her phone. He couldn't place her in this environment at all – walking these roads, talking in that jabber to these people.

'Do you want a cigarette? 555. English brand.'

'They're not English.'

'It says on the packet they're English.'

'They cheat you. They're Chinese. And you're not allowed to smoke on here.'

They got off and Jian began to recognise logos, on clothes and adverts – McDonald's, KFC, Nike – each a small reassurance in the ocean of the unfamiliar. The change in his pocket jangled. He never carried a wallet, Chinese money being mostly notes, but he might need one now.

Here was a shop selling shoes and another selling newspapers, and in between was the Floating Lotus. It looked like a fancy concern, with lanterns hanging outside and a neon sign.

They went in and a bell tinkled as the door closed.

More than any restaurant back home, this place advertised its Chineseness. Limpet-shaped hats and idealised landscape paintings hung above a bamboo skirting, and pride of place went to a back-lit relief of a waterfall. Yet there were no clue as to which part of China the proprietors were from. It was very quiet, there wasn't even any music playing, and the place was so dark Jian wondered if there had been a power outage. There was none of the boisterous vitality he looked for in a restaurant. There were ten or so tables, but only three were occupied. All the customers were white.

Neither waitress was tall enough to be his daughter. No, she was not here, and again hope was cruelly extinguished.

A waitress approached, a slim Chinese girl in a red uniform with nails and lips painted to match. She said something in English, and he asked if she spoke Mandarin Chinese. She looked blankly back – she didn't.

'They're Cantonese,' said Song. 'Like most Chinese people in this country. From Hong Kong originally, I expect. They won't speak Mandarin. You won't meet many Mandarin speakers here at all.'

He instructed her to inquire after his daughter, and opened the vanity book. Wei Wei posed by a balance beam in pink tracksuit, hair tied back, not much make-up. It was the homeliest of all the pictures, and the one he liked best. The inviting smile of the girl in red vanished and her face closed shut.

'She says she doesn't know her,' said Song.

An old man stood at the back trying not to look like he was watching them. Like the girl he had a high forehead, full lips and a receding chin, and Jian guessed he was her father, and the owner. He said, 'Let's ask him.'

Jian pushed the vanity book across the counter. He thought of the Cantonese as cunning, but this old man was no actor. He looked at the picture, scratched his balding pate as if thinking, cast his eyes to the ceiling as if thinking some more, looked at the picture again from another angle, turned the page to look at another picture, then shook his head.

Song translated. 'He says he's very sorry, but he has no idea who that girl could be. He's never met her.'

The old man looked as if he regretted terribly being unable to help. He closed the book and pushed it firmly back.

'He wants to know who she is.'

'Tell him some friends of hers need to talk to her, but they're having trouble getting in touch. Don't say I'm her father.'

The old man was trying hard not to look too curious.

'He wants to know what it is about.'

'Tell him it's a love story – it's about a boy, he's looking for her, the parents don't approve. Tell him the boy is right now on the other side of town doing other Chinese restaurants. Make sure he understands that, that someone is out doing other restaurants.'

'He wants to know who we are.'

'We're concerned friends who want to see true love run its proper course. Tell him we'll have a table for two.'

The mask slipped and the owner looked crestfallen, just for a moment. He escorted them with overdone courtesy to a table far from the counter.

The lighting was arranged so that patrons could see their own tables and little of the rest of the room. It was like going to eat in a cave. The menu was in English and Chinese. Jian read the names of all the dishes because it was good to see words he understood for a change. It was all southern stuff and staples.

'Why did you make me lie to him?' said Song. 'I didn't like it. I thought he was a nice old man.'

'I wanted to test his reactions.'

'Did you think he was lying?'

'A policeman doesn't think, he establishes facts.' Which was rubbish, but the sort of reply that satisfied the public.

He was pleased to discover that they had Tsingtao beer, though at ten times the usual price. He was shocked when it turned up to see how small the bottle was. He ordered crispy fried duck, sweet and sour pork balls, beef and peppers and fried rice. The girl had a glass of orange juice. She said, 'What are you going to do now?'

'I have other lines of inquiry.'

'You must tell the local police.'

Jian had no confidence in that. He knew how missing persons went. You opened a file, sent a rookie out to do interviews, and took the rest of the afternoon off. Every cop knew, missing persons was hopeless. They either turned up or they didn't.

He excused himself. The toilets were downstairs, and there was another door beyond them. It was locked, but only by a catch, so Jian slipped his Bank of China Great Wall debit card into the crack. Back home they called these locks the housebreaker's friend, they were no security at all. But this version was sturdier than its Chinese equivalent and, however he wiggled, the card the catch wouldn't click.

He wiggled harder, a crease in the card whitened and cracks appeared. He imagined a cluttered staffroom beyond the door, and perhaps it had evidence inside and probably not, but he wanted to know one way or the other. The card snapped in two and the broken half flipped back into the corridor. He sighed in exasperation. Things were so much easier in China.

Someone was coming down the stairs. He supposed it was the old man checking up. A lighter footstep was the new arrival stepping off the bottom stair and onto carpet. It was too late to look for the broken half of the card. He stepped into the nearest toilet and got the door closed just as someone padded round towards him.

He considered a vase of plastic flowers on the cistern and a poster of a Hong Kong heart-throb. He did not like skulking around, and especially not in toilets and especially not in the ladies. Really though, what did he expect to find? A rota with his daughter's name, her bag hanging on a hook, her picture in the staff outing photo album? He didn't need evidence, he knew the old man was lying.

Someone still loitered outside, so he put the remains of the card on the edge of the sink and flushed the loo and ran the taps. The card slid off and twirled into the corner. The broken card was bad news, it meant he couldn't use an ATM. He'd be stuck for money as soon as his slim wad ran out. He bent to pick it up and paused. Chinese characters, barely half a centimetre high, were written along the grouting between wall tiles. 'Dull dull dull' – then a doodle of a sunflower with a smiling face.

He spotted another strip of discreet graffiti: 'My boss is a colour wolf' – a sleaze. There was more, but he did not need to examine it. It was just like his daughter, he could see it – the resentful waitress, stretching out a toilet break, venting her frustrations on the only receptive surface.

The owner stood outside, trying to look like he had something to do. Jian nodded and went upstairs.

9

'How about this,' said Song. 'She started a career as a model because she could, she was very good-looking, and she didn't want to tell you because she knew you wouldn't approve. Then she went out to... some desert island on a shoot, and she got into some little trouble and called you, and she dropped her phone, with all her numbers in... She was on a yacht and she dropped it in the sea.' She had come up with a pleasing story to lighten the mood and seemed tickled at her inventiveness. 'I did that once, I mean lost my phone, it was a nightmare.'

She was so happy and straightforward. Jian knew her type. The modern urban Chinese girl, a doted-on only child, well educated, used to getting her own way, brought up in a cosy world that just kept on giving.

Was there ever such a gilded generation as the urban Chinese born in the Eighties? Their whole lives they had surfed the edge of a glorious wave of progress. Taught to aspire to a bicycle and a watch, televisions and fridges had come, then cars and computers. For them, the world could be trusted to just keep on delivering the goods. They had known nothing but bounty, so there was something green about them. They were as alien as foreigners.

His own generation had been blighted, scarred by the Cultural Revolution. In the seventies, Jian had been a Red Guard. Intent on building socialism, he'd got good at hitting people with a brick-filled satchel, as most of his energy had been taken up with fighting other Red Guards.

He'd also put time in humiliating intellectuals, smashing ancient statuary and burning books. He'd smeared ink on the faces of teachers and paraded them with 'cow demon' and 'snake spirit' written on signs hung around their necks.

He had loved and hated as directed and worshipped Mao without reservation. There'd been songs and passion and a sense of purpose. Then times had changed, and the lights he'd been brought up to live by had been shown to lead nowhere. Past struggles had been revealed as a tremendous waste of time, his idol Mao was an old fuck and a fraud. Well, he would not be fooled again. He believed in nothing now – there was only luck and money, and you'd better have one or the other.

He took out a cigarette. It was still a disappointment to learn that 555 was not really English. What about Rolls-Royce, then, and Clarks shoes and gentleman culture?

'You can't smoke in here.'

'What? This is a restaurant.'

'Yes, and you can't smoke in restaurants.'

'What kind of country is this? The bus, I can understand. But a restaurant?' He twirled the cigarette between his fingers and thought how pretty it looked before slotting it back in the pack. 'You're supposed to smoke after eating. It helps the digestion.'

He looked round. The waitress's face was a carefully composed blank, but her fingernails tapped nervously on the counter. The owner was making a call on a mobile. For a moment the men caught each other's eyes and the owner shied away and turned his back. It was good to unnerve them. But it was not wise having civilians around to complicate things. He said, 'I want you to go home, please.'

'Oh. Okay.' She was only discomfited for a moment. 'Are you sure there's nothing more I can help you with?'

'Give me the number of your mobile. I may call tonight, possibly very late. Please keep your phone close.'

As soon as she had gone, he missed her. Bright, sensible, a good citizen – he wished his daughter was more like that one, then guiltily ushered the thought away.

The food was a disappointment. The meat was dry and tasteless, the vegetables chewy, and everything was smothered with starchy sauces. It was a gaudy parody of proper food. He ordered another Tsingtao to wash away the taste.

A couple on the next table paid up and left, and now he was the last customer. He pretended not to notice, got a Beijing Youth Daily out of his case and read a story about a German footballer who might change clubs.

The door opened and a Chinese man strolled in. Leather jacket, jeans, jade and gold jewellery – he looked like an antisocial element. Better dressed than the ones back home, with better manners maybe, but the same attitude. He idled to the counter. The waitress slipped through the door behind it and the old man came out, grinning and rubbing his hands.

Jian watched out of the corner of his eye. They began to chat in Cantonese like the best of friends. But the old man's smile was unnatural and his quickly moving eyes looked scared. The new arrival turned side-on and his eyes wandered. They wandered all the way over to Jian, and for a moment the men locked glances.

The guy ambled over. He was chewing a match. He said around it, 'I hear you're looking for a girl.'

10

He was tall and lean with delicate, almost girlish features. Hooded eyes that didn't seem to blink as much as they should, sharp cheekbones, pale complexion, artfully tousled hair. He could have stepped out of a magazine. But there was a dark birthmark, like a dry sauce stain, below his lower lip. Maybe he chewed the match to take attention away from it.

'Let me see.'

He glanced at the vanity book. No flicker of recognition crossed his face.

'Don't know her. Would like to. What a piece.'

'How come you speak Mandarin? You're from Hong Kong, aren't you?'

'All Chinese should speak the language of the motherland.' He tapped the book. 'What's the story?'

So now he was the one answering questions, the hoodlum knew his stuff. He let his voice rise a little and added a touch of tremulous warble, trying to sound dumb and harmless.

'There's a boy would very much like to find her. They were engaged back home. All we know is, she's a waitress in a Chinese restaurant over here. I've visited so many now they've all started to look the same. Certainly the food always tastes the same – terrible. Why is that, do you think?'

'White people scoff anything. There's no point giving those pigs the good stuff, they wouldn't recognise it. Are you staying around for long?'

'A couple more days. There are plenty more places to check. Depends how the money holds up.'

'What's your name?'

Jian reached into his inside pocket. He had collected the namecards of his companions on the flight and he took one out now. He presented it politely, with both hands, which gave him the chance to glance at the name.

'A refinery sub-manager,' said the hoodlum, drily. 'I would never have guessed.'

This was no idle conversation. So much scrutiny was going on beneath the casual phrases, it was almost like flirting. He remembered seeing the old man on the phone and suspected the youth had been summoned to probe him.

'And you are..?'

'In Mandarin you would say Black Fort.'

Hei lei – presumably it sounded better in Cantonese. It was a hoodlum nickname. At least the lad showed some imagination, usually they just called themselves Dragon.

The manager came over. He was still all smiles but the strain was starting to tell, his cheek twitched. He kept talking and gesturing, and it was obvious he was apologetically saying that he was shutting up. Jian pretended not to get the message. It was always good to give the impression of stupidity – people underestimated you.

The hoodlum said, 'He's telling you he's closed.'

Now, seeing them together, the nervous old man standing and the youth cold and self-possessed in his chair, it was obvious which of the two was in charge.

Black Fort dropped half of a Great Wall card on the table. Jian put his hand on it. The youth put a hand over his. The fingers were long and neat, the nails manicured and glossy as bullets. The palm was hot and soft, but along the edge, below the little finger, he could feel a pad of coarser skin.

Those came from years of practising open hand strikes – it was the sign of a martial artist.

They locked gazes. There was an unsettling yellowish tint to the man's irises. Jian knew Black Fort was lying, knew also that the man knew he was being lied to. A match promenaded across his mouth and he continued not blinking.

'Sometimes it's best to leave things to sort themselves out.'

Jian slid his hand out. 'You're a Taoist.'

'I'm a realist.' The lad pointed the match. 'You know what I think? I think she doesn't want to be found.'

Jian finished his drink.

'Thank you for the benefit of your opinion.'

As he paid, he felt a moment of disquiet at the slimness of his wad. He had taken nine thousand yuan with him, and changed it all up when he arrived, in the expectation that that would pay for all his expenses, including maybe a couple of bribes, then a celebratory meal and presents. He'd gone through most of it already.

The owner escorted him out. Darkness had fallen but there were a lot of lights on – even the adverts on a bus stop were illuminated. Lighting a cigarette, Jian checked out the street in the reflection of the shoe-shop window, and clocked a dark figure lurking in a doorway over the road and a second loitering behind a car. He walked quickly away, and after ten or so paces turned round abruptly. He scratched his head and looked about, pretending to be drunk and lost. He hurried back the way he had come. Both figures had moved. He was being followed.

(11

With all the cars parked at the side of the road and the big shop windows, the street had a wealth of reflective surfaces, and Jian was able to keep an eye on both his followers. On the other side of the road a chunky guy walked with slow deliberation, matching Jian's pace, hands thrust deep into a long leather coat. He was pretty good – at least he looked natural. Further back, and on this side of the road, a slimmer, nervier man skipped along the gutter and peeked round parked cars. He was an amateur.

He was soon convinced that there was just the two of them. Two men were not enough for a tail. It took at least four, spread out in front and behind, with good communications. He was confident he could lose them. He could take a couple of sharp turns, then double back, dive into a bar or restaurant and find a back exit, or just hop into a taxi.

He passed an alleyway where a youth was bent over being sick. Through foggy windows he could see a raucous crowd. Music pulsed. It was an enormous bar. He would lose his pursuers in there, no trouble at all. There might be a cloakroom where he could leave the case. But losing them would achieve nothing. What he needed to do was turn the tables.

Perhaps he would hire a private karaoke booth and a girl to sing with, and then, while his enemies were watching the booth, find a back way to slip out. He could monitor the one outside, and when they realised he had given them the slip maybe he could follow them.

He felt energized. Maybe he had spent too long behind a desk. This was like being an eager rookie again – going on missions, out-thinking bad guys. A man on mean streets living by his wits at least knew he was alive.

It was, he reprimanded himself, an inappropriate response, an undisciplined thought produced by fatigue and adrenalin. This was not a mission, his daughter was in danger, and his anxiety renewed itself.

He stepped into the road and stopped to let a car pass. Its engine roared as it sped up and swerved towards him. It was low-slung and yellow and in the tinted windscreen he saw the distorted reflection of his own startled form and the orbs of streetlights. The passenger door was swinging open. He threw himself back. The bonnet swept by and caught the suitcase and it was wrenched from his grip as the bumper cracked. The open door smashed him in the midriff.

He collapsed and his head smacked the edge of the pavement. He was aware of the squeal of tyres and running footsteps, but it all seemed to come from far away. He could see only lights sparkling in red mist.

His jacket was hauled over his head, trapping his arms and smothering his face. A weight pressed down on his neck. Hands groped inside his pockets. Fury at this violation gave him strength. He twisted and flung a bent arm out. His elbow connected with something and the impact sent shivers to his shoulder.

Pain exploded in his stomach and he gaped and his fingers spread and curled. He tensed for another blow.

Someone started shouting. No new strike arrived. He heard retreating footsteps and an engine growled then receded.

He unclenched and groped for the pavement. The jacket fell away from his head as he rolled out of the gutter. A gurgling sound was coming from his throat. Gravel prickled his cheek. His chest felt huge and sore. Red mist retreated and a white shape resolved itself into a pale and sweaty man with a busy mouth and a chin speckled with vomit.

Jian dragged himself up. The bass thudding from the bar seemed to rhyme with the pain in his head. His suitcase had gone, and most of the contents of his pockets. He'd been done over and robbed. He hadn't even caught a glimpse of his attackers. But it could have been worse. They had left in a hurry, after the puking guy started shouting. He had got an elbow strike in and that had been good.

The white man was making noises of indignation and sympathy and had a hand on his shoulder. The smell of sick was strong and Jian just wanted him to go away. It would be nice to collapse here and let his gaze settle on the sparkling streetlights and observe his breathing return to normal. It would be even better to be several thousand kilometres away in a comfy, familiar bed.

But he had a missing daughter. He got down on all fours and examined the pavement and the gutter. He found half a match and held it to the light. When he pressed the broken end against the back of his hand, he found it soggy. That hoodlum Black Fort. It was not a surprise. So the man had not believed his story. He'd wanted to find out who he was, warn him off and put him out of action.

He staggered to his feet. He found that if he put one hand on his stomach, raised the other to trail along the wall and kept his eyes focused on the middle distance, he could make acceptable forward progress.

He set off back the way he had come. A couple of drunk lads weaved past. It seemed everyone was pissed, maybe today was some local festival. He supposed he fitted right in: he couldn't walk straight, either.

He almost missed the oversized lanterns of the Floating Lotus, the lights inside were off. Now those hanging black globes put him in mind of bombs. The shutters of the restaurant were down, but inside lights were on and through slits in the metal he could see dark figures moving around.

He crossed the road and found a building with a recessed porch, equidistant between two lampposts, and sat with his back against the door. He was in shadow from the road but had a clear view of the restaurant. It wasn't great cover, but it would have to do.

Definitely, he told himself, it could have been much worse. Nothing was broken inside and they had not found his passport and airline ticket, secure in the belt around his waist. He grinned as he imagined them right now rooting through underwear and toiletries. There was hardly any money in the wallet and anyway the credit card was broken. The suitcase had only been slowing him down. They would find his namecard, but so what? It wouldn't mean much to them. He stopped grinning because it seemed to be making his head hurt more.

He lit a cigarette and shaded its glowing end with his free hand. It was reassuring to smoke, it was something other than aches to concentrate on. But when he inhaled, a pain in his side intensified. He discovered the trick was to breathe in very gently. He'd had worse. He rubbed his elbow and hoped it had connected with a nose.

This was tough territory, no place for a naïve young girl. He did not blame his daughter for her lies or her failures, he rebuked only himself. He shouldn't have let her go. No, he had to be honest with himself – he shouldn't have encouraged her to go. How convenient it had been to send her away. He had told himself it was for her own good – but, all along, was it not his own that he had been thinking about? No more difficulties, no more embarrassing incidents. The pain of his battering was easier to bear than these uneasy pricklings.

He settled into the wait. So what he had no money? He'd steal a car to sleep in and beg for food – whatever it took, it didn't matter. No obstacle would be allowed to stand in the way. He was going to find his damn daughter.

GOLD MOUNTAIN

(1 2

Ding Ming lay in a foetal position, inside a sealed box lined with carbon paper, in the back of a container truck. His backside and haunches were sore, his legs numb. The air was so stale that every breath scorched his lungs, his clothes so soaked with sweat they clung to his skin. Sweat trickled along his eyelids and down his nose.

He needed a piss. He could relieve himself into his empty water bottle but he'd lost the screw-on cap, so having relieved himself he'd have to concentrate for the rest of the journey on keeping the bottle upright, he certainly didn't want to be sloshed with his own urine.

It was very annoying that he'd dropped the cap. He risked raising himself onto his forearm so that he could grope for it.

Nothing. He slipped off one plimsoll and fumbled with a bare foot until he felt the plastic rim. With the cap secured by curled toes he brought his foot up and reached down with his fingers. Just before hand met foot, the cap slipped out. He heard it roll, and now he was aggravated at the cap for its disobedience and at the impossibility of bending even this most trivial of objects to his will.

Trying again, his foot kicked the side of the box and he heard paper tear. He'd gone and slashed the carbon paper with his big toenail. If only he'd cut it before the journey. If he'd known it was going to be an issue, he certainly would have done.

He didn't know if the rip was significant or not, because he didn't know what the carbon paper was for. He supposed it was to protect against malevolent spirits or to fool the prying machines of customs officials. That little tear might have terrible consequences, his big toe could have had jeopardised the whole venture. Mental pictures blossomed of a red alarm blaring, men in black uniforms running, evil spirits slipping like smoke through ripped carbon paper.

And he was still desperate for a piss, and the cap still eluded him, and it was baking hot, and breathing the meagre air was like sucking hot sand, and his mind was stretched so thin he couldn't think straight.

The truck stopped moving and the roar of the engine died. An echo of the noise ran round Ding Ming's head, and an echo of the buffetting he'd been receiving from the suspension seemed to be still vibrating his bones.

He heard a suppressed cough and someone shushed. Voices came from outside, and Ding Ming strained to listen. Fearing a customs inspection or a police raid, his stomach tightened.

He'd been caught by the police once before, when leaving, at night, by horse and cart, that country with the wooden houses and the trees with silver bark. The police had kicked him and his companions and turned them all the way back to the gloomy town by the lake.

He felt that his breathing was too loud, surely it was audible to the men in black uniforms, they were craned forward listening with frowns on their faces.

Two booming slaps came, and Ding Ming stiffened. Someone had banged the side of the truck.

Metal scraped metal, and a voice cried, 'Chinky dinkies! Let's be having you!'

13

Ding Ming burst out from his box like a birthday surprise. Others were popping from their boxes, and the sound of splitting cardboard filled the air.

He sought out his wife. Little Ye's hair was matted against her cheeks and her eyes were red, but she was smiling as she stood and stretched. Her T-shirt was so sweaty it clung to her body. The decorative red bows on the shoulders still stood out perkily, though. He took her hand, and together they clambered down from the container.

The truck was parked in a shabby farmyard. A three-quarter moon illuminated rusty machinery, a stack of tyres, weeds growing through cracked concrete. The horizon was bumpier than at home, the trees bushier. It seemed very quiet after the incessant hum of the truck. Just to be still and silent and breathing untainted air was as energising as a cold drink. Ding Ming felt a surge of optimism. Here was an end to feeling like luggage.

Simultaneously, Ding Ming and Little Ye admitted they were desperate for a wee. They laughed and squeezed hands.

Himself, he'd slip it out and piss anywhere, he didn't care, but he respected her need for a little dignity. He peered into a barn. It looked derelict. One corner had fallen in, and pale moonlight streamed through holes in the wall and roof. A container, like the one they'd arrived in, was parked on a lorry flatbed. It seemed like the sort of place where a lady might have a little privacy. He looked back. The other migrants were stretching and chattering. They too were nervous and excited with the adventure of arrival, and for the moment it was conquering fatigue. A white man moved among them, handing out cigarettes. No one was paying him or Little Ye any attention.

'Go here, behind this trailer.'

'I don't want to pee inside, it's not polite.'

'They don't use this place.' He indicated fast-food wrappers. 'It's full of rubbish. Come on.'

But she was stepping carefully between a scattering of rusty metal bars. She stiffened, said 'Ow', and rubbed her ankle.

'What is it?'

'Stinging plants.'

'So come in here.'

She followed him inside, and briskly squatted. He stood before her with his back turned, pissing against the trailer's wheel. It felt good to take a piss in his new home, it was the beginning of coming to terms with it.

'There's a funny smell in here,' said Little Ye.

It was a stench like rotten meat. It added to the gloom and sense of neglect to make the barn a dispiriting place.

A rustling drew his attention to a crowd of black birds gathered in the rafters. Moonlight illuminated a wing, a steady eye, a beak shining like a knife. Ding Ming didn't like the way they were looking at him, so he stamped his foot and called '*Zou kai!*... Go!' and the birds took off, with insolent lack of haste, flapping through the broken wall.

But now the white man, alerted by his call, was hurrying in. He called out things Ding Ming didn't catch, but his tone was stern – though perhaps that was how they spoke all the time.

'I beg your pardon?' Ding Ming said, in English.

'Get out.'

'Sorry, my wife is having toilet.'

Ding Ming had looked forward to speaking English to an English person in England. Now here it was finally happening, a shame the circumstances were not better. He zipped up.

'I don't care if she's having kittens, mate. Out.'

Ding Ming stepped sideways to block his view of the squatting woman, and said the first thing he could think of, anything to stop the man looking at his wife – 'What is your name?' It was the first English sentence he'd learned, one he considered himself good at.

'What? Kevin.'

Ding Ming had seen few white people before and never so close. Mister Kevin was a peculiar sight, tall with a fat general's belly that hung grandly over his waist, hiding his belt. His arms were thick and round, he was like a figure made of rolled putty balls. His skin was hairy and pink as a pig's hide, and stubble bristled on his chin, there was even hair coming out of his nose. With all these details to take in, it was impossible to concentrate on his barking English.

Nervous, Ding Ming smiled, but that only seemed to cause further aggravation.

'What are you grinning about? Out.' Mister Kevin jerked a fleshy thumb over his shoulder. Even his hand was of note – pale, doughy.

But if Ding Ming moved, it would reveal his wife. The more awkward he felt, the more his smile broadened. It was his natural response to awkward social situations. Now it was a rictus grin. He could not think of a new sentence, he was growing panicky.

'What's so bloody funny?' demanded Mister Kevin. 'Heh?' He stepped around and glared at the squatting girl. 'You too – out. Go on – out.'

Little Ye hurriedly pulled up her trousers. What a pity that she could not have gone to the toilet in private. It wasn't much to ask. Now she'd be feeling ashamed.

Ding Ming took his wife's hand and hurried her out of the barn, and Mister Kevin glared at them all the way back into the farmyard.

'I'm sorry about that,' he said, relieved to return to his mother tongue, the Fujianese dialect.

'No, I'm sorry.' She was fastening her trousers. 'It was my fault.'

They watched Mister Kevin closing the barn off by dragging a sheet of corrugated iron across the entrance. He didn't seem to have any more time for them.

Ding Ming felt mortified. He'd caused an uncomfortable situation for his wife, and it seemed he'd broken the rules of conduct of his hosts. He wished he'd never seen that barn.

(14

'It's okay,' said Ding Ming. 'It's fine. This is a thing of no importance.'

'How can you be sure?' She gnawed on her bottom lip in that way she had. He felt foreboding, too. They were in a new country with new rules and new rulers, people who cared about them were too far away to help, and there were no friendly faces to provide a single stroke of comfort.

All the migrants were from China's Fujian Province. The five other men were all from one village, some place on the coast. Tough and taciturn, they'd expected to become fishermen like their fathers and grandfathers.

Ding Ming was aware that they did not see him as one of their own. Never mind that he was a peasant too, a simple village boy whose parents barely scratched a living out of a smallholding. He'd been educated, he could speak Mandarin Chinese and even some English, he didn't smoke, and he'd brought his wife along. They'd left wives and girl friends, and in some cases children, at home, knowing that they would not see them again for years, and they were still working at hardening their hearts. Perhaps it didn't do them good to see a loving couple together.

The two girls were twins from a brood of three girls. Their unfortunate parents had been desperate for a son, and had kept trying, never mind the penalties. Squat and dark and big-eyed, they held hands and sucked their thumbs.

A couple of the men were relieving themselves against the wall of the barn. The girls were going in a ditch and everyone else had turned their backs – that was the way to do it.

Kevin and his lieutenants stood apart, smoking and chatting. Little Ye followed his gaze and said, 'I find them a little frightening.'

He knew what she meant. Kevin and the driver were overweight, and the sense their bodies gave of flesh multiplying out of control was alarming. But even their slimmer companions, with their booming voices and rudely assertive gestures, gave the impression of bigness. To reassure both himself and his wife, Ding Ming said, 'They are no different to you and I.'

Clicking his fingers and pointing, Kevin directed the men towards a dirty white van, while one of his lieutenants began herding the girls to a car.

'I want all the men over here, and the women get in there.'

Ding Ming had no desire to act on those instructions, he did not even let go of his wife's hand.

Kevin's gestures got larger. There was something so peculiar about that babble and the big movements. A Chinese man laughed out of nervousness. Kevin punched him in the face and the man fell down.

'Yeah? That's what happens when you laugh at me.' Kevin rubbed his knuckles.

There was a difficult silence and the felled man rose and wiped blood off his mouth. He waved away the ministrations of his friends and leaned against the lorry to recover his senses.

'Men go to the van, women in the car.'

Little Ye let go of Ding Ming's hand.

'Wait.'

'We have no choice.'

'Let me ask.'

Without looking Mister Kevin in the eye, because he didn't want to be distracted while he formed the clumpy syllables, Ding Ming said, 'Excuse me sir, but wife and me is come together.'

And Mister Kevin said to his lieutenants, 'How about that? That's not bad English, is it?'

Ding Ming pointed with his chin at Little Ye. She looked fretful that her husband had dared speak out like this. 'This my wife.'

'It's regrettable, obviously, but you'll be back together in a few weeks. We got orders, I got quotas. Nothing I can do.'

Mister Kevin put an arm around Ding Ming's shoulder, easily the heaviest limb he'd ever felt. He wore a big gold ring on his finger, now with a smear of blood on it.

'So you're going to have to say goodbye to your lady wife, and she's going to get in the car, and you're going in the van.'

Ding Ming had understood little of the speech but he got the gist. 'We stay together.' He dropped his voice further. 'Please.'

'In a couple of weeks you'll be together again. Say your goodbyes.'

'I go with her.'

'Soon as we get there, you'll get a phone number. You can ring whenever you want. She'll be having a much easier time than you – she's off to pick flowers. Picking flowers is easy.'

The lieutenants gathered round and, because all were much taller than Ding Ming, he fell into a pool of shadow.

'You're doing temp jobs, you go where the work is. I'll make sure you and your wife are together on the next job. Alright? Say your goodbyes.'

'You will give phone number?'

'Yes.'

There was clearly no point arguing any further. Ding Ming hugged Little Ye, chastely because people were looking, then joined the other men in the back of the dirty white van. It was a gloomy space, with torn and muddy seats, and rakes, spades and buckets strewn across the floor. The only window was in the back door. He scrambled up to it, and apologised to a man whose foot he stepped on. He wiped the grimy glass with his sleeve and watched his wife get into the car. As the van was driven away he waved to her, though he doubted she was able to see.

(15

All the migrants fell asleep. Ding Ming was used to travelling with his wife's head either on his lap or against his shoulder, and the troubling absence of that warm weight kept him awake. He made his way forward, thinking to consider the view.

Mister Kevin hunched low over the steering wheel and chewed gum and smoked. The back of his neck was thick and hairy and a gold chain lay half-buried in one of its creases. Outside, cows grazed in giant fields. All that good soil seemed wasted on cattle, and there was a great deal of fallow land where nothing grew but trees. The landscape looked unkempt and desolate, and the sloppy way it was used violated his aesthetic sense. He compared it unfavourably to the Fujian countryside, so compact and efficient, with plots sunk into every scrap of land and the divide between them only wide enough to step along. On the other hand, he was very impressed with the road – a good camber, flat tarmac, the markings crisp and bright.

He could see few buildings, and those there were seemed huge. Perhaps the inhabitants lived in clan halls like Hakka people, or maybe the farms were giant communal ventures. He realised that the paucity of buildings and the desultory emptiness of the landscape were connected – this country was hugely underpopulated.

They came into a city. It was not so unlike the other one Ding Ming had been to, Fujian's capital, Fuzhou – wide, well-lit streets, endless concrete, glass and brick, right angles everywhere and no animals to be seen. The most obvious difference was the advertising. He found the slogans obscure. 'Go Beyond'. It didn't make sense without a subject. 'Just do it'. Just do what?

The van stopped. The street was so empty it was eerie, as if somecalamityjusthadoccurred.Manylightsburnedneedlessly. Ding Ming could see a splendid frontage filled with shoes, and next to it a magnificent restaurant. By craning forward he was able to read the English name, and his lips moved as he formed the words – 'The Floating Lotus'.

A Chinese man came out of the place, got into the front seat and gave Kevin a polystyrene takeout box. Ding Ming salivated at the smell of hot food. The fishermen woke, stretched and sniffed.

The man introduced himself as Black Fort and handed out cigarettes. He was handsome, despite the ugly stain of a birthmark under his lip. He held up a mobile phone. 'You know how it goes. One call each, keep it short, the money comes out of your wages.'

His Mandarin was stilted, it was obviously not his first language. 'The call shows we've done our job and now you and your families have to start honouring the terms of the repayment contract.'

Ding Ming had the number memorised but was shaking with excitement and found it difficult to hit the right keys. He'd given his mother his mobile when he left, for just this occasion.

'*Mama? Mama? Dao le! Dao le!*... I arrived! I arrived!'

'How is it? Is it cold?'

A good line – it was just like he was calling from across the street.

'No, not too cold. Everything is fine. Tell everyone you have an abroad worker as a son now.' He added, though he knew it was inane, 'Sorry if I woke you up.'

'No, I was about to go to market, it's seven in the morning.'
He had forgotten about the time difference.

'Celebrate. Buy some meat.'

Black Fort said, 'Enough. Hand it over.'

'Bye. Bye.'

Ding Ming felt his eyes growing damp, so he blinked quickly. He reminded himself that he'd see her soon enough, that when they did meet again she'd have a fancy phone like that one, paid for with all the money he'd sent back. And after he came home he'd build her a magnificent house, the biggest in the village. He could see the expression of joy on her face when she saw it.

Mister Kevin was eating fried rice and sweet and sour pork balls with a plastic fork. In easy conversation with him, Black Fort worked a match from one corner of his mouth to the other.

He said, 'Yeah... yeah,' which Ding Ming recognised from films as American English slang for the affirmative. He must have been born over here, there was no other way to achieve such an enviable level of English ability. How cool he was, with artfully dishevelled hair, a gold earring, jade necklace, bomber jacket, black jeans. When Ding Ming had money he'd dress exactly like that. He couldn't get taller and paler, and he doubted he could ever achieve that self-assurance, but at least he could buy the look. He craned forward to check the brand of shoes, and the man grew aware of his attention. Ding Ming shrank back.

'*Ni kan shenme?*... What are you looking at?'

'Your shoes.'

Black Fort rested a foot on the dashboard.

'For basketball. They have air in the soles. Like walking on clouds. I understand you speak some English.'

'I did some training to be an English teacher.'

'I have to tell you, you won't be able to use your English here.'

'Why not?'

'They think all Chinese are scum, they won't talk to you. And if you even try, well, that's your lookout. One of our guys, he looked at a white girl a little too long, and he was arrested.'

'Arrested?'

'They kept him in the cells, beat him up. Just for looking at a girl. What you have to remember is, these people think of us as rats.'

'We are rats!' declared a man, who had succeeded in following that much at least of their conversation. 'We are the Fujian rats!' He'd been watching Kevin's fork go up and down. All the migrants, Ding Ming suspected, were wondering when they would get fed.

They made a chant of it.

'We are the Fujian rats!'

Black Fort beckoned Ding Ming closer. 'That guy was lucky.'

'Lucky?'

'We had another guy, he went into the police station to ask the time and he never came out. Rule number one is, you don't have anything to do with authority. You'd be taking your life in your own hands. They're bastards – even worse than in China. They'll knock you on the head and whip out your heart and liver and eyes and sell them for transplants. You go in the police station, you never come out. Tell the others.'

Ding Ming repeated the advice. A man asked him to inquire about prostitutes, and he blushed as he did so, though he was glad to be of use. His Mandarin, it seemed, was proving handy, even if his English wasn't going to be.

'The chickens here are expensive and ridden with AIDS. We provide films and magazines.' Black Fort worked the match to the other side of his mouth. 'I'm not going to lie to you. You've got a lot of hard work ahead. You'll be going to bed tired every day. But keep your heads down, do the job, keep away from those chickens, and in a few years you'll be rich men. Then you can go home and play all you like. You'll have tarts all over you. You'll be set for life.'

What was a few years of hard work? It would pass in a flash. Ding Ming was not afraid of hard work. He asked, apologetically because he didn't want to be seen as bothersome, 'So could you give me some more details about where my wife has gone?'

'She'll be fine. She'll be picking flowers, and that's a simple job.'

'It's just that I worry.'

'You'll be able to talk to her in a couple of days.'

He determined to put it out of his mind for now. Talking to his mother had proved to be without obstacle, and she was much farther away. Black Fort patted his arm.

A man made a sly comment to his friend, on how the failed English teacher was everybody's favourite. Ding Ming pretended not to hear. At that moment he wished that he did not speak any English, and that he had not spent so long at school when he should have been working. He saw that he had too much education to be accepted by people of his own class, and not enough class to be accepted by people of education. He did not fit in. And was that, he wondered, one reason he had been keen to go abroad? The idea was quite new to him. He was experiencing the benefit a distant perspective gives on the problems of home.

Black Fort headed back to the restaurant. Ding Ming watched him though the windscreen. How cool he was, his confidence visible in every stride.

Kevin burped and started the engine. As the van drove away, the headlights swept across a shuttered building, and Ding Ming believed he glimpsed a Chinese man, sitting in its porch. The stocky figure wore a black leather jacket with the collar turned up. The way he was settled, it looked like he had been there some time. He did not look like a tramp or a beggar, perhaps he had just lost his keys and was waiting for someone to come and let him in. It was strange but welcome, as in this vast unknown every sight of a Chinese person brought comfort.

But it was the briefest flash, so Ding Ming could not be sure he had not imagined the scene. Perhaps his tiredness was putting shapes to shadows. He put it out of his mind. The smell of food still hung in the air, and he wondered when he would be fed.

With the migrants buoyed up by their brief connection with home, the atmosphere in the back grew lively – it was like a work unit outing. Following the sighting of a black and white bird and some black and white animal dead at the side of the road, Ding Ming observed that although this nation seemed advanced in many things their animals had yet to make the move into colour. It worked better in his head than out in the open. The migrants looked baffled and when he explained that he meant an analogy with television it rather seemed to drain the observation of its humour.

He curled up and wished his wife's body lay next to him. He recalled the smell of her hair and the feel of it against his face. If she were next to him, her lips would be just here – he put a finger to the spot, then traced the remembered line of her jaw. He let his hand slide down over her neck and collarbone, and he dropped the real hand and an imaginary one followed the rise of her breast, circling a nipple. The hand swooped and stroked and now he could hear her noises of delight, feel skin give beneath his fingers, feel her fingers running through his hair, feel—

The van pulled up. Kevin snapped his fingers. 'Out.' They were parked before a grand two-storey house. Kevin unlocked a door and hurried them in, snapping and pointing.

Ding Ming worried that Mister Kevin's promise to provide a phone number for his wife's work supervisor 'as soon as they got there' had slipped the man's mind. Reminding him did not seem an issue to be entered into lightly, as the big man appeared to have the unpredictable nature of a child, being mild and petulant by turns. He would have to pick his time carefully. He began to form his inquiry in his head, hauling the heavy English words around, groping for politeness and concision. Excuse, please, do you have a phone number for to call my wife?

Kevin was leading them down a corridor. Ding Ming admired the carpet, which seemed a luxurious touch even though it was stained and pocked with cigarette burns, and the floral designs on the wallpaper. He peeked into a room and saw bunk beds lining the wall and mattresses on the floor. There was enough space between the mattresses to walk one foot in front of the other, and this space was cluttered with clothes and packaging. The window was boarded and nailed shut and the room stank of men. He wondered where they all were, who did the cooking and cleaning, whether there were rotas and responsibilities. He supposed it would be like the teacher training college again.

Kevin led them past a shabby bathroom with no door and pointed at a Western toilet, an outlandish porcelain lily.

'English speaker. You tell them, this is a toilet. Pissing and shitting only. Don't go washing in it. You wash with this.'

He gestured at a sink. One tap was marked with a red dot, so Ding Ming asked, 'Is there here hot water?'

'Don't be funny with me, son. Be glad you've got a roof over your head.'

Ding Ming felt awkward. He did not know how to deal with this man at all. Now it would be even harder to ask about the number. Excuse me, please, would it be possible for you to give me a number for to call my wife?

They trooped into a kitchen. Ding Ming was impressed that there was a refrigerator, not something he associated with kitchens. Back home fridges were kept on display in living rooms.

On a table sat a TV with attached video recorder and a pile of videos labelled in Chinese. One video had a picture of a naked lady on the label and Ding Ming looked with guilty fascination at enormous breasts, long legs and an expression of invitation. It reminded him that men without women were animals. He mentally promised his wife that he would not be watching any of those yellow films, and filled his mind with images of her to take away the after-glare of those legs and lips. Her nose was little like a mouse's, her eyes strikingly far apart and big like a squirrel's. He supposed she was now in similar surroundings and he hoped she was getting on alright and not missing him too much.

Kevin said, 'Bucket of rice there, bowls in there. Fill up.'

'Excuse me, please...'

But the man was striding out.

Ding Ming caught up with him on the front step. It was nerve-wracking to be outside, the street was deserted but anyone might walk past, he felt dangerously exposed. All his careful thought, and it came out in a garbled rush.

'Very sorry. I want to ask a thing. You know my wife go to where number, please?'

'What? Oh yeah.'

Kevin looked Ding Ming up and down.

'What's your name?'

Aware that English speakers could not pronounce or remember Chinese names, he used the title he'd chosen at the college.

'My English name is William.'

'William, come into my office.'

Kevin clambered awkwardly into the back of the van, and indicated the seat next to his.

Ding Ming resisted an impulse to squat on his haunches on the floor, which would put Kevin above him and accord with their social rank, and daringly he did as Kevin instructed, and sat next to him. It put him and Kevin at the same level, as if they were equals, and encouraged him to be bold.

'You have got a way me speak at wife?'

He sensed that he had made mistakes there, and worried that with each effort he was only wandering further from the correct construction. It was incredibly hard to talk English to a native speaker, because whenever he got it wrong he felt he was losing face, and grew flustered, and even more incapable of getting it right.

'How old are you, William?'

'I have nineteen years.'

What a strange thing, to be sitting on a double seat with a boss, so close that he could feel Kevin's thigh touching his own. He could see hairs sprouting from the man's ears. The disconcerting sight diverted him so much that he did not hear Kevin's next statement at all, so he said 'yes', but that seemed to be a satisfactory answer.

The man was offering him a cigarette. He knew he should feel grateful for this honour, but he regarded the packet with dismay. To decline would be rude, and might destroy any rapport that had built up. There was no choice, then, but to accept. But that itself had dangers, he didn't know how to smoke. He would have to bluff it as best he could. He would not breathe in.

He took it, and Kevin leaned across and flipped a lighter with a fleshy thumb. The flame spotlit his face. His chin was covered with stubble, every follicle discernible, and not just around the chin, but all over his jaw. It made his face two-tone, pasty above and grey below. To Ding Ming's eyes, used to flatter Asian faces, his nose was enormous.

Ding Ming sucked the filter and breathed out again imme-
diately. The effect was much worse than he'd imagined. The
smoke tasted stale and tickled his throat. He clamped his
mouth shut, and felt his face redden.

'Do you very much want to see your lady wife?'

Focused on stifling his throat's rebellion, Ding Ming was
powerless to reply.

'I've got a phone number here for her manager, so you can
ring and arrange a little chat.'

He took a diary out of the inside pocket of his coat, a
bulky parka. 'And I'll even let you use my phone to call.'
Kevin opened the black book. Metal binders held a sheaf
of loose-leaf pages. He displayed a list of addresses and
phone numbers.

Ding Ming's cheeks bulged and his neck muscles tensed
and his shoulders drew back and his head seemed to swell.
There was no stopping it. A throaty cough exploded. He
bent over, racked with convulsions of coughing, and Kevin
slapped him on the back.

Breathing heavily, Ding Ming waited for the red sparkles
to fade from his vision. He felt like such a fool. Anyway, he
would soon talk to his wife – he'd understood that much. He
might have made a bit of an idiot of himself with the cigarette but it didn't matter. The weight of worry was leaving
his body.

He grinned, not out of social awkwardness for once, but
joy. He brought up his hand to cover his rudely exposed
teeth and saw that the cigarette still burned between his fingers. He thought about giving it another go.

'Which number is it?'

But Kevin put the book back in his coat. His hand now lay
around Ding Ming's shoulders. Their heads were so close
they almost touched. Ding Ming could smell the man, a

musty, cloying odour, quite frightening for being so unfamiliar. When he spoke, his mouth stank of smoke.

'What I want to know is, what can you do for me? Heh?'

Nausea rose from Ding Ming's stomach and made him dizzy. He shifted, worried that he was going to puke. It was that cigarette, it had gone straight to his stomach. He did not feel right at all.

Kevin pondered his own question, tapping his bottom lip with two fingers.

'How about this,' he said, pointing a finger up as if suddenly inspired. 'My balls are feeling heavy and I think I need some help with that.'

(17

Ding Ming did not understand what Kevin was saying but he understood the meaning of the gleam in the eye and the sudden intensity of the man who was almost embracing him.

It seemed very quiet now in the van as Ding Ming fought his queasiness. The silence was broken by the twanging of an elasticated waistband as Kevin slipped his tracksuit bottoms down with his free hand. Grey underpants bulged.

'Will you do this small thing for me?' whispered Kevin. 'Will you put it in your mouth and suck it?' Kevin opened his mouth wide, and Ding Ming looked into a murky chasm framed by a flakey tongue and yellow teeth. Kevin made a hollow fist of his free hand and pumped it up and down before the open maw, miming what he would like Ding Ming to do.

A picture of the task formed slowly in his mind, and his eyes widened and his mouth fell open with dismay. Ding Ming had no experience of that kind of thing, had never met anyone who'd admitted to those practices. Back home he'd heard whispers of a particular public toilet where the comrades, as they were called, those men who bafflingly and perversely liked the bodies of other men, gathered after dark. Fearing AIDS, he had avoided it, even in the daytime.

The forgotten cigarette burned his fingers. The searing blast of pain jerked him up, and he carried on moving, shrugging free of Kevin's embrace, and found the handle of the van and fumbled it open and fell out.

He stood and, feeling terribly ashamed, he said, 'Please, sorry,' before a mist of panic wrapped him.

He hardly knew what he was doing as he ran into the house and through it to the kitchen. His eyes found the back door, but it was boarded up and so were the windows. But, of course, he could not run away anyway: running away was stupid. He should not have run this far. He told himself to run straight back again, but his legs would not obey. He turned circles of distress and confusion.

The other migrants watched him. They were holding bowls to their faces and shovelling rice into their mouths with chopsticks. One explained how they'd put some rice aside, though of course there hadn't been much to begin with. Ding Ming looked dumbly at the bucket. He could not think about food. He opened his mouth to explain, but what could he say? He closed it again. These people would not help him. He was on his own.

Considered in one way Kevin's demand seemed a very small thing. It would not change him physically in any way, it would not hurt, it would only take a few minutes, and no one need ever know. Looked at another way, though, it seemed an enormity, bigger than the sky.

Someone was coming. He tensed, already familiar with that clunky footfall. He supposed Kevin would ask him to come outside, perhaps beckoning with a curled finger, and the obscene act would begin. He summoned the image of his wife – nose like a mouse, eyes like a squirrel – and determined to face his fate squarely. Chewing his lip, he turned.

Mister Kevin was in the doorway. But he did not look at Ding Ming and it was as if nothing had happened. He clapped his hands and called, 'Right, let's get you to work. Chop chop, monkeys.'

THE FLOATING LOTUS

18

Jian killed his ninth cigarette and lined the butt against the shop door behind him. He didn't want a scattering over the pavement to give away his position.

Not much had happened in the last couple of hours. The odd drunk had meandered past, a few couples, and an old lady's dog had sniffed at him before being tugged away on its leash. The only interesting event had been the arrival of a dirty white van, driven by some fat guy. The hoodlum called Black Fort had come out of the Floating Lotus and sat inside. Some twenty minutes later he'd returned to the restaurant and the van had driven away. Pinched Asian faces had been briefly visible in the back.

Jian had plenty of time to think and would rather he didn't. Speculating or worrying wasn't going to bring his daughter back and he didn't have enough evidence to start making any useful conjectures. All he had was a bunch of suspicious characters who knew more than they were letting on. He itched to get his hands on one and start demanding answers.

He rubbed aching knees. He wished he had a car to observe from, and steamed buns and a flask of tea would be most welcome. As would a fistful of painkillers. He lit cigarette ten, took a drag, and winced at the pain in his ribs.

The restaurant door opened and Jian tensed. Four hoodlums staggered out. Two had arms around each other, and found their inability to walk straight hilarious. They were the men who had followed him earlier, he was sure of it. Yes, there was the leather coat flapping. A third man strutted into the road and put his palm out with drunken self-importance and a car slowed to let them cross.

Black Fort walked quickly with his arms thrust into his pockets. He was the leader, certainly – his air of assurance was striking. He did not appear as drunk as his hatchetmen.

It was good that they were drunk, and even better that the owner had stayed inside. But as they made a diagonal across the road Jian noted with disquiet that they were coming straight towards him. This position offered as little cover as comfort. If they saw him there would be trouble: even drunk he couldn't out-fight them and he was trapped in a dead end. He pressed himself back against the door.

As they neared he heard the thump of their footsteps. He held his breath and narrowed his eyes and stood completely still, and he could feel his heart beat. In his pocket, he slipped his house keys between his fingers and balled his hand into a fist.

The trick was to think yourself away and not look anyone in the eye. The first pair came into view and lurched towards him. The man in the overcoat was dressed all in black, exhibiting a taste for the dramatic. His skinny companion wore jeans and a T-shirt with a ponytail projecting from under a baseball cap. Their cheeks were red, their mouths hung open and their eyes were bleary.

Another step and they would blunder straight into the porch. The overcoat squeaked as its owner put his hand against the wall to steady himself. Jian saw four gold rings on chubby fingers and on his wrist the head of a dragon tattoo. The dragon's body curled up the sleeve and out of sight. Its lips were curled back in a snarl and its boggling eyes seemed to be staring straight at him.

Jian stiffened and the nails of clenched fingers dug into his palm. But the man pushed himself away and pitched back

onto the pavement, dragging his friend with him. The baseball cap fell off and the hoodlum caught it and put it back.
His friends laughed. In happy self-absorption the hoodlums
passed.

Jian let his breath slip between gritted teeth and came
away from the wall. Minutes later the waitress came out,
with a bulky jacket over her uniform. She was talking to two
men Jian hadn't seen before, presumably the kitchen staff.
They walked away and the ticking of the girl's high heels
faded. Jian lowered his head, hurried across the road and
slipped into the restaurant.

The lights were off, but an orange glow filtered in from
the street. Chairs were stacked on tables and their jutting
upright legs cast jagged shadows. The manager stood counting money. He looked up and slammed the till shut.

Jian crossed the room quickly, saying, 'I don't want your
money. I just wondered if you had a cigarette.' and watched
fear, then dismay, cross the man's features.

As soon as he was close enough, Jian lunged. He hit him
just under the jawline on the side, but without getting much
weight behind it. He felt the keys pierce the skin and scrape
along the line of the jaw, and the impact sent a shudder up
his arm. The old man's head snapped to the side. Jian leaned
over the counter, grabbed his collar and yanked him forward. Glasses toppled and shattered. This time he was bal-
anced and could have got his weight behind it but he pulled
a punch to the nose. It was just a tap really, to make his eyes
water. The shirt tore and buttons popped. The manager's
flailing hand knocked down a bottle of spirits.

Jian let go, thinking that he'd done enough. It occurred to
him that he was too old for this kind of nonsense. He hadn't
personally roughed anyone up for years, he always got the
keen young guys to do it for him. Obviously he was rusty,

because the old man clambered to his feet, fumbled a door open and ran into the kitchen.

Jian followed. The only illumination came through the open door. The owner was a silhouette. He turned, an edge gleamed and Jian realised with consternation that the man was holding up a chopping knife. He was breathing heavily, talking in a panicky fashion in Cantonese, and backing away.

The restaurant door swung shut and now it was completely dark. Jian could hear the owner retreating. Not fast, but faster than he could move, as he didn't know the layout. He sidestepped and opened a fridge. Yellow light revealed the owner bent before a back door. Keys tinkled as he groped through them with a shaking hand. With the other he waved the chopper.

Jian dragged a bin across the floor and used it to prop open the fridge. He picked up a wok and held it before him, bent his head and charged. The chopper swung and hit his shield with a clang.

Jian slammed into the old man and kept pushing, and felt the man hit the door and tumble. Jian straddled him and lowered the wok until the thin metal edge was against the scrawny throat. He pressed down, and the skin of the neck went white. The old man squawked and cried. Jian tossed the wok aside. He could not help but note how the man's wrinkled brow resembled his own.

19

Jian fumbled in the old man's pocket and found a mobile. He shifted uncomfortably, this position being tough on his knees, and called the student Song. The phone rang and rang – she had better be up – then a sleepy voice muttered in English.

'*Zhe shi zhong guo jing cha*... This is the Chinese policeman. Tell me what this man is saying.'

'*Zenme hui shi le?*... What's going on?'

'He's speaking English, but he's distressed. Just tell me what he's saying.'

Jian held the phone down over the old man's babbling mouth, then put it back to his ear. The girl sounded awake now, and alarmed.

'Is that the man from that restaurant?'

'He knows about my daughter. Tell me what he is saying.'

'What have you done to him? What's going on? Maybe I should call the police.'

'If you hang up, I'll hit him again. Then I'll call someone else.'

'You hit him?'

'He knows about my daughter. I'm going to keep hitting him until I find out what he knows. If you want me to stop, tell me what he's saying.'

He could hear her ragged breathing, and just from that constructed an image of her distraught expression. He suppressed a twinge of guilt.

She said, 'Put the phone on his mouth.'

He did so, and the screen display lit up frightened eyes. He let her hear twenty seconds of jabber, then returned the phone to his ear.

'Well?'

'He says she was here but it's not his fault. He says he's really sorry but there was nothing he could do. He keeps say it. Nothing he could do, nothing he could do. He's very scared. He says he wants to help you.'

'Now what is he saying?'

'Oh, this is too horrible.'

'What's he saying?'

'He says that he really liked her and he's got something to show you. Don't ever call me again.'

'Don't hang up.'

'He's going to show you something. Don't ever call again.' The phone went dead.

Jian hauled the old man to his feet. He was rubbing his neck and whining, so Jian checked for damage. He was okay – a little superficial redness.

The man beckoned with a scrawny wrist and led Jian into the restaurant. He reached behind the ceramic figure of the portly Kitchen God and slid out a thin briefcase.

Jian took two chairs and they sat opposite each other at a corner table. As the old man fumbled with the combination lock, Jian lit a 555 and the table candle. The little flame cast an intimate glow over the two figures and threw thorny shadows round the rest of the room.

The old man took out from his briefcase a pink clamshell phone. He gave it to Jian. A green gonk hung off it. Jian knew that dumb toy, and looked up sharply.

'This is my daughter's.'

The gonk's fur was matted with dried black gunk. More coagulated between phone keys.

The old man reached back into the briefcase, then stepped away and his chair toppled over. He was pointing a gun, a squat six-shooter. Jian looked at him coldly. The barrel wavered, the old man had no idea how to handle it. Perhaps he did not have the strength to pull the trigger. The safety looked to be still on. A couple of seconds passed and he didn't get shot, so he went back to examining the phone.

With a nail Jian scraped gunk from between the keys. He held a flake on the tip of his finger and brought it close to the candle flame. It was slightly translucent, with a reddish tinge. It looked like dried blood. He felt the stone in his stomach turn over.

'What's going on? What's happened?'

The old man reached for the phone.

(20

Some five months previously, Wei Wei had walked into the Floating Lotus restaurant and asked about the job ad in the window.

Mister Li, manager, knew right away he was going to employ her. Possibly she'd be trouble, but it was worth finding out. She was tall and beautiful, her hair was slick and her skin pale and smooth, she moved well and she knew how to dress. She was wearing tight jeans and high-heeled boots and a white blouse. Not much was left to the imagination, but it wasn't too trampy.

They communicated in English, she did not speak any Cantonese. Her manner was forthright, and when she talked, she held Mister Li's eye and did not dip her head, but she didn't come across as too forward, either. It turned out she was a mainlander, pretty much fresh off the plane. That surprised him, as he considered mainlanders rude, ruddy and uncouth. But of course things had changed up there of late: earthy peasant values had gone out of fashion, now they'd got developed they could afford manners. He said he'd pay her four pounds fifty an hour, could keep half her tips, and would she start that evening?

She was good. She picked things up quickly, she was charming and a lot of guys started turning up just for the honour of being served by her. When she wasn't working, she chatted on her pink mobile. It was high end, a clamshell. She liked to film herself on it. She always had good stuff. Young Chinese these days, they spent all their money on name brands and didn't save the way his generation did.

One midweek evening, a Chinese man who he had not seen before, eating alone, let a hand drift over her thigh. She slapped him across the face. He laughed, and when he had finished eating he left her a tip of a twenty-pound note. Li watched her pocket it. She did it well, slipping it into her palm while sliding in its place a couple of pound coins.

If Li had not been well used to the tricks of waitresses, he would never have noticed. He considered what he should do, and decided to leave it, and that was the point at which he admitted to himself that he was infatuated. He loved to watch her work, he loved to make her smile, and he loved to see her happy. He looked forward to her coming in and kept an eye on the rota to see when she was due. He was dressing better these days. He entertained fantasies that she would agree to become his lover. It did not strike him as absurd, as, after all, he was a man of means. But for the present he was content to keep his feelings under wraps, as he had a business to run.

A week later the big tipper came back, and this time he brought three mates with him. Li felt uneasy. They sat in the middle of the dining room and did not seem to care how much noise they were making or how drunk they got. They were playing drinking games, and the place emptied as they grew more raucous.

Wei Wei put a soup tureen down on the lazy susan. Skeletal fish heads with white eyes bobbed in a murky stew. The leader of the group, the good-looker with the birthmark, winked at her. She didn't react. He lunged and she stepped back and he laughed and upended the tureen.

He said, in the English of a native speaker, 'I'm not paying for this muck. Get the manager.' Soup dribbled, fish gaped.

Mister Li had been watching and was expecting something like this. He hurried to the table. Now the men slouched in attitudes of insolent threat. The leader introduced himself as Black Fort. It was just the kind of nickname a tong bruiser would give himself.

'Your food is shit,' said Black Fort, speaking Cantonese, 'but the place is nice.' He broke a toothpick in half and began working it from one side of his mouth to the other.

'Please pay for your meal,' said Mister Li, and then he heard what he been dreading.

'We're in insurance. We'll insure you for one hundred and eight pounds a week. Think of it as luck money. First payment now.'

'You don't scare me. If you are not going to pay for your meal, get out of my restaurant.'

'Pay us now.'

'No.'

Black Fort swept a hand across the table and plates clattered to the floor and smashed. Another guy filled the soup spoon and flicked it. A third picked up a length of noodle with his chopsticks and whirled it around. A piece flew off and splattered into the wall, and the guy laughed like it was the funniest thing in the world.

Mister Li explained to the last remaining customers, a young couple, that he was very sorry but they would have to leave, and of course he did not expect them to pay for their meal. He told the waitresses to go into the kitchen. He stood breathing carefully as the men ripped the limpet hats from the walls and put them on. They knocked the remaining plates to the floor and stamped on them if they didn't smash and turned over tables. Mister Li forced himself not to flinch. He hoped that they did not attack the shrine of the Kitchen God, and that his staff had the sense to stay in the kitchen.

'They'll stop if you pay.'

'No.'

At some signal from Black Fort, the gang assembled, out of breath from their labours. Black Fort and Mister Li assessed each other. Li did not waver. He noticed that Black Fort's eyes were unusually pale. There was something yellowish about the pupils, which combined with his delicate complexion to make him unsettling. And he knew it, obviously.

The toothpick travelled from one side to the other. Black Fort smiled dreamily, as if at some pleasant thought, and said, 'We're going to charge you for redecorating, too. One hundred and twenty pounds a week.' He tucked a black namecard into Li's shirt pocket.

He asked around. The Indian restaurants and the shops owned by whites didn't pay extortion money, but the east Asians had all been preyed upon. Some had made an initial payment, but others, like him, had refused, and nothing had yet happened. The community was bracing itself.

Li sensed that it was vital to stop this rot while it was still possible. If he left it longer, everyone would be paying, the tong would be stronger, and there would be no question of fighting back. Their quiet city would become like London and Manchester, where every east Asian business announced its fealty to one tong or another with a plaque behind the counter acknowledging a contribution to this or that benevolent fund.

Of course the matter could be dealt with simply by bringing in an established triad to deal with these upstarts. One importer had made inquiries of the Wu Song Wu, and a friend of a friend knew a Little Horse in the 14K. But that, he knew, was no long-term solution, for when the smoke had cleared they would be left with another tong to deal with, and, however sympathetic they started out, tongs always reverted to type. They were leeches who lived upon the honest.

(22

The black card held a design of a cocktail glass and a pair of red lips beside the two characters, printed in a script that mimicked brush calligraphy: Black Fort. There was an address in English, in Liverpool, and no phone number.

Mister Li went to the address, in a shabby street at the back of an industrial estate. A nondescript door had an expensive intercom. He buzzed and a girl's voice, in Cantonese, told him to hold the card up to the CCTV camera above the door. He obeyed and the lock clicked.

It led to a dark, narrow hallway. He went upstairs and came out in a small bar lit with garish red light. Plastic bunches of grapes hung from the ceiling. Chinese pop music was playing. Prints of soft-focus nudes in heavy frames were hung against flock wallpaper. A blonde woman whose white dress billowed around her thighs was smiling at him – no, it was a cardboard cutout.

Two men sat at the bar: Black Fort and a podgy, middle-aged white man. Black Fort had his arms around the waists of two Asian girls. He patted them and pointed at a sofa and they wobbled away in platform heels and curled up on it.

He said in Cantonese, 'Good of you to drop in,' and gestured at the stool next to him. 'Drink? On the house.' Another girl stubbed out a cigarette and slipped behind the bar.

Mister Li, choosing to stand, said, 'Thank you, but no.' He was still getting used to the lighting. More details came out of that red gloom – fake flowers, plastic fruit in a bowl, the thick make-up on the three girls which turned their faces into masks.

'A pity. I have very good whisky, single malt. Everything here is of a high quality.' He pinched the barmaid's cheek and she didn't flinch. Obviously he was the man in command here, and wanted to show it.

He switched, without a pause, to English. 'Let me introduce you to my companion. This is my good friend Kevin. Kevin, this is Mister Li, manager of the Floating Lotus restaurant.'

Li found himself shaking the thick white hand, though this Kevin person seemed as uninterested as him in the process. The hand was heavy but the shake limp.

'Kevin is in the people business. If you ever need staff, give him a ring.'

Black Fort plucked the namecard out of Mister Li's hand and gave it to Kevin, and Kevin wrote his name and a mobile number on the back, saying, 'Yeah, I'll sort you out. Very cheap. I do all the paperwork, you get me the cash and they turn up and do the job. Good little workers who won't give you any trouble.'

Mister Li put the card in his shirt pocket and gathered himself, throwing back his shoulders and raising his chin.

'Okay,' said Black Fort, and switched back into Cantonese. 'Let me hear it. I can't pay, overheads, you'll put me out of business.'

'I am inviting you to a banquet. I know the value of a good insurance policy and I want to set the table and talk business. Come to my place on Wednesday night.'

'Around seven okay?'

'Excellent.'

'Will you be cooking some tasty dishes?'

'Yes.'

'Will the tastiest dish of all be there?'

'I'm sorry?'

'That waitress. The mainlander.'

'She will serve us.'

'Excellent. Would you like a girl? Considerate and discreet.'

'Thank you, but I am a little tired. I must attend my business.' He said a courteous goodbye and stiffly made his exit.

(23

Wei Wei did not want to serve at the banquet. He said he'd double her wages for the night and she pouted and crossed her arms and said that it wasn't about the money, she just did not want to see that unsavoury character again, she'd been disturbed by his behaviour and didn't want anything to do with him. Li offered lengthy assurances, and fifty pounds for the night, and she agreed.

Black Fort and his hatchetmen arrived a little early, at a few minutes to seven. Mister Li escorted them into the private banquet room. Black Fort was cordial but cold – certainly he was wary. Mister Li was tireless in his efforts to show that he had no hard feelings, refilling Black Fort's glass often and placing the tastiest morsels in his bowl.

His best dishes were there, a full and complementary range of flavours, among them fish rolls, crisp skinned pork, lemon chicken and sweet white fungus and wolfberry soup. Mister Li was very proud of his food and his Hong Kong-trained chef. Wherever possible, his dishes were made fresh on the premises, and he disdained those competitors who had everything delivered frozen from a warehouse – they were not restaurateurs, he would joke, but reheaters.

They discussed matters such as horse racing and weather and talked about the food a great deal. The conversation was not lively but at least it was there, and Mister Li curtailed any awkward pauses by proposing toasts. They drank pungent Chinese whisky out of thimble-sized glasses. Mister Li was spilling much of it, letting it flow down his chin and jaw and a little later wiping it away with a napkin.

He was introduced to the other gang members. A rather chubby half-Vietnamese man was known as Caterpillar. Though a little slow, and the butt of most of their jokes, he certainly looked the part, with the leather overcoat, the rings and the dragon tattoo. Ponytailed Six Days spent most of the time on his mobile. The third gang member, Blue, didn't talk much. He observed laconically that it got in the way of eating and smoking.

Wei Wei brought in a tureen of egg and tomato soup to finish the meal and tea was drunk as a digestive. Black Fort said, 'I have almost forgiven you for your stubbornness.' This was the first time the business in hand had been alluded to. Mister Li said, 'Likewise,' and they both chuckled, and Black Fort complimented Mister Li on the quality of his banquet. They lit cigarettes.

Mister Li asked Wei Wei to leave the room.

Black Fort said, 'Let's open the door and see the mountain. The premium is one hundred and twenty pounds a week.'

'But at that amount I would go bankrupt in months. I can show you my books. I can afford only two hundred pounds a month. At that, I think I can stay in business – just.'

'I must stand firm by my original premium, or you will make me lose face. You must see that?'

'But I think to lower it would show that you are a man of knowledge who understands the world of business, which is about compromise. A friend is someone who can be compromised with. Compromise makes friends. And a friend is more valuable than gold.'

Black Fort slapped Six Days on the back. 'Listen to this guy. Are you hearing this? A man of knowledge? More valuable than gold? I love this guy. Because I'm drunk, and your soup was so good and your waitress so pretty, I suppose we could accept a reduction to the original amount asked for, which was one hundred and eight pounds.'

'But I cannot pay even that amount. There's the rent, there's food, wages, stock, bills. I have a host of overheads.'

'So put your prices up.'

'Then I would lose all my customers to my competitors.'

'Use cheaper ingredients, they won't notice.'

'I would have to fire my chef and go into the reheating business.'

'You are not in a position to negotiate. The matter is finished. Don't bring it up again or the price will go up again. You are spoiling a pleasant evening. Let's get the cash and go.'

The tong stood, an intimidating presence in the small, smoky room. They might be drunk, but they retained their senses and their faces were hardening.

Mister Li led them out. The restaurant tables had been cleared to the side. Thirty or forty Asian people, mostly middle-aged men, stood in a tight crowd. Mister Li jogged over to stand at their head. He turned around and faced the gang with chest up and chin jutting.

Two of the men behind him unfurled a banner and held it high. Red letters on a white background read, in Chinese and English, 'EAST ASIANS STAND TOGETHER AGAINST GANGSTERISM'.

(24

Li watched with satisfaction the hoodlums look at the newcomers, then at each other, and the cocky self-assurance was wiped from their faces.

Except for Black Fort. His expression was fixed. He laughed as if he had been playing a game, and his opponent had revealed a cunning stratagem, and now he had to hold up his hand in wry acknowledgement. He broke a toothpick in half and plugged it between lips which glistened with oil from his meal.

'We will none of us pay you anything,' said Mister Li.

'I will pay you nothing,' said one man. 'I will pay you nothing,' said the next. They raised their right fists, and chanted together, as Li had schooled them, 'We stand together against tongs in our community.'

Loudest in their shouts were the three ladies, here to back up wavering husbands. A lot of the men had required a great deal of persuasion. 'Why do we have to be brave?' they had complained. 'We just want a quiet life. Let them have a cut.' But the gang's greed had worked in his favour. Someone had made inquiries and discovered that the big tongs usually asked for less.

'We will not let you feed on this community,' said Mister Li. 'None of us will give you anything. Not the restaurant owners or the shopkeepers or any of our businesses. We stand united.'

'Get out,' shouted a lady. 'Get out, you worms.' Mister Li had asked that there were no insults. Always it was the women who were quickest with the insults. There was a way to do these things and it would go easier without such talk.

'I ask you to leave this premises, and never to return,' said Mister Li, projecting his voice to fill the room.

Black Fort walked back and forth before the line, looking all the men in the eye. 'I know who you are,' he said, 'I know you all.' He jabbed a toothpick at them.

'And we know you,' said the lady, 'you leeches.'

'You will have reason to regret this action,' said Black Fort. Mister Li realised that he was clamping his jaw and consciously relaxed it.

He asked that the men with the banner move aside so that the tong could get to the door. The men shuffled, and their banner drooped in the middle, so Mister Li asked one of them to take a few steps to the side to make it taut again. Black Fort yanked the banner down so that it fell to the floor, and trod on it as he left.

Now, of course, the difficult bit started. It was easy to feel brave in a big group of men when you were facing only four. But the gang might come at them individually. If a few broke then the whole group was back where they started. If he was lucky the gang would decide that this community was not worth the effort, and move on. If he was not lucky they would try and chop him, perhaps burn down his restaurant. He did not mind the risk for himself, but he cared for his family. That night he sent his wife and daughter and elderly mother to stay at an aunt's house.

He had bought a gun. It was surprisingly easy, a friend of a friend of a friend had sorted it all out in a couple of days. He'd met the vendor, a young man in a duffel coat, in a suburban pub, in the single cubicle of the gents' toilet.

The squat black Italian-made six-shooter cost him four hundred pounds. The six bullets cost more. They were for a smaller-calibre pistol and had been wrapped in cellophane so that they would fit the larger chamber. Your pea-shooters were easy, the man had hissed, but you couldn't get ammo for love nor money.

Mister Li suspected that he had been passed unreliable merchandise. He didn't like touching the cold, greasy thing, so he put it on a bed of tissue paper in a briefcase, which he kept under the bed at night and in the restaurant kitchen during the day.

He found it hard to concentrate, and swung between trepidation and rage. When he walked into a room he made a mental note of the location of objects that could serve as weapons – ashtray, pen, statuette – and he got into the habit of turning round quickly to see who was behind. Let them come, he would bark at himself. He was ready, he was a tenacious fighter with a will of iron. They had bitten off more than they could chew in daring to challenge Mister Li.

Nine days after the banquet he was woken by a noise downstairs. He knew it was them and he took the gun out of the briefcase. He decided not to put a dressing gown over his boxer shorts and vest, as opening the cupboard might alert the intruders. He determined to shoot that leech Black Fort right between the eyes. But he could not stop his hands from trembling.

He took the stairs one at a time, and there seemed to be more than he remembered. The noise came again. Someone was in the kitchen.

His vision grew used to the darkness. As he approached the bottom step and the point of no return, he wondered if he should not go back to get his glasses.

But he went on. Perhaps, after all, it was only a stray come through the cat flap – then, wouldn't he laugh? He tried to remember what the young man had said about the gun and clicked the safety catch. He was sure that he had turned it to the off position, but it occurred to him that perhaps it had been off all the time, and now he had turned it on, rendering the gun inactive. However he reassured himself, the possibility nagged.

In the hallway he called out, in English, 'Alright you bastards. I'm going to get you.' But his mouth was so dry it came out as a series of rasps.

He kicked open the kitchen door. There was no one there. He went into the dining room, and through to the lounge, stalking with the trembling gun held aloft, and there was no one there. He could not even find how they had got in. He went into the kitchen and drank a glass of water.

A pink mobile phone lay on the counter, a clamshell, open. It wasn't his. It was splattered with some dark-red substance. He picked it up. The red stuff looked like blood. He pressed a button. The screen brightened and showed a brick wall. It was the paused start of a film. He pressed 'Play'.

(25

A brick wall. The camera moved to the left, to show more wall and a corner. It was a wobbly picture, handheld, and the light, coming from above, a bright bulb perhaps, was harsh and flattening.

The camera shifted further and there was Wei Wei cowering, legs drawn under her, arms behind her back, ankles tied with electric cable. The image blurred as the camera was brought closer, then snapped suddenly into clarity. Her lip was split and blood trickled down her chin. Her eyes were bright and damp. She was talking, but there was no sound on the film, her mouth was making the same shapes again and again, she was repeating something over and over.

She slid back, away from the camera, propelling herself along the concrete floor with bare feet until she was pressed against the wall. The camera came in closer until her white face filled the frame. Because of the lighting, all that was visible was big black eyes and the dark gap between her open lips and the black gap between the two front teeth.

A gloved hand grabbed a hank of hair and pulled it up and away from her face and yanked her head back. Her nostrils quivered. She was looking fixedly to the side, at something offscreen.

The hand let go of the hair and it flopped back across the face, and whoever was holding the camera stepped back to widen the frame.

A figure stepped up to the trembling girl, dressed in baggy black clothes, a scarf across his face, a woolly hat pulled down low over his forehead and wraparound plastic sunglasses over his eyes. A knife blade gleamed. He leaned over and down, and with a rapid underhand motion drove the knife a dozen or so times into her torso.

The girl's mouth opened and closed and a shudder passed across her, then she slumped. Blood pooled rapidly beneath her and the knife wielder stepped away.

The picture wavered, then settled, to show the concrete floor and the dead girl and the spreading blood pool. The blank white face of the dead girl grew bigger as the phone holder leaned in towards it, until it filled the screen. Abruptly, the screen blanked.

Jian blinked hard and saw that his hand was shaking. The screen was a tiny thing, much smaller than his palm, but it had swallowed him completely. He was aware of a great heat building in his face. He looked up. He was in a darkened restaurant and an old man was pointing a gun with both hands and the barrel wobbled with his nerves.

He dropped the phone and swept the skinny outstretched arms aside and rammed the little man up against the restaurant wall with one hand and punched the bamboo facing by his head with the other, again and again, until the bamboo crackled and split.

He dropped the old man among the splinters. He looked inside himself and found his body filling with despair. He looked outside, and it was ridiculous and unfair that nothing was different. Here was a restaurant and here he was in it, here was a pink phone, here a hand with scuffed and bleeding knuckles. It was all the same, but it didn't mean anything any more.

The old man was crawling across the floor. Still keeping the gun pointed, he began to fumble with the phone. The film's last frame was a close-up of Wei Wei's blank eye. He was blowing up the picture. He stood and thrust the phone at Jian and retreated to the corner of the room and hid behind his gun.

Wei Wei's pupil filled the small screen. In the corner of the black iris lurked a blurred and distorted reflection of the bottom half of the face of the man holding the camera phone. Almost nothing could be discerned except a dark patch beneath his lip, a birthmark.

Jian put his hands on a counter, then on his face, back on the counter, back on his face, now digging his fingers into his cheek. It was good to have the bamboo splinters burning in his hand, it took the real pain away.

He wanted to think about it. He knew she was dead but he couldn't accept it, because in his head she was alive. But she wasn't alive, she was dead, and there was nothing he could do to change it. He remembered her mother, in the glare of a lorry's headlight, the head lolling, eyes open, blood running down her cheek. In death they were more alike than when they were alive. Mother and daughter – four empty eyes to watch him now.

The old man approached with faltering steps and put the gun down by the candle. He took a black namecard out of his wallet, put it down next to the gun and retreated nervously.

'Black Fort' was written there, by an image of lips and a glass. The old man came forward again and pushed the gun towards Jian's hand, pushed it millimetre by millimetre, until the handle was facing him.

'I get it,' snapped Jian. 'I get it. He killed her and now you'll help me kill him.'

Jian picked the gun up. The old man tapped the name-card. He was pointing at what looked like an address.

(26

Jian examined the gun. It seemed a decent model but the ammunition was a joke: it looked likely to jam or even blow up in his face. He'd have to test it. He pointed it at the old man and rested his finger on the trigger and the man waved his arms and jabbered.

He had worked the story out, it was simple enough – he didn't need to be told. Some guy tries to be brave and the innocent end up hurt, he'd heard it many times. Everything the old man said was an irritation, it was like having an insect buzzing in your ear.

'You think I will become the agent of your revenge?'

Jian wanted him to die. He raised the gun. He said, 'You killed my daughter, as much as anyone. You did. It was you.'

The old man retreated, hurrying behind the counter, talking, talking. Jian stalked after him into the kitchen. The man was scrabbling at the back door.

He fired into the side of a freezer. The shot resounded in the small space and, after, there was a ringing silence and a whiff of cordite. He inspected the bullethole. The bullet had passed through the outer layer of plastic but had not penetrated into the interior. So these shrink-wrapped bullets did not have much stopping power – but at least the gun worked.

'Shut up. You going to help me, or not?'

The old man was talking even faster. Jian had shot the freezer for safety, its plastic surface the only one a bullet would not ricochet off. But let the man think him insane and irrational, it would keep him nervous.

BAD TRAFFIC

He held the pink phone delicately between two fingers and pocketed it. The gun went into his jacket, along with a chopper and a fruit knife.

'Let's go, then. That's right. You piece of shit. Let's go.'

The old man locked the place up. Jian said, 'How fortunate that I should appear, and become the agent of your vengeance. You think you are so cunning, don't you? I hate you.'

The old man smiled and nodded and led him round the corner and into a car.

'I hope you die like my daughter died. You old coward.'

At the dog end of the Cultural Revolution Jian had joined the army, and had fought in an obscure, inglorious and inconclusive war against the Vietnamese. A sensible lad and a bad soldier, he had kept his head down. He'd learned to hate infested bunkers, and he'd spent as much time as he could developing political awareness, because it happened in a dry classroom.

He had come to know the contents of his little red book, 'The Thoughts of Chairman Mao' off by heart. He was taught that, at times of stress, all good communist soldiers calmed themselves with those wise words. Indeed, he had found that, even under fire, by filling his head with the babble of those mantras he was able to function.

Now, in the warm car, woozy with fatigue and anguish, his old survival technique came back to him. 'Exploitation of the working class for profit constitutes one side of the character of the national bourgeoisie,' chanted the voice in his head. 'While its support of the constitution and its willingness to accept socialist transformation constitute the other.' It made him feel like a soldier again.

110

(**27**

Jian considered it quite possible that he was walking into a trap. It would have been a simple matter for the old man to arrange an ambush. But instinct told him that the old man hated this tong almost as much as he feared them. He closed his eyes, thinking to rest for a couple of minutes.

When he opened them the old man was shaking him. He had no idea how long he'd been out. It had been more like a blackout than slumber. They were parked on a dark street without lights. The old man pointed at a door and mimed holding the namecard up to the CCTV camera just visible above it. Jian snatched the card and got out of the car with the gun heavy in his pocket and the car was accelerating away before the door had finished swinging closed.

Jian's breath was juddery and shallow. He was disorientated after his sleep, and there was a black pit at the edge of consciousness, but he could not fall into it yet. He reflected that only on one subject was it worth listening to Mao and that was how to win a battle. Fight no battle unprepared, fight no battle you are not sure of winning, and concentrate an absolutely superior force on the enemy's weak points. He was clearly now acting against the old fraud's precepts. At the least he should have a plan, he should reconnoitre, he should rest.

But his despair was like a sediment: without movement, it began to settle and clog. He could not stand still.

Paint was peeling on the surface of the door. The window for the address was empty. He pressed it, thinking it was the door buzzer, pressed the maker's name, then, third time lucky, got the button.

He had been a bad father. He had not loved the girl's mother – and then, of course, he had killed her. He had not been there for her when she was growing up, every day he had failed her. He had been guilty of sending her away. And now these people had taken her away from him. Killing these people would be nothing. It would not be so hard. Just carrying on, finding the strength to get up in the morning – that, he knew, was going to be difficult.

He did not care that he was one man and they were four. He did not care for the risk, or if he lived or died. His only anxiety was that he be stopped before he had killed any of them. He was anxious to kill the one who called himself Black Fort – the others didn't matter, they were followers, hatchetmen. Even if they had been the ones who... the ones who... his mind wrenched away from that thought, he couldn't allow himself to complete it as words. If he could just kill Black Fort, then it wouldn't matter what happened to him afterwards – nothing would matter.

A voice crackled through the speaker. A girl, Chinese, a bark of inquiry.

He held the namecard up to the camera and the door lock buzzed.

(28

The door led into a dark, narrow hallway. The only decoration was a print of a bare-chested Chinese girl carrying a vase on one shoulder. He knew the picture, it was popular back home. Her big doe eyes and pert tits brightened up a lot of dingy rooms.

Stairs led up. He noted that his palms were not even sweating, a numb fatalism had stolen over him. Let what was about to happen, happen. He felt the gun in his pocket. The chopper was in his waistband and the fruit knife was tucked into a sock.

In his war he had shot and killed one man, a stretcher-bearer. There had been nothing dramatic about it – a retort, a distant figure glimpsed through smoke fell over – and it was a minor event in the great clamour all around, but in retrospect it had grown in significance. He had the taint of violence, he knew what it was and what it did to you, and he knew that to be successful now, he could not falter before the ugliness of it. He opened a door.

A Chinese girl smiled at him from behind a bar. She'd lightened her face with pale foundation and there was a line around her jaw where the make-up stopped and a darker neck began. In the dim light of the room's red tinted bulb she almost got away with it, but in daylight she'd look like a ghost. She said something in Cantonese and gestured at a leather sofa.

Two heavily made-up Chinese girls sat there, one massaging the feet of the other. The girl receiving wore a figure-hugging qipao slit to the thigh. Beneath her black stockings Jian could see blisters on the back of her ankles. Her high-heeled shoes lay on the floor. The other girl, dressed in jeans and a tight T-shirt, kneaded her feet with strong, stubby fingers.

Jian understood. He'd spent enough time in these kind of places, usually in his official capacity, but not always. Aware of the watching barmaid he pretended to be horny and nervous. He sat on an empty sofa and lit a 555. A cardboard cut-out of a half-recognised blonde actress smiled broadly. She was trying to keep her white dress down around her waist as it ballooned up, without much success. On the stale air he smelled cloying perfume, cigarette smoke and a faintly sour chemical undertone, a hospital odour. The ashtray was half full, the carpet peppered with cigarette burns.

The girl behind the bar said something else, and he replied, '*Dui bu qi, wo ting bu dong...* I'm sorry, I don't understand.'

'Oh,' said the girl in the qipao. '*Ni shi zhong guo ren...* you're a mainlander.' She sat up.

'Where are you from?' asked the girl in jeans.

'The northeast.'

'Oh, a beautiful place.' She began to sing a popular song, tilting her head from side to side to mark the rhythm. '*Wo shi yige dongbei ren, wo shi yige hao peng you....* I am a northeasterner, I am a good friend to have.' She had a good voice. He noticed that there was tissue paper tucked into the back of her shoes, to make them fit.

From her accent, the girl was from central China – he guessed Henan. She had a squat build and a ruddy complexion. Like the barmaid, she had tried to lighten her skin with make-up. Though her nails were long, her fingers were thick and calloused. A peasant girl – you could see her in any small Chinese town.

'We don't meet many mainlanders. It's nice to speak real Chinese again. We have to try and learn English.'

The girl in the qipao said, 'Would you like a massage?' and the other girl repeated the statement.

'Yes, please,' said Jian. He pointed at the girl with the jeans on because she seemed more docile.

'How much does it cost?'

'Thirty pounds.'

'Is that all-inclusive?'

'One time. Half an hour. Nothing kinky.'

'Let's go.'

The girl took his hand and led him down a corridor. The red light here was even dimmer. The floor was tile, and a mop and bucket were propped in a corner. Sliding doors led off.

The girl knocked on a door, then opened it. The cubicle beyond held a fold-up bed. Jian pretended to stumble, knocking against the plasterboard division. It didn't feel very strong: he reckoned he could kick through it if he had to.

'Have you been drinking?' she asked.

He looked around for an alarm button but couldn't see one. He stood in front of the door.

'Tell me about this place. How many girls are there?'

'Eight. Give or take.'

'How many are here now?'

'Huh? All of them.'

'And are there men here?'

'Why? Do you like men? That can be arranged, but you'll have to talk to the girl at the front.'

'I want to know how many men are here now and I want to know where they are.'

'I don't think I can tell you that. Why don't you make yourself comfortable?'

She took off her T-shirt, revealing a frilly padded bra. Her arms were bony, with a bluish bruise on the inside of one elbow. It looked like the mark left by an injection. He took her arm and rubbed it. Make-up came off, revealing needle scars. A junkie then. Probably they all were, it would help keep them pliant.

She said, 'Do you like what you see?'

'I'll give you money if you talk to me. Tell me where the boss is.'

'I don't deal with money. You're going to get me into trouble. Please don't get me into trouble. Please, I'll be punished. I can't help you. I just do massage. I don't know anything about anything.'

He guessed that hatchetmen were at the front, and the brains at the back. The building was four storeys high, and now they were on the second. He had to find the stairs.

'I just want you to be satisfied,' said the girl. She put a finger on the inside of her lip, dipped her head and batted eyelashes gloopy with liner.

'Stay here.'

'Where are you going?'

'Stay where you are.'

But she followed him into the corridor. He worried that he was making a mess of this. If he didn't stop her she'd run straight to the club enforcers. He grabbed her arm squeezed, and showed her his gun.

'We're going upstairs.'

She shrieked.

'Nothing is going to happen to you. Shut up.'

She wet herself. Her eyes were huge with fear and she was gibbering and her legs were trembling so much she couldn't walk. He let her go. This was not going well.

(29

A cubicle door slid open and a girl peeped out. Jian supposed she could not see the gun, but she could see her colleague being mishandled, and that was enough. She ran lightly on bare feet into the corridor and back towards the bar.

He left the girl and ran the other way, deeper into the building, and found a door at the end of the corridor. It led to a flight of stairs going up. He took them quickly, three or four at a time. He slammed a door open and found himself in another corridor of closed cubicles, just like downstairs. He opened one. A slim girl sat on a fat man. She turned, and gasped when she saw the gun.

'Where's the boss?'

The man stopped groaning and raised himself. Struggling to sit up, he tipped the girl over and onto the floor. His condommed penis wiggled as he thrashed around.

'Where's the boss?' Jian barked. But either she didn't understand or was too shocked to speak.

He heard running feet behind him. He turned and a man shouted – some threat or curse, probably. Dragon tattoo on the arm, four gold rings. No leather coat now, just a T-shirt, and the tattoo could be seen curling all the way to his shoulder. Yes, he had seen this man before, stumbling along the pavement outside the Floating Lotus.

He aimed and fired. The man looked shocked, then worried. He put a hand on the wall. Jian moved close enough to smell the booze on him and shot him again, and the man fell down. He felt a light sprinkle on his face and wiped it with his sleeve. It was blood. He looked down and saw that his clothes and shoes were similarly spattered. He felt the wooziness of shock steal over him and in his mind babbled to keep it from freezing him up. Sometimes in the revolutionary struggle the difficulties outweigh the favourable conditions and so constitute the principal aspect of the contradiction.

A door slid open and a girl peeked out. Her eyes widened. She ran out, naked and squealing. Jian forced himself to focus. He had to find Black Fort, and flashed the two characters of the name across his mind. Where the girl had run, there must be more stairs.

He found a dim stairwell with bare tile steps. Yellowish light spilled from the floor above, red from below. The walls were mildewed concrete. He could hear the naked girl padding down and now he became aware of more sounds, of pounding feet and shouts and screams. He wondered how long they had been going on for and how he had not become aware of them before. A clanging alarm started to ring.

A portly middle-aged man, naked but for a towel held over his crotch, shuffled in from the corridor. Jian waved the gun at him and he dropped the towel in fright and ran out again. The stairs up led to a dingy stairwell with a normal bulb, not a red one. The shift was abrupt, like breaking out of water into sunlight.

Blinking, his gun raised, Jian banged a door open with his shoulder. The layout of the corridor here was the same as downstairs – plasterboard divisions and sliding doors dividing the space into cubicles. But here there was no attempt at decor. Unshaded bulbs lit a scuffed laminate floor and unpainted walls.

Jian slid a door back. The room beyond was the same dimensions as those downstairs, and held two double bunk beds with just enough space to move sideways between them. Girls' clothes hung from the metal bedframes and from pipes running along the ceiling. Towels and make-up were scattered over the floor and across the beds.

A window was boarded with rotting planks. Underwear hung from the blunt ends of the nails. A picture of green trees and hills, ripped from a magazine, was tacked to the central board. The place reminded him of a cell, and stank of bodies and perfume.

He closed the door out of instinctive politeness and strode past more cubicles. The only proper door opened into a rank little bathroom. A hose with a showerhead attached ran from a tap on the sink. The porcelain was streaky with brown mould. Lines of drying laundry criss-crossed the ceiling. A window was nailed shut and black paint had been slapped over the glass.

This was no good. This was where the girls lived, the boss would be far from here. He should have gone to the front, not the rear. Worrying that he'd missed his chance, he rushed back to the stairs and dropped into the red glow. The clamour of the alarm continued.

Hurtling back along the corridor he almost stumbled on a body and it took a moment for him to realise that he had made the ugly thing. The face was slack, the mouth hung open and the tongue flopped out. Someone had trodden in the pool of blood and now dark footprints led away, partial prints of the balls and toes of small, bare feet. He followed them towards the bar.

(30

The soft-focus ladies still grinned from the walls but the real girls had gone. The table lay on its side and fake fruit rolled back and forth. A bloody smear near the skirting board told him that the barefoot girl had run round the cardboard cut-out of the actress. Strangely, the name of this actress now came to him – Monroe. Behind her, a door hung ajar.

Jian was breathing heavily and motes of light flickered before his eyes. He was thinking in fragments, but screaming at himself to stay sharp. He stood against the wall and extended his toe to poke the door open.

An explosion made his head ring. Stings pattered his side and he flinched, raising his arms to cover his face. Part of the ceiling trellis collapsed with a snap and plastic grapes fell and bounced.

Someone had fired a shotgun at the door. Slithers of wood hung from the hinges, the rest had been blown into the room. The lampshade was torn to shreds, the bulb shattered.

Jian had been hit by splinters and deafened by the noise, nothing more. He dropped to his haunches and knocked a chair over. He hoped its thunk sounded like a dying man. He straightened and took a big, careful step back.

The only light now was a dim red glow from the corridor and Jian almost did not see the shotgun barrel nudging through the doorway. He grabbed it with his free hand and the heat of the barrel was painful as he yanked it, pulling its bearer forward.

Black Fort was on the other end, and now the two men were shockingly close and Jian could see into his yellowish eyes. All he had to do was bring up the gun and it would all be over. He pulled hard on the shotgun barrel and Black Fort lurched forward and Jian's hand came up and his finger was tightening on the trigger.

But Black Fort let go of the shotgun and dropped, and now Jian was off balance, and a jutting elbow struck his gun arm on the wrist and knocked his hand up and the gun fired into the ceiling. Burning powder from the discharge stung his eyes. Black Fort grunted – it had hurt him, too.

Jian was back against the bar, and Black Fort was moving forward, and in a moment he'd banged a bony shoulder into Jian's chest and headbutted his jaw. Jian raised his leg and turned his hips and a knee strike aimed at the crotch whacked his thigh. He brought the butt of his gun down hard on the back of Black Fort's head and the impact jarred his elbow.

Black Fort put his hands either side of Jian's head and fumbled his thumbs into Jian's eyes. Jian beat the gun against Black Fort's back. Black Fort let go with one hand and with the other slapped Jian's gun arm away and pinned it to the desk. The other thumb kept burning into the screwed-up eye. Jian thrashed, death or blindness was a moment away.

Desperation gave him strength, and he leaned right back over the bar, kicked his legs up and carried Black Fort up and into the air. He twisted and turned right over the bar, and with a succession of bruising jolts crashed down onto the other side.

He was lying on the floor and still holding the gun. His eyes were raw and full of water and he couldn't see. He hauled himself to his feet and gritted his teeth against the pains gathering in his ankle and elbow and back.

Leaning against the wall, he pointed the gun and tried to keep it straight. He was aware of a dark form moving in the red light. It went away.

He dragged himself through the open door and around dark shapes that might be furniture. A stereo was playing a catchy ditty, one he had last heard blaring out of a clothes shop back home, and the words came at him clear and distinct. '*Wo zhende ai ni, ni shi wo superstar...* I really love you, you are my superstar.'

He wished his eyes would stop streaming. A square of white light floated before him, rising from the vague redness all around. He dragged himself up to it and realised everyone had gone through this open window and left him alone.

With the gun raised, he felt his way back down the stairs and out the front door. They would return in force, with more weapons, but he supposed he was safe for a few minutes. In an alley he slid down a wall between plastic bins until he was sitting with his legs stretched out in front of him. Pains crowded for attention. He ignored them and reached for a cigarette and was annoyed to find out that his pack wasn't there, it must have fallen out in the fight. All he had in his pockets was his daughter's mobile phone and Black Fort's namecard. He contemplated the phone number scrawled on the back, and waited for his eyes to clear so he could read it.

WILDERNESS

(31

Mister Kevin drove the migrants to the seaside. Ding Ming reflected on what a long day it had been. It would be very good to lie down. He just needed a corner to curl up in and he'd be sleeping like a baby. But he could not rest yet. He contemplated a bleak plain of mud that shaded, far away, into a black sheet of water broken only by the rippling reflection of the moon. He wondered what sea he was looking at.

A Chinese man got down from a tractor and introduced himself as shift supervisor. He handed out boots, rakes and waterproofs and explained that they were going to pick shellfish from the mud. It was very easy, even in the dark, the experienced workers would show them the ropes. They had five or six hours yet before the tide came in, a half-shift. He was from Fujian, and so too, he said, were most of the workers out there, so there was nothing to be afraid of.

And if they worked hard they could earn as much as one pound an hour. Ding Ming was very pleased. That was fourteen and a half yuan, an enormous amount, and just for foraging in mud. Gold Mountain deserved its name. Why, if he was given the opportunity to work ten or twelve hours a day for seven days a week, as he hoped, he'd be earning as much as eighty pounds a week, more than a thousand yuan. Four thousand yuan a month – it was scarcely credible. Back in the village, only a boss or an official could hope to earn so much.

The shift supervisor ordered the migrants onto the tractor's trailer and started the noisy engine. The men whooped to raise their spirits and somewhere a dog barked.

Kevin called Ding Ming back. 'Oi you. William. Over here a sec.'

Ding Ming watched the tractor chug away. He wanted to be given his chance to earn fourteen and a half yuan an hour. He feared another sexual overture and wrung his hands with nervousness.

But Kevin thrust a mobile phone at him. 'I think he's Chinese. What's he saying?'

'Hello?' said Ding Ming.

'Hello?' A man, his syllable a snap of inquiry. '*Ni shi shei*?... Who are you?'

'I'm Ding Ming. Who are you?'

'Who have I called? Whose phone is this?'

'A labour organiser. An English man.'

'A labour organiser... Are you a worker?'

'Yes.'

'Right. Tell him... tell him I'm looking for a job.'

The brusque statements gave Ding Ming the impression of someone used to wielding authority. The accent was northeastern, the Mandarin very clear. This was someone with education.

Ding Ming said to Kevin, 'He say he want job.'

'Tell him to fuck off.'

'He says no.'

The northeasterner said, 'Tell him that a Chinese man called Black Fort gave me this number. Tell him that Black Fort said that I was to ring this man, this labour organiser, and that he was to give me a job. Tell him that.'

Ding Ming translated into English, acutely aware that he was making some shocking grammar mistakes.

Kevin sighed. 'Is he ringing from a mobile?'

Ding Ming inquired. Yes, the man was ringing from a mobile.

Kevin said, 'I'll text him where we are. Tell him to turn up here round about dawn. Give me the phone.'

'The labour organiser is going to text you an address.'

'Can he be more specific?'

Kevin took the mobile and sent the caller a text message. It must have been stored, as it only took a moment. 'Anyway, he'll never find it.'

Ding Ming looked out at the puttering tractor.

'You'll be out there soon enough,' said Kevin. 'When he's dropped that lot off, he'll load up with sacks and come back.'

'One pound for one hour?' It was still scarcely believable.

'But of course we have to shave something off that to cover accommodation, food, work permits, transport to the site, hire of the equipment, administration costs and so on and such like. Then the money that is left is going towards paying off your debt. You won't actually see any money as such for a little while.'

Ding Ming grew aware that Kevin was looking him up and down, and shied from the scrutiny, lowering his eyes. The white man's feet, considered as part of the legs, looked all out of proportion. He supposed a foot didn't get chubby when the rest of you did, it was left behind.

'Of course, certain considerations can be made for good workers.'

'Oh.'

'I believe we were discussing your wife.'

'Yes.'

'And how keen you are to talk to her again.' There was a familiar leer on Kevin's face.

Not this again.

(32

A dog barked, very close and loud, and Ding Ming spun around, expecting to be bitten.

'Bollocks,' said Kevin, and fumbled his mobile out of his pocket. The dog bark repeated. In fact it was nothing but a customised ring tone.

'What?' said Kevin into the mobile. As he listened his eyes widened and mouth opened. 'Christ. You're fucking joking. Shot? With a gun?' Pressing the mobile hard against his head, he hurried into the van. 'Fuck. Well who? Yeah.'

Suddenly it was as if Ding Ming were not there at all, which was a relief, but Kevin's tone was so disturbed and his actions so agitated that he couldn't help feeling a twinge of alarm. This was a serious phone call, dealing with dramatic events. Ding Ming hoped none of that drama would touch him. He sidled away. All forms of trouble were to be avoided.

But Kevin snapped, 'Get in.' And when Ding Ming hesitated, 'I'm not pissing about.'

Ding Ming climbed into the van and Kevin accelerated so fast that he tumbled over. He held onto the seat in front as the vehicle bumped over grassy tummocks towards the road. Kevin was driving far too fast – much more of this and the suspension would break. He wondered whether he could risk asking what was going on, but decided that the best course of action was to keep silent and watchful and not draw attention to himself.

Kevin was talking on his mobile again.

'Christ, I could have been there. Definitely dead? Can't you just dump it in an alley or something? Okay, okay, no, I'm just saying.'

Could have been! What a fiendish language to contain such constructions. What was that – perfective subjunctive? His teacher could have told him. But his teacher would have hardly understood a word of Kevin's slurred and rapid speech. Himself, he was at that frustrating point with Kevin's English, where, though the individual words were generally clear, the meaning was often obscure.

Ding Ming felt that he could hardly remember a time when he wasn't being driven around and told what to do. This was his fate, it seemed, and he'd better get used to it. A cunning person would welcome this chance to grab some rest. He put his forearm along the top of the seat in front and laid his head on it and closed his eyes and went over today's words.

This cake does not 'please' me in the slightest. It is a 'pleasure' to meet you. He was not getting through the dictionary as fast as he'd like, but with all the recent disruptions it was a great effort to keep up his studies. Those people have the manners of 'plebeians'.

He wondered if his wife remembered any of the English he'd taught her. She'd gamely given it a go, but hadn't been very good at it. The oddest words had stuck – choo choo train, amazing, rabbit, doorknob, kitten but not cat. She'd been in awe of his ability and, he suspected, prompted their lessons, not out of desire to learn but to delight in his astonishing talent.

It was impossible not to think about her, so, as Ding Ming was practical in his mental habits, he decided to think about her in English. Darling, sweetheart, honey, my big love, my love person, that one I like the most. My favourite person in the world, the better – no the most best – no the best.

Enough, he told himself, the exercise had backfired, he was nearly crying. He raised his head. The van was travelling a dirt track parallel to the coast. To the right, lights burned, and the lower part of the sky was orange with light pollution, but ahead was total darkness.

They climbed, turned, entered a stand of trees and now all that could be seen was what the headlights revealed: a narrow trail between gnarled trunks. Kevin slowed and turned off the track and the van bumped further into the wood and the tyres crunched undergrowth. Ding Ming flinched as branches lashed the windscreen.

Kevin stopped the engine and turned off the lights, and dismaying silence and blackness swooped down. He got out and beckoned Ding Ming to follow. They trudged downhill, and leaves crackled underfoot. A brook trickled and night creatures rustled and called. As Ding Ming's eyes grew used to the gloom he made out fleshy fungal growths on a rotten log and twigs criss-crossing like the fibres of a net. To be surrounded by trees was to be in an unfamiliar, primal territory. And these trees were grisly and disfigured, their gnarled trunks spotted with breakouts, smothered in moss like a rash. Kevin gave him a spade and said, 'Dig.'

Ding Ming was glad to do as he was told. It was, after all, work, and that was what he was here for.

A thick layer of mulch covered dark, loose topsoil. It was easygoing, the spade biting deep, but it wasn't a practical place for a hole – they should head to higher ground where the water table would be lower. Still, he had his orders.

Kevin sat in the van and chain-smoked. The little red ember, the only point of light in the whole alarming darkness, was a reminder of civilisation. Though Ding Ming feared the man, he was glad to have his presence now, he'd hate to be out here on his own. He considered the man's persistent demands. It occurred to him that perhaps what had been asked for was a thing of no consequence in this country, something men did for each other often and with enthusiasm, something that was more than paid for by the gift of the cigarette. Perhaps it was a token of friendship and he had caused insult by refusing. The thought brought no consolation.

The harder Ding Ming worked, the less he reflected, so he threw himself into his job. He struck a steady tempo – spade in, up, turn and throw, in, up, turn and throw – and took pride in making his crater well and quickly. His shoulders would ache tomorrow, but it was a good feeling to be panting with exertion, an honest feeling. He hoped his wife was having a better time. Maybe she was sleeping now. When she slept, he liked to get right up close and follow the air going in and out of her nose. He fancied the rhythm of the spade to be the same as that of her breath.

He rubbed sweat off his brow. His feet were soaking. As he'd predicted, he'd hit the water table. It was not possible to go much deeper. It was a good hole, more than a metre deep, and with sides as steep as could be expected in this soft soil, and the displaced earth piled neatly.

Kevin turned the van's hazard warning lights on, then tramped over, swishing through leaves. He dropped a cigarette into the hole and it fizzled out.

'It's full of water.'

Ding Ming did not respond, it was not his place to offer comment. He'd done what was asked of him.

Kevin ran his hands over his head. 'You've built a pond.'

A car, growling in low gear, all lights off, swung into view, its bonnet nosing snout-like through the trees. Ding Ming realised that it was following the van's hazard lights. It eased to a halt and Black Fort got out, the man with air in his shoes.

Kevin said, 'I think Albanians. They fill some crackhead with rock, give him a tool, tell him to fuck people up or his family gets it.'

'I know who he is.' Black Fort lit a cigarette and toyed with the burned match. 'A Chinese cop, acting alone.'

'What's his beef?'

'A small misunderstanding.'

'You better keep your head down.'

'He won't find me again, and if he does I'll kill him. I'm going to pick up some shotguns now. I'll go to the farm, start sorting out that fuck-up. I'll pick up the next consignment. You got an ETA?'

'Hold up in Zagreb – now he says five tomorrow morning.'

Ding Ming understood very little of this, as the grammar was obtuse, the delivery rapid and mumbling, and so much of the vocab unfamiliar. Crackhead? Zagreb? Eeteeyay? The only statement he was sure of was 'I'll go to the farm.' Still, he had the distinct impression that this conversation was one it would be better not to hear. He would like to sidle away, but where could he go? He was trapped in this pit. To clamber out would only draw attention to himself. Now Black Fort was pointing at him.

'I'm not happy that you brought him along.' Not wanting to catch his eye, Ding Ming pretended to examine the sides of his hole.

'I'm not digging. You know what my back's like. What's the harm? He doesn't know where we are – he could blab to all and sundry and it wouldn't matter.'

Black Fort opened the back door of his car.

Kevin said, 'William, help him.'

Black Fort straightened and said in anger, 'You brought the one speaks English? Of all the ones, you bring the one speaks English?'

'He was there.'

'Why don't you think?'

'It's fine. He's fine.'

'You idiot. You want to make him one of your boys, fine, but don't let him see things. Think with your head for a change.'

Well aware that it was his presence that had caused the friction, Ding Ming felt embarrassed, and would dearly have liked not to hear any more.

'I'm sorting it out aren't I,' hissed Kevin. 'He was your mate. I don't give a shit.' The men glared at each other. 'I'm doing you a favour here. You're griefing me and I'm doing you a favour.'

'Alright, alright.' Black Fort slotted the match into his mouth and ran a hand through his hair. 'I get short-tempered when my friends die and people try to kill me.' He squatted at the edge of the hole.

'*Ni jiao shenme?*... What's your name again?'

'Ding Ming.'

'Come out of there and give me a hand, Ding Ming. We've got some cleaning up to do.'

He was glad to obey.

'A bad thing has happened.' Black Fort was tugging at something long and bulky rolled up in a blanket and lying in the back of his car. Ding Ming hurried to help, his feet squelching. It was an impressive vehicle, sleek and bright yellow, with tinted windows and flame decals above the rear wheels.

'I told you, didn't I, that people here hate you. We cannot always protect you.'

The blanket fell open, revealing a pale Chinese face with a lolling tongue and staring eyes. Ding Ming stepped away, horrified.

'That was a good man, a man like yourself, in the wrong place at the wrong time. What we need to do now is quickly clean this up, then never talk about it again. You don't ever mention this to anyone. Is that clear?'

'Yes.'

'I'm sorry you had to see this ugliness.'

Ding Ming was sorry too. It was all very frightening. He wanted to believe what he was being told, but could not help a suspicion that he had found himself in very sinister company.

They laid the body down and Black Fort took a white sack out of the boot and dropped it. He said to Kevin, 'You give that kid some money.'

Ding Ming blurted, 'Do you know where my wife is?'

Black Fort was brushing twigs and earth off his trousers and tutting at the state of his shoes. 'Huh?'

'She got taken away to pick flowers and I want a number I can call her at.'

'She's fine, stop worrying.'

He got into his glossy car and drove away, and Ding Ming was left alone with the lustful Kevin and a corpse.

Kevin said, 'Fucking ordering me around. He doesn't even say thank you.' He kicked the body. 'What did you have to die for, twat?'

He turned to Ding Ming.

'What you looking at? Heh?'

'Not look at anything.'

'Heh? Cheeky chinky fucker.' He slapped Ding Ming across the cheek. It stung, but did not really hurt. It was a humiliating affront, and he struggled to wear it lightly. A cool mental voice pointed out the triviality of the incident and the necessity, in trying times, of maintaining clarity. At least it was all Kevin seemed to require. The fat man was calm as he said, 'Let's get this fucker buried.'

(34

Ding Ming was on the legs and Kevin got the arms. The body wasn't even cold. Blood oozed from two raw wounds in his chest and his shirt was soaked. His mouth hung open and Ding Ming kept catching his eye. He had the impression that this person was heavier dead than he had ever been when alive. Perhaps the brute fact of death was a weight that settled in the body.

He'd assumed that Kevin, being twice as big as him, would be twice as strong, but that wasn't the case at all, the white man huffed and puffed. Ding Ming tried to provide a minimum of decorum, but, because Kevin was dragging rather than lifting, the back of the man's head bumped against the ground with every step, and with every bump Ding Ming winced as if his own head were being whacked. He imagined defending himself against an irritated ghost – 'Sorry, I'm just not strong enough'.

To keep the body from sagging as they struggled down the slope, Ding Ming held its thighs and stepped right up between its legs, almost to the crotch. The thing's legs dandled, feet swaying, and its trousers hitched up. It was wearing white sports socks and leather shoes. Blood was still dribbling from its wounds.

Ding Ming looked at his hands – yes, he was getting blood all over them. A dead body radiated ill luck, you could catch it like disease, his exposure was already at a dangerous level. They dumped the body in the hole. Ding Ming was glad it settled face down.

Kevin said, 'Hang on a sec,' and jogged back to the van.

The dead man had a tattoo of a dragon along one arm. It was detailed, in colour, and even the claws on the dragon's feet were picked out. That picture would be lost, and so would the freckles on the back of his hands and that scar inside his elbow.

He was wearing four gold rings: they would be worth hundreds and hundreds of yuan. A person could steal them and no one would ever know. That person would not even really be doing wrong – it wasn't as if their owner had any further use for them. But Ding Ming was not that person. Ruefully aware of his foolishness, he regretted that he could not allow himself to rob the dead.

His first day, and he was making a secret grave for a man who'd died violently. It was not an auspicious start to his new life. He wondered how often he would be asked to do this. Did it happen regularly? Once a week, say?

Kevin returned with the sack. He tossed it onto the body and ordered Ding Ming to split it with the spade. Chalky stuff spilled out, Ding Ming guessed it was builder's quicklime. He supposed its addition was a cultural practice, spirit suppression perhaps, until he saw the lime bubble and fizz as it reacted with the water and realised with a shiver that it had been put there to speed up decomposition. The lime would turn to acid, which would eat the dead flesh, and in a few days the body would have broken down almost completely, only the bones would be left.

'Wait a sec. Take his rings off.' Kevin pointed at a limp hand. 'Get in there and get them off.'

Ding Ming jumped into the hole and picked up a hand as pale and clammy as mushrooms. But the flesh was swelling – the rings were stuck. The lime burned his ankles.

He yanked with hopeless desperation and felt the skin around the knuckles shred, and there they were, four rings flecked with bloody skin, clinking in his palm. He scrambled out and dragged his feet across the earth to get the stinging acid water off.

Kevin took the rings. 'Go on, get him covered.'

Ding Ming determined to get the body buried before the acid started working on it. When it was out of sight it would not concern him any more. He gritted his teeth against the pain in his shoulders and heaved down huge gouts of earth, making sure to cover the head first.

'It's a fucker,' Kevin said to himself. 'I put my neck right out and not even a thank you.'

When it was done, Ding Ming rubbed his arms against a tree to try and get some of the blood off. He needed a good scrub and a drink of water. But Kevin said, 'Get those logs over it.'

The decaying wood felt slimy to the touch, and crumbled and split as he dragged it. He almost tripped on a half-buried boulder, and when he had the logs in position he returned and lugged that over, too. Kevin gathered handfuls of leaves and tossed them over the exposed soil.

Now you would never know there was a body under there. There was nothing to show for their gory work but the smell of freshly turned earth, which would soon dissipate. Ding Ming reflected on the transience of existence. Were we not all destined for such an end? How small, when it came down to it, a life really was.

Kevin's big arm slid around Ding Ming's shoulders and squeezed his neck.

'William, if you ever talk about this to anyone, you're fucked. I will personally fuck you up. Do you understand?' Ding Ming croaked 'Yes', and Kevin pinched his cheek, like teacher to errant student, and let go.

On the drive back, Kevin, in jovial mood, began humming a tune.

Ding Ming's feet and ankles were red and itching, his clothes were filthy with blood and soil, and he felt the taint of death hanging on him. He fantasised about having a wash. He was anxious to scrub the dead man's flesh from under his fingernails.

Kevin parked the van. In the light of the rising sun, the mud was tinted pink. Wading birds scuttered back and forth, working the ooze, and in the distance men could be seen doing the same.

Kevin said, 'Why don't you get in the front?'

Ding Ming was not sure he had heard correctly.

'What, you like it there in the back? I'm saying, get in the front.'

Ding Ming clambered over the seat and sat with his hands in his lap on the passenger seat.

It what seemed an unexpected spasm of generosity, Kevin gave him three coins. They were small in diameter but thick, gold in colour, and they shone appealingly. There was a picture of a woman on one side and a gate on the other and they were each as heavy as nuggets. Certainly it was the most robust currency he had ever felt. He had heard sterling described as stronger than the yuan, but hadn't realised that that was a literal as well as a figurative truth.

'See? Good workers get rewards.'

He was moved to breathe, 'Thank you'. Three whole pounds. His first real wage.

'Big day for you, wasn't it, William?'

'Yes.'

'You're a good lad. You're going to fit in fine. You know where your bread is buttered.'

'Excuse me?'

'Who pays your way.'

'Yes.'

'Now.' Kevin laid an index finger on Ding Ming's cheek, then ran it down to the corner of his lip. 'There's some business that we have to attend to.'

Oh no, not this again. This fat man really seemed to have only one thing on his mind, even a brush with death had not dampened his ardour. Ding Ming felt distance from home as an ache like hunger. How was he going to get out of it now?

35

Kevin began to slip down his tracksuit bottoms. Abruptly he stopped and gripped the wheel, and peered forward, frowning. He said, 'Oh Christ.' And wriggled them back up again.

A colourful car was pulling up, white and black with yellow stripes. A man in a black uniform, some kind of official, got out.

'It's bill. Police.'

Ding Ming blanched. They would ask to see his papers and he would be arrested. They might imprison him, steal his organs. Perhaps he would end up casually shot, like the man he had buried.

He checked that his door was unlocked. If it came to it, he would jump out and sprint. He rested his palm on the handle.

'Stay there,' growled Kevin out of the corner of his mouth. 'Don't do anything. You look a state. Put this blanket over you.'

The policeman's body so bristled with equipment, he looked military. He walked steadily, taking his own good time. A foreboding creaking sound was Kevin rolling down his window.

'What's up, officer?' His voice was light and obsequious.

The policeman stared right across Kevin and straight at Ding Ming. Ding Ming cast his eyes down, afraid to catch the man's eye. His hand tightened on the door handle. He had the blanket pulled right up to his neck, and it completely covered his arms, but he could not hide the smears of dirt on his face, nor his ethnicity.

Ding Ming figured that, with all that equipment, he might be able to outrun the man. But there would be another in the car. And they would call more, who would come in helicopters. Others would bring dogs.

The policeman said, 'Can I ask what you've been doing?'

Kevin said, 'He's been with me all night.'

'Is that so?'

'Yes, officer.'

The policeman addressed Ding Ming.

'Are you alright, sir?'

'Yes.' Ding Ming felt sweat prickling on his brow. His mouth was dry and he suppressed an urge to lick his lips and swallow.

'You look a little distressed, sir. Are you sure you're alright?'

'He gets nervous,' said Kevin.

'I can see that.'

'Tell the policeman you're alright, William.'

'Yes.' Ding Ming grinned with fear.

'Hold up your right hand,' said the officer.

'Excuse please?'

'Hold out your right hand.'

Ding Ming obeyed. He saw that it was shaking. A smear of the dead man's blood was clearly visible on his thumb.

'Alright, put it down. You're in the clear.'

'Excuse?'

'We've investigating an assault on a taxi driver by a man of Chinese appearance. But not one who speaks a word of English, so your friend is off the hook.'

'What happened?' asked Kevin.

'Seems he couldn't pay the fare, and an altercation resulted in a serious assault. Busted the guy's nose and ran off.'

'Ooh, nasty.'

'Have you seen anyone acting suspiciously?'

'No, officer. But if we do, we'll certainly call it in.'

'Have a good morning.'

'Thank you, officer. We will.'

The policeman walked stiffly away.

Kevin leaned back and breathed out heavily. 'Fuck me,' he said. 'Christ.' He watched the police car drive off. 'You did alright there, William.'

Ding Ming's relief was tinged with anxiety. He had been lucky now, but how often would this happen? He might not be so fortunate next time.

Kevin was drumming on the wheel. He watched the police car drive away, let a silence stretch, then turned and said, 'Finally. Come on, then. Suck me off.'

At college Ding Ming had taken up running, he would do laps of the campus. It gave him a feeling of lightness. He thought how lovely it would be to run away, to put his head down and drop into that rhythm where all you knew was pounding feet, heart, breath. The flatness of the landscape invited it. He would take his shoes off and the sand would spurt under his feet. He would run to the horizon. He would run all the way home.

'You don't have a choice, William.'

Kevin sat with his thick legs wide apart and his arms spread across the back of the seat.

Ding Ming saw what he had to do in his mind's eye, and it gave him a cold shiver of disgust. Worse, he saw the whole scene as it would appear to invisible watching eyes, to the ghosts of observing ancestors.

What a big house he was going to build. What a lovely wife he had, would soon be talking to – worth any sacrifice. In a few years, his time in this odd little country would be forgotten, like a dream he had woken up from.

'You could kneel down in front of me here. Or I could lie down in the seat and you could sort of arrange yourself across me, like... no, I don't think that would work.'

The man might be repulsive, but he was better than the alternatives.

He muttered, 'Hand is okay.'

36

'Hand is okay, is it?' Kevin rubbed his chin and pulled faces, twitching first one cheek then the other, which carried his pursed lips with him. What was that expression supposed to mean?

'Alright.'

Ding Ming's teeth were clamped so hard he could feel the tension in his neck. What a terrible thing to be poor, he reflected, as Kevin slipped the grey pants down and a greasy cock sprang free. What was most noticeable about it was how white it was. It flopped about like a dying fish as it swelled before his eyes.

'Come on,' said Kevin. 'It won't bite.'

Ding Ming looked away out of the windscreen as his left hand closed over it. He could see the thing out of the corner of his eye, and the red lump on the end seemed to be looking at him. It was soft to the touch, but rigid underneath and surprisingly hot. He started moving his hand up and down.

'Yeah,' said Kevin, 'yeah. Slower. That's right.' Ding Ming's arm was already sore from all the digging, and it quickly grew tired, so he shifted to bring more muscles into play.

It was more comfortable in the new position, but it did mean he had to look at what he was doing. Kevin's thing extended out of a prodigious tangle of curly brown hair. More hair grew on the man's stomach, below a tattoo of what seemed to be some kind of bird.

Kevin braced one hand against the side windscreen and the other on the dashboard, and settled down in the seat and Ding Ming realised the picture was of a swallow. That seemed an odd thing to have a tattoo of. Perhaps it was lucky in this culture.

Anyway he seemed to be doing it right as Kevin was groaning. 'There's a chinky monkey,' said Kevin. 'That's the way.'

Ding Ming was glad he did not have to put the thing in his mouth – that would be much more unpleasant. He felt he'd been cunning in finding this halfway measure that was less disagreeable and would, it seemed, still get him what he wanted.

It reminded him of milking a goat. Not that he had ever done so, but he had seen a documentary about Tibetan nomads, and what he had seen the women on that doing to their placid animals was not dissimilar to what he was doing now to Kevin. Those women came vividly to mind, with their rosy cheeks and wide smiles and exotic ethnic costumes. Ah, the noble life of a nomad. He tried to remember details from the programme. They cooked on fires made from dried yak dung and put yoghurt on their faces to keep their complexions fair. They put salt in their tea. They were happy as children, living a simple, poor but carefree life on the majestic high plateau of Chinese Tibet.

The more excited Kevin got, the more noise he made. A lot of it wasn't words, or was distorted half-words that Ding Ming did not understand, but he did catch a few adjectives – 'faster', 'harder' – and an imperative command – 'come on!'

Kevin began to slap the window. His face had gone red. His right hand left the dashboard and grasped Ding Ming's shoulder.

More imperatives, and Kevin yelped and his grip tightened until it grew painful. His goo spurted from the end of his thing and fell onto Ding Ming's hand. It was hot and seemed to sizzle there.

Ding Ming let go and the thing spasmed jerkily as more goo dribbled out. He wiped the side of his hand against his trousers, waited what he considered a decent interval, then recited a sentence he had thought about carefully.

'Can I please have the phone number for to call my wife now?'

(37

Kevin was getting his breath back and cleaning himself with tissues. He pulled his tracksuit bottoms up.

'That wasn't so hard, was it? Easy. Should have got some cream, though, you were getting rough.' He sighed, indicating a sudden dip of mood. 'I'm not some woolly woofter,' he said. 'Not some fucking... queeny limp wrist.' He dropped balled-up tissues out of the window. 'It's hot in here. Are you hot? I'm hot.' He took off his parka.

'Number, please.'

'Next time.'

Next time? Next time?

'Telephone number.' This was his right, a promise had been made.

'Well that wasn't the deal, was it?' Kevin circled his shoulders and sniffed. 'The deal was mouths. I can't very well go back on that, can I? Hand and mouth, it's not the same thing. I think there's some kind of misunderstanding. Your English isn't good enough.'

Ding Ming felt his neck muscles tightening. How could this be borne? 'You said.'

Kevin pinched his cheek. 'I'm just fucking with you.' He opened his black book and ran his finger down a list of names. 'Let me see, let me see...'

Ding Ming leaned forward to get a closer look, but Kevin tutted and raised the book, in the manner of a child withholding a toy from a playmate. 'Tell you what, I'll give you one digit each time.'

Ding Ming craned closer to look at the precious page, but Kevin pressed it to his chest. 'Naughty. And the first number is... zero.' Kevin snapped the book shut.

Ding Ming gathered that he had been cheated, that he would continue to be cheated, that this repulsive scenario would be repeated over and over again. He found himself breathing rapidly and shallowly, and his pectoral muscles tensed. A whine escaped gritted teeth. Before he knew what he was doing, he had snatched the book away.

'Tell me where my wife is.'

'Don't get uppy with me, son. Give me that back.'

Ding Ming opened the address book and its pages fluttered.

'What number? What number?'

Kevin punched him, but Ding Ming ducked the blow, and it struck the top of his head. He fumbled the van door open and ran towards the sea. He didn't look back, so he didn't even know if he was being pursued.

Mud sucked at his feet. Perhaps he was crying out, but he didn't know because the wind snatched his voice away. It picked at his hair and clothes, and gulls jeered.

What had he done? Why was he here? Home seemed so far away, it was almost unimaginable. What was he doing, here, now? There had been a grotesque error, a farcical mistake of enormous proportions. His fever dampened, and he stopped and stood disconsolate with hands on knees.

He had watched many counterfeit English language DVDs in the college TV room, with his dictionary on his knee and his finger hovering over 'pause'. Often the films had glitches, and one disc's strange error came to him now. He'd been watching 'Speed', which starred Keanu Reeves, and without warning it had turned into 'The Matrix', also starring

Mister Keanu. It was an analogy for his present disorientation. Like Mister Keanu, he had crossed over into the wrong film.

Though he knew that his only course of action was to turn right round, he could not bring himself to do it yet. He looked about. He could not discern where mud, water and sky began or ended – the entire landscape was a grey sludge, as if he were inside a sodden thundercloud. The only details he could make out were the tractor, piles of sacks and stooped men, and a line of rotting wooden stumps parading down the mud like a lesson in perspective.

A man was watching him. A burly Chinese man in black clothes stood perfectly still, pressed against the back of the nearest stump. His presence was so unexpected that Ding Ming wondered if this was not some malevolent phantom, summoned by his distress. He raised an arm to shield his eyes and saw the ominous figure do the same.

The stranger leaned out from his hiding place, looked around the stump, then stepped forward.

He was no spirit, but still odd. An imposing figure, tall and broad, he wore a leather jacket with a fur collar, and on his belt a pouch for a mobile phone and a clutch of keys. He was boss class. But though his clothes were expensive, his hair was disordered and there was something wild in the set of his features. One eye was completely bloodshot. Clearly he did not care about the ruin of his shoes and trousers as he strode across the mud.

'*Ni hao,*' he called. '*Ni shi shei?*... Who are you?'

'*Wo shi gong ren,*' said Ding Ming, growing conscious of his own wiry frame and bedraggled clothes. 'I'm a worker.'

'I talked to you on the phone.'

Yes, the man who had called Kevin last night.

'The labour organiser. Is that him there?'

Ding Ming looked back. There was Kevin leaning against the bonnet of the van and smoking a cigarette.

'That's him.'

How stupidly he had behaved, Ding Ming reflected – like a petulant child. He hadn't thought, he'd just panicked, and now he'd made things worse for himself. He had done himself no favours. He grew ashamed. In future he would think carefully before acting.

'Let us go to see him.'

'Yes.'

'You speak English,' the man said.

'I can get by.'

'You're an illegal?' He used the derogatory Chinese nickname – *renshe*, a snakeman.

'Yes. Today is my first day.'

It was good to talk to someone, but the more he saw of this man, the more intimidated he felt. The man's fine clothes were filthy and his expression was a scowl.

'I'm Ding Ming. What's your name?'

'What's that book?'

'It's his address book.'

'You took it from him?'

'Yes.'

'Can you read it?'

'Yes. I should give it back.' He did not want to explain further, out of embarrassment.

'Give it to me. My name's Jian.'

If this man returned the book, Ding Ming would save some face from the situation – it was certainly preferable to personally handing it over. Perhaps Kevin would pretend that the burst of ill temper had not occurred, and would not mention it. He hoped so. Pretending it never happened was certainly the best course of action. He handed the black book over and the man put it in his jacket, and now Ding Ming noticed the scuffed knuckles.

He said, 'Did you take a taxi here? Did you attack the driver?'

But the man did not reply. He was moving faster, with his shoulders set and his head lowered. Ding Ming hurried to keep up.

Mister Kevin came away from the van and stood with his arms crossed. 'I'm afraid I have no alternative but to consider docking your wages.'

Jian stopped, turned and said, 'I have to do this now.'

'You have to do what now?'

He punched Ding Ming in the head.

Ding Ming fell over, too surprised to cry out. Dazed, he watched his attacker walk up to Kevin and hit him. Kevin staggered backwards and put his hands up.

Ding Ming's lip was split, and he tasted the coppery tang of blood in his mouth. He blinked. He couldn't believe it. He got shakily to his feet and croaked, 'What are you doing?'

Jian back-handed Kevin and followed it with a swinging left. The fat man hit the ground with a dull thud. Jian riffled through his pockets and took out car keys, wallet and a packet of cigarettes.

Ding Ming gathered his senses. He was horrified. This man was dangerous, probably insane – he had to run. He got to his feet and stumbled away, but Jian stepped up, pulled him round and hit him again, and the sky went out.

(39

Pain was the first sensation Ding Ming felt as he returned to consciousness. His head felt like it was splitting open. Even his eyes seemed to be throbbing. There was a sharp ache in his side and a dull one in his neck. His mouth was raw, his arm numb. He thought for a moment that he was seven years old and he'd fallen off a wall, then he remembered, no, that was the last time he'd been really hurt, and this time was worse – no one was about to kiss it better.

He wished he was still unconscious and wondered if closing his eyes again would deliver him back there. But pins and needles were lancing and his neck was so sore it seemed like, if he didn't move, something inside would snap.

He lugged himself upright and his head lolled. He laid its weight back and a moan escaped his lips. Here was a whole new set of unpleasant sensations. Circulation was returning to his right side and it felt like tiny balloons were bursting in there. The back of his head was just getting sorer.

'*Ni zenme yang?*... You alright?' said a voice to his right, in Mandarin Chinese. He had no inclination to find out who it belonged to. The slightest effort, a flutter of the eyelids or a completed thought, might collapse his whole system. So he looked at the ceiling. The roof was grey and moved like water. It took him a few heartbeats to realise that he was looking at it through smoke.

Encouraged by this successful deduction, he let his attention grope outwards. He was sitting in a moving vehicle. He wondered why there was no steering wheel on this side, then an alarming set of realisations clicked in: he was in Kevin's van, his wife was missing, he was very far from home. He looked round. The big crazy man called Jian was driving.

'I was worried I'd hit you too hard,' he said, and took a drag on a cigarette. The man drove with his hands on top of the wheel at five to midnight. They were brutish hands with scuffed knuckles.

Ding Ming wasn't sure what was going on, but knew he was in a lot of trouble. He needed to know who else was here so he swivelled, ignoring the pain. He expected to see Kevin and maybe a bunch of migrants in the back, but it was empty. They were alone.

'Where is everyone?'

'That's your first question? Where is everyone?'

'Where are we?'

'You know as much as I do.'

It was raining hard, and the windscreen wipers sloshed water. The broken white line at the centre of the road shot into the distance, but that was all that could be discerned with any certainty. The road was lined with – nothing. A plain of mottled green and purple rolled as far as the eye could see in all directions, before being swallowed in mist. No people, no buildings, not even trees. It was a wilderness.

'What's going on?'

'Do you want a cigarette?'

'Why are you driving this car?' But as soon as he asked the question, the matter clarified. 'You've stolen it.'

In his alarm Ding Ming forgot his aches. He had been kidnapped by a dangerous lunatic. He did not care for what purpose, he had only one concern, which was to get out. He opened the door and a howling wind buffeted him. Rain pelted his face. Papers were swept up and dashed about, and ash from the cigarette burned his arm.

He lurched towards the blur of the road, but something pulled him back. He tried again, and found himself once more restrained. Jian reached across and pulled the door closed.

'Idiot,' he said. 'You'll kill yourself.'

The seat belt had checked him. The effort left him exhausted, and his head felt more fragile than ever. '*Lao tian a...* Oh heavens,' he said weakly.

'You've ruined my cigarette,' said Jian. 'Let me tell you how it is. I want you to find a man's address.'

'What?'

'You find it for me. In here.'

Jian showed him Kevin's black address book. 'You're looking for Black Fort.'

'A Chinese name?'

'Look for it in there. In English. Black Fort.'

'What if it is? Then you'll take me back?'

Jian dropped the book in his lap.

'Is it there?'

'You want me to find an address for you and then you'll take me back?'

'You find the address. You get me there. Then I'll take you back.'

What a fate, to be at the mercy of this madman.

'You don't have a choice. If you don't help me, you don't get back. Look around. Which way will you go? You were out for ages, you have no idea where I've been driving. You could set off in the wrong direction. Maybe wolves will catch you. Or, if you're really unlucky, cops.'

Jian yawned. He settled forward in the seat and shook his head. 'Help me, then I'll take you back. It's your only chance.'

'You stole this car. The police will catch you.'

'Find that fucking address.'

Jian was scowling blearily across. He yawned again and Ding Ming realised he was fighting fatigue.

Ding Ming wished he had never learned English. To placate the lunatic, he flipped through the book, looking for Chinese characters, but there were none. Perhaps the name was labelled under its odd English translation. There were no entries at all under B. Under F there was a Fianb and Fian, or perhaps Frank and Fran, Mister Kevin's spidery handwriting was not east to decipher. In Pinyin, the system of transliterating Mandarin Chinese into English, the name began with an H, so he tried there. He tried under C for Chinaman, E for Easterner and O for Oriental then went through all the names from A to Z and back again. It didn't take long, Kevin didn't have too many friends.

'Is it there?'

He felt nauseous, aware that every second he was borne deeper into wilderness. The van drifted off the road and bumped over the verge. Jian yanked the wheel. Ding Ming lurched and the book slid off his lap into the footwell. He said, 'Watch the road.'

'Is it there?'

Ding Ming flicked despondently back and forth. As well as lists of addresses there was a day planner, with scribbled notes like 'dentist', 'farm' and 'vet', and there was even a foldout map of the world, divided by time zone. Automatically, his eyes found China. It was not in the centre of the page, where he was used to seeing it, but out towards the edge.

'There's no address. It's not there, there's nothing. Take me back, please. Take me back.'

The van veered again. Ding Ming clicked the seat-belt release, opened the door, and jumped.

(40

His shoulder hit first, a thud that he felt all the way to his feet, then the impetus took him and more impacts jolted his body until it seemed he would be broken apart.

He found himself motionless and tasting earth. He got to his feet. He was winded and his head was spinning. His body had made a great smear ploughing across the grass. He had been lucky: he had slid right between two boulders.

The wheels of the van squealed as it braked. Ding Ming sprinted heedlessly away. The steep incline was carpeted with wiry bushes that scratched his ankles, it was like trying to wade across fibreglass. He tripped and the plants stung his face.

He scrambled up and looked round. The road below was a grey strip winding along the bottom of a valley and vanishing into fog. There was no sign of the van. All around was the wildest landscape he had ever seen, offering no shelter or hiding place.

He stilled the yelps of alarm that filled his head and tried to work out what to do. He had to find Kevin, and to find Kevin he had to find the sea. Perhaps he had not been taken far, perhaps he had only been unconscious for a few seconds. He would continue climbing, and from that ridge he would find out. He could see the view in his mind, the sweep of the bay and the glimmering mud, and because it was so vivid there the conviction rose that it must be true.

Climbing with his head lowered, rain trickled down his neck. Slithers of water seeped into his shoes. The raindrops were not plump and warm like at home, but small and cold, and they came lashing in from an oblique angle. The dismal sky seemed a weight that hung just above his head. He looked up and the pale peak seemed to have mockingly receded.

He heard voices, snatches borne on the wind – a line of song, a chatter of laughter. There was something so unexpected about them, he first thought they were inside his head. No, they were real, people were coming. Bulky figures breasted the ridge, carrying sticks.

Ding Ming threw himself to the ground. He was in a shallow gully, and by rolling to the side he was able to lie out of sight. But his whole body was now being jabbed by the infernal bushes.

Boots tramped closer, trousers swished. There were four of them, walking in single file, and they wore waterproofs, and carried rucksacks on their backs like soldiers. Perhaps they were hunters returning from an expedition with packs full of dead game, or landowners, prowling for poachers.

A woman said, 'I believe I can see the faintest smidgeon of blue sky.'

'Mad dogs and Englishmen', sang a man, 'go out in the morning rain.'

When they were past, Ding Ming sat up and pulled branches off his wet backside. The group were on a path, one he had missed, marching on enormous shoes. The path veered up again and took them back over the ridge. When he was sure that they would not hear him, he rose and struggled on.

The peak came upon him suddenly – he looked up, and he was there. He was above the fog now and could see for kilometres.

He was in a vast and forbidding emptiness. There was only more grass and scrub, on more hillsides, going on and on, fading into blueness, then the grey nothing. It was horrific – it was what death would look like.

It occurred to him that it was really quite possible that he was going to perish. If he fell over and turned his ankle, if he simply sat down, that would be it – the elements would kill him. It struck him as odd that he could contemplate this possibility in such a theoretical way, without it worrying him. No, he only worried when he thought about the terrible effect, both emotional and financial, that his demise would have on his wife and his family. He was a man with responsibilities: many others depended on him. Despair and defeat were luxuries he could not afford.

He could see the walkers again. They were certainly headed somewhere, and any somewhere was better than this huge nowhere. For want of any better plan, and because the fact of other people was a comfort, Ding Ming set off after them.

His body and clothes were so filthy that he was effectively camouflaged, and he knew that as long as he was careful to be quiet and to stay away from the skyline, they wouldn't spot him. There was little chance of losing them – their bright kagools would be visible for kilometres – but when they disappeared over another hilltop he could not help feeling anxious and quickened his pace.

He thought about Kevin, the man's flabby bulk coming vividly to mind. Now it represented security, how rash he had been to be repulsed by it. Had Kevin not kept him safe from the policeman? Did Kevin not know where his wife was? Kevin was all he had, Kevin was shelter. He tried to recast the man's actions in a favourable light. The big man paid well and promptly and handed out bonuses for good workers. He was a tough but fair employer, just a bit lonely.

Still the ramblers rambled, striding the emptiness with the confidence of ownership, down a valley and up a hill and down another valley. Ding Ming followed with his arms crossed over his chest. At least he was not getting any wetter. He was already saturated.

He started stumbling and falling over. He could no longer control his shivering and it was hard to complete a thought. He no longer worried about being seen. Everything was a blur but for the bright kagools, which stood out like buoys in an ocean.

The group strolled to a road, and it dawned on Ding Ming that it was rather familiar. Why, this was the very first hill he'd climbed, all those hours ago. There were the bushes he had trampled, here the gully in which he'd hidden.

The group had tramped in a giant pointless circle, and for no reason at all. It was baffling and infuriating. As Ding Ming watched, they passed the rocks he'd slid between when falling from the van, and the woman pointed with her stick at the marks his body had made on the turf.

What a stupid waste of time. Ding Ming slapped his cheeks with consternation. This world was not merely uncaring, it was malevolent, a player of monkey tricks.

Feeling sorely hard done by, Ding Ming followed them to a car. Crouched behind a bush he watched them make a jolly picnic inside, with sandwiches and steaming thermoses. He heard snatches of laughter and the crumpling of packaging.

They were in a car park surrounded by dripping trees. A building in the corner looked quaint and self-sufficient – the local equivalent, perhaps, of a pagoda. Its overhanging roof offered shelter from the rain. Ding Ming dashed from tree to tree, then flattened himself against the brick wall.

A woman from the car approached, a robust, clomping figure. Fearing she was coming to challenge him, he prepared to slink into the bushes. But she went inside the building and that's when he spotted the stick-figure signs. He was outside a public toilet.

The woman came out, the car drove away, and Ding Ming slipped into the gents. He found an astonishing opulence. The space was larger than his family home and much better equipped, with electric lights, fancy plumbing and running water.

Having slaked his thirst from a tap, he washed face, arms and feet in a glorious stream of hot water. There was no plug, so he stuffed the plughole with a sock and filled basin after basin. There was a mirror over the sink, but he was careful to avoid considering it until he'd finished.

His upper lip was swelling where it had been split by Jian's punch. It was tender to the touch. Bruises on his shoulder were the result of his tumble from the van. Even Kevin's slap had left its mark, a cut where the man's ring had nicked his cheek. His shirt was stained with the blood of a dead man. He looked tired, slovenly and furtive.

He dried himself under a hot-air dryer. It was a clever device – certainly these people had a genius for convenience – but it didn't work properly, it kept switching off. Using the paper towels would have been easier, but he had a nagging feeling that an attendant would appear and charge him for them. Great good fortune should not be pushed.

He locked himself into a cubicle. At least here he did not have to deal with the vastness outside. He slumped and let his thoughts drift, enjoying the after-sting of the hot water. It was the first time he'd been really comfortable in what felt like weeks. He determined to sit in this reassuringly compact space for a few minutes and recover from his ordeal, then work out what to do.

He awoke with a start. His worries thudded down like blows and he slid off the toilet. The light outside was dying, he must have slept for many hours. He could not believe what he had done, he felt guilty – as if he'd let everyone down.

He was no further towards any solutions... just hungrier. Night would come soon, and then he would be colder. He wished he could return to his dreams.

Clearly, he could not stay here. Men might come to use the toilet, someone would arrive to lock the place up. And if he was discovered, who knew what would happen? They might kick him for sport, one would hold him down while another phoned the police.

Outside, the sky was the colour of mildewed sheets. It had stopped raining, but he could feel sogginess in the air. He peeked into a litter bin to see if the walkers had left any edible scraps, but it held only packaging. A flock of birds flitted from tree to tree and he wondered how he would go about catching one. They flew over a dirty white van and Ding Ming caught his breath.

Fearing it a mirage conjured by desperation, he was reluctant to allow himself hope. He approached as if happening upon it casually, expecting it to resolve itself into an unfamiliar vehicle. But no, it continued to look like Kevin's van. The evidence grew incontrovertible – there was the mud-spattered back door, the dusty windows, the rusted wheel arch.

But there was no Kevin inside. Instead, there was, of course, the madman Jian. He was collapsed in a dead sleep in the driver seat, head on his shoulder with his mouth open and the tip of the tongue protruding, snoring as loud a chainsaw.

So, after Ding Ming had jumped, the man had driven on for barely a kilometre. He had simply pulled up at the first discrete spot and fallen asleep. He had not even taken the time to cover himself with the blanket, take off his jacket or lock the passenger door.

The madman was better than the wilderness, just – as least he offered a chance. Ding Ming got in and tapped him politely on the shoulder. Jian grunted, stirred and looked around, and Ding Ming could almost see the man's own concerns banging into his consciousness.

Ding Ming said, 'I know where Black Fort is.'

交通差 LOST

(41

The events of the previous night were still fresh in Ding Ming's memory, but the chronology was confused. The smell of fresh, turned earth, a slither of moon glimpsed through trees, the feel of a spade handle, the sting of a slap, Kevin saying something about a rock, Black Fort saying, 'I'll go to the farm.'

It was the only entry under H, and it took up the whole page. 'HOPE FARM' was scrawled in capitals, in red biro. The address underneath was in spidery running script: 'BLOODGATE HILL, SOUTH CREAKE, NORFOLK'. Under that, in blue, in the same hand but written more patiently, were what looked like directions. 'A435 FOLLOW SIGN FOR SC LEFT AT WAR MEMOREAL TRACK ON RIGHT'.

Ding Ming jabbed the page with his finger. 'That's where he is.'

Ding Ming wondered how sure he was. Black Fort might have said, 'I'll go to the firm,' or perhaps it was 'I'll goat the palm,' which might be a dialect phrase. He was pretty sure, say eighty percent sure. But of course, just because this was the only farm listed in the address book didn't mean it was the one Black Fort was talking about. It might be – but it might not be. So, sixty percent. And maybe Black Fort was lying to Kevin, and even though he said he was going to the farm, he actually wasn't. Or maybe he changed his mind, and later decided after all not to go to the farm. Fifty? Forty?

'I'm one hundred percent positive. Now I've told you where he is, will you take me back?'

'No.'

'What do you mean, no? I've helped you.'

'You're going to get me there. You're going to read a map.'

'Why can't you read a map?'

'I can't tell a thing in this language, it's all squiggles to me.'

'How are you going to be able to take me back?'

'I've got an address. Your boss texted it to me.'

'Well, how did you read that address?'

'I didn't, did I? I showed it to a cabbie.'

'And then you beat him up.'

'What else could I do? I didn't have any money. Can you read a map in English or can't you?'

'I suppose.'

'Then there's no problem. You read a map, you get me there, then I'll take you back.'

'It could be anywhere. Anywhere at all.'

'This isn't China. This is a tiny little country. You could drive from one end to the other in a day. You'll be gone a few hours, if that. When I take you back, tell them you escaped, wandered round, and found your way back by yourself. They won't be angry with you. They'll be angry with me. Tell them I'm crazy.'

'That's true.'

'They saw that you didn't come willingly. When I return you, you won't get into trouble.'

'Where is this map?'

'There'll be one in here somewhere.'

'You haven't even got a map?'

'Have a look round.'

'You said you had a map.'

'I never said I had a map. Look in there.'

In the glove compartment Ding Ming found a pair of sunglasses with one arm missing, a mobile phone charger, pens, sweet wrappers, a dog lead and a chew toy. He pulled a newspaper out of the door compartment and was confronted by an enormous pair of breasts, staring out at him just like that. They seemed out of proportion – fascinating, but wrong. The girl they belonged to smiled invitingly.

'Like a cow,' said Jian, and Ding Ming stuffed the paper back in the door. He hoped his wife was getting on alright and having more luck than him. There was no map here. He cursed. '*Lao tian a.*'

'We'll drive until we find a town and buy one,' said Jian, and started the engine.

'Why do you want to see Black Fort?'

'That's my business.'

Ding Ming wondered what was going on back at the mud flats. Everyone would be talking about it. The migrants would be nervous – would their pay be docked? Would the wrath of Kevin fall upon them? Mister Kevin and his lieutenants would be gathered round a table, swearing bloody oaths of vengeance.

The sky was darkening. They were driving east, away from the setting sun. Big birds circled and Ding Ming wondered if they were vultures.

'What are you looking at?'

'I'm scanning for helicopters.'

Perhaps they were being tracked right now by radar, satellite or unmanned surveillance drones. Perhaps, in a control room somewhere, a man in a black uniform was following a red dot on a screen.

'Why?'

'Police helicopters. Looking for a stolen van.'

'They won't send helicopters.'

Surely it was only a matter of time before they were stopped, arrested and delivered into the butcher's hands of the immigration authorities. And say they weren't caught, he didn't trust this madman to make good on his promise. And say it all went well, and after some obscure and no doubt dangerous quest had been completed, the madman did make good, and delivered him back to the mud – well, what then? He'd have to tell a clever story about how he had jumped out of the van and wandered for hours and hid in a public toilet, then found his way back all by himself – what if Kevin didn't believe him? And what if Kevin – who did not, after all, seem a particularly rational person – believed him, but blamed him for the loss of his van? Perhaps Jian would bring down some calamity on Black Fort, and Kevin would blame him for that?

And what about his wife? Would they tell her that he had been kidnapped, and condemn her to endless worry? Would she be punished for his perceived transgressions? It was too awful, all of it. He worded a silent appeal to higher forces, let what was to happen, happen, but let his wife be spared, just let her be fine.

Simply to hear something other than the incessant fretting inside his head, he said, 'I don't think you should drive so fast. I think those signs are a speed limit.'

He knew that if you broke the arcane rules of the road, a cop car would flash his lights and chase you. And some cops travelled in cars that were exactly the same as normal cars, and you only knew they were cops when they put a hand out of the window and attached a light to their roof and made their sirens whoop.

'I can walk faster than thirty kilometres an hour.'

'You don't know where we're going. We're going nowhere. What does it matter if you go there at thirty or three hundred?'

They were passing through smallholdings and villages of stone houses and good land left for nothing but cows and trees. The road widened as the van approached a roundabout. It was the first time they had encountered other traffic. Jian leaned forward and shifted on the seat. He barely slowed for the turn. Horns blared.

'You're going the wrong way! Go round the other way!'

'I know, I know,' muttered Jian, and the van shuddered to a halt. Ding Ming was thrown forward, and if he had not braced himself quickly on the dashboard would have bumped his head on the window. Now Jian was reversing the van rapidly straight back into the road he had come from. A din of clashing metal and Ding Ming was thrown against the passenger door. The window of the driver's door shattered and glass tinkled.

The van juddered to a halt. A lorry had swiped them. Ding Ming watched it pull up in a lay-by up ahead. He felt very still. The crash, which had taken barely a heartbeat, seemed now to be reverberating into the present. His ears were ringing.

This was it, then, the beginning of the inevitable – capture was surely imminent. The driver of the lorry got down into the road and circled his shoulders. Jian accelerated hard, turned the right way into the roundabout, and took the first exit off it.

'We're going to get caught,' moaned Ding Ming.

'No, we're not. He didn't get our number, we're fine.' He swept broken glass off his lap.

'Where did you learn to drive?' asked Ding Ming.

'I used to rocket round in a squad Toyota. You put the lights on and everything gets the hell out of the way. It's a lot easier than this.'

'You were a policeman?'

'I am a policeman.'

Ding Ming fell silent. It made sense. The man had the temperament: he was fierce and short-tempered. And he drove like an official – arrogantly, hogging the middle of the road. The knowledge made him even more uneasy, he had never had anything to do with officials. They were no use to a peasant, they only took your money as taxes and in a dispute would never side with the poorer man.

'So you're here to arrest Black Fort.'

'I've said too much already.'

'Show me the address again.'

Jian took out the black book and opened it to the right page.

'Give it to me.'

'I hold it, you look at it.'

Ding Ming examined the instructions and looked words up in his little red dictionary. He discovered that a mile was a unit of distance and that there was no such thing as a 'memoreal', it was probably a misspelling of 'memorial'.

They were heading into a small town, where traffic was heavier. Ding Ming flinched every time a car passed and turned his face from every pedestrian. The only shop he saw was a florist's.

He said irritably, 'It's getting dark. You think we can find a map? Where's a bookshop? *Lao tian a.*'

He wanted to cry from sheer annoyance. They wouldn't find this farm in a few hours. They wouldn't find it in a week. He should never have returned to the van, he should have wandered the nothingness, living on squirrels and rabbits, washing in public toilets, until one day he saw the sea.

They'd be there and back in no time, the policeman had said. He was quick to make promises, like Kevin, and would take them as lightly as that pervert did. Mister Kevin Pervert. Mister fat lazy pervert Kevin. Ding Ming was shocked at his own vehemence. The anger he had been so careful to repress had broken through. This was all Kevin's fault, the fat lazy pervert pervert. He wanted to shout at the man.

He discovered that in his anger he had torn the tissue-thin pages of the dictionary. He smoothed them down and put the book away in his pocket, chastened. Kevin was his only hope, Kevin was his future, Kevin would tell him where his wife was. He rebuilt his mental dam and stored his feelings behind it and insisted to himself that the man was not so bad.

'There,' said Jian. He pointed at two neon Chinese characters, 'Happy Duck', which seemed to jump out at them. Just the sight of a Chinese character was enough to raise the spirits after all this foreignness. And a duck was a good omen. It was, of all things, a Chinese restaurant. 'Let's ask them.'

(42

Kevin's bulky green parka was draped over the back of the seat. Ding Ming did not like wearing a wet shirt poisoned with blood, and certainly didn't want to be seen in it, so he took it off and put the parka on. It came down below his knees and his hands were swallowed in its sleeves. Its fur-lined collar was soft against his neck. He put the hood up and it swallowed his head completely, it was like his own personal cave. He supposed he might have some difficulty moving in the thing, but it was very snug.

Emptying packaging out of its pockets he found a quarter full cola bottle. Jian hadn't seen him – he could drink it and the man wouldn't know. But he decided it was more to his advantage to be seen to be trustworthy, so he shared it.

'You look like a giant baby in that.' The policeman bumped the van over the kerb, stopped it, and they got out. The street was eerily quiet, with none of the life Ding Ming was used to: no hubbub of conversation or hum of machinery, no gangs of old women playing mah jong or youths play-ing pool, no theatre, no colour. There were people around – their televisions glowed behind drawn curtains – they just weren't very social.

The only figure in the whole scene was a woman push-ing a pram towards him. He stepped off the pavement to let her pass. As with all white people, he could not tell her age, she could be anything from fifteen to thirty-five. She was a vision of class and beauty. Her lovely red hair – red hair! – was scraped back from her head and tied up with a pretty band. Gold teeth gleamed when she puffed upon her cigarette, and silver hoops hung prettily from her ears. She swept regally past. Jian grabbed him by the arm and pulled him back onto the pavement.

'Stop running away from them.'

'They hate us.'

'They don't hate you. They don't even notice you.'

A fantastic car was parked up ahead. It looked like it had been poured rather than moulded. No rivet or flaw disturbed the flow of its curved surfaces, as lovely as a woman's. It sparkled with reflected light. To Ding Ming it hardly seemed possible that he and it occupied the same world. An ache grew in his breast, the pain of aesthetic rapture. A daring notion occurred to him – what if he were to touch it? He dismissed the idea as the sort of thing that would get him into trouble, but there was no harm in taking another step and craning forward. He moved a little to the side so that he did not see in that lovely surface the mundane interruption that was his own reflection.

A hairy head leaped, and jaws gaped and wet teeth glistened, and a terrible howl of threat began, and hanks of hair shook as the demon mouth opened and closed. Ding Ming jumped back with shock and, even after he had realised that it was just a dog – and a small yappy one at that, disturbed in its slumber on the passenger seat – he was still shaky with alarm. Worried his trespass would set in train further unpleasantness, he hurried after the policeman.

Ding Ming suspected that any restaurant proprietor who saw him looking like this would assume he was begging and chase him out. Still, he wanted to bathe in the reassurance of the familiar, so, sticking to the shadows, he slunk to the restaurant and peered in. It was a small, bright space with a counter that stretched the length of the shop. There were no chairs or tables, but there was a flashing entertainment machine, which seemed an odd touch. A middle-aged Chinese man stood behind the counter in a white smock. Ding Ming pressed his face against the window and yearned to be that man. To have created a decent clean restaurant – that was an achievement he could understand.

Jian tugged him in and said, speaking Mandarin, '*Ni hao, bang ge mang xing ma?*... Hello. Can you help us, please?'

The man was frying potato slithers in a vat of oil. He replied in Cantonese. Ding Ming knew only a few phrases in that dialect, picked up from pop songs and films, such as 'I like your hair', 'you are my precious one,' and 'die, bitch.'

'*Ni hui shuo putonghua ma?*... Do you speak any Mandarin?' Jian asked.

Obviously he didn't, because he said, 'You want chips?' His English was easy to understand, though Ding Ming didn't know what chips were.

'We want help.'

'I can't hear you under there.'

When Ding Ming took the hood down it made him self-conscious of his battered face. He said to Jian, '*Gei ta kan dizhi*... Show him the address.'

'No.'

'He can tell us where it is.'

'Just ask where we can get a map.'

Ding Ming frowned as he shaped the lumpy sounds. 'Where we can buy map. Country map. Map for England.'

A Chinese girl, pleasantly plump and round-faced, had come in from the back and was watching them, wiping her hands on her smock. She said, 'You'll have to go to the petrol station.' Her English was rapid and fluent, harder to understand than the man's. 'Are you in a car?'

Embarrassed at his abject appearance, he shrunk from her gaze. He wished the lights were not so bright.

'Yes.'

The man put a sheet of paper on the counter, licked the end of a biro, and began to sketch a diagram of how to get to this 'petrol station', whatever that was.

Ding Ming's attention was drawn to the food on display. What magnificent sausages, the biggest he had ever seen. And those fried in batter looked even more delicious. He realised he was very hungry.

'Do you want some chips, duck?' She winked. 'On the house. Free.' She began ladling fried potatoes onto a paper sheet. He felt overwhelmed by her kindness and wanted to linger in the warm shop. He saw something heroic in this man and his daughter. They were pioneers who had gone boldly into the territory of the barbarian and carved out a life for themselves. It was inspiring. He was moved to say, 'This a good place.'

But Jian said, 'Let's go,' his manner curt and distracted. Obviously he saw these people only as potential witnesses, an added danger.

The girl gave them each a punnet. 'Good luck on your trip, ducks. Goodbye.'

Ding Ming said, in Cantonese, 'I like your hair.'

(43

It was chilly back in the van, but the chips warmed Ding Ming's hands and stomach. The salt stung his wounded lip. Jian started the engine.

'Can't we wait?'

'We're going to that place. Navigate.'

The restaurant was marked with the character for duck, the 'petrol station' with a star. Instructions in English accompanied the drawing.

'Straight on, past two sets of lights. I wonder how much money they make in a day. Very simple business, but a strong one. It's good to have hot food, a person can't do anything on an empty stomach. These would be better with some spice on them.'

'Shut up. Where now?'

'I don't think you should tell me to shut up when I'm navigating.'

'Now where? Now where? Okay, talk all you like. Where are we going?'

'Left.'

They headed out of town and onto an unlit road that curved around a lake. He pointed at a pool of light. 'I think that's it.' Jian slowed. It was a garage with a four-pump forecourt and a shop at the back.

Why didn't you stop?'

'I don't want them to see the van.' The policeman parked in a lay-by a hundred metres or so further up the road.

They got out and started walking back. The lights of the town tinted the lower part of the sky orange, but all else was shaded blue by the moon. On the left ran a wall of uncut stones. It had been made without mortar and this pleased Ding Ming's sense of aesthetics – it was clever, efficient and frugal. To the right lay the lake, its surface rippling in the breeze, and those dark humps beyond were hills.

Ding Ming had never seen stars in such abundance, more than you could possibly count. He craned his neck and his mouth hung open. He grew intrigued at the variation in colours and brightness of the twinkling heavenly objects, and wondered what that pale milky streak was.

'That's nothing,' said Jian. 'You want stars, you come up to the northeast.'

'Are they the stars we see? Are they the same as the stars over China?'

'Of course they are.'

The sight stirred the poet in Ding Ming. Here was something that all mankind shared, be they peasant, policeman or foreigner. Were they not each and every one an inhabitant of the same small globe spinning in space? Looked at in cosmic terms, his epic trip across the seas was nothing but a small step, and this alien and baffling country was after all not so far from home. And how petty were the affairs of humans, compared with the timeless magnificence of the cosmos? He wished his wife were here to share this.

An owl hooted and when it ceased Ding Ming wondered if he had ever experienced such a profound quiet before. Feeling enveloped by absence, he wanted to shout, just to add some humanity to the setting. He began to twist his feet when he planted them, and to scrunch his chip punnet, just to break the spell of silence.

The petrol station was closed and no one responded to Jian's banging and shouting. Ding Ming peered between shutter slats. A dim light illuminated prodigious racks of confectionery and magazines. 'Motoring World' struck him as a very lyrical term. One big green book, he could swear, was called 'Map of the Road'. He pointed it out.

'We'll have to break in,' said Jian. 'I could maybe smash this shutter with a rock.'

'You're a madman. As soon as you break that window, there'll be a screeching noise, and a metal sheet will slam over the door.'

Ding Ming spotted a CCTV camera. He'd seen one before, in a bank in Fuzhou, but it was frightening to see one out here in the wilds. He turned his back on it, only to see more, trained on the forecourt. He put up his hood, and swivelled a raised arm, pointing them out.

He whispered, 'They have pictures of us. They have pictures of the van, too. They'll send cars to catch us. Helicopters will go across the sky pointing lights at the road. They'll hunt us down like rabbits.'

'Shut up about helicopters,' snapped Jian, but he obviously didn't like it, either. 'I'm going to look on the roof. There might be a way in from above.' He rolled a wheelie bin over and stood on it. The plastic lid bent under his weight. Grunting with the effort, he hauled himself up to the flat roof, the toes of his shoes scuffing brick. A crunching sound was him walking around up there.

Ding Ming stepped round the side of the building to get away from the implacable gaze of the cameras. A yellow phonebox was attached to the wall. It had a slot for coins. So... here was a phone, he had money, his captor had left him unsupervised. An unlikely opportunity had arisen and he remembered his own stricture to be cunning. He picked up the receiver. It was surprisingly cold and heavy. He was not a cunning person, deception did not come naturally, neither did nerve. But they had never really been required before. He heard banging and scraping. The policeman shouted down.

'There's a skylight, but there's a metal grille over it. I'm going to see if I can get it off. Stay there.'

Ding Ming observed that his hands were shaking as he fed one of his precious gold coins into the slot.

(44

Ding Ming could not believe what he was doing – it was as if it were happening to someone else, and he was watching. He dialled the country code for China, and the township number, then the number of his own mobile. He held his breath as the phone rang loud and clear.

Twisting the receiver's metal cable with his free hand, he imagined his request shooting into the night sky and being picked up by a satellite and hurled back down and hitting the bottom-of-the-range silver flip-top mobile with the scuffed case.

His call was answered.

'Hello?'

'Mother? It's me,' he whispered.

'Ding Ming? Is that you?' There was a slight delay but the voice was as clear as if she stood beside him. He cupped his hand over the receiver and hissed, 'Mother, has Little Ye made a call home? I need to know where she is.'

'My son? Where are you? You have to go back. Please.'

'What?'

Another voice came over the line, gruff, male, speaking Fujian dialect. 'Is that the foreign guest worker Ding Ming?'

'Who are you?'

'Never mind who I am. What do you think you're playing at? Listen to me. We've been here for hours and we're bored and angry. Your mother's not having any fun, either. We've got her tied to a chair.'

'What?'

'I'm going to strap this phone to her head, and then I'm going to pull out the teeth she's got left and you can listen to her screaming. And then we're going to find the rest of your family and do something worse.'

Ding Ming reeled as if he'd been hit. His hand squeezed the cable. His throat seemed lined with thorns.

'Stop,' he croaked.

'This is what happens to runaways. We fuck their whole family. You owe us a lot of money and we're not going to let you run away from your debt. We own you, do you understand? Is that clear?'

Something scraped above and the policeman shouted. 'Hey. You.'

Ding Ming supposed he had been discovered. He dropped the receiver and it clattered against the wall, and the way the cord lashed as the receiver swung reminded him of an angry snake. It even glittered like snakeskin.

'Ding Ming,' shouted the policeman. 'Are you there?'

'Yes.'

He backed into the forecourt until that thing was out of sight. He was unsteady on his feet and could feel blood draining from his face. He couldn't think, his head was full of static. He looked dumbly up. The policeman was frowning at him. He supposed the man would punish him but he didn't care about that now. He only cared about what was happening to his mother.

'I need something to lever it. Go back to the van and fetch that spade.'

Ding Ming continued to stare. The man was a black silhouette against star-sprinkled blueness.

'What's up with you?'

'I... I saw a snake.'

'Get the spade. Hurry.'

Ding Ming turned and ran. He could see the scene: toughs arriving on a motorbike, his mother wringing her hands, and then the cord, the feeble struggle. He even knew the chair she was tied to, the cracked grey plastic one with the metal legs – it was the only one with a back. With every pounding step his mind added a detail, and each was a twist to his guts. Minute after minute, she had sat terrified, and the toughs had lounged around, bored, cracking sunflower seeds with their teeth and spitting the husks on the floor. They'd told her he had run from his boss, from his debt, and what a bad son he was.

When he reached the van, he fought back the desire just to keep hurtling on down the road and into blackness. He tugged the spade out of the back. The blade was grimy with earth and touching the handle brought an image of the lolling tongue of the dead man he had buried. What viciousness the world contained – he was surrounded by it. The sound as he slammed the door seemed doleful.

But he was not a bad son, and not a runaway. The policeman had stolen him away, so it was all that man's fault. Anger brought some mental clarity and he resolved to sort this nonsense out. His two remaining coins chinked in his pocket. He would call those men again.

The forecourt cameras made him self-conscious, and he pulled the hood tighter over his head, which narrowed his vision still further, to a tunnel. To look round he had to move his whole head. The policeman stood on the roof, smoking. As Ding Ming climbed onto the bin, a crack in the lid widened and he smelled a fetid odour. Hands snatched the spade away.

'If I can just get this grille off, I'm in. An alarm will probably ring, ignore it. You stand outside peeking through the shutters, and point out the map book. When you see I've got it – and only then – run to the van. Alright?'

'Yes.'

'Say it.'

Fearing that his turbulent emotions were written all over his face, he looked aside at the wall as he mumbled, 'I point out the book and wait till you've grabbed it.'

He jumped down and hurried round the corner and saw the phone receiver hanging. Right, more cunning was required. He noted with consternation that his hands were shaking even more this time. Softly he slid his second heavy, shining coin into the slot and winced as it clinked through the innards of the machine. He dreaded hearing the crunch crunch of footsteps on the roof – that man only had to take three or four steps and look down and the subterfuge would be discovered. But all he heard above was clanging and grunting.

He called home again, and settled the receiver deep into the fur-lined hood to muffle it. The plastic grew warm with his panting breath. The call was answered, but all he heard were vague shuffling sounds.

'Hello? Hello? Mother? Is that you Mother?'

Abruptly she was screaming at him. 'Oh, my son, my son. I can't feel my arms any more, they tied the rope so tight.'

His stomach lurched. He scrunched up his face. He guessed a hand was holding the phone up to her mouth. 'They say they're going to pull my teeth out and other things. He wants to talk to you. You have to do what he says.'

'Guest worker?' a male voice drawled.

'I didn't run away. I was kidnapped...'

'Shut up. Ring this number.' He began to dictate. Ding Ming put his finger into his mouth and wrote the digits in spit on the wall. He pictured a substantial figure, red-faced with booze, speaking without hardly moving his lips. 'One five three nine...' Such a casual tone – it was the voice of a man dealing with a minor nuisance at work.

His mouth was parched, he could work no more spit into it. 'No, wait – the last four again.'

The phone cut off and buzzed tetchily in his ear. He found and pressed a 'next call' button. He could only see his spit-drawn digits by laying his cheek against the wall and looking at them obliquely so that the liquid caught the light. With shaking fingers he dialled the new number. It was difficult to see the keypad through his tears and he fumbled the second 6, hitting 5 by mistake. He depressed the receiver's cradle so that he could start again, and the machine hiccuped and the display flipped down to zero. He put his last coin in.

Was it 2265 or 2256? His numbers were already fading. A phone began to ring. It rang a long time and Ding Ming looked at the lake. The water was black and still. Even to drown himself would not help, money would still be owed. Up above, the policeman cursed, and metal rasped.

'Hello?' A sleepy voice, speaking English. Ding Ming whispered, 'Hello? Hello?'

'Who is this?' He knew that tone, and the lazy way those syllables ran together to make 'hoossiz' – Mister Kevin.

'My name William.'

'Who?'

'I work in mud. Touch your... little brother with my hand. Got take away.'

'Oh, yeah, the little Chinky takeaway. I've got some nasty bruises off your friend. You'd better get back right away.'

'He no my friend. He take me. I no... I no can choose. I want go back. Please, understand. I no want my mother be hurt.'

'Are you still with that guy?'

'Yes.'

'And the van?'

'Excuse me please?'

'The car, he took my car, where's my car?'

'Car is here.'

'Tell me where you are, we'll come and get you. I'll make sure everything is smoothed over back in Chinkyville and we can pretend none of this happened. Okay?'

He felt a surge of gratitude. Mister Kevin was harsh but fair, a lonely figure in need of love, a reasonable man of his word, soon to inform him where his wife was.

Something clanged into the forecourt and Ding Ming caught his breath. He turned his head and saw the spade skitter across concrete and come to rest against a petrol pump. The policeman yelled, 'Fuck. I can't get in. We'll stay the night and come back in the morning and buy the fucking thing.'

Now his feet could be heard scrambling for a footing on the lid of the bin. He was climbing down. Ding Ming realised he was too late, the man would be round the corner in a few seconds. He winced at a sharp crack. The policeman swore again. He was very close, but there were no footsteps. Ding Ming put the receiver on top of the phone and scurried to peek around the wall. One of the policeman's legs had plunged through the broken lid, and with much grumbling and swearing the man was clumsily extricating himself. He ran back to the phone.

'At petrol station,' he blurted.

'I need more than that.'

Where were they? He had no idea. He rummaged his head furiously for the right English words, hopping from one leg to another in his haste.

'Got lake, close by town. Town got Chinese restaurant name Happy Duck.'

'Happy Duck? That'll be in the phone book. Alright... me and the lads will be down soon as. Sit tight. Stay out of the way when it kicks off.'

He heard a thud. The policeman had jumped down from the bin. Footsteps – now his tormentor was walking in the forecourt. They came unhurriedly closer. A few more steps and his captor would see him.

'No hurt my mother. Tell me where my wife is.'

'Huh?'

Ding Ming put the receiver back and hurried round the corner and walked right into the policeman. Feeling that just to catch the man's eye would be to give himself away, he lowered his head, and saw that one of the fancy leather shoes was filthy with crud. It had packaging stuck to it and what looked like smears of banana.

'What's up with you? Seen more snakes?'

'They're everywhere.'

45

Ding Ming and the policeman returned to the van. Ding Ming figured that when Mister Kevin and his lieutenants arrived, the important thing would be to get quickly out of the way. Perhaps, after it was over – the van returned, the policeman punished – Kevin in his gratitude would let him talk to his wife. He looked forward to returning to a world that might not be pleasant or comfortable but was at least safe and familiar.

He regretted his earlier hesitation at performing the action Kevin had asked of him. If he'd just done that then, perhaps this wouldn't be happening now. His predicament could be seen as an instructive tale about the consequences of disobedience. Well, he'd learned his lesson. Those people owned him, he had to do what they wanted. His spirit was sick at the thought of that greasy cock in his mouth, but he imagined such troublesome selfishness would diminish over time.

He said, 'Let's go to sleep.'

'My body is on Chinese time. It thinks it's the morning. It's telling me I should be getting up.'

'If you get some sleep you'll feel fresh tomorrow. I'm very sleepy. So tired. So sleepy.' He conjured the term and, imagining his eyes a projector and the head of the policeman a screen, beamed the characters across: *shui jiao, shui jiao.* He heard tapping and rustling. 'What are you doing?'

'I've run out of cigarettes. I'm trying to build new ones by collecting tobacco from the butts in the ashtray.'

'You could go to sleep and buy more cigarettes in the morning.'

'Back home, the old guys smoke tobacco in rolled-up newspaper. When I was growing up, that was normal, we didn't know any different. It's harsh but you get used to it. I'll smoke that page you were looking at... that picture of the lady with the huge tits. Might make for a smoother smoke, what do you think?'

He would return to Kevin, and he would be welcomed back, and after a rocky start that in years to come he would laugh about, his life here could begin. After some weeks he and his wife would be put on the same work detail and allowed to toil side by side. Their debt would steadily diminish and the money that they sent home would pay for all sorts of treats. 'Good old Ding Ming,' people would say. 'A man at last, earning for his family.' A burst of coughing and spluttering hacked the reverie apart.

'*Wo cao!*' said Jian. 'This is rough.' He coughed again. 'Fuck me, this is rough.' He looked gloomily at his cigarette, a tube of rolled newspaper, cocked upright to stop tobacco falling out of the end.

'Stop smoking it, then.'

But the man persisted. It took him more than ten minutes to consume the thing, and when he finally stubbed it out and stopped coughing, the van was full of smoke and smelled of rank tobacco and burning paper.

'My mouth is raw. I'm going out for a drink.'

Left alone, Ding Ming squatted on the seat with Kevin's parka wrapped round him, and waited for Kevin and his lieutenants. He hoped there were many of them, that they would come suddenly, and that whatever was to happen, happen quickly.

Minutes passed, and he grew anxious at the policeman's continued absence. What if he had taken it upon himself to go for a walk? The man was restless, it did not seem unlikely.

If he'd wandered away, then he'd see Mister Kevin and company arrive, and would hide from them, and Kevin would come up to this van and he would ask Ding Ming, 'Where's the other guy?' and Ding Ming would have to say that he didn't know, that the man had decided to wander off. 'In the middle of the night?' Kevin would say. And the suspicion would be there: 'You warned him, didn't you? You told him we were coming.' And Kevin would be angry with him, and perhaps he would say, 'I'm disappointed in you, William, so I won't tell you where your wife is.'

He decided to look for the policeman and encourage him to return. His excuse for going out would be, he wanted a drink too. He took the empty cola bottle, he could fill it up. He was relieved to discover the man standing barely twenty paces away, throwing stones into the lake.

Ding Ming splashed a scoop of water into his face and rubbed it about with his hand. He could feel the pebbles beneath the thin canvas of his shoes. Bending to dip the bottle, his feet grew damp. He had holes in both soles.

'Fill it right up,' said Jian. 'I don't know if I can afford to buy anything for us to drink, I might have to spend all the money on petrol.'

'So what will we do for food?'

'Maybe we'll see an orchard.'

'Or get invited to a feast.'

'I could do with a steamed bun.'

'Beef noodles.'

'Hotpot.'

'Fish soup.'

'Just a proper cup of tea,' Jian said.

Ding Ming realised this was a good place to be when Kevin and his men came, he'd be able to run away. He'd head left, along the pebble beach, then turn onto the road and run uphill where it curled around the lake and up a ridge. If he got on that road he could outrun anyone, and from that ridge he'd be able to see everything that transpired.

He looked at the policeman's big hands and remembered how they had struck him and probed his split lip, still sore, with his tongue. Yes, much better to be out here than confined with him in the van. All he had to do, then, was keep the man talking.

He brought up a topic that was much on his mind. 'Have you ever...' It was difficult to give it voice, but he forced himself on. 'Have you ever had a woman suck on your... little brother?'

'What a question.'

'What was it like?'

'There is no greater joy.'

'Was it your wife?'

'You won't get a wife to do that. You have to pay a whore.'

'Do foreign men do it? Is it something that they do to each other? I mean, is it normal?'

'Who can say what the habits of these people are? Why are you asking?'

'I saw it in a film.'

'No, you didn't. Your boss asked you, didn't he?'

Ding Ming lowered his gaze. The policeman was astute. What else had he noticed? 'Yes.'

'And that's why you were running away.'

'Yes.'

'I suggest you bite it off. He won't ask again.'

'Thank you for that advice.'

'I'd get another job if I were you.'

But Ding Ming, writhing with embarrassment, was desperate to change the subject. 'What's being a policeman like?'

'It's a job. At least I don't have to suck cocks. Well, not literally.'

'Lots of banquets?'

'Invitations most nights.'

Ding Ming knew the kind of banquets policemen held – dozens of courses, as much booze as you could drink, and all on state funds.

'But... Sometimes you have to let the villains go, just because someone with clout told you. These days it's all the wrong way round. I see scum driving big cars and being the big boss when they should be in jail.'

He threw a stone. Ding Ming threw one after it and was disappointed to see that his went barely half as far.

'Sometimes we get told when to hold executions by the hospital. They've some guy in, he'll pay a lot for new corneas, can we shoot one of our rapists? You start to lose... you get lost... everyone's making money, you want to be in on it. Everyone else has an Audi, you want one too. I found out about this colleague of mine, guy under me... he took a bribe off a murderer to get the charge dropped. The victim's family bribed him even more to reopen the case. He went back to the murderer, got even more money. You know what I did when found out?'

'What did you do?'

'I took a cut.'

Ding Ming threw another stone, a little further this time.

'How glorious to be an official.'

'When I was young I wanted to make a difference. I was stupid and wrong, but I cared. I wanted to build socialism – we all did. Then you find out it's just another racket, and you're a foot soldier for the biggest tong of all.'

To Ding Ming this was hardly news. Any peasant could tell you: the government were a bunch of gangsters. The emperor might be benign but his officials were venal and that's how it had been for five thousand years. You didn't expect to hear it, though, from the mouths of policemen.

He said, 'I wanted to learn English. I got up every morning and studied under the bedclothes and at night I studied
under streetlamps. I won a prefecture scholarship to teacher
training college and I was very happy. I had top marks in all
my classes and my English level was better than my teachers. But the township said the college has informed us that
you are not suitable, and they took my scholarship away.
They gave it to the cousin of an official in the public security bureau. I met that man, the cousin. He could not speak
one word of English. Not one word.'

Ding Ming threw a stone, and this one went twice as far as
the last.

'That's a pity,' said the policeman quietly.

Ding Ming did not want to dwell upon past injustices, to
do so, he knew well, was to paralyse himself with pointless emotion. He turned away from the lake, as it seemed
the sight of all that dark water was encouraging this morbid
bout of reminiscence.

'Because I didn't graduate, I can't be a teacher. I should
never have tried to get an education. It was a waste of time
and money when I should have been working.'

'How did you get over here?'

'Snakeheads smuggled me.'

Ding Ming shivered as he remembered. The journey had
taken three and a half months. In between trips by truck,
cart and boat, he and Little Ye had been hidden in safe houses and forbidden to leave. Subsisting on rice and bread,
sometimes they'd gone weeks without seeing sunlight. The
people who dealt with them obviously did not see them as
anything but a troublesome cargo that required a certain
minimum quantity of air and food.

He had fallen out of the habit of asking what city or country he was in. His only concern, day after day, had been

when would they be moved again? On a map, he would be able to trace very little of their route.

'And how much did you pay for this?'

'Twenty thousand dollars.'

'US dollars?'

'Yes.'

'Where did you get that kind of money?'

'I didn't. That is how much I owe to the snakeheads. I pay it off while I am working here.'

'How long do you think that will take?'

'A couple of years.'

'How much are you earning, with that man?'

'A dollar an hour, maybe. I'm not sure.'

'Do the snakeheads charge interest on the loan to you?'

'Yes.'

'I think it'll take ten years. Twenty.'

'At least it is a chance.'

'You couldn't get a job at home?'

'Easily. For fifty yuan a month. No chance to save. There are no good jobs for a peasant in China. Not without connections or qualifications.'

'What about your girl? You going to let her sit at home and play mah jong for ten years? Eyeing up the lads who stayed?'

'She's in this country, but another place.'

'She came too? She also owes twenty thousand dollars?'

'Yes.'

'You shouldn't have brought her. It's no life for a woman.'

'She insisted.'

In fact it was Little Ye, Ding Ming's sweetheart since the age of fourteen, who had convinced him to go. The couple had married a few days before the trip. They'd had a small do in a restaurant and there had not even been time to get the disposable camera's pictures developed before they were packed into the pitch-dark hold of a Taiwanese fishing vessel.

Ding Ming added, with some pride, 'She is a modern woman.'

'She is, is she? Maybe she will suck you off, then.'

Offended, Ding Ming turned away. Underneath this man's hard shell was only sourness. He saw a car approaching. Here they were, then. Finally it was going to happen.

46

The engine of the car grew louder, the headlights brighter. Ding Ming sidestepped along the beach. Why was it so slow? He wanted it all to be over with quickly, but the thing was taking an age just to arrive. He began to jog, and pebbles crunched.

Jian called, 'Where are you going?'

Ding Ming looked over his shoulder. It was a small car, shaped like a beetle with a chugging engine, and driven by an old woman. A second stared with a pale pinched face out of the passenger window. It seemed to Ding Ming that her lips pursed and her eyes narrowed, and for a moment he saw what she saw – two Chinese men with wild hair and dirty faces, one holding a stone. The car sped up and in a few moments it had chuntered past.

There was a bench here, and, oddly, a litter bin. He gestured towards them and started talking, just to prevent having to make up an excuse for his odd behaviour.

'This must be a beauty spot. Perhaps poets come here to write about the moon reflected in the water and the hills like...' a pause stretched as he tried to think of a clever metaphor... 'fish heads in soup.'

'Where I come from, it looks like this. I could almost believe I was home.'

'I've heard the northeast is beautiful.'

'Some places. We have landscapes that can make your heart sing.'

Jian tried to skim a stone, but it dropped in without bouncing. 'My daughter had an idea to open a travel company.

That was going to be its name. Singing Heart Travels. History tours, photography tours, wildlife tours...'

'Wildlife – to eat it?'

'To look at it.'

Jian tried skimming and again had no success. Ding Ming skimmed a stone and it bounced twice.

'You have to pick flatter stones. And it's a flick of the wrist, it's not about power. So you have a daughter.'

'She spoke English like a native. Even better than you, I think.'

'Where is she now?'

'I see. It's a toss, not a throw. She's dead.'

Jian's stone again vanished with a plop. He watched the ripples spread out and diminish and rubbed a hand over his face and bent over with his hands on his knees.

Ding Ming said, 'I'm sorry.'

After some time, Jian stood and said, 'She's dead and now I'm going to go and kill the men who killed her.'

Ding Ming would like to have asked more questions but delicacy held his tongue. To have a child die was a terrible thing. He stood with his hands clasped in an attitude of sympathetic mourning, as if the blackness before them were not a lake but a grave. He let his respectful silence stretch and grew aware of the midges buzzing round his head.

The policeman took his jacket off and said, 'The arm needs to be more free. I'll get it now – you watch.'

When he laid the jacket on the bench it made a clunk. Ding Ming was alarmed to see a gun butt poking out. The policeman would shoot Kevin and his lieutenants dead, then, cursing traitors, turn the weapon on the man who had betrayed him. Nauseous with worry, he tapped his damaged lip with nervous fingers. The policeman had presented his back to him as he sifted through pebbles. Ding

Ming contemplated the thick neck. He guessed that the man, in the grip of strong emotion, was composing his features.

'This is a good one. Flat and round. Watch this.'

The man drew his hand right back. Ding Ming pulled out the gun, pincering the butt between thumb and first finger. It was so unexpectedly heavy he almost dropped it. He put it in the pocket of the parka.

The stone arced across the water, dipped, and bounced.

'Got it.' said Jian.

Ding Ming's fretting did not abate, for now, at any moment, his theft might be discovered. But there was, too, a giddy sense of achievement. He could hardly believe what he had done, he had never been so reckless.

'Do it again,' he said, struggling to control a flutter in his voice. 'That might have been a fluke.'

'What's your record?'

'Five.'

'I'll get six – you watch.'

'You'll be here for years.'

Ding Ming stepped to the shore and the gun banged against his thigh. He put his hand in his pocket and held it still, fingers around the cold barrel. He watched the policeman skim stones and realised that he had to keep the man busy at his childish activity – as soon as he put his jacket back on, the theft would be discovered.

'Two. You see that? I got two.'

'Not bad.'

'Not bad? Watch this.'

But his next stone did not skim.

'It was the wrong shape. You do it again. I want to watch.'

There was something dark about the policeman's enthusiasm, it had a touch of mania to it. Ding Ming groped among the cold pebbles with shaking hands. He shut his eyes hard in the hope that when he opened them his captor would have vanished from his life. Why had this man, with his grief and rage, come into it? Were his own troubles not large enough? He opened them and saw a hand holding a stone.

'Here.'

It was the ideal shape, smooth and flat. He arranged trembling fingers around it and tossed it. It turned in the air and splashed straight in, a couple of metres out.

'What's wrong with you?'

'I just didn't do it right that time.'

'You look terrified. What is it?'

'I was wondering if there are fierce animals here. Bears or wolves.'

'I think they are the least of our worries.'

Now, at the same level as the insect noise, a distant engine hummed. Ding Ming looked about. Yes, a vehicle was approaching, its headlights burned through the darkness.

Jian said, 'I'll take you back tomorrow morning.'

'What?'

'After we get the map book, mark upon it where I have to go. I'll find it myself. It's not fair to take you with me. I'll take you back to that place tomorrow. You've only missed a day's work. I don't think they'll be too angry with you.'

The noise of the vehicle grew louder, and Ding Ming could see it now, a boxy green truck. He recognised it, he was sure, yesterday it had been parked by the mud. He told himself that the policeman deserved whatever was about to happen.

He squeezed his eyes shut as hard as he could, opened them and stepped away as he said, 'Men are here. Run away now.'

'What do you mean?'

'I called my boss. That's him – run away. Men have come for you. I'm sorry. Run.'

(47

Headlights swept across the beach and spotlit the two men in a yellow glare, and their long shadows fell shimmering over the water. The tyres crunched pebbles and the engine cut out.

Ding Ming stepped away and implored, out of the corner of his mouth, 'Run!' If Jian left now, there was still time. He'd be swallowed by the darkness and perhaps they would never find him.

But instead the man grabbed his jacket, swung it, and plunged his hand into the pocket. Consternation crossed his face when he found it empty. He must have realised what had happened, but he did not even look at Ding Ming. He picked up the litter bin, turned it over and shook it out. Cans clattered, packaging drifted. He grabbed a bottle and smashed it against the side of the picnic table. Jagged glass glinted.

The doors of the truck opened and two figures got out – things like men but with huge heads, giving them the proportions of monstrous children – and one had a brutal spike in place of a hand. This one pointed at Ding Ming and a deep voice said, 'You, go and wait in the van.' The second aimed a shotgun at the policeman and said, 'You're going to fucking get some, you fucking fuck. Down on the ground.'

Jian hurled the jacket and lunged after it. He knocked the gun barrel aside and rammed broken glass into a neck. The gun roared and shot made momentary fountains of the lake.

The thing dropped slowly to his knees and clawed at pebbles and said, 'Fuck, I'm stabbed,' and blood splashed over his fingers. Ding Ming saw that they were, of course, only men, given a fierce aspect by the motorcycle helmets they wore and the tools they carried.

The second figure swung a spanner and the policeman stepped away. But now another man was coming down from the truck carrying a bat. Jian retreated into the shallows and the men closed on him with their weapons raised.

Ding Ming pulled himself away and sprinted to the van. He fumbled the passenger door open and sat in the dark, gnawing at his knuckles, his head bobbing.

He could not see the fight now, the truck was in the way – all he could see of it was ripples spreading on the water. He remembered the awful weapons those men carried. They meant to kill, there was no mercy in them, they would batter and gouge and smash, and the body of the Chinese policeman would be ruined. And it would be his, Ding Ming's fault, as much as if he had wielded the instruments himself.

Ding Ming realised that another man was sitting in the truck, in the driver's seat, hunched over the steering wheel and watching the fight. The man turned and looked at the van, and Ding Ming recognised him, and just for a moment Ding Ming and Mister Kevin locked gazes. Kevin winked.

Ding Ming shrank from that podgy face and scrambled over the seat and into the back of the van, where the darkness was complete and welcome. He curled up on the floor with his arms around his knees. His stomach was tight with cramps. He wanted to be sick, and he wished he could be sick because then the feeling might stop.

He heard running feet. It was over, then, the white men were coming to take him away. The front door of the van opened and Ding Ming wondered what he could possibly say. But it was the policeman, dripping wet and panting.

Cursing under his breath, he started the engine. The van lurched off the verge and into the road.

Ding Ming, terrified, bit on his hand to stop a gasp escaping. The man would want revenge. He cracked open the back door and jumped out, hands raised to protect his face. He glimpsed the grain of the road between fingers before impacts jarred his arms, then his side, then he was sliding on tarmac, then rolling on grass. He came to rest on his back, looking up at throbbing stars.

He heard gruff voices, speaking English.

'Quick,' said Kevin, 'Get him in.'

'He's bleeding loads.'

'Just get him in. Come on.'

Ding Ming found a host of new pains laid over his old ones. His arms were burning where they had scraped the road. His head felt like it was splitting open. He touched it and screwed up his face at the pain, then looked at his finger. Thankfully, there was no blood. Something lumpy was jabbing into his side. He rolled over and realised it was the gun in his pocket.

He got to his hands and knees. He was sore but he was functioning. He winced and told himself, 'I've got to stop jumping out of moving vehicles.' The thought made him giggle. Of all the times to start laughing, part of him observed. He thought that he was very silly, and that made him giggle again. Pain slammed down and he had to lie grimacing on the cool grass. The stars stopped moving and behaved themselves.

He rolled and looked at the road. The truck shot past him. Someone had written 'cleen me' with a finger in the dust on its rear. Beyond it, the van sped away, engine roaring. The back door swung, then, as the van turned onto the ridge, slammed shut.

The green truck accelerated after it, its engine noise a high whine. The van sped up and the truck sped up, too, and the engine noise dropped to a rumble. The truck got faster and bumped into the back of the van and the crunch of metal carried across the water.

Ding Ming stood. Now he couldn't see much more than the slashes of distant headlight beams. The truck, big and dark and loud, bore down again, and rammed the back of the van, and metal crumpled and the lights burst with a pop.

The van veered off the road and dropped bonnet first into the lake. A splash, and in a fraction of a heartbeat it had vanished. A ripple fringed with foam swelled, smaller undulations followed, and the moon's reflection wavered.

Ding Ming watched in distress. He had the impression that the ripples were not going to stop, they were going to come all the way across the lake and up the shore and overwhelm him. A voice in his head said, that policeman is drowning and it is all your fault.

The wave subsided and Ding Ming realised the truck was receding. He stood and shouted and waved his arms. 'Mister Kevin! Wait! I'm here!'

It seemed impossible that they could not hear him. But the truck did not stop: its headlights receded, and the drone of the engine faded away.

'I'm here!'

He shouted himself hoarse, but the truck was gone. The only sound was the slosh of water and the tick of insects. The only light came from the empty petrol station and the moon and the stars. He crossed the road, sat at the picnic table and drank a long glug of water from his bottle. It chilled his stomach. He had never been so alone. He drew the coat around him and shivered.

交通差 JOY

(48

When Mark came into the Happy Duck chippy, Joy caught her breath and turned so that he wouldn't see her flush. She hadn't seen him for three days, not since they'd swapped spit on the bench by the lake.

He'd said he really liked her and that he'd certainly be dumping that Jessica, and he'd stroked her face and looked into her eyes. The moon had been almost full, the stars had been glittering and she hadn't felt the cold at all.

She'd wondered how it would feel when she saw him again, and now here it was. It was a jittery, pre-exam feeling.

He strolled to the counter. In real life he was more commonplace than the Mark she'd built in her head. He was only okay-looking with his small features and gingery hair. But he was solid and the fact of his presence thrilled her. It was his confidence that made him appealing, really. You could see it when he moved.

She caught his eye and grinned and turned aside. She looked a right state, in her work apron, no make-up on, tired. It was unfair of him to walk in on her like this – she almost resented him for it.

'Alright?' he said.

'Alright.' The last time she'd seen him his lips had been glistening, his mouth hanging half open, tongue heavy and wet. She was glad now that she hadn't let him touch her tits, though it had been a close thing at the time.

Any sort of flirtation was out of the question in front of her father. She looked sidelong at him, then back at Mark to signal the danger. To her dad she was still a girl who played with plastic ponies.

Mark put both hands on the counter and repeated, 'You alright?' He was looking her in the eyes, and she ordered herself not to wilt beneath that clear-eyed cheeky gaze.

'I am,' she said. 'Yourself?'

'Alright.' He looked around the shop.

'What you want?' asked Joy's father.

Mark looked disconcerted for a moment, thinking perhaps that the old man had sensed something he disapproved of. In fact, he always sounded abrupt when he spoke in English.

'A small portion of chips please, sir,' said Mark.

She liked it that he called him 'sir'. The opinion of her friends was that his manners were rough, but around her he was courteous.

Joy's father scooped chips. Joy put her hands in her apron pocket and wrung them. She wondered what she could do – pass Mark a note with the ketchup?

'That'll be eighty pence, please,' she said in a voice that was sterner than usual. She didn't call him 'duck', which was how she usually addressed customers.

'Have you got change?' He was holding up a five pound note. There was something suggestive, almost rude, about the way he wiggled it back and forth. She plucked it and held it to the light to see if it was fake.

Having checked that her father was busy wrapping, she pressed coins one at a time into his cupped palm, each a stolen kiss. His hand closed and he winked at her. He took his chips and she said, in a softer voice, 'Salt is here.'

'Have you got any… mayonnaise?'

He checked that her father wasn't looking and blew a kiss. She snatched it and swallowed it – was that what you were supposed to do?

'We do not have mayonnaise. But we do have… garlic sauce.'

'Thank you. I'm a big fan of… garlic sauce.'

'Good.'

'Well, I'll be seeing you. Thank you,' he said.

'No problem at all.'

The bell above the door tinkled as he exited, a fluttering tinkle like her heart. So that was it, then. It was official. They were going out.

It was quiet – probably that on-off drizzle was keeping people at home. She had a textbook open, with a sheet of transparent paper over it to protect it from spatters, but however hard she looked at it, nothing was going in. Her euphoria began to be tinged with anxiety. Should she have been more forward? What if, in fact, he was still going out with that Jessica? He'd not said clearly that he wasn't. Perhaps, after all, she was reading too much into things and he had only come in because he was hungry? Why had he specified a small bag of chips?

She chided herself and wondered if it was going to be like this all the time from now on – queasiness, difficulty concentrating, fluffy dreaminess alternating with spiky paranoia. She told herself she would not be letting her college work suffer. But here was another voice, a whole unexplored aspect of herself, saying 'Bugger work – open your mouth in the rain, watch flowers turn to the sun, laugh, sweat, snog.'

Around ten o'clock the Community Support Officer came in, a chunky girl called Sandy. Joy knew she wasn't proper police, she couldn't even make an arrest. Her job was telling underage drinkers to go home and being a highly visible use of taxpayers' money. She wore lifts in her shoes.

She was escorting two real policemen, a man and a woman with radios attached to bulletproof vests and utility belts as big as Batman's. They had flat hats, which perhaps meant they were a higher rank than your usual tithead.

Sandy the CSO nodded good evening, and called them Mister and Miss Cho, showing off to the regulars how well she knew her beat. She asked how business was.

'So-so,' said Joy's father. He was stiff and suspicious around anyone in a uniform, even parking attendants, so she wondered how he would handle this.

The policeman took off his hat. 'We've had reports of suspicious behaviour by two Asian-looking gentlemen up at the lake.'

'I went to check it out,' said Sandy the CSO, 'and I found a broken bottle with blood on it. Someone's been stabbed.'

She looked puffed up with self-importance, or maybe she'd put bigger lifts in. Real trouble would look great on her CV – she probably dreamed about it at night. She looked at the proper policeman keenly, like a faithful dog. She either fancied him or, more likely, his uniform. He was quite good-looking, this policeman, but he had a moustache.

The real policewoman glared at Sandy, obviously for saying too much.

'A broken bottle?' said Joy. 'That sounds terrible.'

'Yes,' said the policeman. 'Our witnesses said that that the suspicious characters were... Chinese in appearance.'

So of course you came here, thought Joy, though she didn't say anything.

'We were wondering if you had seen any... people of Chinese appearance tonight.'

Again the pause. The policeman seemed aware that 'people of Chinese appearance' was a clunky term. Perhaps he was wondering if it might even cause offence.

Joy recalled the mainlanders who had come in earlier, a big old one and a skinny young one. They had looked furtive, but they hadn't looked like criminals. She composed her features into what she hoped would be read as blank indifference.

'You mean, apart from each other?' she said.

Joy's father said, 'No.'

Joy said, 'No.'

'If you don't mind me asking, how many people are in your family?'

'Dozens,' said Joy.

'Living here.'

'Only us.'

'How many members of your family live in the area?'

'None, nobody,' said her father. 'We no got anybody since my wife pass away. Not another Chinese family near.'

'Have you seen anything out of the ordinary today?'

'No.' Joy was nodding, pouting a little, trying to look as if she would love dearly to be able to help. 'What happened exactly?'

'We're not sure.'

'So we're talking to everyone,' said the policeman.

'Should we be worried?' said Joy.

'Be alert and aware,' said the policewoman, 'but don't get anxious.' She had a surprisingly high-pitched voice. 'Please give us a call if you see anything odd – anything at all out of the ordinary, however small.' She opened the door.

'And don't go down to the lake,' said Sandy.

'We certainly won't,' said Joy. She thought that was it, but the policeman looked determined to prolong the encounter.

'Those chips look tasty,' he said. Joy offered him some and he refused. The women left, but he took his time. He suspected something, she could tell, and she had to suppress gestures of nervousness and impatience as he looked round, stepped towards the door, looked round again, put on and adjusted his hat.

When he reached the door she expected him to do a Columbo, come back with a finger raised saying, 'Just one more thing...', but he didn't. The bell tinkled, they were gone, and she puffed out her cheeks.

Joy's father said, in Cantonese, 'I think it's slow tonight because of the weather.'

'Yes.' Joy waited but there was nothing more. She wasn't going to bring it up if he didn't. The matter, then, was closed. They were co-conspirators now. She reflected that if she had been with any of her friends, and they had lied to the police, they would afterwards acknowledge and discuss the transgression. But to her father, who after all had come from a very different world, it was just a simple fact, not even worthy of note, that you did not talk to cops.

（**49**

Joy went back to the textbook but the words were just not adhering. She'd served a few figures, and turned a clutch of pages, when Jessica came in. She was wearing her bulky black bomber jacket with the fur-lined collar and she was backed by that lanky girl with the gappy teeth.

Joy considered stepping away and letting her father deal with them, but only for a moment. This had to be done, she supposed, and anyway there was a counter between them. She squared up. She wondered how Mark had done it, and hoped he hadn't been brutal. Of course, there was no easy way.

Jessica was a small, pretty girl, but now she had a mean set to her jaw and red blotches high up on her cheeks.

She said, 'I want a pickled egg.'

Joy got an egg out of the big jar and waited for the punch-line.

'No, I don't want a pickled egg. A pickled egg is white on the outside but yellow on the inside. That's the wrong way round.'

The other girl, the tall one, giggled. Joy dropped the egg back in the vinegar.

'I want a piece of fish.'

'You're sure, are you?'

'Yes, I'll have that piece there.'

Joy took the battered cod out of the cabinet and wrapped it in unnerving silence. She was aware of the girls watching her and was careful to do it properly. They were just trying to psych her out.

Joy said, 'That'll be two pounds forty.'

Jessica unwrapped her parcel and considered the battered fish. She broke it open.

'Thing about this is, it's yellow on the outside but white on the inside, isn't it?'

'Like a banana,' said the tall girl.

'Two pounds forty,' repeated Joy.

'Just like a banana. Yellow on the outside, and white on the inside. So you could say it lies about what it is.'

'Does it cheat, as well?' said the tall girl.

'I should think that for something like that, that lies about what it is, cheating is something that comes natural.' Jessica lowered her voice. 'A liar and a cheat.'

'A liar and a cheat,' repeated her friend.

'Fuck off,' said Joy, 'you little twat. You little wee tart. And you, you stupid cow, you can fuck off and all.'

'Bitch,' said Jessica, and dropped the fish on the floor. 'I don't want that. It's off, anyway. It smells gross. Though maybe that isn't the fish – maybe that's the little chinky. You'll have to come round here now, won't you, chinky bitch in your little apron, and clean it up.'

'I'll have you for that, Jessica, you cow.'

She wanted to throw something at them, and picked up the ketchup bottle, but the realisation that that was what they wanted stayed her hand, and the girls left the shop stiffly, chins in the air, and Joy was left clutching the bottle so hard that sauce oozed from the nozzle and dribbled over her fingers.

Her father got out the mop, but she told him not to bother, she'd do it. She told him it was just a stupid tiff and nothing to worry about. Kneeling to clean up the mess, she was glad he couldn't see her, as the hand gathering fragments of fish onto a sheet of paper was shaking with fury.

'If they come in and do that again,' said her father, in rapid and loud Cantonese, 'I will strike them. I cannot allow people to come into my shop, insult my daughter and take my fish without paying. I will strike them.'

'You can't hit them,' said Joy, adding a reasonableness to her tone that she did not feel. 'They won't come in again. But if they do, just tell Sandy the CSO and then, if it's really necessary, we can get an ASBO against the little bitches.'

Joy was speaking Cantonese, as she usually did with him, but she said 'Sandy the CSO', 'ASBO' and 'little bitches' in English. It was common for her to swap between the two languages like that – she did it without thinking.

'I'll hit them.'

'Father—'

Someone tapped on the window. It was such a tentative sound she hardly heard it. She turned, expecting to see the girls again, but it was a strange slim figure swallowed up in a hooded parka, rapping with a knuckle. She only recognised him when he pressed his face up to the window and squinted in. That Chinese guy, the skinny one. She pointed at the door and he slipped in.

(50

Just to look at him you could tell he was a long way from home. His desperation and foreignness made Joy uneasy. She remembered that someone had been stabbed with a broken bottle. With no counter for protection, she felt exposed.

She said, 'Duck, take your hood down so we can hear you.'

He looked a sorry state, dishevelled and dirty with a nasty cut on his lip and bruises on his cheek. His wide eyes moved rapidly back and forth.

He said in English, 'Please, can I use telephone?'

Joy looked at her father. In the past he had refused exactly that request – but that had been from drunk white people. He beckoned for the man to duck under the counter, and led him into the back room. The guy said 'thank you' about eight times.

Joy dumped the broken fish in the bin, which happened to be close to the door. She pushed it open a crack and peered in. The mainlander was sitting on the chair and her father was standing next to him holding a saucepan, so no funny business. The phone was on the counter by the freezer. The guy tapped a couple of numbers in, screwed up his face, tapped a few more, gazed at the ceiling with his mouth opening and closing, tapped a few more, then concentrated so hard that a whine escaped between gritted teeth. Joy's father said, 'You sure you know what number?'

'No sure,' said the guy, 'no sure,' and jabbed a last digit. He held the phone hard against his ear. His legs were crossed and his foot flexed rapidly up and down. Joy could faintly hear a dial tone beep-beeping and held her breath waiting for a reply. The man's nervousness was infectious – this was an important call.

The dial tone stopped and the man straightened and said, 'Mister Kevin? Mister Kevin?' Joy could not make out what was said at the other end, but it did not seem to be what he wanted to hear, as he repeated, 'Mister Kevin? Are you Mister Kevin? Do you know Kevin? Ke-vin, yes Kevin, sorry I Chinese, English no good, Kevin, Kevin, yes, Kevin. No? No? No? Oh.' And the poor man's face fell, and his head drooped as he said, 'Sorry, I got number wrong.'

He put the phone down and left his hand on it and asked, 'Can I call China?'

'China?' said Joy's father, in an exasperated tone.

'Have to call home. Sorry.' Asking the favour really did seem to be causing the man considerable distress – he was squirming, and his foot went even faster.

'China's very expensive.'

Da-ad, thought Joy, come on.

'Very expensive.'

'Sorry. I go another place.'

'Go on. Be quick.'

A phone number was dialled, with confidence this time, and a connection made. The beep-beeps went on, and Joy was interested, waiting for the pick-up. But the beeps just carried on and she grew frustrated, first with the people at the other end, then with this mainlander, who wouldn't accept that there was nobody home. Finally she was bored. The man would not give up. Perhaps he would have sat there for hours, waiting with the phone pressed to his ear, but finally her father said, 'There's no one home.'

The man put the phone down gently with two hands and said, 'Thank you very much.'

Joy retreated a few paces and pretended to be interested in her textbook as they returned. The mainlander was reserved and stiff. He'd been desperate because he had hope. Now, plainly, there was no hope, but at least that meant he could act with dignity. He said that he was very sorry to have troubled them both.

Joy asked him what he was going to do now.

'I will go outside,' he said.

'After that.'

'I will do some thing,' he said. She could see his only idea was to get out of the shop. The fact that he had asked a favour had lost him face, and he just wanted to get away from the scene of that humiliation.

'Do you want some food?' she said.

'I no hungry, I have eat full. You potato very delicious.' He slipped out the door so discreetly that he hardly disturbed the bell at all.

'What do you think his problem was?'

'He asked to use the phone and I let him. I do not want to think about it more than that.'

'What if he's in trouble?'

'Of course he is in trouble. I will not have him bringing his trouble into my shop any further. I want no more to do with him.'

'He's Chinese.'

Joy had only said that to probe how far her father's racial solidarity would go.

'He is a mainlander. Mainlanders are not like us.'

That was not unexpected. He'd been brought up in Hong Kong and Hong Kongers pretty much thought of themselves as a race apart. But she did not feel that way. Having been brought up in Britain, she was simply British Chinese, or Chinese British, and set little store by her father's regionalism.

In all her time serving chips no other Chinese person had come into the shop who wasn't a relative. She was irresistibly curious.

'I'm going to take him a can of Coke,' she said.

'What?'

'He looked thirsty.'

'If he was thirsty, he'd ask for a can for free. He asked to use the phone for free, and then he called China. He wasn't proud.'

Joy already had the can out of the cold cabinet and was heading for the door.

(51

She ran into the street and looked up and down, and at first she thought she was too late, he'd gone, but as she turned to go back she spotted him squatting on his heels in the doorway of the newsagents. He looked befuddled. Presumably he was considering what to do and coming up with no answers. She thrust the can at him.

'I thought you looked thirsty,' she said.

'No no no,' he said.

'Take it.'

'No.'

'Take it.'

Bloody Chinese, thought Joy. Her relatives were the same. You couldn't give them anything without them refusing it twice first. The mainlander stood and drank.

'Better than Pepsi,' he said. 'Every person like Pepsi, but I like Coke.'

'I'm a Fanta girl myself.'

'What is Fanta?'

'Orange-flavoured. Well, orangeish. What's your name?'

'Ding Ming.'

'I'm Joy.'

'Very lovely name.'

'Thank you. What are you doing here?'

'I need to give call Kevin, he my boss. I have to go back.'

'Back to where?'

'Work place.'

'And where's that?'

'I don't know. By side sea.'

'Side sea? You mean seaside? We're miles from the sea. Have you got any money? Anywhere to stay?'

'No.'

'What are you going to do?'

'I do not know.'

Then, as if the weight of his troubles were a physical burden carried on his back, he sank until he was squatting on his heels again. She didn't have the flexibility to squat, so she sat down cross-legged on the cold stone.

'Where's the other guy, the guy you were with?'

'He got... he go away.'

A couple of lads were approaching, and Joy grew self-conscious. She knew the guys, though she couldn't remember their names. There was a fat one and a really fat one.

'Alright, Joy?' Said the fat one.

'Alright.'

'We've been down the Ferryman's. Saw that Jessica. She's well pissed off with you. She was mouthing off. You want to watch out.'

'I saw her.'

The fatter one ducked behind a car and a tinkle began as he pissed against the wheel. 'Sorry,' he mumbled. 'Caught short.'

'Any trouble,' said the fat one, 'and you call on us, right. We're on your side.'

'Yeah.'

'Who's your friend?'

'This is Ding Ming.'

'Relative, is he?'

'No.'

'Nice to meet you,' said the fat one, and thrust out a hand.

'He wants to shake your hand,' Joy whispered, and Ding Ming stood and did so, grinning nervously.

'Where are you from, then?'

'China.'

'Oh aye?'

The fat one turned and considered the street, perhaps trying to look at it through alien eyes. 'This must be a bit different for you then, eh?'

'Yes.'

'You, er, you eat a lot of rice, do you?'

'I like rice very much.'

'Do you know any of that kung fu?' He struck a fighting pose and waved his hands about in a vaguely martial way. Ding Ming looked alarmed, and stepped back, and the fat lad dropped his pose and slapped Ding Ming on the arm with drunken camaraderie.

'It's alright, Grasshopper. Just messing about.'

The fatter one shouted across the car, 'He has a few and thinks he's Chow Yun-Fat.'

Ding Ming said, 'Chow Yun-Fat?'

'You know him?' said the fat one.

'He is number one star.'

'Yes, he bloody is,' said the fat one, with passion. 'I'm always telling people: you can take your Arnie, you can take your Stallone, Chow Yun-Fat would have them both. Easily. He is the man.' He punched his own hand and repeated, with alarming vehemence, 'He is the man,' as if someone had cast doubt upon the assertion, or even suggested that he wasn't the man.

'He is number one star, you are so right, my friend. With the two-gun action.' He made gunhands – two fingers curled back and cocked thumbs – and started shooting at Ding Ming: 'Bang bang bang bang!'

The fatter one came round from behind the car, and he was doing it too, going 'Boom boom boom boom!' and the two men circled, shooting each other, and Joy, and Ding Ming, and the street.

Ding Ming made guns out of his hands and shot back – 'Pam pam pam!'

Joy reckoned it a guy thing. She'd seen The Killer and Bullet in the Head – supposedly Chow Yun-Fat's greatest work – and found the stylised, slow-motion violence at first alarming, then numbing. She'd called it ballet for men.

The fat lads mimed getting shot in the chest, throwing their arms in the air and their heads back, then flapping their hands to simulate blood spurting from ruptured bodies, and letting their tongues hang out and wobble. They laughed and slapped Ding Ming on the back and repeated what a man the incomparable Chow Yun-Fat was.

The fatter one muttered to his friend, 'Let's leave the lovebirds to it, heh?'

'Lovebirds?' said the fat one, and looked at Ding Ming in a new light. It was explained to him in a whisper that carried clearly to Joy's ears – 'Arranged marriage, isn't it.'

Joy was too shocked to say anything for a moment, then realised that outraged protest might offend Ding Ming, and by the time she had formulated a sensible response the lads had taken their leave.

Joy said, 'Never mind them – they're just pissed.' Ding Ming's burst of gaiety had faded, but it seemed to have improved his mood a little.

'Internet,' he said.

'What?'

'I can send email my cousin, he go see my mother, get Kevin telephone number. MSN Messenger.'

'What?'

Joy understood what he had said, it just seemed such an unexpected thing for the man to know about.

'MSN Messenger. Have this place got computer bar?'

'No. Ding Ming, I want to ask you a question. Please tell me the truth. Have you attacked anyone tonight? Have you stabbed someone?'

'Stab?'

'Like this.'

'No. No.'

She looked him in the eyes as he said it, and believed he was telling the truth.

'I've got internet. On my laptop.' She looked back at the chippy, the street's only lighted shopfront.

'My father wouldn't like me taking you up. Tell you what: we'll close up soon and then he goes to bed. Wait here for an hour or so, then I'll come and get you. OK? You understand?' She remembered the policeman. 'And don't let anyone see you.'

She led him to a dark alleyway and made doubly sure he understood her plan. He put his can at his side, saying he preferred his cola flat, and squatted between bins with his arms folded across his knees and his head dropped, resigned to the wait.

She returned to the shop and told her father the guy had taken off. This was the second time she'd lied for the mainlander – he'd better be on the level.

It didn't look like there would be any more trade, so they closed up and in silence wiped surfaces and cleaned machines. She was free to think about Mark – she'd earned this right, surely? – but as she tried to whip up a soft-focus reverie of gentle hands, wet lips, adoring eyes and so on, she kept being disturbed by the thought of the man squatting between the smelly bins, in the cold, in his oversized coat.

They went to the flat above the shop and her father cooked fried rice.

Joy said, 'Father, I'd like to go to the ancestral village. I think it would be interesting.'

Joy had been to Hong Kong a few times, but never to the village in Guangdong Province that the Chos traced themselves back to.

'One day,' he said, 'but we will be expected to take a lot of presents. No one is more popular than a rich man going home.'

'We're not rich.'

'You'll be surprised the number of relatives a rich man can have. I'll take you when you have finished your education. But it would be better for you to spend time in Hong Kong. You can meet a good man there. You won't meet one on the mainland.'

'I could meet a good man here.'

He chewed slowly, and changed TV channels with the remote. As always after work, he was sat with dinner on a tray in his lap and an apple pie, a mug of green tea and a packet of Royals waiting on the armrest. He found football and grunted with satisfaction.

Finally he said, 'You can meet a good man in Hong Kong.'

Joy was not going to push it. She went to bed and lay fully clothed and wide awake in the dark with her door ajar, waiting for her father to finish up. It took him ages. The LED on her alarm said 12:43 when finally he shuffled to his room and the door clicked shut. She gave it another forty minutes, then slipped out.

She'd snuck out on other occasions, to go to parties or meet lads, and knew where all the creaky floorboards were. Still it was a risk. The tricky bit was getting down the stairs. She carried her trainers and put them on when she got outside.

She'd been more than two hours, but not only was the mainlander still in the alley, he was still in the same position. He looked up sleepily at her approach. That was a clever trick, to be able not only to squat on your heels for hours, but actually to doze in the position.

'Right,' she said. 'We go into a hallway, then up a flight of stairs and we get to a corridor. My room is at the end of that corridor, but we have to pass my father's room. Any noise will wake him up and then I will be in such deep shit. Take your shoes off.'

Ding Ming seemed to take this all very seriously, and she was relieved to see that he was light on his feet. He didn't even need to be told to step at the edges of the stairs not the middle, and when they were in the hallway he followed in her footsteps as she crept along the wall.

She heard the rhythmic breathing of her sleeping father and for a moment it did not reassure her but made her worry, for he was not conscious to offer his protection. It occurred to her that this particular adventure was really daft. Inviting a possible murderer into your room in the middle of the night did not now seem like the action of a smart person who considered things carefully. Anyway, she got him in without incident and closed the door.

The room was barely big enough for two people. A smart person would also have already got the computer started and the broadband connected, but she had to do it while he stood looking round. She was embarrassed by her muscle-guy screensaver, her girly trinkets and all the clothes heaped on the floor, especially the pants.

But he was not looking at her pants, he was looking at her shelves.

'So many books,' he whispered with reverence. 'Very good.'

He unzipped his parka, revealing a bare, bruised chest. Why there was not an ounce of fat on him and you could see all the ribs, like on a greyhound. She tutted at the state of him and gave him an old T-shirt. She motioned for him to sit at the desk and he typed 'www.sohu.com' into the address bar and some Chinese homepage opened. He closed pop-ups.

To her, China was important, but an abstraction. It was part of her experience but not her life, a background image like a distant unclimbed mountain. Now, here was an envoy come down from the mountain, earthy and real. His skin was darker than hers. There was something different about his body language — it was less demonstrative, almost demure. He even smelled different, completely unlike anyone she knew. How could that be? Was it simply diet? Or was he in some essential way Chinese?

One-fingered, Ding Ming typed an address and password, and an email account opened. But it was garbled. The icons all worked, but the text was a jumble of symbols. He tried refreshing and the same page popped up. He opened an email and the text there was all rubbish, too.

Ding Ming chewed a lip. 'What China language your computer got?'

Joy could not read Chinese. She had picked up Cantonese from her parents but had never formally studied, she could read only a handful of characters. So she didn't have any Chinese language software on her computer. Because she didn't have Chinese language software this guy couldn't send an email from her computer to back home in China. She should, she felt, have anticipated this problem. She should, she felt, have learned how to read and write what was after all her own fucking language.

She was ashamed and upset.

'I don't have Chinese language software,' she admitted. 'I'm sorry.'

The man, it seemed, was inured to disappointments. 'Thank you for help me,' he said carefully. 'I will try to call my mother on the telephone again in some time.'

But the phone was in the hall and the shop was closed. She couldn't let him do it here. And she was tired now.

'Why don't you sleep in the shed behind the shop? Then try again tomorrow? How about that? Come into the shop in the morning and I'll convince my father to let you have another go at calling your mum. Okay?'

'Thank you. You are very kind. You are the most kind person ever in the world.'

She took blankets and a sleeping bag and led him out of the flat and down the alley. A door here led to the yard behind the shop, where the shed stood. When they'd moved a broken bike, he assured her that it was quite spacious enough.

For the second time she snuck back upstairs. Only this time she pushed open her door to find her father standing in her room with his arms crossed. He'd put trousers on over his pyjamas, but he was barefoot.

'I will not have you sneaking around at night. You think I am stupid. I'm not stupid. Do not test me in this manner. You are seeing boys, aren't you?'

He moved into English, which he only did with her when he was upset.

'Are you bad girl?'

'Don't say that,' shouted Joy, speaking English now too, a easier language for her to argue in. 'It's not like you think. Why do you think the worst all the time? I helped that—'

Her explanation was cut short by a scream. They both fell silent. It came from downstairs, either the alley or the yard. The only window that looked over the yard was in the bathroom, and that was frosted. She would have to go and look for herself. Was it that Ding Ming? No, it had sounded too girlish. But what would a girl be doing there? She ran downstairs.

'What is going on? What is going on?'

He paused in the hallway to put shoes on, and she rushed out alone.

Someone hurtled past, an elbow caught her in the stomach, and she was knocked against the wall. It was a small figure with a hoodie pulled up, and over it a bomber jacket. It was clutching a spray can. It sped around the corner. That bloody Jessica.

In the yard, Ding Ming stood contemplating the wet letters sprayed in blue paint along the wall by the back door, the word 'Chin'.

He said, 'I hear noise, come out, person paint on wall, I grab him, he run away. Run away very fast.'

Joy wondered what Jessica had intended to write. 'Chinky bitch', perhaps, or something similarly uninspired. She touched the paint and her fingertip came away blue. Perhaps it would be easier to clean up while it was still wet, but she couldn't be bothered. Leave it till the morning.

Her father arrived and inspected the damage. He ignored Ding Ming completely, you'd think he hadn't noticed the man at all, but on his way out he said, in English, 'I want him go out first thing in the morning.'

Ding Ming said, 'Thank you.'

'I saw her and I know who it is, so we can go the police,' said Joy. They were on their way upstairs.

'No police,' said her father.

'We slap the bitch with an ASBO, she gets arrested if she comes near the place.'

'If you want to let people stay in my yard, you ask me first.'

'We could go and tell her parents. We should take a picture before we clean it up.'

'I don't understand young people today,' said her father, and Joy wondered if he was talking about Jessica or her, and got no chance to ask for clarification as he went back into his room and shut the door.

'That's right,' she said, to the door, in English. 'Why don't we ever have a proper talk? We talk for, like, minus a second a day. Oh well, whatever.'

Finally, she got to go to bed, but jumbled memories from the day were bright in her head – Mark's smile, a hand-drawn map to a service station, broken fish, the word 'Chin' in blue paint, Jessica's vicious eyes.

The notion took her to learn how to squat the way the mainlander did. She didn't much feel like sleeping, so she got out of bed and gave it a go. She managed for about ten seconds, then the strain was too much and she collapsed on her bottom. It made her laugh. 'How daft are you,' she said out loud. 'Look at yourself.' Someone knocked on the front door.

She slipped bare feet into trainers and put a coat over her nightdress and buttoned it as she clumped downstairs. It was either that Jessica or that mainlander and they were both trouble. If it was that Jessica she would punch her in the gob, definitely. She wound herself up to do it as she unlocked the door. It was on a chain and she saw a radio on a dark uniform and a moustache on a serious face. The police. That one from earlier, and behind him his wingpig, the woman who looked round a lot.

'May we come in?'

'It's a bit late.'

'Your lights were on.'

'Okay.'

She took off the chain and opened the door and said, 'How can I help you, officer?'

'We are investigating reports of a serious assault. Do you have a young Chinese man staying at this address?'

'What do you mean, assault?'

'An attempted rape has been reported.'

'That's ridiculous. It was that Jessica, wasn't it? It wasn't an assault. She was spraying graffiti and he chased her off. I don't think he even touched her. She's a vandal – go and arrest her.'

'Nonetheless the allegation has to be investigated. It's the second incident involving a Chinese gentleman tonight, and we need to talk to him urgently.'

Her father joined her at the bottom of the stairs, with his gravest face on.

'Your co-operation is advisable. We can drag you in for questioning and get warrants if we believe it's necessary.'

The girl cop said, 'If an offence has been committed and you do not co-operate, you could be in a lot of trouble. Where is this man?'

'I don't want any trouble,' said Joy's father. His jaw was set, his eyes fixed at a point above her head. 'He in the yard. He stay in the shed.'

The policeman said, 'Take us there, please.'

Joy led them round to the alley. She guessed that even if Ding Ming was innocent, he'd be in bother. Probably he was an illegal immigrant, in which case they'd – what did they do? Did they put you in prison, or fine you, or deport you? She coughed and scraped her feet on the tarmac, with the idea that the noise might alert Ding Ming. If he was quick he'd have time to run away.

'This is stupid,' said Joy, loudly. 'You should be round at her house arresting her. She's the one done wrong, she's a vandal.'

'He's in there? In the shed?'

'Yes.'

'Stand back. Back. Does he speak English?'

'Yes.'

The policeman knocked at the shed door.

'This is the police. Come out of there, please, sir. Come out of there, sir. If you do not come out I will open the door. I'm opening the door.'

Ding Ming hurtled out, head down, arms flailing, and crashed into the policeman. They went down together. He got up and rushed towards the alley.

The policeman got him round the waist and the police-woman steamed in, and after a flurry of limbs they had him down in the dirt on his front, the policeman planting a knee in his back and wrenching his arm round and going, 'Oi oi oi oi oi.'

Both cops were puffing and had lost their hats. Even as they were cuffing him he squirmed and fought, and it was horrible to observe, like watching the spasms of a dying animal.

'He hasn't done anything wrong,' said Joy. 'He's just scared shitless.'

'And why would that be?' The policeman was flushed. He was in control of the situation, and the satisfaction of victory was in his voice.

'We're taking him down the station. We'll need statements from you and your father, but we can get them in the morning.'

The girl cop was frisking Ding Ming. She said, 'Found a gun.'

'A firearm? He had a firearm? Is it loaded?'

'I don't know.'

Joy could see they were struggling to contain their excitement. A real live gun! It was well out of the ordinary. This arrest was getting better and better – now it was a story, what kudos they'd get down the cop shop.

'Make sure the safety's on. Take the bullets out.'

'I'm not sure how.'

'Just put it away. Carefully.'

She lowered it into her upturned hat.

'Look at all this trouble,' said Joy's father, in English. 'Look at it. Trouble and more trouble.'

Ding Ming glanced at Joy as he was led away and the awkward feeling rose in her that perhaps he thought she had betrayed him. She waved at him, trying to convey her sympathy, and bit her lip the way he did. She hoped it would be okay for him. She had no idea why he would need a gun, it seemed completely out of character, but she was certain that if he did there was good reason. She felt that she had glimpsed the edge of a secret, and would now never know its full shape.

'It's a shame,' said her father, in Cantonese.

'Yes.'

The cops took Ding Ming over the road to a squad car. They put him in the back and the man with the moustache got in with him and the woman climbed into the driver's seat.

Joy took her father's hand.

'Who's that?' he said, pointing.

'Huh?'

'I thought I see somebody. There.'

'It's nothing.'

'Yes. I made mistake.'

His hand was hot. She hadn't held it like this since she was a kid. She supposed she should let go, but she didn't. Her bottom lip was trembling.

'Let's go inside. I can't watch.'

SPEEDING

(52

Jian opened the back door of the police car, slid in and put Ding Ming in a headlock. He pressed a shard of glass against Ding Ming's neck, behind the windpipe.

The peasant sat still, wide eyes moving rapidly. The policeman on the back seat glared across the peasant's exposed neck. He was annoyed, his moustache twitched. Jian moved his hand to show him the glass, show he knew what he was doing. A few pounds of pressure and the carotid artery would get severed. The policewoman in the driver's seat turned off the engine.

The policeman sighed with irritation. The girl adjusted the rear-view mirror so she could check out the back seat drama, and Jian glimpsed his own reflection. He looked like a wild man, a savage come out of the woods. When he was in his twenties, he'd helped to chase down two robbers – brothers, one retarded, the other evil. His unit had tracked them to a cave, where they had shot one – the idiot it turned out – who died complaining he was hungry. Now he looked like those brothers, and it wasn't just the dirt. It was something sullen and furtive in the eyes. He said, '*Jiao zheige nan de...* Tell the man to take out a set of handcuffs.'

With his head up and back, eyes bulging, Ding Ming croaked, 'I don't know what handcuffs is in English.' He swallowed and his Adam's apple bobbed up and down beneath the fragile skin.

Jian worked to keep his breathing shallow and level, it helped in keeping the pressure of the glass blade steady. It cut into his palm. The pain was welcome, it kept him alert.

'You can manage it. Say, 'those things you tie people up with' or something.'

The command was communicated in a croaking rasp, Ding Ming's English now sounding more like frogs than birds.

The policeman took cuffs out of a belt pouch, slowly.

'Tell him to put one around his right wrist.'

The policeman slipped it on.

'And secure it. Properly. Now tell the girl to put the other cuff round her left wrist.'

The policeman leaned forward and put his arm out, and she reached back and did as she was told. Neither looked too happy about it. No doubt they were thinking, the idiot doesn't realise we can get these off in a few seconds. But that was fine for Jian, let them think him a fool.

Now they were cuffed together, the policeman leaning forward, the policewoman leaning back, hands joined over the handbrake, an awkward position for both.

'Tell them to take off their radios and drop them on the floor.' Ding Ming croaked, and the two police unclipped the radios from high on their torsos and dropped them.

'Tell them to kick them under the seats. Tell the girl that if I see her touching the radio on the dashboard, I'll kill you.' Ding Ming babbled some more, his voice a little higher.

'Now tell them to take off their belts and drop them on the floor and kick them under the seat as well. Him first. Good. Now tell the man to put his left hand on the back of his head. Good.'

The peasant licked dry lips. A bead of sweat ran down his neck, touched Jian's thumb and dissipated.

(53

Jian had been lucky when the car went into the lake. He'd taken some knocks but nothing debilitating.

Water gushed in through the broken side window. He grabbed the door handle and tensed against the force of the rushing tide and waited. Feeling the van revolve, he hoped he didn't end up trying to open a door jammed against the bottom.

When the interior was almost full of murky water he took a deep breath, ducked, pulled the handle and, with one foot braced against the steering wheel, forced the door open. He wriggled out and kicked for the surface.

When he came up he took a quick breath and went straight back under – he didn't know if his enemies were watching. He struck out for the far side of the lake and swam for ten minutes before reaching shallow water.

He knew that he needed to get dry and warm before considering anything else. Having broken into a fishing cabin, he crouched in front of a fan heater for half an hour. It was a glorious experience – the comfort so unexpected, the hum and the heat lulling him into drowsiness. He still had the black address book but the ink on the vital page was so smeared it was illegible, and his life started to look without purpose. Then, realising where the peasant was bound to have gone, he cursed himself for wasting so much time.

Ding Ming said, '*Ni bu mingbai*... You don't understand: snakeheads had my mother, I had no choice—'

'You don't talk to me, only to them.'

He didn't want the peasant too frightened, so he added, 'I don't want to kill you. Do what I tell you and it'll be fine.'

He was keeping his expression and his tone neutral. If he showed fear, uncertainty or craziness, it would encourage the cops to act. He was wondering how he'd react if he was on the job in this situation. He'd do what the idiot with the weapon said. Citizen getting knifed in the back of a squad car would look very bad – black marks on your record and a big dry-cleaning bill. He'd co-operate, and let a stand-off drag on. Sooner or later, back-up would arrive. Then you'd be looking at a siege and cops always win a siege.

He was concentrating hard. The pressure on blade had to be kept constant, the police and the peasant and the road had to be watched, he had to anticipate and calculate. He'd been involved in these sort of situations a couple of times, on the other end, and things had never finished well for the hostage taker. But they'd always been cornered men in the grip of strong emotion. He reckoned if he played it well his chances were good, but it was no sure thing.

He began talking in a low, level tone. 'If you stay with them, they'll deport you, at best. Stay with me and you've got a chance. You help me, like we agreed, then I'll take you back to your boss and that's what you want, isn't it? It's the only chance you've got. Tell her to open her door.'

This was going to be the difficult bit. 'Now tell them to leave the keys in the ignition and get out of the car.'

Ding Ming relayed the instruction but nobody moved. Jian had expected that he'd have done the same thing. Get the guy irate and talking, see how far you could push it. See how it played and maybe, after a few hours of threats and coaxing, rush him. Unless back-up turned up first.

The guy began to turn in the seat, saying something in a reasonable tone.

Jian took hold of Ding Ming's left little finger and said, 'Either I pretend to break this finger, and you scream really loud, or I really break it, and you scream really loud. Which is it to be?'

'Pretend, pretend. I'll scream.'

'Scream and thrash about. But don't move your head, I don't want any accidents.'

Jian bent the little finger back, and made sure the woman could see it in the rear view.

'Tell them that if they don't get out of the car now I'm going to break the finger.'

The command was relayed, but still nothing happened.

The peasant's hand was warm and damp with sweat. It was clean and unblemished, the skin soft and supple. His own aged hand was grimy, with dirt ingrained in knuckles as gnarled as wood knots.

'Ready? Really scream. One two three...'

Jian pushed the peasant's hand down so they couldn't see what he was doing any more, then pinched the back of it hard.

Ding Ming screamed and thrashed about, then sobbed and breathed in ragged gasps. Jian worried he was rather overdoing it. But it worked. The policewoman got out and pulled at the handcuffed hand of the man and he scrambled over the seat division into the front and half fell out of the car.

'Tell them to walk forward twenty paces. Now tell them to lie down on their faces.'

Jian clambered quickly into the front seat, put the car into first gear and stamped on the accelerator. He got the car into the road, kept his foot down, and changed up. He checked the rear view. The uniformed figures were getting to their feet, but diminishing fast.

He reached across, dropped the blade onto the road and pulled the door closed. His palm throbbed where it had pressed against the glass, and he wiped blood off onto his trousers and shook it to take the sting out. Still, he supposed he could have come out of that worse.

Ding Ming said, 'I had to tell my boss, I had no choice. They tied up my mother and they were going to pull her teeth out. Please understand – they have my mother tied up.'

Jian flipped switches on the dash and turned on heating and a fan before he found the siren. A two-note wail built and he saw the reflection of the flashing roof lights on the bonnet. The speedometer hit eighty on some unfamiliar scale.

'Do you remember the address?'

'You won't get ten kilometres. They'll hunt you down.'

Jian hit third gear and moved into the centre of the road. The dotted lines coalesced into a strip.

'Do you remember the address?'

Jian showed him the black book. He'd dried it in front of the fan heater and now the vital page was crisp and warped. The ink had run and the words were a cloudy blur.

'Look at this, it'll jog your memory. You're going to get me to that farm. Then I'll take you back to your boss.'

'They'll catch you and shoot you.'

'We're going to get a map.'

'When they catch us, tell them the truth. Tell them you forced me to help you.'

'They saw me stick a blade to your throat – I think they know that already.'

'Tell them.'

'I'll tell them I forced you. Will you read a map?'

'Heaven, this is so awful.'

'You're better with me than them. Will you read a map?'

'I'll read a map. I remember the address. But you won't get ten kilometres.'

Jian glanced at the lad in the rear view. He was squirmed round, looking out of the back window, no doubt on the lookout for helicopters. This time those fears might be justified. His own force would put out everything they had if a squad car was stolen, though they might be slow to alert other forces, out of sheer embarrassment.

The handcuffs gleamed. The lad wasn't going to be able to read a map with his hands cuffed behind his back. He hoped the key was on the belt under the seat and not back at the station.

It felt natural to be behind the wheel of a squad car with the siren wailing over his head. These roads, without pot-holes or meandering pedestrians or unlit donkey carts, just invited acceleration. Trees and houses flashed past. He could feel his palms prickling, as they always did when he drove fast.

'When we get a map,' said Ding Ming, 'I'll mark where you have to go and write the address down in English for you to show people, and then you can take me back to the mud.'

'You're coming all the way.'

'But you said you'd take me back. When we were at the lake, you said, you said.'

'I remember, just before you tried to get me killed. Maybe you'll try and cheat me, and when I get a map you'll just mark any old place. Could be you'll call your boss again. So you're coming with me all the way. I'm taking you back only after you get me there, not before.'

Black and white stripes loomed, alerting Jian to a sharp bend. He stamped the brake and tugged down hard at the wheel and the tyres squealed in complaint. The bumper scraped the sign before he got the thing back on the straight. A bump in the back was the peasant falling against the door.

'*Lao tian a, lao tian a.*'

(55

Jian bore rapidly down on a set of tail-lights. It was a boxy estate doing maybe seventy kilometres an hour, a man driving and no passengers – just what he was looking for. He overtook, swerved in front of it and slowed. As hoped, the driver pulled up. Jian stopped ahead of him and switched off the siren. His ears were ringing.

The peasant sat up. 'What are you going to do now?' There was curiosity as well as fear in his voice.

Jian tapped the wheel and looked the driver over in the wing mirror – a man waiting patiently for the police, unclipping his licence from behind the driver-side visor. He reached under the seat and pulled out the utility belt. It annoyed him that there wasn't a gun attached to it. A gun made things simpler. The only weapons were a telescopic baton and a spray can. He'd read about these sprays. The Russians used them. They dispensed a gas that made the eyes and throat burn.

So he could just hit the guy with the spray and steal his car. And that would buy him, what, a couple more hours. No use. He had to make sure the guy didn't report his car as missing. Maybe he could get the cuffs off the peasant and cuff the driver to a fencepost and leave him for the night.

He said to the peasant, 'Stay here.'

He reversed until there were just a few metres between the cars. He tucked the baton into his belt and held the can in his hand, finger poised over the nozzle. He'd spray the guy in the face, shut him in the boot of the cop car, drive it into the corner of some field where it wouldn't get found till morning, then come back – hauling the peasant – and take the estate.

He reminded himself to check the guy for a mobile phone before slinging him in the boot, and, all the while, keeping an eye on the peasant. So, better idea – lock the guy in the boot of the cop car, shut the peasant in the boot of the blue car, then dump the cop car in a field. That would work.

The driver was winding his window down. Jian got round there quickly, raised the spray to a puzzled face and saw a wide eyed toddler in a child seat in the back.

He faltered and lowered the can. The presence of a kid complicated things too much. The driver scrambled down by the handbrake, and Jian worried he was going for a weapon and after all would be forced to spray him, until the window started rising with a hum. The automatic window button was down there. He was jamming it with the fingers of both hands, as if that would make it go faster.

The driver whacked the car into 'drive' and it pitched forward, straight into the back bumper of the police car, smashing a headlight. Broken glass tinkled and the man got his car into reverse and it shot back, tyres screeching. He stopped, turned and drove off.

Jian considered his decision not to spray the man. It was a good decision – he did not want to endanger a life so innocent – but if he was to be honest it was not cold consideration that had stayed his hand but that soft face and the big curious eyes.

That hadn't worked, what now? He opened the police car boot and found a medical bag and a toolkit and a couple of traffic cones. His mood of fragile optimism was waning. He had made a hash of this, the logistics were a nightmare, the whole operation was a mess.

Back in the squad car he got a police utility belt out and found a stubby metal key on a chain. He got into the back seat and pushed the peasant's face against the window.

'So you phoned your boss.'

Ding Ming's cheek was pressed against the glass. He blurted out of the side of his mouth, 'When you took me, he told the snakeheads in China and they tied up my mother and I called her—'

The handcuffs chinked as slender hands shook. Beneath the coat Jian could feel the bobbles of his spine and he realised how malnourished the lad was. Poor kid was just a civilian, hapless and unlucky, and he felt a twinge of guilt.

'How did you contact him?'

'I called him.'

'Will you call him again?'

'Of course not, no, no.'

He unlocked the handcuffs and the kid scrambled into the front passenger seat. He envied the lad his youth and his future and his innocence and even his fear. To have fear was to have hope.

Jian got out and into the driver's seat. The peasant was pointing a gun at him. He groaned with exasperation. He recognised the gun – he'd shot that hoodlum with it... was it only yesterday?

The peasant said, 'Take me back to the mud.'

'Where did you get that?'

'In the glove compartment.'

'I wondered where it had got to.'

Ding Ming held it with both hands and still the barrel shook.

'Take me back to the mud, now. Take me back.'

'Or what? You'll shoot me?' He leaned forward and pointed as he said, 'Did you see any cigarettes in there?'

He knocked the peasant's arm away and grabbed his wrist. With his other forearm he forced the lad back against the door, rising off the seat to get his weight behind it. But the idiot still didn't let go of the gun, so he headbutted him.

The peasant cried out, dropped the weapon and slapped both hands over his face. Jian fished the gun out from under the handbrake, checked the safety was on, and put it in the driver's door pocket.

The peasant said, 'Ow ow ow. Stop hitting me.'

'Let me look at it.' He prised Ding Ming's fingers away. 'Can you see okay? Any sparkles in your vision?'

'No.'

'Any disorientation? How do you feel?'

'Tired, hungry, terrified.'

'You're fine.'

It would sting for a few more minutes and he'd be dazed, and soon enough have a bump and a bruise. The lad's eyes were watering, with pain or possibly frustration.

'Stop hitting me, just stop hitting me.'

'I'm sorry. Okay? I'm sorry.'

Jian pointed at the glove compartment.

'Is there a map in there?'

'Yes.'

'Excellent.'

(56

Jian was pleased to see the peasant pull out a road atlas. The lad said, 'What are you going to do now?'

'Hijack a car. One with no kids in it.'

But he drove for minutes and saw no other traffic. He didn't like not knowing where he was going and losing time. The next vehicles he saw could be a posse of police cars.

The peasant said, 'You can't just stop someone and take their car. People have guns.'

'Is that so? Look at the map. Find out where we are.'

Ahead, a car was turning off. Jian accelerated to catch it, but overshot the narrow sideroad and had to brake and reverse. The car was a few hundred metres ahead but he could see its brake lights winking as it travelled the winding lane.

It was a good location – the hedges were high, there were no buildings around and there were fields either side he could dump the police car in. He gained on the vehicle, it turned again, and he followed it into a secluded car park fringed with trees. His quarry slowed.

Jian shifted in his seat, psyching himself up. He would be ruthless, whoever was in there. He reached to turn on the siren but paused when he saw the odd, busy scene. Six or seven cars were parked up. A gaggle of men bent to peer into a roomy estate, and one aimed a video camera through steamy windows. The back door of a van hung open and a man knelt on the tarmac before it, his head and shoulders inside, moving rhythmically.

The squad car lights swept across an interior painted red and a tangle of pale arms and legs. Why, there were naked people in there. They seemed even more surprised than him.

The sight of the police car spread panic. Half-dressed figures scattered for cars, the van door was pulled shut, a man shuffled, holding up his trousers.

'What's going on?' said the peasant.

Car doors slammed and engines started. Headlight beams swiped back and forth as cars rushed away.

Jian put the siren on and took the squad car forward. A white van and a black sports car were parked side by side with their front doors hanging open. In the front of the sports car, three figures hastily rearranged themselves. Doors were pulled shut, the vehicle reversed and swung around, and, as it shot past, Jian glimpsed a bare-chested man driving and an awkward couple with flushed faces squeezed into the passenger seat. He slid the squad car towards the only vehicle remaining, the abandoned van.

'A sex party,' said Ding Ming. 'They were having a sex party.'

'Stay here.'

But, though the van's front door was wide open, there was no sign of the keys. Presumably the driver had been driven off in the sports car. He cursed. He'd wasted so much time. He'd get back on the main road, set up a roadblock and hijack the first vehicle that came along. Or break into a house and steal some car keys. The thought of terrorising more civilians, and the logistical hassles any plan he might come up with would entail, caused dismay.

'I could maybe start it,' said Ding Ming. 'There are four wires under the ignition, you have to bind three of them and then touch them to the fourth. Don't tell anyone I helped you. Tell them you did it yourself.'

'How long would it take?'

'I'd have to have a look.'

Together they considered the housing behind the steering wheel.

'First, you have to get that off. Fiddly. Needs a screwdriver. Then you can get to the wiring.'

Jian found a hammer in the squad car toolkit. He smashed the housing until it cracked, then turned the head and wrenched it away with the claw. Underneath the gouged plastic, coloured wires ran along a metal shaft.

'If anyone finds out I did this, you forced me to help you,' said Ding Ming. 'I didn't have a choice.'

'That's right. I said I'd break your fingers if you didn't.'

The peasant squatted and poked his head under the steering column. Jian stood behind him pointing a police torch.

'My cousin showed me. He's a lorry driver. They all know how to do it because they get drunk and lose their keys. Can I have more light, please? There's the wires.'

'Can you start it or not?'

'It's fiddly. What about all those people, having a sex party out here? I feel sorry for them. They can't have loving spouses.'

'Get it started. Someone is going to come back for this soon.'

But the peasant stopped work.

'I'll start the engine if you grant me a favour.'

'Cunning peasant.'

'Can I call my mother. Please. I'm worried about her. They've tied her to a chair.'

'I'll get you back to your boss and everything will be straightened out.'

'I want to make a phone call.'

'Your mother is fine. Think about it. Your boss and his men saw the van go into the water. They thought you were in it with me. They think we're both dead. Your boss will have told the snakeheads back home, and they'll have told your mother and left her to her grief.'

'I must call her, I must call her.'

A vehicle was approaching. The headlights were white and low. It was the sports car.

'Get that van started,' barked Jian. 'You can call her. But you will speak only Mandarin to her and you'll say nothing except that you are alive.'

'She doesn't understand Mandarin.'

'She'll understand your voice.'

He leaned into the police car and turned the siren on. The flashing rooflights illuminated the scene and the peasant could be clearly seen tinkering. So Jian turned the headlights on full beam to dazzle the new arrivals.

The sports car stopped and a man got down from it and stood shading his eyes and calling out.

'Tell him to stay back,' said Jian. 'Sound like you mean it.' The peasant shouted at the guy, who took a couple of steps closer. Ding Ming said the same thing, louder this time, and now the man stopped. He was wearing a shirt but no shoes or trousers, and was hopping from one foot to the other. Perhaps the tarmac was pricking his feet.

Ding Ming said, 'He wants to know what we're doing. He said he wants to get into his van. And some other stuff, but I didn't catch it.'

'Tell him to turn round and put his hands on his head.'

Ding Ming relayed the order and the man obeyed and Ding Ming returned to fiddling with the wires. But now a woman was coming out of the car and calling. Jian said, 'Tell them to lie on the ground with their hands on their heads. Sound annoyed.'

The man got down on his front but the woman stepped forward. She wasn't buying it.

Ding Ming said, 'They want to know if we're Chinese police and what we're doing. They say they were just having a party and it's not against the law, and some other stuff I couldn't catch.'

'Tell them we've found a bomb.'

'I don't know how to say that in English.'

Jian ran a hand through his hair. So here I am, he thought sardonically, trying to steal a car from a bunch of sex maniacs on the wrong side of the world.

'Then tell them there's a man with a gun. He's hiding around here somewhere. For their own safety they must lie on the ground.'

'That's difficult.'

But Ding Ming leaned back out of the van and shouted, and at least now there was some authority to his voice. The woman obeyed and a second man got down from the sports car, and he lay down, too. The lad went back to the wires. The engine of the van caught and he grinned in triumph.

Jian got in. An image of his daughter rose unbidden. She was sitting in the passenger seat talking about a film she'd seen. She put the seat belt on and tugged to check it was secure. Her voice and her deft hands were as vivid as if she were really there, but the image vanished and a sense of emptiness welled. She was not an absent presence but a present absence. So was her mother. What great gaps he carried.

Ding Ming said, 'What is it?'

'Nothing, it's nothing.' He wrenched the steering wheel. It did not obey, and he slapped it in frustration. It was locked – it would move a few centimetres then freeze. Some kind of security device. He should have known, they had the same thing on the squad cars back home. Ding Ming's smile faded.

(57

'Fuck this,' said Jian. He got out of the van and pointed his gun at the figures on the ground, holding his arm out straight to make sure they saw the ugly thing. The woman gasped, and a man reached across and grasped her hand.

The keys to the sports car were still in the ignition. Black leather creaked as Jian got in. He was reclined far back and much lower than he was used to, and the pedals were small and close together.

'Quickly, quickly,' said Ding Ming, clambering in.

Jian ran from first to third and back again, getting used to the tight shifts, and varied pressure on the pedals to get a sense of the engine's response. The thing was so powerful and sensitive it would take some getting used to.

He drove to the police car, and got out and chucked the utility belts, the medical kit, the tool kit and the map into the cramped space behind the bucket seats.

'Hurry – they're getting up.'

Jian put his foot down, sweeping the car right around the car park, and glimpsed upraised puzzled faces as he turned into the road.

'This is a car,' said the peasant. 'Will you look at this? There's a button here to change the angle of the wing mirror. That's a CD player. I think this is air con. It's like a spaceship.'

'Don't touch anything.'

Tilted back in the bucket seat, surrounded by illuminated dials and readouts, Jian felt more like a pilot than a driver.

The thing ate up road, but he still didn't know if he was going in the right direction.

'Get on and read that map. Find out where we are.' He pointed. 'There's signs everywhere.'

'That's an advert. Keep going – we'll come to a town, and then I can look it up in the index and work it out. Can you put a light on in here?'

Stealing this car had solved nothing. Those sex maniacs from the car park would ring the police and a call would go out, would be going out now: Chinese hostage-taker now travelling in black sporty number registration whatever whatever, take him dead or alive. Across the force, the crime would be taken personally. Every cop in the country would yearn to catch the man who'd stolen a squad car.

'You said I could make a call. Can I borrow your phone?'

'No.'

Jian no longer had his daughter's pink mobile. He'd lost it in the lake, along with the wallet. It must have slipped out when he was swimming. He'd been concentrating on keeping the address book, he hadn't given those others a thought.

'You said as long as I spoke Mandarin to her, you'd let me. We had an agreement that, if I started the engine of that van, you'd let me phone my mother. I started the van.'

'But it wasn't any good, you set off the steering lock. Our agreement is void.'

'Please.'

'My mobile is out of charge.'

Which, he told himself, wasn't really a lie.

'I have to call my mother. They tied her to a chair.'

The man was like a scratched record. Jian repeated his earlier argument, working to keep the impatience out of his voice.

'Think about it. They thought you died, with me, drowned in that van. There's no longer any reason to threaten your mum. Or any of your family. You're free. You know what? You pulled off a great trick. They think you're dead, so they won't collect the money you owe.'

'Oh no – they told us quite specifically. If we die we still owe the twenty thousand. They'll collect from my family.'

'It's going to be fine. Everything will work out so long as you help me get where I'm going.'

He injected an upbeat tone that he did not feel. This was like talking to children, something he had never been good at. He gave the peasant the address book. 'Find this place.'

Out of the corner of his eye he checked that the lad was considering the road map. He would rather they travel in silence, but he couldn't afford for the lad to start sulking.

'Have you found it yet?'

'The village isn't marked. I think the scale is too big. This map only has towns.'

'Find the province.'

Ding Ming showed him the back cover, a picture of the whole lumpy island.

'It's here. See? England is shaped like a squatting woman, and we're heading to her big bottom.'

'And which direction is that?'

'I don't know, do I? When you take me back,' said Ding Ming, 'do you think they'll punish me?'

'What's in it for them? They'll put you straight to work.'

'I'm worried they'll realise I helped you.'

'Your story is, I abused you, then you escaped and made that phone call to your boss. After the van went in the water, you got that nice Chinese girl from the restaurant to help you find your way back.'

He prattled on, trying to sound convincing.

'Just have that straight, and stick to it. Be glad you're so beaten up – that'll help convince them. They'll see you've had a very bad time.'

Ding Ming fingered the bump on his forehead.

This was a future so distant it wasn't worth thinking about, the peasant's concerns were touching but absurd. The poor lad believed everything was going to work out. They'd get where they were going, and the peasant would wait in the car twiddling his thumbs while the people who needed to be killed got killed, and then they'd just drive back. As if this was all some country jaunt.

'Everything is going to be fine. Can you work out what road we're on?'

'I'm looking, it's difficult. You go so fast I can't finish reading the signs. What are you going to do after?'

'After what?'

'After you drop me back at the mud.'

Jian reflected guiltily that, without the texted address stored in the pink phone's memory, it would be much harder for him to return the peasant. In fact, it would be almost impossible.

'That's no concern of yours.'

Jian hadn't thought about it and didn't care to start thinking about it now. When he imagined the killing of the men who murdered his daughter, he could see possibilities, strategies and outcomes. But he could not envision a life afterwards. The prospect of more days to fill wasn't pleasing. He realised that he expected to die.

58

Jian accelerated but he hardly felt it at all. Looking out of the windscreen was like watching TV, the car handled as if it was on rails.

'This is a lovely car. She drives like a bullet. Chunky in lower gear, but when she gets over fifty she's flying. Listen to that purr.'

A sniff made him look across. Ding Ming was gripping the edges of his seat and looked like he was about to cry.

'What's the problem now?'

'I never thought I could be sitting in such a wonderful thing, but it isn't making me happy.'

How could a great car make you sob? But the peasant had to be jollied along.

'Don't worry about it. Your mother is fine, you're fine. I'll get you back, you can save up and one day buy one of these.'

The snotty sobs irritated Jian. As if he didn't have enough to deal with of his own. At least the lad hadn't watched a film of his daughter being killed. His hands tightened on the wheel and he pushed the accelerator. A box at the side of the road flashed.

'That was a camera,' said Ding Ming. 'They took a picture. They know where we are.'

You're paranoid. Look, there's a sign. Where are we?'

They entered a suburb and Jian slowed. He felt uncomfortably conspicuous around traffic, pedestrians and buildings. He stopped at a red light.

Ding Ming pointed. 'Is that a police car?'

The squad car, unmistakable in its waspish war paint, sat in a layby ahead, hazard warning lights blinking. Jian considered turning and taking off, but then they'd certainly pursue. He could outrun one, but how many more would come? Roadblocks would be set up, marksmen deployed.

Perhaps after all, when the lights changed, he'd be able just to cruise past. His fingers drummed on the wheel. A man was crossing the road, pulling a dog on a lead. What was it with these people and their dogs? They appeared to dote on them more than children. Another car pulled up behind. Feeling boxed in, he shifted uneasily. Ding Ming was groping around the back seat.

'What are you doing?'

'I'm your hostage.' The lad fumbled a handcuff onto a wrist and was about to snap it closed.

'Don't be an idiot.' Jian snatched the cuffs away and sat on them. The lights changed to green. Ding Ming opened the door. Jian grabbed his collar and yanked him back.

'I wasn't going to go. I just thought I'd leave it open.'

The car behind parped its horn. The map book slipped off Ding Ming's lap, out of the crack in the door and into the gutter. Jian pulled the peasant's head close. He said, 'One two three. Get out, pick up the book and close the door.'

The car behind tooted again.

'Okay?'

'Okay.' The peasant got out, picked up the map book, got back in and pulled the door to. Jian took the car forward at a stately pace, past the police car, which was empty. He turned off and pulled in.

'Are you going to panic all the time?' he said. 'Are you going to run around like a monkey? You're no use if you're just going to lose your head. If things are getting on top of you, count to three.'

He chucked the handcuffs in the back.

'Don't think you have to act fast. Think about what you're going to do, then do it. Slow is sure and sure is fast. Read the map. Where are we?'

'We're in— the lad jabbered in English, a fluid twitter of birdsong. 'We have to go through town and get on the – birdsong – which leads us to – birdsong – and then we head straight south on the – birdsong. And then we're in the right province.'

'About how far?'

'Two hundred kilometres.'

'We'll get to the province, then take a better map.'

Driving in the town was stressful. Back home Jian rarely bothered to indicate and, if he felt like going the wrong way around a roundabout, no one was going to stop him. But here he did not want to draw attention to himself, so was careful to try and obey the rules of the road. But really, there were just too many of them. Certain streets only allowed traffic in one direction, on others right or left turns were forbidden, this lane was for turning off, this for going straight, this just for buses. Traffic lights, pedestrian crossings and speed bumps turned the road into an obstacle course. The sports car didn't like crawling in low gear and he kept stalling it.

At least Ding Ming seemed to be throwing himself into his task. He found a page in the book which explained what road signs meant, and when a sign appeared would flick to it and frown through the explanation and shout, 'You were meant to stop there', 'Dead end, dead end', or, 'this is a one way street, turn round, turn round.'

They were aiming for a road labelled with a letter and the number 46. After an exasperating series of roundabouts, they appeared to be on it. Jian realised he was craned so far forward in the seat that his chin was almost touching the steering wheel.

The road opened up. It was a scene with few human referents – just lines and lights, and, at the side of the road, illuminated numbers and diagrams. Robotic and entrancing, it was a system a person plugged his car into, a system designed for speed, and Jian put his foot down. He kept the speedometer hovering around the ninety mark, about a hundred and forty-five kilometres an hour. He'd never had such a feeling of swiftness in his life. Even trains didn't go this fast.

Ding Ming kept peering out of the side window. Jian could discern nothing that might be holding his attention. The roadside was deserted – no food stalls or cheap hotels like at home, just a barrier, then fields. It reminded him of the wilderness back home, because that too was a harsh unpopulated environment a man felt all alone in.

He realised that was the first time he'd thought of home in hours. He cast his mind over his recent life like a man probing a bad tooth with his tongue, inviting a lancing shot of pain. He could not recall with much accuracy the faces of his colleagues or the bodies of his girls. He looked at this figure who caroused and cultivated connections and hankered after his very own Audi, and he saw an inconsequential man with silly preoccupations. Here was a house with a big TV and a karaoke set and a PC, all showy and hardly used. What a daft frittering-away, all of it.

A phone was ringing, he answered, and he asked how her studies were doing and what she was eating, and he was hurrying her along because he was drunk and didn't want to be bothered. There was the pain, right there, and masochistically he jammed the sore point again – hurrying her along because he didn't want to be bothered.

'What are you doing?' screeched the peasant, and Jian swung the car back into the right lane. 'Concentrate.'

'I'm fine, I'm fine. What are you looking at?'

'Cows.'

'Where?'

'They're all over. You spot one and then you see lots, like mushrooms. I don't like them. They look selfish.'

'What are you talking about?'

'One of those cows has more land than a Chinese family. It's disgusting. And another thing. I look out and all I see are cow fields. Where are the vegetables? And where are the factories and the mines? It doesn't add up.'

'The fields and factories and mines are in other countries.'

'They're cow people.'

'What are you talking about now?'

'They're like their big stupid cows. Their life is the easiest it is possible to imagine: they wander around their lovely park, all day going munch munch munch. Nothing to worry about, just munching the stupid grass all day long in a lovely big field. And people like me, we are the rats. We live in the ditch and eat shit and watch out for the hawks, and our life is bitterness and struggle, and we're terrified all the time.'

'Rats don't eat shit.'

They shot past a police car parked in the hard shoulder.

'Police, police.'

'Fuck.'

In the rear view Jian saw the squad car set off and flash its lights.

(59

No doubt he could outrun the police car, but that would solve nothing – other cars would join in the chase, road blocks would be set up, etcetera. His only chance was to avoid pursuit long enough to change vehicles again. He pushed the car harder and the speedo crept to a hundred and twenty.

'What's the next junction?'

The peasant was rigid with fear. 'You're going too fast.'

'The next junction... When's the next junction?'

The lad ran a shaking finger along a red line.

'Thirty-four. Quite soon. We can go north or south from there.'

'We'll get there fast and he won't see where we've gone, and there'll be four options. We'll turn around and go back the way we came, he won't expect that. Put your seat belt on, then help me with mine.'

The cop had started his siren, but the wail was growing fainter and the flashing lights in the rear view were diminishing. If they could get to the roundabout a few seconds early, there was a good chance. The tricky part would be getting off the road without losing control of the car.

'There's a sign for when a junction is coming up: three stripes, two stripes, one stripe... then you're at the slip road. Oh, you're going too fast, too fast.'

Jian reminded himself to breathe. He felt he was about to take off. The road was a blur of flickering lines. He wasn't even blinking, conscious that a tiny lapse could end in disaster. There was just the lines, all he had to do was stay inside them. He wondered how fast they were going, but did not dare take his eyes off the road to look at the speedo. A blue sign winked in and out.

'Here,' shouted the peasant.

Jian stamped on the brake and swung the car onto the access road and the wheels screeched in complaint.

The road canted upwards and veered away from the expressway but it was short, too short, and he was braking hard and the car shook, but still the speed was alarming and now here was the roundabout, a mound of grass and more road and lines. There was no way he could wrestle the car round it in time. He kept the car straight and a judder passed over it as it hit the mound, a rumble filled the shaking vehicle, and in moments they had clattered right across the grass to the other side. Jian took his foot off the brake and aimed for the nearest turnoff.

The peasant was breathing in shaky gasps. He shouted with fear and exhilaration at being alive and showed Jian the map book, which, in his anxiety, he'd torn almost in two.

Jian told him to find out where they were. He hoped there was a town coming up, so they could lose themselves in it. He had only been lucky and he was furious with himself – that was reckless. He had endangered the life of the youth.

'You were breaking the speed limit. That's why he wanted to stop you.'

'The police will be looking for us. We're going to dump the car and steal a new one.'

'Not again. It's impossible.'

'What do you suggest? You want to take the train?'

'It's not my problem. You think of something.'

'I could break into a house and steal some car keys.' Jian tried not to sound as dismayed by this prospect as he felt.

He didn't want to prey upon the innocent and he had a low opinion of housebreakers. 'It'll be easy. They don't even have bars on the windows.'

They've got guards, dogs, guns.'

'What does that sign say?'

'Service station.'

'We'll find a car in there.'

'*Lao tian a*... Heavens.'

'You curse like a girl. Curse like a man. Say fuck your grandfather. Say it. *Cao ni da ye de*.'

'No.'

'*Cao ni da ye de*.'

'Don't say that to me.'

'*Cao ni da ye de*.'

'*Cao ni da ye de*,' said Ding Ming quietly.

'That's better.'

'*Cao ni da ye de, Cao ni da ye de*.'

'Feel better?'

'No.'

'Is this the service station here?'

'Yes. *Cao ni da ye de*.'

'We're going to steal a car, and you're going to do your trick again.'

'*Lao tian a*.'

60

Jian stopped in the darkest corner of the car park. He turned off the engine and listened to the silence and watched the illuminated dials fade.

'Look.'

The peasant had discovered a pair of trousers in the back footwell. They had a wallet inside, which Jian took. It was stuffed with notes, more than a hundred pounds, and there was a picture of kids and a woman. In the car boot, Jian found a can of petrol and a golf bag. He emptied the clubs out of the bag and put his equipment and the map book and the petrol can inside. He put the gun in his waistband and a police spray in his pocket.

In a children's playground he sat on the edge of a plastic fort and the peasant squatted at his feet.

'I don't know how to get into a car – just how to start one. And I don't know how to break a steering lock.'

'Don't worry about it. You're always worrying.'

But Jian was not confident. The car park was well lit and the service station windows looked out onto it. Video cameras were attached to walls and lampposts, and there were too many people around.

'We'll go for an old car, something clapped out. It won't have alarms or a steering lock. I'm going for a look round. That means I'm going to leave you alone. Are you going to try anything?'

'No.'

'I'll get us some food. Give me that coat.'

'Why?'

'So I look less like a beggar. Don't worry – I'll give it back. Now empty your pockets.'

'Why?'

'I want to see that you haven't got any money.'

'What do you think I'm going to do?'

'Sneak off and phone your boss, like you did last time. Show me.'

'See? I have nothing to my name except a dictionary and a toothbrush.'

Jian felt inside Ding Ming's socks and around his crotch and patted him down. The lad winced when his bruises were pressed.

'You should stop jumping out of cars. Wait here.'

There were ten or so vehicles in the car park and they were all newish models. A BMW arrived and parked close to the doors, and two men in suits got out and stretched. A woman came out of the service station and got into a hatchback and drove onto an exit lane. There was no obvious weak point to the system, and no dark corner to operate in. At least there didn't seem to be any security guards. He wondered if the staff parked round the back, but there seemed to be no way round there.

He'd have to catch a lone traveller as he was getting into his car, squirt him with the policeman's spray or wave a gun at him, throw him in the boot, and snatch the car. The guy could be safely disposed of in a field, trussed up to be discovered in the morning.

The prospect did not fill him with enthusiasm. His conscience nagged at the idea of brutalising more civilians, though not enough to make him change his mind.

An automatic door opened and he entered a warm lobby. The place reminded him of an airport waiting lounge. Unsettlingly bright lights made the goods on display look appetising and the people look ill.

In a shop he filled a wire basket with sandwiches, crisps and bottled drinks, and took two polystyrene cups from a coffee machine. Catching his reflection in a mirror atop a rack of sunglasses, he was perturbed at how rough he looked – any security guard would certainly have him pegged as a troublemaker. Perhaps he was already being followed on camera. He picked out two England football shirts and a black hooded sweatshirt.

There was a whole rack of maps. He selected four, to cover the entirety of the fat lady's bum. At the counter he mimed smoking a cigarette and was given a pack at a scarcely believable price, you'd think they were made of gold. He bought three lighters, too.

In a cubicle in the gents he changed into a football top and stuffed his shirt behind a toilet. The rest of the purchases went in the golf bag.

A bald man was taking a piss. Perhaps he was on his way out. Jian took his time washing his hands and followed him, with his hand resting on the gun in his pocket. He focused on the back of his neck and imagined threatening to hit him there. He halted when he saw the man join a woman and a child.

The automatic doors opened and two uniformed men strolled in. One talked into a radio, the second strutted with his thumbs hooked on his utility belt. More police. Jian veered into a photo booth, pulled the curtain across and sat on the little stool. The damn security forces were everywhere – this whole poxy little country was locked up tight.

He peeked out. The policemen proceeded down the corridor towards him. He imagined the reports that had come through on their radios: be on high alert for a middle-aged

Chinese man, hostage-taker and car thief, armed, dangerous, desperate.

The bald man and his family were heading for the exit and for a moment the policemen's view was obscured – this was his chance to move. He stepped quickly out and into the café. He joined a queue. At least that meant his back was to them. He shifted forward, keeping his head down, and smelled coffee. A blonde girl in a green apron was addressing him. He pointed at a display and was given a cake.

He stared at the girl to stop himself looking round for the police. She was pretty, plump with pale skin, and she smiled as she gave him his change. Strangely, she had two Chinese characters tattooed on her arm, *nu* and *li* – 'girl strength' – but the writing was childish and out of proportion.

He took his cake to a corner and allowed himself to glance around. He was sitting next to a young couple, the entrance doors opened for the bald man and his family, and the policemen were strolling ever closer. He couldn't see a back way out. He assumed there would be emergency doors, but opening them might set off alarms. He could not recall seeing any windows in the toilets. If the policemen challenged him, he would have to point his gun at them. Then what? Take a hostage? He imagined the people around him running, screaming, hiding. What a mess he was making.

He opened a discarded magazine and pretended to study it, with a hand on his brow to obscure his features. There were photographs of cameras and cars and girls wearing almost nothing. It reminded him of Wei Wei's vanity book. In his mind a grainy film ran again – his daughter cowering, a knife blade gleaming, blood pooling. Older memories surfaced, just as awful, of his wife's dead eyes, blood running down a cheek, a smashed headlight. He ran a hard hand across his scrunched-up face. It was gone, he was here, he had work to do.

He became aware of raised voices. The couple next to him were hunched over coffee, arguing. She was jabbing the table with a fake plastic nail and talking rapidly. She looked tired, and her mascara was beginning to run. Even beneath heavy make-up, a flush could be seen on her cheeks. He was rubbing his fingers along the sides of his nose and Jian guessed that all he was thinking was, 'Please keep your voice down.' His car keys glimmered on the table.

Jian tapped the man on the shoulder and thrust before him a picture of a girl rearing in a bikini.

He said, 'I'm going to borrow your car. Look at this picture while I steal your keys.'

Both looked baffled. Jian tweezered the keys with his free hand and, holding them behind the magazine, grinned and winked and said goodbye, hoisting his golf bag over his shoulder.

He walked out of the café without hurrying and glimpsed the policemen in the restaurant, queuing up with a tray, their backs to him. The exit got closer and he kept a steady pace, and nobody tried to stop him.

He repressed a grin. He'd arrested a few pickpockets in his time and he knew their tricks, but it wasn't something he was practised at. Probably it had only worked because he hadn't considered it, he'd just done it as soon as think it, and if he'd paused it would never have come off.

The sound of the automatic doors opening was like a sigh of relief. All he had to do now was find the right car, and again luck was with him because it was the third that he tried, a little red runaround, with no babies or dogs inside and a full tank of petrol. He started the engine and the radio came on – a chirpy tune. He drove the car round to the children's playground, where he'd left the peasant. The peasant wasn't there.

61

Jian went twice around the car park, then up and down the access road. Possibly the lad had run away... No, of course, he'd got it into his head to phone his mother. Or his boss – he wouldn't put that past the little rat. He must have had some money hidden on his somewhere. He parked the car and cursed – '*Cao, cao, cao*' and slapped the steering wheel.

He went back into the service station. One of the policemen was sitting in the restaurant, the couple in the café still argued. No – now they were getting up to leave. The peasant wasn't by the phones. Jian ran a hand across his head, feeling the pressure. The couple were looking around the table and might look up and see him. He strode quickly away and into the bathroom.

The peasant was washing his hands in the sink.

Jian grabbed his arm and hissed, 'Get out here now, you idiot.'

Ding Ming shrugged him off.

'There are policemen out there and I've just stolen a car. Let's go.'

'I'm not going out if there are policemen out there. We could hide in a cubicle. The doors have got locks on.'

Jian put a hand on the lad's elbow and led him out. He wished this place wasn't so bright.

'I told you to stay put. You're going to get us both killed.'

'I needed to go.'

'You couldn't have gone in the bushes?'

'It was a children's playground.'

'Keep talking as we go for the exit,' said Jian. 'Talk fast and walk slow, don't look round and don't catch anyone's eye. Don't look at them and they won't notice you.'

Jian was finding it hard to obey his own command. His eyes swivelled left and right, scanning for the policemen.

'What do you want to talk about?'

'It doesn't matter. Anything.'

'Er... I'm impressed with the high level of sanitation in public conveniences. When you press a button, soap comes out of a nozzle.'

'Is that so?'

Jian glimpsed the second uniformed figure putting money in a vending machine. He fought the impulse to speed up.

Ding Ming looked at a bank of phones and said, 'I want to phone my mother.'

'Not now.'

The lad shook himself free.

'I'm not moving until I can phone her.'

'Stupid peasant. I'm sure she's fine.'

A clunk was the vending machine dispensing a can. The policeman bent to pick it up. The couple in the café were looking under the table. The man got down on his hands and knees. Other people were beginning to look round. The policeman approached his companion.

Jian pushed Ding Ming into the phone cubicle, a transparent plastic bubble. At least in here they were not so noticeable. He slotted change into the phone and said, 'You speak only Mandarin to her. Just say you're fine. If I hear a male voice, I'm pressing the lever.'

Ding Ming dialled and waited. The phone rang and rang. Jian wondered, had his daughter done this? Had she rung and rung and waited in desperation for an answer? No. He had answered. If he had failed her, it had been when they talked.

'Okay, she's not in. Let's go.' Jian took the receiver out of the peasant's hand and replaced it on the cradle. The lad had been pressing the phone to his ear so hard that it had left a red mark.

Jian put an arm around his shoulder and steered him towards the exit.

'I'm not a stupid peasant.'

'I will never call you stupid again. Just look straight ahead at the door and keep chatting. Talk to me.'

In the café the woman was feeling in the crack at the back of the chair.

'I don't like being called stupid. Stop pulling me around. Give me some face.'

Jian resisted the temptation to observe any more or hurry Ding Ming along. He talked, hardly hearing what he was saying, concentrating only on those automatic doors.

'There's a big guy at the station and everybody calls him Titch. It's the same when I call you stupid. It's funny because it's so obviously the opposite.'

'I don't think it's funny.'

'I won't do it again.'

They were passing the restaurant. If the policemen looked up they would certainly be spotted.

'There they are,' said Jian. 'Act normal.'

'Them? They aren't policemen.'

'Don't look.'

'I'm telling you they're not policemen. You know what it says on their back? It says 'Emergency Breakdown.' They're mechanics.'

(62

Out in the car park, the peasant said, 'When did you see a policeman with a spanner on his belt? What do they call down the station? Do they call you Brains?'

'Hey. They call me Head-cracker because of what I do to funny guys. Do you like my shirt? I bought you one, too. This car here.'

'You want me to drive?'

Jian realised he'd opened the passenger door. Of course, the steering wheel was on the wrong side – it was easily forgotten. They got in and Jian handed Ding Ming his gift.

'Good material. Look how stretchy it is... that's quality. Look at these lions – they're quite like Chinese lions. I've never had anything this nice before. It says it was made in China. I don't know who Rooney is.'

Jian had his eyes closed to savour his first pull of a cigarette in what felt like weeks. It was a very good smoke, with no rough edges at all. Sparkly sweetness diffused through his body.

'He's the young firebrand of Manchester. Very fierce. A good striker of the ball. You should be pleased. Who have I got?'

'Lampard.' Pronounced in Chinese, *Lan Pa Du*. The rock of Chelsea, a sturdy man of steady character, and a clinical finisher. That was a good omen.

'Can I have the coat back?'

'You know you look ridiculous in it.'

'I know.'

'You look like a baby.'

'I know.'

'Don't put the hood up. I can't hear what you're saying.'

Jian looked through the window of the coffee shop as he drove past, and saw the woman peering under the table and the man down on his hands and knees looking at the floor. He could hardly believe it: he had got away with it so far and he was continuing to get away with it, and maybe he would get away with it all the way until everyone he wanted dead was dead.

He accelerated as he hit the access road. They were back on the expressway. This car was clunky, but much less obvious. The radio was on.

'I like this song. I used to learn English to it.'

'Look at these maps.'

It took more than five minutes but finally Ding Ming said, 'I've found it – it's marked. Look.'

Jian pulled up on the hard shoulder. Ding Ming showed him a cluster of brown oblongs on a white ground.

'That's the village.'

Jian pointed at a box with a cross on it.

'What does that symbol mean?'

'A temple.'

'You know where we go after we get to the village?'

'The hill of the bloody gate.'

'I don't think you're stupid. I think you're one of the cleverest people I ever met. For someone like you to go and get himself an education, that's amazing. Really. You're a credit – you know that.'

'Get there and do what you have to do, then get me back.'

'I'll try.'

63

Ding Ming pointed at a giant plastic strawberry marking a farm turnoff. 'Imagine having a real strawberry that big. You could jump into it and eat your way out.'

They had left the expressway. Now the land was lush and flat. Houses were far apart and kept private and sheltered by trees. Jian felt more secure on these small roads, but there were lots of the annoying roundabouts. He was careful to keep the speed down, hovering at around fifty, and in the villages even slower.

'I think you should dip the headlights for oncoming traffic. Look, he's dipped for you, you should do it for him.'

Jian imagined he saw his daughter in the back seat of the passing car. The hypnotism of the road was stealing over him. Perhaps a conversation would keep him focused.

'What's your wife like? Apart from modern.'

'Very lovely.'

'Pretty?'

'Very pretty.'

'Obedient?'

'Not really.'

'She speak English?'

'She left school when she was twelve.'

'So you're more educated than her.'

'I don't care.'

'Of course you don't care. But they don't believe that.'

'No.'

'You worry that she worries about it.'

'Exactly.'

'You miss her?'

'All the time. I don't know where she is.'

'Why not?'

'They took her away to pick flowers.'

The peasant choked down a sob. His hands fluttered about his face as he fought strong emotion and the map book slipped off his lap. Jian squeezed the steering wheel in exasperation. Was there no end to the man's tales of woe? He wished he'd never started this now.

'I'm sure she's fine.' He put as much honey in his voice as he could muster. 'She'll be okay, of course she will, and you'll see her soon.'

'You think so?'

'Definitely. You dropped the map.'

They hit a roundabout with three exits.

'I'm worried. I didn't know they were going to split us up. My boss said he would give me a telephone number to call her. But...' he tailed off. He was sitting on his hands and rocking back and forth.

'You should both go home. I'll make sure you're okay.'

'Really?'

'The force needs upright citizens. You'd be an asset.'

'You mean that?'

They'd been all the way round the roundabout. Much more of this, Jian felt, and he'd be too dizzy to drive.

'Of course I mean it. You dropped the map.'

This time the lad retrieved it.

'We'd still owe money to the snakeheads.'

'They wouldn't dare touch you if you worked for us.'

'That exit there.'

Jian could see the man's mind working, and knew what was coming next before it was said.

'Don't kill Black Fort. It won't change anything. Leave him alone. Go home.'

'I have to do this. I sent my daughter abroad because she was an embarrassment to me. I took a bribe to let a murderer go.'

'I don't understand.'

'I don't want to die a bad father and a bad policeman.'

Jian wondered if any more arguments would come up. He could think of plenty. The fact that he was one against many, for example, and of course the old 'it won't bring her back' and the 'forgive and move on' stuff. But the peasant didn't push it.

'What was your daughter like?'

'She was trouble. She was wild.'

'Like her dad.'

'She hung around with the wrong sort.'

'Like her dad.'

'What does that mean?'

'A policeman spends his time with criminals, doesn't he?'

'Arresting them, not... You don't know a thing about it.'

'I expect she just wanted you to pay her more attention. You only noticed her when she did wrong. That's why she went wild.'

'Your opinion has been duly noted, Granny Wang. Read the map. Think about strawberries.'

Jian decided he didn't like hedges. They turned the road into a tunnel. It was like being a rat in a run, scurrying through undergrowth. A rat... Perhaps he had heard the peasant talk about it too often, he was starting to think like him.

Ding Ming pointed at what looked like a fortress. The crenallated battlements of a tower were crisp against the sky.

'That's it. That's the temple.'

Jian stopped the car.

'Definitely? That's it?'

'The village is just up ahead.' The peasant was excited. For him it was merely a step on the way to his objective.

An old man was approaching, the first pedestrian they had encountered in a hundred kilometres. Jian watched, mentally ushering him away. He was stooped and his round glasses gave him an owlish look. He opened a wooden gate and shuffled between stone stele in the temple garden, and gave no indication of having seen them at all.

'Where now?'

'There should be a road round here. The name is the hill of the bloody gate.'

'What do you mean round here? Where is it?'

'I don't know.'

'Look at the address, then.'

'It's all blurred.'

Jian closed his eyes and rubbed his face, working to keep irritation out of his voice.

'You can't read it and you've forgotten what it says.'

'I got you this far. It's really close. It's just... round here somewhere.'

Jian looked balefully across and the lad shied away. Over his lowered head Jian could see the temple. The garden was unkempt and its stele jutted like bad teeth. With narrow windows and rough stone walls, the place really looked like a citadel. The old man was unlocking a door.

'You're going to ask him.'

64

The gloomy worshipping hall emanated a forbidding silence. Above the altar hung a macabre effigy, a hanging man, dead or dying. The old man sat on a bench with his head lowered. Jian walked up the central aisle, with the peasant hanging close behind. Their footsteps rang on the stone floor and even the sound of their breath seemed a noisy imposition.

'*Lao tian a*,' whispered the peasant, and crossed his arms.

'Just ask how to get to the hill of the bloody gate – that's it.'

The old man looked harmless, though anyone could phone the police. Jian pushed the peasant forward. While they conversed in hushed tones, the peasant bowed and the old man bobbed clasped hands. He got the impression that they were trying to outdo each other in politeness.

He turned his back on the unhappy image of the dying man with his crown of thorns. He had no time for theology. It was a ruse by the ruling classes to justify their wealth and power, it was nothing but superstition, people succumbed to its allure from fear of death and an inability to accept that they were not important. Modern people should learn to overcome this weakness. He did not fear death and he knew that there was nothing after it and he knew he was nothing and he was not afraid to face that, either. His gaze passed over baffling accoutrements of worship – a wood carving of a lamb carrying a cross, statues of men in dresses – and settled on the homely sight of dried flowers.

The peasant bowed some more and took his leave.

'Well?'

'He said he was happy to meet such early-rising worshippers. He said—'

'Did he give you directions?'

'He thinks it's on the other side of the village.'

'Fuck.'

'Please don't swear.'

'Let's go.'

'Wait.'

The peasant kowtowed before the altar, touching his forehead three times against the floor. 'Give something,' he urged.

'Do you even know what this religion is?'

'They're the gods of this place. We should leave them an offering for luck. Please.'

There were two notes left in the wallet, a twenty and a five. He slipped one out, and saw it was the twenty. He picked out the five, but realised it was too late: the gods who were not there would remember only his parsimony and not . his generosity. He put the twenty-pound note on the altar and asked that this god that he did not believe in look after him and his cause and, in particular, look after his daughter in a spirit world that did not exist.

As an afterthought, he put the wallet down. It would be returned to its owner, who'd be glad to get back his credit cards and pictures. Yes, he was glad that had been done. He left feeling naked, and told himself he was ready for battle and death.

Outside in the garden the peasant said, 'Do you know what he said? He said the name 'rings a bell'. I think it's an idiom meaning to remember something but not clearly.'

Jian pointed at steles. 'These are graves.'

'Who would surround a temple with graves?'

'They are. Look, there are dates on them.'

Jian considered a headstone topped with a statue of a winged woman. She had closed eyes and an expression of serene repose. So humans everywhere tried to gloss their brute end with prettiness. It reminded him of a Buddha statue he had seen many decades ago. Red Guards had toppled it and he had stood on its shoulders and smashed that composed face away with a sledgehammer. He'd felt good about it at the time, and sour ever since.

The peasant stood close. 'Then this is a shrine to the god of the dead.'

'He'll look after us as well as anyone else. Maybe better.'

'There are ghosts. Let's go.'

The headlights of a passing car flashed across the angel, illuminating spots of lichen on her cheek and the chiselled feathers of her wings. Jian glimpsed a tinted windscreen, a yellow roof and a gaudy fire design above a rear wheel arch. An ache tweaked his hip and he remembered how that vehicle had smacked him. He grabbed the peasant's shoulder and tugged him behind the grave and hissed, 'That's him. That's Black Fort.'

65

Jian ran to his car and started the engine. But the peasant was still crossing the graveyard, scurrying left and right. It was like watching a rat navigate a maze. The idiot didn't want to step on any tombs. He got to the path and sprinted. As he scrambled in, Jian accelerated hard and cursed him. The peasant lurched, the passenger door swung onto his leg, and he cried out in pain.

The road was narrow and winding, so Black Fort should not be too far ahead. Jian bent low over the wheel. He swung the car round a corner, the wheel clipped the verge, and the door slammed shut. The peasant rubbed his shin and, with his other hand, braced against the dashboard.

They passed pretty houses decorated with hanging baskets. Low walls of red brick lined the road and behind them great blooms flourished in gardens.

At the next corner he thought he saw a flash of a yellow roof, some two hundred metres up ahead. The gun, where was the gun? In his waistband. And the spray was in his pcoket. The rest of his weapons were in the golf bag on the back seat. It was a pity he was not in a larger vehicle that could ram and crush. He felt his armpits prickling and licked his lips. His fatigue had vanished.

The road widened as they came into the village. They passed a red booth and a stone sculpture on a lawn and came to a duck pond. On a lane just beyond it, a brake light winked. Jian followed. The hedge was thick and high and he could not see far. His enemy might be just around the next corner. But when he turned the car into a straight that cant-ed uphill, there was no sign. He squinted for the gleam of moonlight on metal and squirmed in agitation. It would be very annoying to lose the man now.

Ding Ming was sitting on his hands and rocking.

Jian said, 'Put your seat belt on. If there's contact, keep your head down.'

But when the car breasted the rise, Jian saw only trees and empty road. Perhaps the man had grown aware that he was being followed, and was lying in ambush. He stopped, turned off the engine and the radio, and wound the window down.

'What are you doing?'

'Be quiet. I'm listening. Stop breathing so hard.'

'Sorry.'

There. It was the throaty hum of a powerful engine in low gear, far to the left and some way behind. Jian reversed for a hundred metres or so and now he saw the turnoff. The entrance was partially obscured by a stunted tree, and easy to miss.

The hedges were so overgrown there that twigs buffeted the car. The tarmac was worn and spotted with clumps of grass. Not wanting to make too much noise, Jian kept the car at walking pace. His quarry would be far ahead now. Never mind, he would catch the man at his destination. He turned off the lights. The peasant shifted uneasily.

'What's that?'

An unsurfaced track wound away.

'This might be it.'

Jian stopped the car.

'Stay here.'

He got out, closing the door softly. Branches stirred in the breeze and night creatures called. There was not a building in sight. They could be anywhere, any time. The thought brought a flash of identification with a remembered figure from a TV drama – a disgraced mandarin, his pigtail shorn and his robes of office stripped away, tramping in lonely exile through the void beyond the Great Wall.

A sign lay in the verge. Two short words were burned onto rotting wood. He gestured for the peasant to come out and have a look, motioning him to be quiet.

'This is the place,' whispered Ding Ming. 'The farm of hope.'

'Get back in the car and keep quiet.'

He reversed and eased the car onto the verge, against the hedge. He had time now, he must prepare himself. He clambered into the back seat and filled the two glass bottles he'd bought at the service station with petrol from the can. They were a nice shape – good for throwing. He tore the polystryrene cups to shreds and dropped those in.

The peasant watched in the rearview mirror. 'Why the plastic?'

'Makes it stick like napalm.'

A sulky little arsonist had told him that trick. Bright lad, but he wouldn't stop setting fire to public buildings. They'd had to put him away in the end.

Jian tore two strips off his shirt, soaked them in petrol and jammed them in the end of the bottles. He hadn't made a petrol bomb since he was a Red Guard, but you didn't lose the knack. They stank, and he reminded himself to leave it a while before having a cigarette.

It was good that his hands weren't shaking. He didn't feel ready, but he knew from experience that you never felt ready. You just had to know what you had to do and maintain enough presence of mind to do it. He clipped the police utility belt on. The two gas sprays went in there, and the handcuffs and the torch and the extendable baton. He took a hammer from the toolkit and secured it in the belt. He wrapped the petrol bombs in his shirt so that the glass did not clink, and put them in a plastic bag from the service station.

He became aware of squeaking plastic. The peasant was rocking harder. He put a hand on his shoulder.

'Hide. When I'm sure I've killed them all, I'll come back to the car and shout your name.'

'What if you get killed?'

'Go to the temple. Maybe they'll help. Or the police. They're not as bad as you've been led to believe.'

He opened the door.

'Wait. Look at the time. Wait one minute, please.'

The peasant was pointing at the dashboard clock. Blue figures said four four four – *si si si* – it sounded like death, death, death. 'It's an unlucky time. Wait a minute.'

Jian got out. Was it his imagination, or did the breeze carry just a tang of the sea? His body was stiff from all the driving, but he supposed it would soon loosen. He hoped his knees would hold up.

'Don't kill anyone. Please. Take me back.'

'I'll do my best to stay alive.'

The peasant opened the passenger door. His face was damp with sweat or tears. 'You said you wanted to be a good policeman. That isn't just killing criminals. You kidnapped me, so you should get me back.'

Jian took him by the neck.

'If I think you're going to go and warn him, I'll kill you now.'

'No, no – not at all.'

'Go and hide.'

He watched the peasant scuttle forlornly away. He rubbed earth on his face and over the hammer, so that they didn't shine, and put the hooded top over his football shirt and pulled the hood up. He mumbled 'surmount every difficulty to win victory', and set off down the track.

(66

Jian advanced along the verge, bending low to minimise his silhouette. Grass swished and dew dampened his trousers. As his night vision grew sharper, he made out flowers and berries. Moonlight filtered through overhanging trees and dappled the track. The muddy surface had been recently churned by thick-wheeled, heavy vehicles. A black shadow hurtled past his ear and he ducked. It was nothing, merely a bat, and he ordered himself to be calm.

His sleeve caught on a thorny branch and he stopped to pull it loose. He was pleased to discover no mental snags to his progress. But he was a little detached, an observer of himself. He tried to put thought away and concentrate on sensation. Leaves rustling in the breeze, his rapid breath and heartbeat, the pressure of plastic handles on the pads of his fingers. He peered round a clump of thistles and considered a dilapidated farmyard. Black Fort's car was parked before a two-storey house. Two lights were on downstairs, and one up.

He stepped carefully over rubble to a tumbledown barn. He crept past a corrugated-iron sheet blocking off an entrance and he kept his mind busy estimating distances to and between yard, car and house. At least there did not seem to be a dog – it would have barked by now.

He skulked to the house and peeked in a window. A yellowing net curtain hung with its ragged edge a few centimetres above the sill. A bare bulb illuminated a tatty kitchen. The floor tiles were peeling or loose and the surfaces splotched with mould. The only signs that it was not disused were the fridge and portable hotplate, and dirty cups and bowls beside the sink.

The windowframe was speckled with woodworm. It would split easily, but make a lot of noise in the process. The windows were not double-glazed, so he could hurl a petrol bomb in without worrying about it bouncing back or breaking on the window.

The front door creaked open. Jian flattened himself against the wall. He was completely exposed. He put his bag down and slid his hand around the cold gun. Had they heard him?

A torch beam wavered over the yard, across the yellow car, a heap of rusty poles, a stack of tyres. It found the sheet of corrugated iron and held there. Two men strolled out. Jian recognised a ponytail and a bristling flat-top. He had seen these men outside the Floating Lotus restaurant – they were Black Fort's henchmen. The bigger man, flat-top, held the torch. He yawned and covered his mouth with his hand while his companion tugged the metal aside. They went into the barn.

This was a good chance. Jian stepped towards the dark entrance. The gun in his pocket was reassuringly hard and heavy. If things went wrong he could show it to frighten them. It was easy to be quiet on the concrete but he watched his step for puddles and loose stones.

Light flashed round inside the barn. Standing at the side with the hammer raised, he thought about how he'd do it. He'd take the bigger one first, then catch the second before he could run. It would be tricky, and these things came down to luck, but it was possible: they'd have no night vision because of the torch and after the first strike the second man would freeze. He just had to make a good first strike.

His heart was pounding and he was gripping the hammer so hard that he felt it in the tendons on the back of his hand. The contradiction between the proletariat and the bourgeoisie is resolved by the method of socialist revolution. The unbidden words trilled. He heard scraping, footfalls, the men chattering in Cantonese. The hammer was shaking and he willed them to come out, just come out. The contradiction between the working class and the peasant class in socialist society is resolved by the method of collectivisation.

The men came, dragging a slight and skinny girl. Her ankles were tied with a rope that forced her to take mincing little steps. Wails of complaint were muffled by a gag. A length of electric cable bound her wrists and the bigger man was pulling her along the way you'd lead a donkey. He held the torch and, as he yanked the girl, the light played over the house. The second man guided her by tugging her hair. They moved fast and the big man was already too far ahead.

Jian swung the hammer at the back of the second man's head and caught it where the skull joins the neck, beneath the band of his ponytail, and there was a crack and he went down. His hand was still holding the hair of the girl and he dragged her down. Now she was between Jian and his new target. The man let go of the rope and ran for the house and torchlight swung wildly.

Jian shoved the girl out of the way and drew his gun. But his target made the front door and slammed it shut. He cursed and put a hand on the back of the felled man's neck, behind the comma of black hair. A mental picture came of the last time he had seen him – staggering drunkenly with his friend's arm round his shoulder, his cheeks red and his mouth hanging open. Now his spine was cracked and he was dead. This was an ugly business.

The girl was shuffling away. He caught up and took her by the elbow. He swept bedraggled hair out of her face. She was Chinese, only young, with small frightened eyes. He tugged her gag down and held her head level with a hand on her chin and said, 'How many of them are there?'

She looked at him blankly and he worried that perhaps she did not speak Mandarin or was insensible. Her face was filthy except below the eyes, where tears had washed it. Her cheek was livid with bruises.

'They said they were going to break us.'

'How many?'

'I don't know.' She began to sob. 'Have you come to save us?'

'No. Run away.'

Jian let her go and turned his attention to the house. Surprise had been his only advantage and he had squandered it. They knew the ground and perhaps they had weapons. He had to act while they were still shaken.

He had to concentrate. First, where to put the hammer while he lit the bombs. He clamped it between his teeth and tasted mud and blood. The lighter, where was that? In his pocket. Now get it to light. It seemed smaller than he remembered, his fingers bigger and clumsier. The flint sparked twice, and on the third attempt a ghost of flame appeared.

He picked up a petrol bomb and lit the soaking rag. His instinct was just to get the thing away but he fought that, took aim, and hurled it as hard as he could. It revolved in the air and he saw its looping path as a retinal streak. The kitchen window smashed and the bottle shattered against the far wall. With a sucking sound, a fire whumped into being, and heat pressed a moment on his eyebrows. Now that it was going on he was glad. He stepped back and planted his feet wider to throw the second bottle. It went through the other downstairs window and flame blossomed.

Stepping forward he held his arm up to shield his face. Fire tendrils jumped and snatched and a flurry rushed up the curtains. A crackling sound, and the house shimmered in the heat.

The door was thrown open, and the man with a flat-top haircut ran out, his head bent low and his arms raised high. Screeching, he turned on the spot and beat at the flames flickering round his shoulders and down his back. Jian smacked him with the hammer and he fell and was still as fire played over him.

Movement glimpsed in his peripheral vision made him look up. A figure stood in an upstairs window. A pale face was framed by black hair parted in the middle, and lit from below by the gentle glow of a candle, which accentuated the elegant cut of the jaw and the high cheekbones.

Jian gaped at that silent, motionless form, more familiar than his own reflection. He felt as if he had been punched in the stomach and staggered back.

'Wei Wei?'

The features did not add up to an expression, her face was as vacant as those of the statues in that temple. It wavered in the heat haze. The big dark eyes were giving nothing away. Jian called again to the image of his daughter.

'Wei Wei?'

But the face retreated into darkness.

SNAKEHEAD

67

When Wei Wei walked into the Floating Lotus and asked about the job advertised in the window, she knew that she would get it. She was not sure, though, that she wanted it. She told herself that the discipline would allow her monkishly to discover a new aspect of herself and, thus romanticised, it did not seem so bad, at least for the first couple of weeks.

Bending to clear the plate of a solitary Chinese diner, she felt a hand slide across her thigh. She slapped him on the cheek. He did not seem disconcerted, but held a hand up in obviously unfelt apology. Only now did she notice the birthmark under his lip, the jade jewellery, the attractively dishevelled hair. Actually this guy was quite good-looking. When he said he was sorry, he was smiling, and the toothpick he was chewing rose suggestively.

He left her a twenty-quid tip. She was not impressed, she thought it vulgar. She palmed the note and replaced it with coins. That was one skill, at least, that the Moping Locust had taught her.

When she finished work, this guy was waiting by a flashy yellow car parked across the road. He got out and addressed her in English.

'What are you doing?'

'I'm getting a cab.'

'Would you like to go out?'

'Do you have nothing better to do than hassle girls?'

'I don't do it often – you should be flattered.'

'I'm not, and I'm not cheap enough to be bought.'

She felt his eyes on her as she walked briskly away, and resisted the urge to look back.

At the house she ate her takeout in the dingy kitchen. Someone had left textbooks on the table. Feeling a guilty twinge, she moved them out of her eyeline. Dropping out of college had not been a conscious decision, she had just stopped attending. Back home, as a student of English, she had excelled – it was the first requirement of the world she wanted in on, so she had worked hard. But Tourism and Leisure? It seemed commonplace, marginal. The idea of opening a tourist agency had been little more than a whim and it had evaporated as soon as hard graft was required. The hospitality industry seemed, on closer examination, to be all tedious practicality and distasteful servility. She knew she didn't have the temperament for it.

She flipped through a fashion magazine. It was full of promise. 'Be all you can be, discover the new you' – even the ad copy seemed to speak to her. This glossy world was what she wanted. She had no idea how to get there, though. She had sloughed off her unwanted identity – the police-man's girl from the cold backwater – like an old skin, but no new one had grown.

Song came in. Wei Wei supposed they ought to share a bond, being the only Chinese girls in the house, but she found her housemate haughty and dull. Her white boy-friend was with her. Annoyingly, he was quite presentable. She was pretty sure he was called Paul. They were always watching TV curled up together on the couch, in a state of what looked like comfortable mutual boredom. Now they were making cocoa. Just for something to say, Wei Wei complained about how cold her food was.

Song said, in Chinese, 'Why don't you heat it in the microwave?'

'Oh yes, I'll do that.'

It was typical. The girl was always offering advice, and Wei Wei sensed a familiar subtext – You're just a hick, I'm a proper city woman.

'Not that one. You press this button here.'

'I know,' said Wei Wei.

Paul was considering the magazine. 'She is far too skinny.' He looked at Wei Wei as he said, 'I like curvier girls.'

'Nice dress,' said Song.

Wei Wei said, in English, 'It's pleasantly understated.'

'Huh?'

'It means simple and uncomplicated.'

'Not showy,' said Paul. 'Just elegant and sexy.'

'Exactly.'

'And ridiculously expensive,' said Song. She took the drinks out and the boyfriend said he would follow her up in a minute, he was just going to root round for some biscuits.

Wei Wei watched her food rotate in the microwave, drumming her fingers. 'Root is a verb?'

He put a hand on her arm and whispered, 'I'm crazy about you.' The hand moved to her shoulder. She consciously emptied her face of expression as he blundered on. 'The way you move, the way you look in that nightdress, how you tip your head when you're thinking.' His fingers touched her cheek. 'I totally agree with what you say, about living like an artist. Living in the moment.' She was backed against the counter, there was nowhere to retreat to. 'Well?' he said. 'What do you think about that?'

The microwave pinged.

'Excuse me. Dinner.'

He moved in to kiss her. His greedy tongue reminded her of a cow's. Two in one day – it was unprecedented. But neither, of course, was suitable. His chin was stubbly and he had an offputting odour. She thought of kisses as having a colour – she'd read it in a book – and this one was definitely pale green.

She grew aware of movement in her peripheral vision, then squealed as she was drenched with cocoa. A cup clattered to the floor. Song had returned, and caught them, and now, having hurled her drink, was standing with her knees together, her face crinkling. Wei Wei brandished her magazine, swatting at the air with the confused idea that this troubling couple could be made to disappear like wasps.

Song's expression hardened and she pointed an accusing finger at her boyfriend. To avoid a tedious scene, Wei Wei ran to her room and propped her table against the door. It wasn't as if she asked for this, she reflected, it was just the sort of thing that seemed to happen to her. She was still hungry but thought it best to avoid the kitchen for the time being, so she skinned up a joint and watched a recording of 'EastEnders' on her little television. She liked that there were all these strong women who castigated wavering menfolk, and hoped that Song was giving Paul a similar hard time.

But when she came down for breakfast the next morning to closed, hostile faces, she discovered that a picture of the drama in which she was cast as a rapacious harridan had been circulated and accepted. She was informed with a note, written in red capitals, and signed by all her housemates, that she had been 'sent to Coventry'. What a phrase. It seemed that English, just like Chinese, concealed unpleasantness with quirky euphemism. Well, she told herself, it wasn't as if she spoke to those dullards anyway.

Her what-the-hell defiance lasted the restaurant's evening rush, but as her shift wore on she felt her spirits sag. Her qipao dress was constricting, the customers banal, the tips measly. Perhaps recent experiences had left her more sensitive to certain signals, but it occurred to her that she really didn't like the way twinkly-eyed old Mister Li watched her. Really, it was too much. This was not the sort of place a girl might be discovered by a model scout or acting agent. She was just wasting her time. Skulking in the ladies – it was the the only opportunity to sit down – she expressed her feelings by writing 'My boss is a colour wolf' in the grouting between wall tiles. She was dull, the job was dull, she was not being all she could be, and had no idea how to start discovering the new her.

So she was almost pleased when, leaving the restaurant, she saw the yellow car again. The Chinese guy leaned against it with one ankle tucked behind the other and hands behind his back.

'Why didn't you come in?'

'I wasn't hungry.'

'Then your trip is wasted. You're not my type.'

He gave her a red rose. It was not the usual cheap article guys fobbed you off with, but the real deal, a full bloom with a heady scent. 'Thanks. Not sure what to do with it, though.'

'Keep it by your bed.'

'Maybe in the bathroom. Goodnight.'

'At least tell me your name, beautiful stranger.'

'You can keep calling me that.'

She walked away. She heard footsteps behind her and planned her next move. It was hard to strike the right balance, in English, between cutting and flirtatious. Perhaps she should say 'Can't you take a hint?', or just 'What is it now?' as if he were a pesky puppy.

When her pursuer was right behind her, she swivelled on one heel, affecting weary resignation with head cocked to one side. But it wasn't the handsome Chinese man. It was creepy Paul. He looked broody and furtive.

'How did you find out where I work?'

'You left a flyer. Me and Song split up. So we can go out.'

'I don't think so.'

'What?'

'I don't want to.'

'Hey, you can't just—'

'Yes, I can.'

He gripped her elbow and squeezed and she smelled booze on him. She wriggled. 'Let go.'

'Yesterday you wanted to—'

Paul jerked as he was grabbed from behind. His arms flailed as he was twirled round. The Chinese guy punched him with the base of an open hand and Paul fell, clutching his face. The Chinese guy cracked him with an elbow. She grabbed his arm and placed herself in his eye line. His expression was impassive, like that of a man solving a problem.

'Don't. Please don't. Stop it.'

The guy jabbed a heel into Paul's foot.

'What do you think you're doing?'

He stepped back and ran his hands through her hair. They watched Paul stagger away. She felt giddy. Something dark in her had liked what she had seen and she was angry about it.

'My name's Black Fort. Come for a drink.'

'I'm going to see that he's alright.'

'Tomorrow, then.'

After that he picked her up most nights. He took her to hotels, which was a lot better than going home. It turned out he was a hoodlum, with a gang and dreams of unlimited wealth and respect. His unsuitability was exciting, it made her feel like a tragic heroine. Every song now seemed addressed to her. Nothing was banal any more. Perhaps, after all her false starts, her life here really was beginning.

(68

Wei Wei cowered, her legs drawn under her, arms behind her back, ankles tied with flex. Her eyes were bright and damp. She said, 'No, please, no,' over and over again.

Black Fort pointed a camera phone at her and she slid back, propelling herself along the concrete floor with bare feet, until she was pressed against a brick wall.

'No, please.'

Six Days grabbed a hank of hair and yanked her head back. He wore baggy black clothes, a scarf across his face, a woolly hat pulled down low over his forehead and wraparound plastic sunglasses over his eyes. A knife blade gleamed.

Her eyes widened. She thought to herself, this is it, I'm going to die, I'm going to die and there's nothing I can do about it. He let go and hair flopped across her face.

'No, please. No.' A tear ran down her cheek. A mental voice screeched, I don't want to die, I don't want to die. Six Days leaned over and down, and with a rapid underhand motion drove the knife a dozen or so times into her torso.

Wei Wei's mouth opened and closed and a shudder passed across her. She slumped and blood pooled rapidly beneath her. She felt Black Fort's warm breath on her cheek as he brought the camera right down to her face.

She thought, this is it, I'm going now, I'm dying. Nothingness seemed to close in. Her eyes unfocused. The blur that was Black Fort drew away and snapped the phone closed. It was over.

She sat up and said, 'Cut!' and the brisk syllable helped banish that grim persona. It was an uncomfortable place she had inhabited and she was disorientated as she came back into herself. She stretched and shook briskly like a cat coming out of water.

She untied her ankles and removed the tape holding the blood bag to her stomach. A fish hook snagged in the bag was attached by fishing line to her thumb. When, out of shot, she'd jerked her hand, the hook had ruptured the bag and fake blood had spurted in satisfactory, gory fashion.

That had been her idea, as had the extra lights and the two rehearsals – the gang had proved quite clueless in this regard. She'd bought the stage knife from a theatrical supplies website and made the blood with food colouring and corn syrup.

She dabbed fake blood off her chin with a tissue, and wiped off the smears of eye shadow that had made a convincing bruise.

Black Fort replayed the film. Its purpose was, she knew, a mean trick, but that was possible to overlook when the challenge of it seemed so delicious and fitting to her talents.

Watching herself expire, she felt pride in a thoroughly professional piece of work. Dying convincingly was a difficult trick. She clapped to show her approval and gasped at sudden pain. She had forgotten about the fish hook and it had slid into the flesh of her palm.

Black Fort teased it out, but the barb widened the wound and it was alarming how much she was bleeding. Six Days was sent to buy plasters.

She began to feel woozy and was aware that her face was turning pale. She felt annoyed with herself for this weakness – she wanted very much to be tough.

Black Fort said, 'Hold your hand in the air. Sit down.'

She said, 'Rub the blood on the phone.'

'You're a natural.' He kissed her. 'Come on, baby. Be brave. Don't look at it. It's okay. I'm here. It's okay.'

(69

For the deception to work, Wei Wei had to leave town. She was not sorry. Black Fort helped her move out when all her flatmates were at college. He drove her to Liverpool and put her up in a bedsit. It was smaller than she had been led to believe. He assured her that it was only temporary, and soon they would be living together in a mansion. They spent a torrid two weeks christening it, then, for three weeks, he didn't visit once, and was evasive when she called. It was hardly satisfactory.

He'd bought her a new mobile – black, boysy, with a wealth of pointless functions. She rang her father.

'How's life?' he asked.

'Interesting.'

'How's your course?'

'Okay, not bad.'

'What sort of marks are you getting?'

'Around sixty-five percent.'

'Try for seventy. How is the weather?'

'It's warmer now and the sun is shining at last.'

'What did you eat this week?'

'Yesterday I had spaghetti.'

'Was it good?'

'It was okay. Sorry, Father. Someone else is calling. Hang on a moment.' She put him on hold.

'Hey, babe.'

'I'm talking to my dad. In China. Are you coming round? I don't see you at all these days.'

'I'll see if I can get away. I'm super-busy. What are you wearing?'

'I'm not wearing anything. I'm lying in bed touching myself, and I'm not wearing anything. Are you coming round or not?'

'Stay like that and for sure I'm coming round.'

'I'm putting you on hold.'

'I don't hold. Later, babe.'

She returned to the first call, and to her native tongue.

'Sorry, that was my classmate. She wanted some home-work.'

'Where are you now?'

'I'm in college. I have a lecture in a minute.'

'Study hard and success is assured.'

Quoting the Chairman at her again, though maybe the phrases were so ingrained he never even noticed he was doing it. She said, 'I'd better say goodbye.'

'Goodbye.'

'Same time next week.'

She discovered she'd been twisting the sheets and smoothed them down. Really, she should have got up before ringing her dad – it was weird to talk to him in her night dress. She didn't like lying to him, and told herself, as she did every time, that it was just until she found her feet. She hoped it would not colour her day, and promised herself that, no, today would be a phoenix day.

Breakfast was instant coffee and a Marlboro Light. What a funny word 'bedsit' was – but not inappropriate, as the only chair was covered in clothes and she did, indeed, sit on the bed. More clothes hung on hangers on the cupboard door and windowsill. Dirty laundry was on the floor, and that was the extent of her housework system.

She supposed she should clean up and wash clothes, but they weren't phoenix-day things. No, she would take a bus into town and explore. Chancing down alleyways, she'd discover hidden gardens and quaint locals sitting out in traditional dress.

But Liverpool city centre looked just like Leeds. She felt nostalgic for the excitement of her first few months away, when everything was new and interesting. She tried wandering down an alleyway but it smelled of piss, and a beggar leered at her. The people of Liverpool exhibited no distinctive customs beyond speaking at high volume in a harsh vernacular.

She went home to prepare for her man's arrival, and tried to invoke him by thinking seriously about his body, the way, she imagined, a Buddhist meditates on a crystal. Tattoo, birthmark, hairless chest, a match in a lopsided smile. She built him in her mind, but as soon as the figure was perfect it evaporated, so she snuffled in the pillow for the scent of his hair gel. She wrote him an email on her laptop – just 'Hello, thinking of you' – and in a final act of extravagant devotion that only she would ever know, changed her Hotmail password to 'blackfort'.

The tingle of expectation made it impossible to settle, so she flipped through her magazines. These had taught her many new words, such as 'culottes', 'orgasm', 'anorexia' and 'gigolo', and now she looked up 'compatibility' and 'nit-pick'. But by midnight there was still no sign of him. It was very exasperating. She rolled a joint and lay down as the buzz took her. She liked being stoned, that feeling of peace and light on a high plateau, but, increasingly these days, getting there was a bumpy ride through paranoia foothills.

In the abstract, her situation was interesting, glamorous – the bad boy, the exotic foreign land, love in a dangerous world – but in reality this sitting around 'twiddling her thumbs' was completely unacceptable. It didn't help that the flat he'd put her up in was so mean, she could hardly get from bed to shower without banging her shin.

Thoughts sparked, spiralled and fizzled out, and underlying all was a sour note of loneliness and loss. 'Kitchenette', what a funny word. So the tiny washroom should be a 'bathroomette' and she, right now, felt like a 'girlette' living a 'lifette'. This was no phoenix day. It had curdled into yet another dog day.

Her thoughts drifted to her father. He had a mistress parked in a flat, just like this. She'd seen the girl in the passenger seat of a squad car, a country lass with stubby fingers and a guileless smile, and when she'd asked about her, he'd said yes, she was his girl and he looked after her. Perhaps she, too, killed time all day. Of course that had been years ago – he'd probably finished with her by now, taken up with another one. Or two, maybe. Perhaps he had them in flats all over town, one for every occasion.

She sat up so fast it made her dizzy. Now it made sense. Why her man was absent, evasive, distracted. Tremors of alarm spread from her stomach. She laughed at herself for being too dumb to have noticed what was right in front of her. He had another woman.

She looked up an article – 'Love emergency! What to do when your man cheats'. She should confront him, apparently, and give him a hard time about it. She certainly should not ask herself, 'Where did I go wrong?'

She asked herself where she went wrong. Was she too assertive, too docile, too simple, too complicated? Was she, when it came down to it, just too naïve and unsophisticated? The need to know more, to be certain, gnawed.

The entry system trilled. She was totally unprepared, stoned and confused, no make-up on and the place a mess. She was desperate to please him, hating and loving him, and not really wanting to see him. Worried it would all show on her face, she buzzed him in, then began making a pile of her dirty laundry.

Black Fort kissed her cheek, barged past, fell on the bed, lit a cigarette and started taking off his clothes. He'd been drinking.

'It's late.' She wanted to express her dissatisfaction but could not bring herself to confront him. It was on the tip of her tongue – Is there someone else? You can tell me. But she said, 'You haven't been round for so long.'

'Work is insane.'

'Why?'

He never talked about work and she'd been happy not to ask. Now, when she needed to know everything, it was too late, the rules were set.

'Don't worry your pretty head. I don't want you getting frown lines.'

'You are the most secretive man I ever met.'

'It's for your own protection.'

'That is such an old line.'

He started pawing at her clothes.

'Really, what have you been doing?'

'I robbed a bank and killed a policeman. Then, in the afternoon...'

'Please.'

'I run the club. I make sure people get paid on time. I make sure other people pay me on time. Today I did accounts.'

He had described his gambling club so well, he imagined that she knew it. The metal door, then the smoky room with the fantail table. A croupier made a pile of counters, then swiped them away in groups of four, and punters bet on how many would remain at the end – none, one, two or three. And that was all there was to it – an arid, male environment.

Again, she wanted to ask, Is there someone else? but what she said was, 'I think I should get a job. I'm tired of doing nothing.'

'No girl of mine needs to work.' No girl of mine? Implying she was one of several? 'Very soon, I'll move you into a nicer place. I promise.' He stroked her neck. 'You talked to your dad today, huh? That always puts you in a bad mood.'

'That's true.'

'He kill any bad guys lately?'

'He shuffles paper and goes to banquets.'

'Could I take him in a fight? If he came over to defend your honour?' He tickled her.

'Leave him out of it. Tomorrow is four months from when we first met. So what I would like is for us to go out and have a...' – her eyes went up to the tatty lampshade as she recalled the English phrase – 'slap up do.'

'Not tomorrow. I'm taking my uncle to the races. We'll celebrate the week after, okay? The four months anniversary of when we first... you know...'

The uncle again. She had never met him, or any of Black Fort's family, about whom he would give no details, and wondered now if they were nothing more than a collection of knee-jerk excuses.

He started kissing her belly. She would have liked a little more getting to know you, but the feel of his face on her was reassurance that he was still, at least, interested.

She ran a finger along his dragon tattoo, from the bewhiskered, boggle-eyed head on his shoulder to the scaly tail at his hip. He practised wing chun and his torso was toned and taut. How hard and soft his body was. It was the perennial fascination of men.

'Why don't you get a tattoo? Just here on your thigh. A dragon to match mine. A dragon for a dragon queen.'

'I'm a princess, not a queen. And it's a phoenix for a girl.'

There was a great deal to like about him. His birthmark, for example. He flinched when she touched it. The fact that he was sensitive about it – she liked that, too. He was a whole other country, she an excited tourist.

Her breathing settled. If only it could be like this all the time, to be the absolute focus of attention. When she was with him she felt whole and protected, but she had to have him all to herself.

Later, while he slept, she took his clothes into the bathroom, where the light was better. Squatting in the shower stall she went over them minutely, all the time telling herself how silly she was being. Under his shirt cuff she found a long yellow hair, black at the root. There was a smudge of lipstick on his boxer shorts.

She felt a moment's relief – she was not going nuts, her 'female intuition' was 'spot on'. She stared hard at the hair, trying to picture its owner, and a sense of grief came, black and overwhelming.

His wallet was on the bedside table. Riffling through it she found, as well as a few hundred quid in notes, a couple of one Euro coins. In the back pocket of his jeans she discovered the stub of a boarding pass – a flight from Rotterdam, dated today. So he had lied to her – easily, naturally. What had he been doing in Europe?

He moaned and rolled over and his arm flopped onto her pillow. Curse him for lying and for being in her head so much. A mania had descended that could only be satisfied with more evidence. She went back through everything, worried that her rapid breathing would wake him but unable to stop.

Tucked behind his debit card was a business card for his gambling club – lips, cocktail glass, characters. Written on the back in a girlish scrawl, in capitals, was an address:

Hope Farm, near a place called South Creake. And under that a time, 4pm, and a date – tomorrow – when he had said he was going out with his uncle. And at the bottom were the words, 'DON'T BE LATE! K.'

Some uncle. She imagined her rival, Miss K – a fresh-faced country girl in a headscarf, singing as she scattered chicken feed. She decided she was damn well going to find out what was going on and put a stop to it. She took a picture of the address on her phone, wincing as it clicked. He rolled over but didn't wake.

(70

When Black Fort got up, with his usual brisk efficiency, at ten, Wei Wei pretended to be asleep, and huddled under the duvet. He kissed her goodbye – how could he still be so tender? – and she waited for the door to slam.

It was the work of a few minutes in an internet café to find out where South Creake was, book a bus ticket to the nearest city, King's Lynn, check the timetable of local buses and to print out a map of the village and surroundings.

She called her father.

'Did you finish the accounts?'

'Is anything wrong?'

'It's about my course.'

'What about your course?'

'I wasn't... I wasn't telling the truth.'

She wanted to say, I've made a bit of a mess of things, I dropped out, now I'm this hood's moll, which isn't as exciting as I thought it would be, and I think he's cheating on me.

'My... marks have gone down a bit. Fifty percent.'

'That's not so bad. How has the weather been?'

'It's warmer – the sun is shining.'

She gathered her forces to try again to surmount the formidable barrier of habit.

'Dad?'

'What is it?'

'I feel bad.'

A silence stretched. She wished she could see his face.

'You stick in there. A few bad marks is nothing. The important thing is to keep your head down and work hard. Don't let anything stop you.'

He was slurring his words, and she could hear laughter and conversation in the background. Perhaps it was not a good time.

'I'm just... I'm having a bad day today.'

She was floundering in unfamiliar territory and realised it was distressing him as well.

'Application is not easy. You have to be strong. You have to be determined.'

'I'm not sure what I should do. Maybe I should just let things go on the way they are or try to change them.'

'Always try to make things better. Always push for improvement.'

He sounded like the Party Commissar off some crappy old film, spouting slogans. Her patience left her, she didn't want to be thrashing around in this murk, causing discomfort.

She said, 'For breakfast I had a chicken sandwich.'

'How was that?'

'Too dry. I miss steamed buns.'

'I'm sure bread is very good for you.'

'I'll say goodbye. Thank you for... I'll say goodbye.'

'Goodbye.'

She pressed 'end call'. She felt stupid – all she had done was worry him. It was an embarrassing incident that would never be mentioned. She resolved, next time they talked, to be relentlessly upbeat.

She squeezed her eyes closed so that when she opened them the last few minutes would have gone away. It struck her that one of her father's characteristic gestures – the hand drawn over the screwed-up face – had the same purpose. She opened her eyes and, yes, it was gone. She was elsewhere.

She'd get there just after four and catch them in the act. She composed a mental diorama – the wronged girlfriend at the centre, her anger magnificent, the contrite boyfriend wilting before her. The other woman – cheap slut, painted hussy – was banished to the shadowy edge. Like the women on the television, she would point and say, 'You are out of order!' It was such an exciting image that her face flushed.

(71

As the local bus wound through rural Norfolk, Wei Wei reflected that all this fresh air and nature would be invigorating in other circumstances. She had not realised that England could manage such bucolic charm. South Creake was so twee it made her want to laugh. She could imagine the cottage where Black Fort's lover lived, with ivy climbing the walls and flowers in baskets hanging from the porch.

According to her googlemap, she had to walk past the duck pond, turn left and there would find a turnoff that led up Bloodgate Hill. But she couldn't find the turnoff, so she asked at the only shop, a studio selling artistic weather vanes. The sculptor said he'd ask his cleaning lady, who told her that the track didn't lead anywhere since they'd built the new road, that Bloodgate Hill was windswept and no use to anyone but birdwatchers, and finally that the overgrown track was just past the duck pond.

Heading up the hill, the landscape changed into one more fitting her mood. Here were thick woods and empty fields and no sign of human habitation. It was all, she guessed, because of the wind whipping in from the coast, not so far away. Trees rustled and shook, and those atop the hill were bent and stunted by the pressure of that ceaseless agitation. She recalibrated her mental picture – the other woman was a gypsy, living in a cabin in a wood.

Perhaps there had been a mistake. Really, there was nothing here. It was almost four. A voice told her to go home, be reasonable, get sensible. She ignored it, searched the hedgerows for gaps, and found wheel ruts either side of a tummocky ridge. The track ran along a hedge, then curled and was swallowed by a wood.

In the hedge she found a rotted plank. She tugged it out, breaking the grasp of knotty tendrils and exposing worms and woodlice to the light. Two words had been burned onto it with a soldering iron, now just readable: 'HOPE FARM'. She tossed it aside. Right, then.

The track fell into the shade of tall trees and unkempt hedges. It led to a dilapidated farmyard. Wilderness seemed to be taking possession of the place. Weeds grew through cracks in the paving of the yard and rusted machinery lay half subsumed in tangles of foliage. Birds flitted about the gaping roof of a barn, and their cheeping, and the rustle of leaves in the wind, was the only sound.

Black Fort's flashy car was parked beside a dirty white van, before a tumbledown cottage. Certainly he was here, but this did not seem right at all. It occurred to her, for the first time, that she had got entirely the wrong idea. What girl would accept such a home? Only the wildest kind of wench. Perhaps the desolation added a frisson to their coupling.

She picked her way across the yard and peered in at a window, with hands shading her face, but she could see nothing beyond the drawn curtains. She heard a girlish moan of pleasure and froze. Indignation swelled, and her frustrations gathered, preparing for tumultuous outlet. Her heartbeat quickened and she was aware of blood thudding in her temples.

She tried the front door and it opened into a dingy corridor. Her senses were keen and she was quivering. Though impatient for the release of confrontation, she slowed and stepped carefully. She did not want to be heard, she wanted masochistically to catch them in the most explicit of acts.

She did not yet know what she would say, but was confident that the right words would come, at the right volume. Perhaps no words would be needed. From behind a closed door another groan came, and now the torment could be borne no longer. She wanted to break things. She shoved a door and stepped into a room.

Six or seven surprised faces turned to her. A lot of big men idled in a small space. Caterpillar and Six Days smoked on the sofa. A pall of smoke hung at head height. On top of a television with a shattered screen sat a laptop. Its display showed a busy profusion of flesh and straining faces.

A strangled sound came from Wei Wei's throat and she closed her mouth with an audible pop. An ashtray fell to the floor and a beer can clinked as it rolled. Everyone was now standing up.

A fat white man said, 'What the fuck?' The porn on the laptop continued, and a girl moaned, 'Oh, baby, that's so good.' Foaming beer dribbled off the table.

Black Fort grabbed her shoulders, span her round and rushed her out into the yard.

'What the hell are you doing?'

'I thought you had a girl here.'

'You looked through my stuff? What am I going to do with you? Get out of here.'

He raised his hand and she thought this is it, he's going to hit me, but all he did was gesture up the track.

She saw herself with his eyes, and she was pathetic. She sat, feeling tears well.

'Look at you. You're a mess.'

Yes, she was a mess. She'd been a mess for a long time and there was something wrong with her. She was worthless, he should have hit her, it was what she deserved.

'I'm so lonely.'

'Come on. Get up.'

It was embarrassing that she could think of nothing to do but cry, but she could not stop. Men came to the door, looked at her, then went back inside.

'Let's get you out of here.'

Black Fort helped her to her feet, and with a hand on her elbow steered her away. Her eyes were blurred, and the scene before her was a green mass. She noticed the way that sunlight coming between the leaves dappled the track. The sobbing fit was winding down in a trickle of sniffs and heaves. She stumbled and leaned against him, and the feel of his firm hands supporting her was great reassurance.

She said again, 'I thought you had a girl.'

'It's just you, babe. Mind your feet.'

She dried her eyes with her sleeves. She was relieved and ashamed and there was a surge of self-pity. Her mind-state of only a few minutes ago seemed bizarre – how could she have worked herself up like that?

'I just... I don't know what I'm doing here. I'm lost. I should have stayed at college. I feel like it's all a mess.'

'Hey, you're fine. You're doing well. You're having an adventure, aren't you? You're finding yourself. That's what you said you wanted, remember? This is you, finding yourself.'

'Can we have a talk?'

'Huh? Yeah sure. I'll come and visit soon. I promise.'

'Really promise?'

'Really.'

'Okay.' She sniffed and wiped her face. 'What's happening at four?'

'Business.'

'Is it that?'

A truck was rumbling down the track in low gear. Dust swirled behind it.

Black Fort said, 'Go on, get out. I'll call.'

He steered her onto the verge, out of the way, and she felt his eyes on her as she walked away. The haste with which she had been dismissed was disquieting. She turned to see his face again, hoping for an encouraging smile, but he was jogging back to the farmyard.

The men were coming out of the cottage. She ducked behind a tree to watch him join them. She did not like them. They were thuggish and frightening, and to see him among them, being matey and relaxed, was to see another side to him. Did he belong there, or with her? Perhaps, in a sense, there were rivals here, after all. She wanted to call him away. He was so much better than them. He had capabilities – for humour, for passion – that they surely did not.

The truck passed her. Now she found her relief tainted with indignation. So the other woman had been a ridiculous fantasy brought on by too much thinking and unhappiness, but the fact remained that he had lied to her. There was that whole matter with the uncle, and Rotterdam. Really, she did not like the way she had been sent so quickly away. There were still things that needed to be discussed. She was not in the wrong, he was not exonerated. She was going to demand some candour. She had half a mind to walk right back to the farm and start on him now.

She heard oaths, and looked up. The truck was parked in the yard and the men were gathered round the open back doors of the container. It was a curious scene, and she stepped closer and peered around a tree.

A man called, 'Hello? Hello? Oi. Get up!' and reached in to shake a limp arm.

Another said, 'Oh fuck, fuck, fuck.'

Black Fort said, 'This is a mess.'

'Some might be alright. We should get them down. Get a mirror – see if they're still breathing.'

Though all she could see of the men was the backs of their heads, their shock and consternation was obvious. Six Days was kicking the ground. Blue had his hands over his face.

'Look at their tongues,' said Kevin. 'Look at their bleeding fingers. They tried to claw their way out.'

Black Fort tugged at something, and it tumbled out of the container, hitting the ground with a dull crack.

He said, 'Fuck.'

In dismay the men retreated from the object, stepping slowly backwards as if being repelled by an invisible force, and now Wei Wei had a clear view. She blinked watery eyes and the scene sharpened into awful clarity.

An expression of bug-eyed terror was frozen on the waxy face of the man on the ground. A second body flopped over the edge of the container, arms dangling. Many more were strewn behind, limp and in awkward attitudes, like rag dolls. A woman lay with her skirt in disarray, exposing pale thighs. She clutched a child to her chest, and his T-shirt had ridden up over his head, and his skinny torso was arched in a way that looked subtly unnatural.

Wei Wei put one hand over her mouth, and with the other reached out to steady herself on the tree trunk. She couldn't stop looking but the meaning of what she was seeing was slow to penetrate. Perhaps, after all, one of the figures would get up and this obscenity would be refuted. She wanted to go and pull the child's T-shirt down and tidy the woman's skirt. She willed one of the men to go and do it, but they were still retreating.

Someone shouted, 'That girl. She saw.'

Many eyes considered her. She shrank back. A man stepped forwards. She turned and sprinted away.

72

Wei Wei ran blindly. She stumbled when she came onto the road and put her hand down, and the rasp of tarmac on her palm brought her to her senses. She looked back and could see no pursuit, only a bland view of trees trembling in the wind. She heard nothing over the din of her own blood and breath. Remembering that harsh voice, she forced herself on.

She ran all the way to the village. When she came to the pond she bent with her hand on a 'Ducks Crossing' sign, chest juddering as she gasped. Exertion had kept the images at bay, but they flooded back now – a limp hand with cracked fingernails, a dead head on concrete, lips stretched back from pale gums. She blinked them away. The village continued nestling snugly, being cute and clueless. The only movement in the landscape was a bus trundling along a lane. A harsh scream at her feet made her jerk in shock.

It was only a duck. It looked at her with beady eyes, then screeched again. More were approaching, geese too, and they took up the refrain, calling her stupid, calling her mad, telling her about the corpses up the road. She shouted at them to stop, then threw up into the rushes. Ducks hurried to investigate the spatters of vomit.

She dropped to her hands and knees and her fingers sank in cold mud. Those poor people. She imagined being curled up in total darkness with panic prickling as the air grows thinner. A feeling like your lungs being pinched, and that grip growing harder, and you bang on the metal walls for help, suck hard but no air comes, your mouth wide open with chest heaving and still no air, scratch at the metal and the sound echoes, rasping, your eyes bulging, lungs burning and still nothing to breathe. Get me out get me out get me out.

An instinct to hide joined a sense that she must punish herself. She crawled into the reed bed, the stiff stems crackling as she pushed them aside. Her hands splashed in murky water. Ducks waddled towards her, quacking away, patient, monstrous. This was ridiculous. Cruelly her distress had been robbed of dignity. It occurred to her to get out of the reeds, but she did not want views, she did not want to see the quaint village – the sight would be as mean as the ducks.

She was so alone. Everything had gone wrong. She couldn't be here any more. She had to be home. An image rose of her stolid and reassuring father, a man who knew what to do in a crisis. She fumbled out her mobile and called him with trembling fingers. The ducks mocked her as the phone rang and rang at its own unhurried, infuriating pace. Her breathing had still not settled and she cried out between gasps, '*Baba bang wo...* Daddy help me, please, help me. Pick up please, help me, pick up, daddy help me.'

Her quacking, she felt, was only adding to the general uproar. She was a duck, too, a stupid creature, lost far from shore.

'Daddy, help me, help me. Help.'

Her hand was wrenched back. She dropped the phone and it splashed into the water. Black Fort picked it up. He took the battery out and put it in his pocket. He held tissues out towards her.

'Look at you, you're filthy. We've got to clean you up.'

She hurried away, thrashing through the reeds, and he waded after her.

'Hey babe, there's nothing to be afraid of. Come on.'

His soft voice, so reasonable and persuasive, was comfortingly familiar. But something awful had happened and she wasn't sure if she really knew him any more.

'Babe, this isn't helping.'

She stumbled onto the village green. The bus was approaching. She waved at it.

He said, 'I'm sorry you freaked out. Let's sort this out. What do you think is going to happen? Come on. You're my girl. You're angry, you're confused – at least give me a chance to explain. Let me take you home. Come on.'

The bus stopped and the door opened. He stood by the war memorial, hands open, palm uppermost. She backed away.

'You're my girl. I'm your man. Talk to me.'

She crossed the road towards the bus.

'Where are you going to go in that? You don't even know where it's headed.'

He pointed at his car, parked by the pond.

'Come on, I'll take you home.' There was no hint of pleading or desperation in his voice or on his face. His tones had a numbing effect. He sounded so fair and practical. Was she just being silly again? The last time she had jumped to conclusions, she had made a dumb mistake.

The bus driver scowled at her. 'I can't sit around all day.'

Black Fort, strolling across the road towards her, called, 'You look a state. And look at me. I'm covered in shit. Let's clean up together. I got more tissues in the car. At least let me take you home.'

The bus driver said, 'How about you have your tiff on your own time?'

Black Fort said to her, 'Give me the chance to explain. Just a chance.' He held out a hand.

'You getting on, or not?' said the driver. His passengers looked at her with annoyance.

What did she think she was going to do – just head off into nowhere, on her own? She didn't have anywhere to go and she didn't have anyone else. He slid a match into his mouth. The familiar gesture served more than his words to sway her.

'Come on, babe.'

She grasped his hand and he squeezed gently. The bus door closed with a whoosh of compressed air and the bus lumbered off. She took his tissues and began to wipe her face as he led her away.

'Who were you calling?'

'My father.'

'Yeah, that would really help – get the Chinese police involved.' He pointed at her chin. 'You've missed a bit. Actually, you've missed a lot. Look at my shoes. They might be ruined. Have you got wet? I've got soggy feet.'

The ducks were waddling after her again. He shooed them away. 'They just want to get fed. I owe them a favour, though maybe I wouldn't have found you if it wasn't for their racket. I'll throw them some breadcrumbs tomorrow. You really scared me, you know. I thought you'd lost it.'

'I'm scared.'

'We'll talk about it when we're cleaner, okay?'

He opened the car door for her, and climbed into the driver's seat. She took the bottle of water out of the side door and rinsed it round her mouth to wash out the taste of vomit.

'You silly thing. It's fine. Everything's fine.'

He shook his head, as if at an errant child, then punched her in the face. Her head snapped against the side windscreen. Dazed, she tasted coppery blood in her mouth. Watery sick dribbled down her chin. She blinked and groaned, 'What?'

He slid behind her and got an arm around her neck and pulled her back. A man came out of the ditch and opened her door. He grabbed her arm and rolled up her sleeve. A hypodermic needle glimmered. Her eyes widened. The arm was pinned.

'Don't fight it,' hissed Black Fort.

His arm around her neck was choking her. Her feet lashed in the footwell. She felt a jab on the inside of her elbow, and she gasped and shuddered as a wave of numbness crashed over her and she filled up with white noise. Her heavy head drooped.

She was swimming in a drowsy dreamland. The vehicle was moving and she seemed to be flowing with it. Lights blossomed and swirled. Now he was talking on a mobile. The words seemed to drift towards her from a great distance.

'I've got the girl. Kevin, stop panicking — it's fine. Get the container in the barn but leave it on the flatbed. I'll straighten it with the snakeheads. They won't kick up a fuss, this shit happens all the time. Nobody is calling anything off. Everything is fine.'

It was all coming to her as if she were a mildly interested observer of herself. She knew she should be feeling something, but she didn't feel anything. Her body was made of hot jelly. It occurred to her that she had been probably been given heroin and she was pleased to have worked that out. The numbness was coming in waves, higher and higher, she would soon be subsumed. He kept barking into the phone.

'No, no, Kevin, you listen. We need an earth mover. And twenty bags of lime. From different suppliers, no big orders. Yes, a digger. No paperwork and you pay cash, see if you can blag it off a mate of a mate, have a story set, I don't know, you're putting in a patio or something. We rip up the ground behind the house, it won't take a couple of hours, chuck them in, lime it, done. It's a morning. In a couple of weeks, we concrete it over. No drama Kevin, it's fine. Tell the others, and don't let anyone leave.'

A wave took her and she knew she was not going to stay awake for the next one. She groaned.

He turned to her and started talking. She knew that he was talking to her because his eyes were looking at her. They were large eyes and a shade too pale. She had always liked that.

'You know something that could put me away for life. Fifteen, twenty counts of manslaughter. I can't have you holding that over me. Sorry, babe.'

He talked on, but she could no longer make out what he was saying. A comfortable stillness settled, then her senses dimmed to nothing.

73

Wei Wei woke. Her blackout had been a dreamless pit, and she had not yet fully crawled out of it. Her mind was slow and memory hazy.

She lay on a mattress, facing faded wallpaper. Over the regular pattern of repeated flowers a second design of random blotches of mould was imposing itself, and soon the mould would win. Her attention groped outwards. The thin mattress had no sheet or pillow. It lay on a wooden floor and there was no other furniture in the drab room.

She knew she was in a lot of trouble and ought to do something about it. But mental effort was a terrible strain – she was pulling a dead weight that wanted to drag her back to the pit. First, it was necessary to be aware that she had been drugged. She knew all about strange states brought on by chemicals, the trick was to know when the drug was talking. Just because she did not feel alarm did not mean the situation did not merit it.

Black Fort lay behind her, spooning, and she grew aware of his murmuring voice. He seemed to be talking half to himself.

'That – what you saw – that wasn't anybody's fault. These things happen. It was just bad luck. Teething trouble. Too many of them maybe... customs delays... whatever.'

His hands dabbled in her hair.

'It's a headache to sort out, but once the route is in place the money rolls in. There is so much money in it. More than drugs, more than girls. There's money in it like you wouldn't believe. I can't tell you how excited I am. I'm going to be big-time. Premier league.'

Often she had lain with him in the dark and listened to his dreams and ambitions, stated in a low and level tone, just like this. She mumbled his name. He started to kiss her neck. He always started around there or along the jaw, a preliminary circling before tackling the lips.

'I wanted to tell you. I wasn't excited just for me. For both of us. I had so many plans.'

She said, 'Love you.'

'I love you too. Love your skin, love the way you move, your eyes, tits, everything. So it's such a pity I have to do this.' He ran a hand across her breasts. 'Tell me your Hotmail password.'

'What?'

His fingers tapped out the syllables on her cheek as he said, 'Tell me your password.'

She felt him slipping off her trainers and socks. The mould on the wallpaper came into focus. She had always been quick to feel disgust and it came now. Fear and despair followed. Emotions were beginning to return, she was re-inhabiting herself.

'Why?'

'You can't just disappear. Not with that influential daddy. I don't want some Chinese cop fretting, making calls, kicking off investigations. I figure on sending Daddy emails from your account. Sorry I didn't ring, my phone is playing up, weather is this, my marks are this, the food is rubbish. I like emailing, it's cheaper, let's do it like this from now on. Only need a couple of months, I'd say – long enough to cover all traces, but you know what? I really don't think he'll ever notice.'

He wrapped tape around her ankles.

'I won't help you. You want to kill me.'

He whispered into her ear. 'I don't own a gambling club. It's something else. There are girls there. These girls, they do okay, but first they need persuading. They need to be broken.'

He bit down hard on her earlobe and she cried out.

'I know a lot of ways to persuade people. You'll agree to whatever I want. You'll give me your password.'

The pain blew through her befuddlement.

She said. 'I won't help. I won't help. Please, just let me go. Let me go and I won't say anything. I promise. Why? Please. Darling. Baby. No.'

He taped her wrists together behind her back and ran tape from there to her ankles. She was trussed up like a fowl. 'You know the first thing we do when we break someone?'

He slid a gag over her mouth and fixed it carefully.

'We give them time think about it.' He planted a kiss on her nose and left the room.

(74

As the drug wore off, the pain in her jaw grew bothersome. Despair stole over her but she pulled herself out of it by trying to think practically. There was no give in the tape, but she discovered it was possible to shift herself by small degrees if she lay on her side and wriggled. She slid off the mattress and experimented, moving around the room, and gritting her teeth when she banged her head or shoulder. The only break in the wall was a plug socket and she could not think of any way to make it serve her. There were no useful splinters jutting out of the floor or the skirting board.

It occurred to her that there was a great deal she needed to think about, primarily what she could say to make him change his mind. But these musings led to others, distressing or irrelevant, such as how this could happen, what could have made him like this, how ridiculous she was. The situation could not be as simple as it looked. It was impossible to accept, for so many reasons. How could she fall for such a man. How could her instinct be so wrong. How could a man who had loved her do this. So in her mind it grew many complications. He had gone temporarily mad, was being manipulated or blackmailed, had been replaced by an evil twin or doppelganger. Perhaps this was some kind of test.

As the hours stretched on, her mind ran over and over the same territory, and she grew irritated with herself. She was tired and thirsty. Her mental and physical labours began to look pointless. There was only waiting and discomfort. Subtle signs convinced her that a rat was in the room, and she began to listen out for it. She drifted into troubled sleep. When she woke the gag was like gravel in her dry mouth and the pain in her jaw insistent.

A moth settled low on the wall and it was interesting to watch. There was something like a silver dust on its wings, she had not noticed that about moths before. She passed into a light-headed state of acceptance and clarity. He was a cold-hearted killer and she a silly little girl. She'd lived under a set of foolish illusions and was now paying a price. What shit she talked, believed, did. It was a shame that she was not to be given a chance to redeem herself. She had made a mess of a great many things.

She believed she heard voices and engines outside. She seemed to hear a man call, 'Chinky dinkies! Let's be having you.' It was incredible that there were real people, just out there beyond the window. She must be clever and find some way to use this. She forced her way towards the window and made as much noise as she could by banging her head and knees against the wall. But the vehicles departed, and she was left alone to her well of fear and pain, tired and defeated.

Her thoughts grew impossible to control. Sometimes she wanted to giggle. The fact that the password he was after was his own name, for example, could be seen as drily amusing. She thought about her mother and her father and listed in her head all the things that she wanted to do. It struck her that many interesting thoughts had occurred to her and maybe this was just one of them. There were more rats now, though they were cunning enough to stay out of view.

Aches and pains and the rage in her throat made it impossible to complete a thought, though many were begun. Each minute was tediously the same, a cycle of pain, despair, hope, worry, thirst, exhausting and unstoppable. She wet herself, and was annoyed that she had not done so away from the mattress. She began to black out, for a few minutes at a stretch. Waking, and realising where she was, was awful, each time worse than the last. Once she thrashed furiously, and banged her head on the wall, first by accident, then deliberately.

She watched the wallpaper darken. Another night was coming, perhaps her third. She slipped from nightmare to reality and back again. The floor was thronged with rats, a great sea of them writhed, if she slept they would gnaw her. Her stupefied gaze took in a slither of moon, mocking shadows, a phone smeared with blood, a curlicue of hanging wallpaper, a pair of basketball shoes. Her eyes closed and coloured shapes ebbed and flowed. Her eyes opened, and the shoes were still there. Black Fort helped her up, slipped down her gag and poured water between her flaking lips.

Wei Wei leaned against the wall with her mouth open, and water splashed over her chin. When she began to choke, instinct brought forth effort, and she coughed and swallowed. Her stomach tightened as the water hit it, and it was a surprise to her that her body still had the strength to manage that response.

He held her head steady as she drank. That soothing trickle was like a thread sewing her back together again. As her senses gathered, she grew aware of moonlight filtering through the window, and saw in its pale glow a dragon-shaped pendant of green jade. She knew it well, had often rubbed it. His face above held no expression, and she observed the familiar line of the jaw and the birthmark. Her eyes were always drawn to that mark – it made his face more interesting. She had tried to make him see and he never understood. His skin was soft and clear. She wondered at her own mind, that it could bring up these irrelevancies, and reminded herself that he was not her lover but her torturer.

Hot fluid touched her lips and a metal spoon tinked against her teeth. Perhaps he was trying to poison her. She clamped her mouth shut and wrenched her head away and the liquid dribbled down her neck.

'It's soup,' he said, and showed her the polystyrene cup. She licked her lips and tasted tomato. Patiently he tried again and this time she let the spoon enter and tip. Creamy smoothness filled her mouth.

'Okay, here it comes again. Open. Careful. Slowly. There we go.'

Her spirits stirred. He spoonfed her so tenderly that the intoxicating thought grew that things were back to how they were – perhaps, after all, he was the man she knew. It was such a delicious hypothesis that she did not dare test it until the cup was finished.

'Let me go.'

'I can't do that.'

'Please.'

'I told you, I can't. Do you want a cigarette? Last meal and a last smoke. I figure it's the least I can offer.'

'Last? Oh, please.' She coughed. It was not easy to talk, her words seemed to take her breath away with them. Hot tears welled. It was better when she was numb.

'I guess not. Then we'll get on.'

He laid the spoon down between a candle and a little plastic bottle shaped like a lemon. Next went a hypodermic needle in a transparent plastic cover, a blue packet of cotton balls and a baggie of beige powder. He laid it all out neatly, in two rows, like instruments in a hospital.

He held an oblong of white card up to her face. The strain of her eyes refocusing hurt. She made out her own surname, Ma, under the PSB logo of Tian'anmen Gate. It was her father's namecard.

'He's dead.'

He struck a match and lit the card and held it by the corner. She watched Tian'anmen blacken and curl, then the name.

'He got here very quickly. I guess you managed to call him after all. Bad luck for him.'

With the flaming card he lit the candle. He shook the card and the flame went out and black flakes swirled. He dribbled wax onto the windowsill and stood the candle in it.

'He drowned in a lake.'

He squirted drops of liquid from the lemon-shaped bottle into the spoon, then added powder from the baggie. His movements were precise and patient, as ever.

'So no need to get your password out of you. It doesn't matter any more.'

He moved the bottom of the spoon over the candle flame and the metal glinted, and shadows on the walls loomed and receded.

'When things are messy, I feel itchy. You know that feeling? Maybe you don't.' His voice was as steady as his hand. 'Very uncomfortable.' He pinched cotton off a cotton-wool ball, rolled it between his fingers, and dropped it in the spoon. 'Itchy,' he repeated.

Focusing her energies, she stumbled through a prepared statement – 'I beg you, think about what you're doing and remember all the good times we had and trust me as I've... trust me as I trust you.'

'Huh?'

She realised she had addressed him in Mandarin and began to repeat herself in English. He hit her with an open palm. 'You don't say anything. Every word I hit you again.' Finally his voice had an edge to it. 'You fucked this all up, not me. All I'm doing is cleaning up.'

She lay and sobbed and watched him put the needle of the hypodermic against the cotton. He pulled the plunger, held the syringe upright and tapped it.

'A hot shot. Smack and strychnine. You'll just float away.'

He freed her ankles and pulled her legs straight and she gasped as pins and needles prickled in her hips and thighs. Her feet were very pale and the paint on the toenails was chipped. There was so little feeling in them, it was quite possible they were someone else's. She mustered all her strength and kicked out at him, but he batted her legs aside with ease.

'No. No.'

He pulled one leg of her jeans up and tied a belt around her calf. She could see her flesh constricting but hardly felt the squeeze. She drew the other leg back, lashed out and caught him across the face. He reeled and dropped the syringe. She pulled her other leg out from under him and rolled off the mattress onto her stomach. She groped for the syringe with a foot. She had the idea that she could grab it between her feet and stab him with it.

He straddled her, grabbed a hank of hair and yanked her head back.

'Move again and I smack your face into the floor.'

She felt him lean back. He was retrieving the syringe. She tried to wriggle, but he held her fast between his thighs.

Waiting for the prick of the needle, her senses seemed to sharpen, and she considered the immense rich detail of the scene – the grain of the wood on the floor, the wallpaper design, the splotches of mould. An oblong of yellow light flitted across the wall, as someone outside swept a torch across the face of the house. She heard running feet, then the sound of glass smashing, then the rumble of an explosion, just beneath her. Still the jab did not come.

Black Fort clambered off her and went to the window. She rolled over and laid her cheek against cold wood. What a stupid little girl she was. She realised she was going to die miserable and desperate, and this seemed a shame. A second explosion thundered, this one closer. Black Fort cursed and sprinted out. She raised her head.

76

Wei Wei scanned the room for the needle, but he seemed to have taken it with him. Fear of it gave her strength. She pulled herself to her feet and staggered to the window. The sky was just beginning to silver – it would soon be dawn. A sputtering orange light, coming from the downstairs windows, lit the yard. His car was parked there, looking incongruously urban. The metal sheet that covered the barn door was off, and a figure lay near it, and by the awkward arrangement of its limbs looked to be injured or dead. Movement caught her attention, and she saw a slim girl shuffling away with an odd, mincing gait.

She followed a flickering shadow back to its source and saw a thick-set, hooded man, standing with one hand shielding his face and a hammer raised in the other. The front door opened and a figure staggered out, beating at the flames that wreathed his shoulders. The hammer swung, the figure fell. Wei Wei flinched.

The man looked up. Dirt smeared across his face, giving him a demonic aspect. Dark eyes blazed up at her, then he staggered backwards as if punched. He shouted her name. Alarmed, she shied away. When she returned he had gone.

Adrenaline was giving her strength. She could move, she could think, though she was aware that she was drawing on the last of her reserves and complete collapse was not far away. The candle still burned on the windowsill. She turned and pulled her hands up behind her until her shoulder blades were crunched together. Leaning back, she tensed in anticipation of pain. At the first scorch of the flame she jolted away, but thoughts of the needle pushed her back. She quivered as her skin seared, and gritted her teeth. She could smell acrid plastic as the tape burned. She cried out – this was as much as could be borne – and tumbled forward. The tape parted as she brought her hands round to break her fall. The skin of her wrist, on either side of the black ring of tape, was red and enflamed.

The door was locked, and too sturdy for her to break. The window was divided into panes too small to fit through. She yanked at the windowframe and it rattled and shook but didn't budge. In frustration she rested her forehead against one pane of glass and slapped another. The side of her hand caught on a nail-head and she realised the frame was nailed to the sill. Disappointment drained her, and she slid down the wall.

Smoke was coming under the door. The house, she realised with a start, was on fire. Wood snapped and split and the room grew hazy. Inhaling brought a tickle to her throat. Down here it was easier to breathe and her eyes didn't smart so much. She slumped to the floor. It would be good to curl up and close her eyes. No, she barked to herself, she had to get out. But now she was coughing, and the effort of it was stealing her energy.

Something smacked into the door from the other side, and the wood vibrated and the handle shook. The frame split with a crack, splinters flew and the door swung inwards. A figure lurched in, borne on a billowing tide of smoke and sparks, emitting a ferocious coughing and spluttering. It became her father.

Her mind was stretched too thin to register much of an emotional response. He rammed the claw end of his hammer under the windowframe and tugged until the wood split. He smashed and jabbed to knock out glass splinters and wooden crossbeams. She wondered what to do to help, but he was so furiously busy she did not want to get in his way. He picked up the mattress, and, grunting with the effort, folded it and heaved it out. She was grabbed and borne aloft and a breeze touched her face. He was straddling the sill, half out of the window, and taking her along with him.

Her insides lurched as she fell. She opened her mouth to scream, but her body smacked the ground and the air was knocked from her lungs. A detonation went off in the back of her head and hip. She took a juddering breath and pains ground over her. She took shallower breaths and they ground harder.

She was lying on the mattress, half on top of her father. He must have turned as he fell so that his body would cushion hers. When they'd hit, her head had smacked him in his face. She shook him and called his name but he did not respond.

A black blizzard of sooty flakes churned. Sparks burned her legs and she yelped and scrambled forward. They had to get away from the fire. She tugged at the mattress, until it seemed her shoulders would be ripped from her sockets, and it slid for a couple of metres before catching on uneven ground.

Beyond the crumbling concrete edge of the yard, long grass sloped down into a tangle of bushes. She heaved him off the mattress. Another roll took him to the edge and she winced as his head bumped. She scrambled down, grabbed a leg and pulled, and he tumbled past her and settled in the undergrowth.

Black Fort came round the house. She lay beside her father in the long grass and watched him open the back door of his car and pull a shotgun off the seat. He loaded it and it clicked as he snapped it shut. He crouched and swivelled. The smoke was obscuring his view, or he would have seen them for sure.

She lowered her head and it touched her father's dirty cheek. His chin prickled with stubble. He smelled of soil, smoke and blood. He'd come so far to help her and she had done so little to deserve it. Never mind her fatigue. She was going to be strong and if necessary she was going to fight. They were going to get out of this. At least then she'd get the chance to apologise.

HOPE FARM

77

Ding Ming waited in the verge. The hatchback was around fifty paces away, just around a bend. He didn't feel safe near it, as the policeman's enemies might find it, but he didn't feel any safer away from it in the wilds, either. The call of an animal made him uneasy, and he imagined he was being watched by the twinkling eyes of wolves and snakes.

With every passing minute it seemed more likely that the policeman would never return. He would have to give up this vigil at some point, and then what would he do? He would have to try and find Mister Kevin by himself, no easy prospect.

He contemplated a smear of roadkill. A man could live off such fare, perhaps if all else failed it was possible just to survive. He imagined living in a cave or dell, trapping rabbits and drinking from streams, tending a secret vegetable patch, picking wild fruit and mushrooms. He might be happy doing that, he considered. But even that option was not open to him — it was doom for his family, saddled with their crippling debt.

He heard a car approaching. Some night animal scuttled away. A rat, he was sure of it. It was busy, he should be too. Thinking would not get him very far, he had done too much of that in his life already. It was time to be practical.

He stepped into the road and waved his arms. A van stopped and a man got out. The sight of a uniform was dismaying: it was just his luck to have stopped a policeman. But he spotted 'Post' written on the side of the van and hoped it meant what he thought it did.

His encounter with the temple caretaker had altered his opinion of the natives. Perhaps they were not all bad, and he had merely been unlucky with the specimens he had encountered. He was not quite so scared of them any more. Still, he could hardly believe he was being so reckless.

'Excuse me? Hello?'

He was like a boy approaching a big creature, not sure if he was going to get a lick or a bite. He took off Kevin's parka and held it out.

'Would you like to buy this coat?'

'You what?'

'I have to call China. I need small money for telephone. Please buy this coat.'

'China?'

'It's a very good coat.'

'You've been in the wars, haven't you?'

'Excuse me?'

'Keep your coat, you'll need it. I've got about a quid in change. Here.'

'Thank you. Thank you very much.'

'England fan, are you?'

'Sorry?'

'You like football. Your shirt.'

'Yes. Rooney very good. Good kicker of the ball.'

'He is that.'

'You are very kind.'

'You mind how you go.'

The man took his leave. Ding Ming considered for a moment the unexpected kindness. 'Mind how you go' — take care in the manner of your passing. It was a beautiful phrase.

He ran to the village. It was good to feel the jar of the road on his feet and his body settling into a rhythm, if only he could outrun his difficulties, if only it was a simple matter of will, pace and endurance.

He rushed into the red phone booth and called his mother. He imagined the mobile ringing, and with each trill the picture expanded. There was the phone sitting on the shelf, there was the photo of a car he'd cut from a magazine, mud walls covered with newspaper, a calendar advertising a button factory, chillis hanging from the rafters to dry, a naked bulb, a boarded-up window, sink, pots, oven, radio, stool, bed. The phone was answered.

'Hello?'

'Mum? Mum, it's me. Are the men there – the snakeheads?'

'Who are you?'

'It's me, Ding Ming. I need to talk to the men.'

'It is not possible,' she wailed. 'You are dead. You're a ghost because you died hungry in a foreign land, and now you are tormenting me on the telephone.'

'It's really me. There has been a mistake. What did those men say?'

'They said you were killed in a car accident. Are you ringing me from heaven or from Gold Mountain?'

'I am in England. I was not in that car, mother.'

He wanted to say, 'Many things that I was told about Gold Mountain are not true. My boss is not a good man and I want to go home.' But he did not. He said, 'I am fine. All is fine.'

'I thought you were dead. Look at this – I cried when the men told me you were dead, but I am bawling even harder now.'

Tears pricked his eyes.

'I'm so sorry. I tried to phone before, but there was no reply.'

'I went to the temple. But I was so blind in my grief I walked without knowing where I was going and I walked and walked. I miss you so much. My son, my son.'

A set of pips sounded, and Ding Ming realised he had better be quick.

'I miss you too. Do you have the phone number for my boss?'

'I can't believe it. I'm so happy. You can't imagine what it was like. The men said that even though you are dead our family still owes them the money. Oh, I can't believe you're alive. Tell me again it is you.'

'I'm not dead, everything's going to be okay, I'll earn the money to pay off the debt.'

'You have to go back to your boss.'

'I know, I'm trying. Give me the num—'

The line went dead.

Ding Ming ambled in a daze to the village green and put a hand against the war memorial for support. A wreath of plastic poppies sat at its base. That blood-coloured flower of tragedy was more appropriate than the gaudy blooms in their baskets. He was deeply ashamed for all the hassle he had caused and the upheaval he had put his family through. He was here to try and help – their hopes rested on him – and now he had done this to them. He would make amends. He'd work until his hands bled, and if it was necessary for him to suck on another man's part then he'd do that, too. He was a poor man and the lot of a poor man was the consumption of bitterness, he would suffer so that others might be more fortunate.

The rumble of an engine drew him out of himself. A green truck slowed to take the turnoff past the duck pond. The interior light was on and the passenger was talking on a mobile phone. He looked remarkably like Mister Kevin, and even wore a similar shirt. But, of course, all white people looked fairly alike, with their big noses and round eyes, and fat people in particular looked the same. It really did look like Mister Kevin, though. The truck turned. 'Cleen me' was written in the dust on the back. He had seen it at the mud, and again last night by the lake. It really was him.

The familiar face was as reassuring as a hug. At that moment, Mister Kevin the abuser was his guardian angel, who could guide him out of this wilderness. He stepped out and waved.

'Mister Kevin! Mister Kevin!'

But the truck roared on. Ding Ming ran after it. He tripped on a bollard, fell into reeds, and when he got up he saw the back of the vehicle fade into the gloom.

Better not to have seen the man at all than glimpsed him and lost him. Twice now he had been taunted by a view of that truck's rear end. It was cruel beyond endurance. It was a bad joke, more monkey tricks. The universe was a bully with a poor sense of humour. He slapped the ground in frustration.

Then the truck's brake lights burned new holes in the darkness, the engine note lowered as the gears were changed down, and the truck took the turn towards Hope Farm.

Ding Ming ran after it. He grew giddy with excitement as he realised that a way out of his mess had improbably opened up for him. Mister Kevin must be protected from the mad policeman, he must be warned. Mister Kevin's life was there to be saved, and perhaps his reward would be his wife.

(78

Ding Ming hurtled down the track. An odd crackling sound ahead of him rose in volume, but he did not realise what it was until he rounded a curve and the cover of trees parted onto a confused and disturbing scene. Tongues of flame lapped from the windows of a house and churning smoke formed a black column against grey sky. He was too late – the murderous business was in hand.

Shading his eyes he peered harder. Through a shimmering heat haze he saw the green truck and Black Fort's yellow car. There was Black Fort and, yes, there was Mister Kevin. That bulk was unmistakable. He was fiddling with some kind of stick – no, he was loading a shotgun. There were two other men there, and they had guns too. He felt a twinge of dread. He stepped back and a twig snapped.

A man pointed and yelled, in a harsh bark of English, 'There he is, there.'

Another voice growled, 'Get him.'

A gun flashed and boomed and leaves and twigs crunched as they were torn apart.

They had mistaken him for their enemy. Ding Ming turned, put his head down and sprinted heedlessly away, a shrill note of panic ringing in his head. He tripped, and when he put a hand down to right himself felt grass and earth. He put the hand in front of his face. It was shaking, and smeared with mud. He saw bark and leaves. He had run right off the track and into the wood. A man yelled 'There,' and another voice said, 'Head him off.'

Ding Ming rushed on. It was so dark that he did not see the tree trunks until he was almost upon them, and he had to veer and lurch. Dew glistened on barbed wire. He planted a hand on a wooden post and vaulted into darkness. His heels dug into soil, thorns tugged his thigh, then he was sliding and rolling down a muddy bank. He came to rest in a stream of cold water, one leg curled painfully beneath him.

Above, a torch flashed and he heard his pursuers slow.

'You hold it down. I'll go over.'

The wire twanged as the men climbed the fence.

Ding Ming picked himself up and careered into the wood. Twigs whipped and flayed. His head banged a branch and the shock brought him up short. He realised he was making such an uproar crashing through the undergrowth that pursuit was simple. He had to hide.

Rotten wood split as he crawled into a hollow below a fallen trunk. He curled up and clasped his knees, his cheek against spongy moss. His mouth was very dry and he licked his lips, tasting earth. The parka covered him completely. He was glad it was green, and dirty, it made good camouflage. He remembered how the policeman had smeared his face with dirt as a disguise and did the same.

He could hear nothing over the din of his pounding blood. No, there, tramping feet approached. The torch's tunnel of light grew brighter. If they found him his only chance would be to very quickly explain that it was not his fault, that he had done nothing and he was only a poor peasant and victim of circumstance. He feared that they would not believe him, or even care to listen. He realised that he should not have run – that made it look bad. He should have stood there on the track and shouted, 'Mister Kevin, stop, I am so glad that I have found you, there is a man come to kill you and your friends, and you must run away.' And that might have sorted it out.

He curled up tighter and wished he could make himself small enough to vanish altogether. The swish of feet in undergrowth grew louder, then stopped. There were two men. He could see clods of earth on their shoes and burrs stuck to their trousers. The barrel of a gun swung into view.

'Where did he go?'

An animal chattered.

'This way.'

Their steps receded. Ding Ming realised he was holding his breath and exhaled. He crawled out, but this time fought the instinct to charge off. Slow is steady, he told himself, and stepped as quietly as he could. It helped to imagine himself an animal whose survival depended on stealth. He resolved that when the new day came he would think of a plan. But his only immediate idea was to get away from his pursuers and get through this awful night.

He came to a clearing. Birds twittered and pale streaks slashed the sky – it was soon be dawn. Black smoke rose in a column. He looked round a tree and his spirits fell as he realised that he must have travelled in a loop. He had come all the way back to Hope Farm. It was very frustrating. He was reminded of the time he had followed the ramblers and only ended up back where he started. It seemed his destiny to make great efforts and get nowhere. He tried to orient himself, looking for the track he had come down on. That would lead to the road, and then the village, and perhaps he would be safer there, where people were kind.

As he scrutinised the scene, a suspicion that it was familiar grew to a startling conviction – why, yes, that yard was where the lorry had parked, and that was the barn where he'd taken a piss – this was the very place he had arrived at, not two days ago. The tree he had his hands on right now he had admired, in those happier times, as one of the bushiest he had ever seen.

He supposed he should have thought of it. In retrospect it was obvious – Black Fort and Kevin were friends or business partners. Of course there was only one 'farm' that they used. All it meant was that he knew for certain he was at least three hours' van drive from the mud.

A female voice cried out. Someone else was in trouble and they were coming this way. He ran to another tree and peeked round it. A girl was lit by a raking beam of light. She was trying to run, not very successfully, as her ankles were tied together, and there was something pathetic about that mincing shuffle. Her T-shirt was ripped, and one of its red bows hung loose and flapped. He knew her in an instant, and it hit like an electric shock. It was his wife, Little Ye.

(79

Little Ye was making a noise he had never heard her make before, a yowl like a cat. A man jogged after her. He too was familiar, the sinister Black Fort. And watching and holding the torch was Mister Kevin. Each man, like his pursuers in the wood, carried a long, stout gun.

Ding Ming's fingers dug into bark. He kept on looking although he wanted more than anything not to see. He couldn't believe it. She'd gone nowhere, she had stayed here all the time, it was the most appalling monkey trick of all.

He stretched a hand towards her, then put it in his mouth and bit down, and kept biting as he watched Black Fort catch up with Little Ye and grab her shoulder. She swung at him and Ding Ming saw that her wrists were tied together. Black Fort slapped the clumsy blow away and raised the shotgun, threatening to hit her with the butt. She fell over.

Ding Ming hopped from one foot to the other and took his bleeding hand out of his mouth and splayed his fingers over his face. His eyes felt huge between them. He watched Black Fort slap Little Ye and grab her by her matted hair.

'Stop messing about,' hissed Kevin, and the torchlight went up and down to signal his impatience.

'*Bu, bu, bu.*' she sobbed. She looked terribly small and delicate and Ding Ming wanted to choke. Black Fort dragged the rope that hung from her wrists until she scrambled to her feet. He pulled her by the rope and she shuffled after him. Kevin turned towards the barn, swinging the torch, and the scene went dark. Ding Ming reeled. Lurid after-images lingered, of pale limbs and long shadows.

It was impossible not to follow. He was aware that a simple turn of the torch would reveal him, but was determined not to let his wife out of his sight. When the group headed up a rise towards the barn, he dropped to his stomach and crawled. The fire raged in the house. Roof beams collapsed in a storm of sparks. Tiles fell and shattered with a sound like a string of firecrackers going off. Black dust swirled. It settled on Ding Ming's coat and smudged his skin and made his eyes smart. But he was glad of the smoke and the uproar, it masked his presence.

They took his wife into the barn. He stole along the wall towards the entrance. With every step he knew he was just being more and more reckless, but he could not stop himself – a wilful demon seemed to be in command. What were they doing with her in there? It was tormenting. Bitterly he remembered his feelings of hope and trepidation when he was in there all those hours ago, back when he was young and stupid. He felt like crying. He had lived so long at a pitch of high emotion that his exhausted mind could barely function.

Metal clinked beneath his feet. Rusty bars were scattered at the base of the wall. He picked his way to a stack of tyres beside the barn entrance. He was alarmed to see a man lying just a metre or so away, a slim Chinese man with a neat ponytail. His head was twisted unnaturally to the side and his limbs were flung out carelessly. Ding Ming realised he was dead. He wanted to go and turn that head away. The eyes seemed to be looking right through him.

Black Fort and Kevin came out quickly. Ding Ming was so close he could see swirls of decorative engraving on the stock of Kevin's gun. He was trapped: he could not retreat for fear of making a noise. He ducked out of sight behind the tyres.

They loitered in the entrance, and Ding Ming could hear not just their voices but their heavy breath and footfalls.

A beam of torchlight shone into the pale face of the dead man. Kevin whined, 'Oh Christ, look at that poor fucker. Can't we just get out of here?'

Black Fort said, 'As soon as it gets light, someone will see the smoke and call the cops. If they find any bodies, they'll come after us. We have to clean up. I want you to call the driver and tell him to get a move on.'

'We should tell him to stay the hell away.'

'No. When he comes, we put the new arrivals and the girls in your truck. We unhitch the container and hitch up the one in the barn. Chuck all the other bodies in there and get the fuck out. When the cops turn up, all they find is an empty container and a smoking ruin. It's just some arsonist been playing around. They'll shrug and leave it. If we do this right, we can still get away.'

He remembered the last time he had eavesdropped on these two, the night before, while standing in a puddle in an open grave. That time he hadn't wanted to hear. Now he craned with his senses trembling. The girls – they were talking about what to do with his wife.

Kevin said, 'You can't throw those girls in with new arrivals. They'll talk about what's been happening to them and we'll have a riot on our hands.'

'True. It's hassle we don't need. Okay – we'll kill them.'

Ding Ming blinked. Had he just heard what he thought he heard?

Kevin said, 'Jesus Christ.'

'Throw them in the container with all the other bodies.'

'Listen to you.'

'We can't afford to mess about.'

'We can't just—'

'You want to come out of this or not?'

'Christ.'

'You want all our hard work to go to shit? Fifty years inside? We got, what, twenty corpses to deal with – what's another three?'

'Listen to yourself.'

'We clean this up together or I sort you out as well – understand?'

'Are you threatening me?'

'Yes.'

'Christ. You want to go in and kill them? Just... stick a shotgun in there and shoot them?'

'I'll do it. You don't even have to watch.'

Ding Ming paled. They planned to kill his wife. He couldn't breathe, the knowledge was like a pebble in his throat.

'I'll get the others. Phone the driver and stay here in case he turns up. He's going to see the fire and the bodies and freak out. Tell him it's under control. If he tries to leave, wave your gun at him.'

'Can't you stay, as well?'

'What is it? Don't you want to be left alone?'

'I just... Christ.'

'I'll be two minutes.'

'What about the psycho? What if he's here?'

'Shoot him.'

Ding Ming heard Black Fort jog away. He peeked over the tyres. Kevin had his back to him. He was trying to make a call on his mobile but kept looking up and glancing nervously round and swivelling his gun.

Ding Ming knew what was required of him now, but felt inadequate to the task. He wished he was as strong and mad as the policeman but he was just an ordinary person. He wanted to break into a sob and screwed his face up to force it back.

He picked up a metal bar. He couldn't believe what he was about to do, and he knew that if he stopped to think about it would fail. He remembered the policeman's advice and kept counting in his head – one two three, one two three – until it drowned all else out. But still his hands shook with nerves.

He ran forward and smacked Kevin on the head with the bar. The impact jarred his arm to the shoulder. As Kevin fell, Ding Ming hit him again. His features, he could feel, were contorted into an arrangement they had never held before.

He started towards the ruined body, needing to see what he had done, then turned because he couldn't look, and he put the metal bar, now repellent to him, down on the ground. Something warm trickled down his chin and he tasted blood and realised that he had bitten his own tongue.

(80

Jian became aware that he was hurt. His head was humming, his vision swam. He forced his consciousness outward and realised he was lying on his stomach, in a tangle of plants. He hauled himself onto one elbow and grunted as pains stamped down on him. He took a breath and sharp jabs lanced his chest.

The pain wasn't unbearable, he told himself. It was just a cracked rib – and he kept saying it in his head until, with an exhalation, that twinge subsided and duller aches yammered for attention. His hand and wrist were scraped raw, something was wrong with his ankle and the back of his head throbbed. He'd have a good bump there tomorrow, if he lived that long. The sight of blood spatter down his arm alarmed him, until he realised it was someone else's.

A voice was murmuring – someone was here, very close. He fumbled the gun out and pointed it at a dark form. That was too much effort, so he brought the other hand up to support his wrist, but still the barrel wavered. Wei Wei whispered, 'Dad, it's me.' He tried to say, '*Dan ran*... Of course,' but it came out as a groan. Hands were laid on his shoulders. 'Don't try to get up.'

He grasped her with both hands. The contact stung where his palm was scoured, but still it was welcome. She was alive, she was gloriously here. She was just like his mental pictures but smaller and denser. Her face was pale, with hollows round her eyes, flaking lips and a bruise on her cheek. She had raw scrapes all along her arm. Her wounds caused him more pain than his own.

He did not want to take his eyes off her, as if to do so were to break the spell and she would be dead again. His sour dream of rage was over in an instant, and new emotions took hold. Foremost was the fear that she would go again, he could not stand to be robbed twice.

A sharp crack drew his gaze. A strip of guttering, warped with heat, peeled away from the roof of the house. It twisted free, fell and slithered down the slope. Grass sizzled and leaves shrivelled. It came to rest barely a footstep away.

Their location was perilous. He got to his feet, thrashing branches aside, and, with arms raised to shield his face from the heat, tested the weight on his ankle. It would slow him down but he could still walk – it was just a strain.

In the yard he saw a new arrival, a green and dusty lorry. Jian knew that menacing radiator grille, now dented. It had forced him off the road last night. More enemies had arrived.

He had to get her away from here. It was not far to the wood, then they could find the road which would lead to the car, then they could drive away. The further he planned, the more fretful he became. How quickly his mind had normalised. Like any intense pain, the rage could not now even be recalled. Mundane emotions had streamed into the gap – fear, nerves, vexation.

He took her hand. It was hot and damp with sweat. A few paces across open ground, then the sanctuary of the dark trees. Then the road, the car, safety.

She whispered, 'Wait,' and pointed at the barn. 'They put a girl in there.'

So what – it was clearly not his problem. It was necessary to get her out, delay only endangered them both.

'Dad, we have to help her.'

He felt mortal, tired, and old. He was so battered that there did not seem any part of his body that did not ache.

He wiped sweat off his brow and looked at the welcoming cool darkness.

With disappointment he realised that he could not fail himself again. Now he was trapped, there was the inconvenience of duty. He looked at the barn through churning smoke and flakes of soot.

'Let's see what we can do.'

(81

Jian led his daughter across the yard. The fire spat and growled at his back like some caged angry animal, and smoke stung his eyes. A new body lay sprawled in the barn entrance – that fat boss, who didn't look like he'd be getting up any time soon. His shirt had ridden up his back, exposing pouches of folded flesh.

'Someone hit him and went in,' whispered Wei Wei.

He motioned for her to stay behind him, drew his gun and took a long step over the body. As he slipped into the barn he was mindful not to make a silhouette in the doorway. Weak moonlight came through holes in the roof and a ragged gap in the back wall. He made out the edges of a container. A dark figure stood before it, fiddling with the door. He raised the gun and his finger tightened on the trigger. He recognised the outline of a bulky fur-trimmed hood and lowered it again. It was, of all people, that peasant. The lad had a habit of not staying where he was put.

'Hey, clever.' The lad looked around. Jian was used to seeing the kid in distress, but his expression was of a subtly different order now, his features slack with shock. His face was smeared with mud and shone with sweat.

'They didn't take her anywhere.' His voice was oddly flat.

'Take who?'

'They didn't... My wife. They kept her here.'

He fumbled at the container door with shaking hands.

'She's in there?'

'I can't get it open.'

Jian pulled a lever. Metal clunked, then hinges creaked, as the door swung open. An arm dropped through the gap. The skin was blotchy and grey, the fingers swollen. He gagged on the stench of rotting flesh, and stepped back and held his hand over his mouth and nose. The door swung further, revealing the puffy face of a dead boy, mottled with lividity. Behind it, a throng of limbs and torsos stretched away.

The peasant wailed in dismay. Jian swung the cold arm back, then closed the door and pulled the lever down to secure it.

'She's not in there.' There was something brutally matter-of-fact about dead humans. He blinked to get images of blank eyes and toothy grimaces out of his mind and turned his back. Wei Wei swayed in the entrance, silhouetted by a guttering orange glow. How fragile her limbs now appeared. He hoped she had not seen that obscene mass.

The sight seemed to have galvanised the peasant. He dashed about in a frenzy of agitation. 'Little Ye?' he howled.

'Be quiet.'

'Little Ye?'

An answering moan was heard. At the far end of the barn a metal panel was propped against the wall. The lad hauled it aside, revealing stone steps leading to a square wooden door, held fast by a metal bar fixed between brackets. He tugged out the bar.

The cellar door was pushed open from the other side and arms bound with rope and electric cable stretched forward. Hands patted and groped. Jian smelled the sourness of confined bodies. There was only room for one girl to crawl out at a time, but three were trying it. Wei Wei hurried to help.

Jian hurried to the barn entrance. There was no sign of his enemies, but they must be close. He was frustrated. They were losing time and these girls would slow them further.

Who knew how they would react? He rolled the fat man over, rooted in the pockets of his greying tracksuit bottoms and remembered doing the same thing not two days ago. This time he found loose notes and change – of course, he'd stolen the guy's wallet – cigarettes, phone, lighter, shotgun cartridges and a set of car keys. He prised fleshy fingers off the shotgun and checked that it was loaded.

Back in the barn, two bedraggled Chinese girls clung together. A third shuffled to join them, sobbing snottily. He recognised her – he'd freed her once tonight already. Ding Ming flung his arms around her and pressed his face to hers.

There was no time for this. 'Listen,' barked Jian. 'There is a truck out there. I have the keys. I'll open the back shutter, then start the engine. When you hear the engine, you come out. You get in the back, pull the shutter down and lie on the floor. When the girls are in, and the back shutter closed – and only then – Ding Ming, get in the front passenger seat. Then we go. Do you all understand?'

Three solemn nods. He waited for the two younger girls to acknowledge him. It would only take one losing her wits to get them all killed. He felt frustrated at the delays and the burden of these extra lives. And the girls could not move faster than a shuffle. But he only had to get them in the truck and get the truck onto the lane. Those men would pause before firing on a vehicle they recognised. He just had to keep a cool head.

A call came from the yard, a bark of English. Jian dropped and the stone floor was cold against his stomach. He glimpsed three men running with guns.

He waved at the others to retreat into the shadows.

Wei Wei's face was ashen. She said, 'They know we're here.'

When outnumbered, do not attack. They could all go through the gap in the wall at the back of the barn and quickly lose themselves in the woods. All he needed was a small head start. He would show his enemies that he was armed, and probably they would be too wary to pursue.

'Lie down.' He pointed to the gap. 'See that? Get ready to run there. Not yet. You're going to follow me out.' He yelled to his enemies in the yard, 'We're armed too. Let us go and no one else will be hurt.'

The reply came in Black Fort's stilted Mandarin.

'You're going nowhere. You're dead. You're all fucking dead.'

'Fuck your grandfather.'

Jian fired both barrels through the entrance. The roar made his ears ring. He told himself they had a good chance now – no one wants to chase a man with a gun. He got up and rushed to the back and broke the shotgun open.

The smell of cordite triggered memories of his last firefight, still sharp after all these years – men with guts blown out and limbs sheered off, shrieking with fear, shitting themselves. He had been a stupid kid then, reckless and daft, he was old now, too old for this. Breathing shallowly, he ordered himself to stay focused as he slotted cartridges into the barrel.

Someone fired in and shot pinged around the walls. He hoped that the girls and the peasant kept their nerves and stayed hugging the floor.

He eased forward and looked through the gap at a grey sky slashed with pink. Woods and fields ran all the way to the monotone horizon.

He heard scrambling and panting, then a low whisper. Men were running round the side of the barn. They'd anticipated him, and cut off the retreat. They would have time enough to shoot them all in the back if they tried to run to the wood. It seemed that, after all, these men would fight.

Probably they had left one man laying down suppressing fire through the front and now the other two were coming round the flank and soon all would be able to fire in. He could keep running between the two exits and firing out and nothing would be achieved – he would only keep the enemy at bay until he ran out of ammunition. They were trapped.

Stones chinked. The men could not be allowed to get much closer, they would soon have an angle to shoot in. He fired through the gap and heard someone slither to a stop. Again a blast was fired through the front and shot ricocheted.

White powder hissed as it poured from ruptured sacks. With all this metal flying about, the civilians would get hurt. Jian ran to his group and pointed to the stairs. 'Get down there.' He could no longer hear his own voice over the ringing in his ears. 'Down, go, quickly.'

The stunned girls moaned and swayed. It irritated him. It was terrible to be burdened with the weight of all these lives. He gave the fat man's phone to Wei Wei. 'Call the police.'

He gave his pistol to Ding Ming. 'Hold it with two hands. The safety is not on. The trigger's stiff. There's only one bullet, it's in the chamber.' The peasant nodded, biting his lip. 'There's only one man out there. If you're sure that I'm killed, sprint through the front. Wave the gun around, hope that he keeps his head down and all of you run out.'

Jian reloaded the shotgun and clambered out of the gap at the back of the barn. Make a noise in the west to attack in the east. He hurled a broken brick to the left, where the flanking force was waiting, and heard it land and roll. Hopefully it sounded like a man stumbling. He took his finger out of the trigger guard – easy enough to shoot yourself in the foot – and ran round the barn to the right.

When he turned the corner he pressed his back against the wall with the warm shotgun raised against his shoulder. He was panting very hard. Yes, he grimaced – too old, too old. But not dead yet. He was sure they did not know his position, he had to keep this advantage. If the enemy expects defence, attack.

A blast came through the front, followed by a second. Both barrels had been fired and the shooter would have to reload. He could hear his target, there behind the yellow car. In his head he saw the man kneeling with the shotgun broken. He knew what he had to do but it took a great effort of will to move towards gunfire and he filled his head with babble. The contradiction between the proletariat and the bourgeoisie is resolved by the method of socialist revolution.

He sprinted forwards, skirting close to the house so that the smoke plumes obscured him. Blood pounded in his ears. His vision narrowed to a tunnel. Heat pressed against his side and his eyes felt raw. His teeth were gnashed together so hard that his jaw hurt.

It was hard to run in the dark with a bulky gun and a damaged leg, and the conviction that he was not going to make it grew into bleak certainty. He would be shot here, he would bleed out in agony, many others would die afterwards.

A figure rose behind the car and wriggled in the heat haze. Jian was still ten, fifteen paces away. A gun swung round. Jian threw himself down and gasped as a jolt passed through his shoulder and a spike of pain jabbed his ribs. A boom, and he felt the whoosh of displaced air as shot whizzed over him. He laid his gun flat along the ground and fired under the car, and the man screamed as his feet and ankles tore. Jian ran round and fired the second barrel into his chest.

His ears rang from the blast and that din added to a sense that he had stepped outside time. He hauled his mind back into the present. The contradiction between the working class and the peasant class in socialist society is resolved by the method of collectivisation. He wiped sweat out of his eyes and realised he was parched.

He hoped the other hoodlums had heard the screams and the shots and were running away. No, he heard scuffing feet – they were going into the barn. They were astute. Now his only cover was the vehicles, and they had brick walls. And maybe hostages. The thought made his stomach lurch.

He picked up the dead man's shotgun. The barrel had been chopped down. Open near ruined feet was a box of cartridges. He put a handful in his pocket. Always keep moving and fight in territory that you choose for yourself.

He got into the cab of the truck and started the engine and put the handbrake on and the gearstick into neutral. Watching his hands as they ran through these tasks he was pleased to see that they did not shake, but he felt disconnected from him, as if they were someone else's. Bent over the pedals he jammed the butt of the sawn-off shotgun against the accelerator. It stuck there, with the barrel rammed hard against the seat. The engine whined. He depressed the clutch, slipped the truck into first, and pulled the steering wheel round.

An explosion – the windscreen shattered and broken glass sprinkled his back. They were firing at the truck thinking he was going to drive away. He clicked the headlights onto full beam. As he slid into the passenger seat, keeping his head down, he let off the handbrake. The truck lurched and he jumped out.

He hit concrete and the shock jarred his hip and ankle. Struggling to maintain balance he whipped his gun round. A figure stood in the barn entrance aiming a gun out. It roared and spat flame and the headlights of the truck popped. Jian aimed at the brief tongue of flame and fired both barrels. But he was off balance, and thought his shots had gone high.

The truck pitched forward and its left-side front bonnet crashed into the wall of the barn and crumpled and the truck wheeled round, tyres screeching. It struck the wall and cracked and wrinkled. The wall buckled, collapsed, and bricks showered inwards. Roof beams sagged and split, and tiles tumbled, smashing in the yard. A cloud of dust rose.

Jian reloaded. He guessed he had a few seconds, while the dust cloud hovered and they were still blinking away the after-image of the headlights. He ran into the barn. A man was rising drunkenly to his feet. Perhaps a brick had hit him, or the earlier shot had been accurate. Jian fired and the man sat heavily, his head went down to his lap, and then his leg spasmed and he rolled onto his side and was still.

Dust swirled. He could see nothing but vague shapes and built a picture of the place in his mind – container, sacks, stairs. Beams slanted down. Bricks clinked as they settled. Streaming powder hissed.

The fat man's upper body protruded from a pile of brick. A horrible croak was coming from his throat. His hand extended and grabbed Jian's leg. He pulled and Jian lost his balance and fell. He turned and fired into the man's bulk and the hand loosened. Jian broke the gun open and emptied out the spent cartridges.

Black Fort staggered forward, one arm around Wei Wei's throat, holding her before him like a shield. She sobbed and wriggled.

Sprinkled with brick dust, he looked like a ghost. Blood made a vivid channel down the dusty cheek. He was moving stiffly and the light in his pale eyes was dim. The barrel wandered dreamily, looking for a subject.

Jian grew aware of movement to his left. Underneath the trailer of the container, a familiar over-sized coat was worming forwards. Ding Ming was holding the pistol out and pushing it before him.

Jian tossed his gun away. He forced his mouth into a grin. The corners of Black Fort's mouth twitched in response. Now Jian could see the livid gash above the man's ear. The man's gun seemed to have made up its mind. Jian looked into the barrel's full stop.

'You're a realist,' he said. 'I understand that.' He just needed to get the man talking. 'Kill me, but leave my daughter.'

Acutely conscious of the peasant's movements, he had to resist the impulse to glance across. He stretched his hand towards the man and tapped the floor, hoping Ding Ming understood.

Black Fort said, in stilted Mandarin, 'I'm cleaning up. You're all dead.' His voice was slow and slurred. He stumbled and, as he regained his balance, squeezed Wei Wei's neck. She gagged.

'You can watch her die.' Black Fort pushed her away and swung his gun towards her. She screamed.

Ding Ming skittered the pistol across the floor. Jian dived for it, grabbed it, turned and shot Black Fort in the head. The shotgun halted, drooped and fell, and without fuss the man tumbled after it to the floor. A puff of dust rose. One white shoe twitched. Sprawled untidily on broken brick, he seemed to stare at the fat man and the fat man seemed to be looking right back.

Jian said to Ding Ming, 'You never stay where you're put, do you?'

They helped the girls into the long grass behind the barn. All moved shakily and slowly, with stunned acquiescence. It was almost peaceful here in the long grass. Jian was shaking, too, as the adrenaline left his body. He was like a child, putting names to the things he saw – sky, tree, daughter. A gentle breeze animated leaves. Rooks flapped across grey sky, past a slither of sun garlanded with rosy streaks. He realised how much his body was aching.

The buzz of an engine rose in volume. A heavy vehicle was coming up the track. Jian pointed to the trees. 'Hide. Ding Ming, come with me.'

Jian picked his way over loose bricks into the barn. The dust was settling, but sooty flakes swirled and thick blood pools ran. He took the car keys out of Black Fort's pocket.

Ding Ming called, 'There's a truck coming.'

'I know, I know.'

Jian came out and watched it edging forwards. It was only just wide enough for the track, and branches lashed it. Jian fired his gun into the air, then aimed at the driver.

'Ding Ming, tell him to stop and get out.'

The command was communicated, and the man got down with his hands in the air. He was another portly bald type.

'Tell him to empty his pockets. Good. Now tell him he's got a minute to run as fast as he can, then we're coming after him.'

Before Ding Ming had finished talking the man was sprinting away. When he looked back over his shoulder Jian raised the shotgun. He ran faster.

Jian said, 'I reckon your English might be getting better.'

'What are you doing?'

'I'm going to get this truck into the yard.'

'Why?'

'It's blocking the track.'

'There are migrants in the back, you know. That's what they do here, they—'

'Direct me.'

Jian scooped up the driver's wallet and mobile. The cab smelled pungent and was full of empty crisp packets. Easing the truck into the yard, he developed a new appreciation for the skills of their drivers – the thing handled like a brick.

He opened the container at the back and peered into the gloom at large cardboard boxes. He clapped, and the cardboard began to rip from the inside, like square eggs hatching. Hands appeared through the gaps, then pinched, frightened faces. Frightened, hopeful eyes looked back.

He said, 'All of you stay there.'

A Chinese man said, 'Is this Gold Mountain?'

'No.'

A girl piped up, in stitled Mandarin, 'Please, sir. Can we get out and go to the toilet?'

'No.'

A distant siren began to wail. Once more he had to be quick. He took Ding Ming aside.

'Give me that coat.'

'Why?'

'It's very distinctive. Give me the football shirt, as well.'

'I don't understand.'

'There.' Now you're just another migrant.' He considered the man's bruised, pale torso. 'A very skinny one.'

'What are you doing?'

'You tell them that you arrived in that truck, with that lot, stuffed in a box. You and your wife and the two girls, you know nothing about anything. You just got here.'

'Tell who?'

'The police. You're going to wait here till they arrive. All of you are.'

'No. They'll take my organs.'

'Who told you that? Think about it for a second. The snake-heads told you. You believe them?'

'You told me.'

'Did I? Alright, I told you. For the same reason they did. I needed you to be afraid. Don't believe everything you're told. Nothing will happen to any of you. You'll get deported, that's it. They'll shrug and send you home.'

'You're going? You're just going to leave us?'

The kid had rubbed soil over his face, and on top of this layer was a coating of soot and dust. Even through all this, he could still see the split lip and purple bruise over his eyebrow.

'I'm Inspector Ma Jian of the Qitaihe Public Security Bureau.' With his index finger, he traced the two characters of his name on his palm. 'Its in Heilongjiang Province, Qitaihe Prefecture, Liberation Road. You know what it means, me telling you this? You could tell the cops here and get me into a lot of trouble. But I trust that you're not going to.'

He laid both hands on the lad's bony shoulders. 'I trust that you're going to keep quiet, and let them deport you, and when you get back home you're going to look me up. And I'll sort you and your wife out. And those other two. I said

I'd get you a job, I'll get you a job. And you won't have to worry about any snakeheads. Anyone comes near you, I'll sling them in jail. Just get yourself home, then you're set. In front of my daughter, I promise.'

Ding Ming nodded. 'We all just arrived in that truck.'

'Good lad. We did good together. Go and brief the others.'

Ding Ming's face broke up.

'You nearly got me killed.'

He lashed out. Jian parried blows.

'You'll need to work on that. Try and get your shoulder behind it.'

Ding Ming swung again and, as instructed, put his shoulder into it, and landed a punch on Jian's jaw. Jian staggered and put a finger to his lip. It came away smudged with blood. Ding Ming bobbed with an expression of pain on his face and his fist tucked up in his armpit.

'How do you say 'Goodbye' in English?'

Ding Ming told him, and he gave it a go.

Jian laid the parka around Wei Wei's shoulders and hurried her into Black Fort's eye-catching car. He supposed it was his own body that had made that dink on the passenger door. Bright yellow, with a flame decal, sooty and peppered with shot – the thing was hardly inconspicuous. At least the windows were intact.

'I'm sorry, Dad, I'm so sorry—'

'You got that credit card I gave you?'

'Huh? Uh, yes. It's in—' A flutter of birdsong. Her ease with English had always impressed him, and that sudden eruption reminded him of his pride. She was a bright girl, she'd do okay.

He unzipped his money belt, prised out a filthy, sodden passport, and put it on the dashboard to dry out.

'Where's yours?'

'That's there, too.'

'First we pick up your card and passport. Then we have to get to an airport.'

'Why?'

'Why do you think? We're going home.'

The seats were reclined quite far back, but he was getting used to that now. He turned the ignition and slid the car into first gear and it shot forward with surprising force. He supposed it had been souped up.

'Do you smoke?'

'Yes.'

'Here.' He tossed cigarettes and lighter into her lap. 'And light one for me.'

He turned the car out of the lane and put his foot down. Driving towards the sunrise, he laid his hands high on the wheel. Another long journey was beginning – he could not rest yet. Gesturing at the glove compartment he said, 'Is there a map in there?'